THE TIDES OF LOVE

"But you still expect me to marry you?"

"Why not? You have nothing to fear from me. I only prey on overseers and heiresses."

A wave of healthy anger flooded over Sabina, and she suddenly surged toward Myles like a small tidal wave. "Stop it!" she shouted, hitting her fists futilely against his chest. "How dare you speak to me so? Is it because I have nothing—*am nothing!*—that you treat me like this? Do you think you own me just because you saved my life? Is that all I am to you? *Flotsam!*"

She felt her wrists suddenly seized, as he roughly pulled her against his body, the amusement wiped clean from his face. Her shawl had slipped to the floor, and she felt his hands slowly slide up her bare arms, stopping only to caress the soft flesh just beneath her shoulders.

Slowly, he pulled her still closer until his body felt like an addition to her own. Then his lips descended upon hers, and it was a physical relief to feel his breath mingle with hers.

THE SEA WIFE

HOLLY COOK

LEISURE BOOKS   NEW YORK CITY

To Venus and Helen.
Two Classic women in more than name.
Thanks for the unfailing support.

A LEISURE BOOK®

May 2003

Published by

Dorchester Publishing Co., Inc.
276 Fifth Avenue
New York, NY 10001

ISBN 0-8439-5207-5

Visit us on the web at www.dorchesterpub.com.

THE SEA WIFE

PROLOGUE

Dimly, as if through a green mist, she saw the hand stretching toward her—masculine, strong and imperative, like a hand from an old biblical painting.

And like the hand of an ancient prophet, it offered her a chance at life. A fleeting sadness fluttered at the edge of her consciousness. It was too late.

Too late. The current swirled; velvet fingers dragged at her, pulling her deeper into the silent darkness. With detached interest she watched the tendrils of long brown hair swirl about her head like those of a mermaid. Upward they floated, foolishly curling around the wrist that flailed above her. *Too late . . .*

Her eyes closed; after the terror of the last hours she was strangely peaceful, disinclined to reenter the maelstrom above her.

My name, she thought dispassionately, *is Sabina Grey, and I'm dying.*

The hand, however, was arrogantly insistent.

Pain ripped through her scalp as the fingers tangled

1

into her hair and pulled fiercely, jolting her back from the strange half-world of exhaustion she inhabited. She struck out at the fist, gripping it with a mermaid's strength, pulling both herself and her rescuer farther into the depths of the murky, churning green.

More pain. And then she was rising. Half dragged, half propelled by a sudden furious desire for survival, she broke the surface with a wild gasp for breath. The waves slapped into her open mouth, and she choked, ready to slip back into the peace below, but a man's face suddenly appeared close to hers, his arm gripping her shoulder. He mouthed something she couldn't hear above the crashing of waves and the dreadful sound of the sinking ship behind her. He was as sleek and smooth as a young seal, his hair plastered to his face with blood and seawater, his broad shoulders supporting her against buffeting waves.

He was clearly a selkie, one of the legendary water creatures from childhood legend, assuming human form to seduce and destroy foolish maidens. Mindlessly she lifted a hand to touch him, prepared to tell him that she was not so foolish, only to find that her free arm had slipped around his neck. She was dragging them both down.

His hand moved toward her once more, and this time the descent into darkness was so sudden that she had no chance to cry out or struggle against it.

CHAPTER ONE

She awoke in a coffin.

Caught in the fragile world between waking and sleeping, Sabina instinctively kicked off the rough woollen shroud and struggled onto her elbows, gasping wildly. She gulped in great breaths of air, and sagged with relief.

The wooden bunk with its high, rough-hewn sides was deep and coffin-shaped, but despite the fact that her head felt as if it were about to roll from her shoulders, she was very much alive.

And still very much at sea.

The creaking of timbers and the rise and fall of the bunk would have told her she was on the sea even if a lamp left hanging on a hook near the door hadn't cast a dim light over the cabin, outlining in detail the meager furnishings and the trappings of life aboard ship. Yet she was no longer on the *Margaret Rose*. She had watched its death throes some thousand miles off the coast of Rio de Janeiro, while clinging to a piece of wreckage, rocked by huge waves, half in, half out of the water. . . .

She moaned softly as she remembered the *Margaret Rose*, a beacon of flaming timbers, with everything and everyone she had left in the world sinking inexorably into a churning ocean.

Involuntarily, her hands went to her face, and she was startled to find it covered in grease. Her hands, too, she realized, were bandaged from the palms to the wrists, leaving only the swollen, red fingers bare. *Sausages,* she decided in horrified fascination, stretching her arms straight out in front of her, the better to view them, freezing there as the cabin door suddenly opened. A man entered and stood framed within the arc of her bandaged hands, like the subject of an artist's portrait.

The portrait of a pirate.

He was not a comforting sight. To begin with, he seemed to completely fill the cabin, his height forcing him to lower his head as he passed through the doorway, his breadth of shoulder dwarfing its already cramped proportions. He was apparently bent on a mission of mercy, as a towel was draped over his arm and he cradled a bowl in one hand, but some instinct caused Sabina to shrink from him, drawing herself into a tight ball against the pillows.

The man saw the gesture and paused, the fingers of his free hand curling into a fist. Automatically, it seemed, his stance stiffened into the defensiveness of a soldier in unknown terrain. Eyes of a brilliant blue examined her carefully from beneath a crop of wild, dark curls; one black eyebrow quirked upward in silent interrogation.

She too was being studied, she realized. By a pirate, tanned to a deep mahogany by the elements, the angles of his face partly obscured by a short dark beard.

All that was missing was the earring and the cutlass between his teeth.

Unexpectedly, the man threw back his head and laughed, his smile white against the darkness of his beard. She realized that the small frog croak she had just heard was her own voice, and she made a small, embarrassed movement, tucking her feet firmly against her body. The man ignored her further retreat, dumping the bowl on a small table, and then shockingly placed one long brown hand on her forehead. She jerked back, but his face was impassive, his fingers moving over her head with impersonal interest.

"So you are finally coherent. You've been tossing about in a high fever for the last four days. How do you feel?" The question was abrupt, his deep voice slightly hoarse as though he had been calling into the wind.

"I ... ." Sabina paused, uncertain how to answer. Uncertain if she could answer. However, a lifetime of polite drill led her to say primly, "I thank you. I am well."

Her voice was weak and hoarse, and the man frowned, suddenly straightening to his full height, arms crossed, legs braced. She flinched at the unexpected demand of his next words. "How much do you remember?"

Too much. She remembered too much.

She wanted to sink back beneath the blanket and return to the soothing oblivion of sleep, but the unspoken command was inescapable. "I remember you," she heard herself say dully. "You were the Man on the Raft."

She had *hated* the Man on the Raft.

And why not? He had made her do things she had not wanted to do. He had done things she had fought against. He had sheltered her in the shadow of his body when the sun seemed to flay the very flesh from her bones; he had shouted her awake when she would have given her immortal soul for the chance to close her eyes and drift into sleep; he had kept her lashed to the timbers by crushing her beneath him as he resisted the waves' efforts to wash them into the ocean.

He had kept her clinging to life when it would have been so much easier to let go.

Sabina expelled a shaky breath and lowered her eyes, plucking shyly at the edges of the discarded blanket. She was uncertain how to phrase the words. "I remember that you saved me from drowning." She raised her eyes to his and added simply, "Thank you."

For all the notice he took of her words, she might as well have been thanking him for the bowl beside her.

"You were sunburned, but it's not as bad as it could have been." He smiled and examined her with the professional eye of a slave trader. "You'll be all lilies and rose petals once again."

There was deep mockery in his words, and his smile unsettled her. Sabina shifted uneasily, conscious that her feet were bare. She pulled the rough blanket up over her knees before asking quietly, "Where are we?"

He moved to the other end of the cabin where he filled a pewter tankard from a jug that perched on the edge of the table. "I told you the sea-lane was our best chance of survival," he said over his shoulder. "The *Ellen Drury* picked us up eighteen hours after the ship went down. She's a merchantman bound for Plymouth. The master is an old sea dog from Devon called Scully. We couldn't have been more fortunate if we'd ordered her directly of the Fates."

"Eighteen hours!" Sabina shivered at the thought. "But what about the . . . others? Where are they? Was . . . wasn't anyone else picked up?"

He stood with his back to her, contemplating the tankard.

"No." His voice was cool, and Sabina felt herself suddenly shrivel inside. She hadn't been traveling alone. The Marchands had extended their help after her father's sudden death in Rio de Janeiro, arranging her passage with them back to England. A jolly middle-aged couple who enjoyed simple jokes and simple acts of kindness, they were far too fond of life to have lost it so easily.

"What . . . no one? But surely if *we* were lucky enough . . . I can't believe there wasn't a sign of anyone else! Didn't the ship turn back to *see*?"

"There was nothing to see," he replied brutally. She shrank in bewilderment from the harsh finality of his words. He turned to face her, the chiseled features betraying all the softness of a marble effigy, and then crossed to her side, proffering the tankard. "It's water mixed with a little wine. You've been throwing up for the past three days. You must be as parched as a mummy."

6

Perversely, she wanted to slap the tankard out of his hands and give way to the dreadful hysteria she felt rising within her. "I don't want it," she told him angrily, thumping the bunk in a gesture of futility. "I want the Marchands. I want Captain Feeney and all the others!"

"What we want and what we get in this world are two different things."

"How can you talk like that?" she demanded hoarsely. The man's indifference lashed her into a sitting position, despite the pain to her head and arms. "Don't you have any human feelings?"

He seemed more amused than offended by the question. "Very few, my dear. That's how I've survived in the world as long as I have." He looked down at her, the tankard still outstretched, his face carefully devoid of expression as he added harshly, "You can go into mourning for the whole ship for all I care, but if you don't want to get sick and follow them, you'll drink this. I didn't pull you out of the sea to watch you go into a decline."

Sabina had never in her life been spoken to in such a blunt manner. Indignation battled with the last fleeting feelings of gratitude. And won. "You heartless b . . . bear. I wish I'd been saved by anyone but you! Real pirates! I hope . . . I hope . . ."

Even to her own ears, she sounded more like a peevish child than a mature woman of two and twenty, but she was powerless to stop herself. She was not surprised that the man's amusement increased. "Drink. By the time you've finished it, I'm sure you'll have thought of some fitting punishment for me."

Close to tears, she shook her head. "I don't want it."

"Naturally," he replied smoothly, "You've been fished out of the Atlantic and lain in a fever for almost a week. You have neither hunger nor thirst. You are indeed a remarkable young woman." He set it down on the table next to the bunk. "Drink it." His voice suddenly softened as he added, "I'm a realist, Sabina. You can grieve sensibly, or you can grieve like a fool. Get your strength back. No one on the *Margaret Rose* will grudge you a swift recovery, you

7

may be sure of that. Don't look upon survival as a burden you have to bear. Don't torture yourself because you are alive."

The unexpected gentleness of his words poured over her like honeyed balm. She turned her head slowly toward him, grateful that he somehow seemed to understand exactly what she was feeling. It was true—she *did* feel guilty that she still lived while the Marchands and the others had perished. It made it difficult to be thankful for her own miraculous salvation. She smiled a little tremulously, one hand outstretched, prepared to take the tankard, and raised her eyes shyly to his. But she faltered and then dropped her bandaged fingers, shocked by the calculating brilliance of the man's suddenly narrowed gaze.

She felt like an insect pinned against a canvas, ready for the scientist's dissecting knife.

Sabina inhaled deeply, struggling to maintain some sort of composure. She wanted to ask him what he meant by it, but somehow words she had not meant to utter were startled from her. "What sort of man are you? Haven't you any feelings for what happened? Haven't you ever lost anything you loved?"

In the silence that followed, she was quite sure that the entire ship would be able to hear the heavy pounding of her heart. The man drew back, his expression unchanged, and replied evenly, "No. You must tell me what it feels like sometime." He left the cabin as suddenly as he had entered it.

It was as if she had been slapped.

She was torn between a desire to call after the man and an even stronger urge to throw the tankard at the door, but she found that she could barely lift her bandaged hand, let alone grasp the handle. She reached out, determined to make up for her former childishness by drinking down its contents, and accidentally knocked it to the floor, watching in dismay as the liquid soaked into the rough boards. She moved her tongue across her cracked, dry lips, suddenly conscious of how thirsty she was, conscious of how very alone she felt.

I have nothing and no one left, she realized in quiet horror. *I can't even feed myself, and I made the Man go away.*

The Man. She didn't even know his name. During those terrible hours they had spent fighting the sea, it had seemed immaterial. He was just there—the center of her precarious world.

And yet . . . wasn't that in itself highly unusual? One could hardly travel in the restricted environs of a ship for nearly three weeks and not know every soul on board by sight. Particularly a man as overwhelming as this one. He couldn't be a common sailor, not with his educated voice and his air of easy command. A reclusive passenger, then, stricken with seasickness, green and groaning in his cabin . . . ?

The scenario seemed so unlikely that a small, bitter smile tugged at the corners of her mouth. She could more likely believe that he was a merman emerged from the sea to save her from a watery death. Darkly handsome and strangely sinuous in his movements, so unlikely for such a tall, well-muscled man . . .

I'm beginning to hallucinate, Sabina decided, touching the grease on her face and neck with uncertain fingers. Whoever he was, whatever he was, she owed him more than she could ever possibly repay. She remembered her harsh words to him, and felt panic rise within her.

What if he didn't come back? What if he washed his hands of her and left her to the tender ministrations of the crew? He owed her nothing. He had already done his duty by her as a fellow member of the human race. . . .

Again the cabin door opened and the tall frame ducked under the narrow entrance. This time he carried a bowl whose tempting aroma promised more nourishment than water and wine. Sabina stifled the exclamation of relief that sprang to her lips, and sadly contemplated the tankard, which continued to roll about the floor in lazy circles.

His expression darkened. "I thought I told you to drink it."

"I . . . I couldn't," she admitted. Mutely she held up her bandaged hands.

He swore, the words sending her back against the rough pillow as if she had been pushed. "I can't help it," she added tearfully, ashamed of her own weakness.

"Don't," he growled. "I'm not angry with you." The Man put the bowl on the table and ran one exasperated hand through his hair. It was a curiously vulnerable gesture, and Sabina's own confidence suddenly soared. The Man was at a loss. It didn't matter that he was the picture of rude, animal health, standing on his own two feet and glowering down at her from a great height. He was suddenly all masculine confusion, confronted by the great mysteries of the sickroom. "I've never nursed a woman before." His tone was rueful, and Sabina impulsively responded to his softened voice with an outstretched hand.

"I know I must be a trial to you. And I'm sorry. For all those horrid things I said about you. And for being so annoyingly helpless. I'm not used to being an invalid, you know." She paused, and asked wistfully, "Aren't there any other women on board?"

"Only you and a female monkey," he replied dryly. "And she obviously knows more about this kind of thing than I do." After contemplating her extended hand, he took the fingers gently in his and sat down on the bunk. With his free hand he lifted a spoon from the bowl and thrust it toward her mouth with grim purpose. "Eat."

Sabina ate, the embarrassment of having to feed from his hand keeping her silent. Swallowing was difficult, and her arms had a tendency to tremble when she tried to hold herself up. It was not until she cast a discomfited glance at some spilt soup that she noticed her lack of clothing. She wore a thin shirt, which, though dry, left nothing of her body to the imagination. With a startled sound, she slid beneath the blankets, clutching them to her chin.

"I'm almost naked!"

One dark eyebrow quirked skywards. "I hadn't noticed," he said politely. "It must be the fact that I've been looking at you in your chemise for the past six days." He smiled grimly at her outraged gasp and raised the spoon to her lips, adding matter-of-factly, "Your sense of decorum must be pleased that the storm left you that much. I've seen men stripped naked by the force of the waves."

She swallowed, noting that he was dressed respectably, if roughly, in a seaman's garb of white trousers, shirt and short jacket, a kerchief carelessly knotted beneath the collar.

"Do I have any clothes left? Or will I have to borrow from the monkey?"

"You must be feeling better if you are thinking of your wardrobe. Eat and stop talking."

"But what on earth am I to do? I can't . . . I can't wear breeches!"

The spoon, held only inches away from her mouth, trembled slightly, and she realized that he was laughing.

"I'm glad you find the thought so hilarious," she said primly.

"Hilarity isn't exactly the emotion that image evokes," he said dryly, "but I won't go into explanations. Rest assured you won't have to borrow off the crew. Captain Scully's daughter sailed on the *Ellen Drury* last voyage and left some things in a sea trunk. You'll have at least one skirt, and a brush and comb of your own."

Sabina raised her hands self-consciously to the tangle of curls that spilled over her shoulders like pieces of hempen rope. A brush and a comb. The thought pleased her, and yet made her remarkably melancholy. It was the realization that these objects were now the sum of all her worldly possessions. Everything she had possessed in the world—her clothes, her meager jewelry, her father's books and sketches—everything was at the bottom of the ocean. She tried to make a pleased response, but could only hang her head to prevent the man from seeing the moisture rolling down her cheeks. She was ashamed that the thought of her lost belongings should finally move her to tears, when the memory of her lost friends had evinced only an angry denial. She turned her head to spare herself the expected taunts.

"It's all right. I shan't let you arrive in England looking

11

like a beggar." He was amused, but there was a curious gentleness in his tone that made Sabina lift her head and gravely study his face. Beneath the beard she detected the clean, hard angles of his jaw, casting into sharp emphasis the high-bridged nose, the strongly marked brows and the extraordinary cornflower blue of the thickly lashed eyes. It was an intelligent, uncompromising face, yet bespeaking a sort of restrained aggression with which Sabina was totally unfamiliar.

The men in her rather sheltered experience had been scientists, like her father—botanists and natural historians who had treated her with either paternal indulgence or a kind of detached reverence. Adventurous, perhaps, in their pursuit of knowledge, but hardly able to be described as adventurers. At seventeen, she had left school in England to travel with her papa to the West Indies and the colorful countries of South America in search of the fascinating bird life of these areas; along the way she had met with sickness, storms and death. It was not the usual life for a young woman of gentle upbringing who had expected to run her father's small household in a respectable part of London, transcribing his notes and dusting his sketchbooks. But although she had encountered both scholars and scoundrels on their journeys, she had never met anyone quite like the man who sat mere inches from her now, his eyes holding hers with a fixed, incalculable gaze.

"I don't think I understand you at all," she finally admitted, her head tipped to one side. The Man . . . strange that he should still figure in her thoughts in capitals. She suddenly gave a small gurgle of laughter that caused him to straighten and examine her with cool detachment.

"I take it you aren't giving into hysterics," he inquired politely.

"No, I don't think I could raise even a decent scream at this stage." She carefully wiped the moisture from her face and attempted a wavering smile. "It's just that . . . well, I realize I haven't even asked you your name. You were here, and it seemed totally beside the point if you had a name or not."

"Oh, I have one."

"Naturally. And like Rumpelstiltskin, you don't wish to share it. And yet you know mine."

This time his eyes glinted with a light that made her edge the blanket closer around her shoulders. "Even a recluse like myself managed to notice you aboard ship, Miss Grey. You were . . . eminently noticeable."

"I was?" Sabina cast her mind back to her behavior on the ship, anxious to recall any lapses on her part. Surely she had been the very picture of ladylike circumspection. She had refused to play card games on Sundays, and had never walked on deck in the evening without Mrs. Marchand as her chaperone. Well, almost never. "What do you mean?" she asked suspiciously.

He lifted the spoon and began to feed her more soup. "I don't suppose Feeney spent so much time in your company merely to teach you navigation. No, don't splutter at me. I feel I'm getting rather good at this cosseting business, but I need your cooperation to actually get the spoon in your mouth."

Sabina swallowed indignantly. "Captain Feeney was very kind in his attentions. He knew that when Papa died in Brazil, I was left stranded without a penny to my name."

"Yes, I always took Feeney for a philanthropist. Good works seemed natural to that old sea buzzard."

The spoon once again stopped Sabina's robust reply, and after she swallowed, she merely said meekly, "I suppose you are paying me some sort of compliment. Either that, or," she hazarded, "fobbing me off from discovering who you are."

"There is no great mystery. I am Myles Dampier."

Sabina's mouth clamped down on the spoon and she swallowed with difficulty. No mystery? Why, the man was *all* mystery. She wondered why she hadn't guessed his identity earlier.

Myles Dampier had kept to his cabin on the *Margaret Rose*, refusing to consort with the other passengers and only emerging to walk the decks of an evening. He had occupied one of the privileged saloons under the poop deck; the other, used by Mrs. Marchand and Sabina, should have afforded them more than the rare glimpses they actually had of the man. He was rich, he was reclusive, and he was arrogant—that much was known. Even those who had traveled in his company all the way from New South Wales could add little more to the general sum of knowledge about Myles Dampier.

Sabina would have had little to add were it not for one memorable encounter.

"I'm a fool not to have recognized you, even with the beard," she said slowly. "We met one evening on deck when I was alone."

"*Met* is not an accurate term, Miss Grey. You took one look at me and darted off as if I were about to eat you."

"I did not!" she replied indignantly. "What a ninny you make me sound. It's just that . . . well, while I might not recognize a compliment, I can recognize a leer when I see it."

"That was not a leer. It was merely a glance of masculine appreciation." Sabina was unconvinced, and he asked innocently, "How long did you live in South America?"

"Five years. Why do you . . . ? Oh. I see. Well, foreigners may be forgiven for leering, but you don't expect such appreciation from an English gentleman."

"English, certainly. Gentleman, now . . . that is debatable." There was a sharp edge to his voice, which was at odds with the cool amusement of his words.

The sharpness caught Sabina's attention. "You are the most curious man I've ever met. You save my life, I spend a day and a night with you in the middle of the ocean, I find that for days I lived less than ten feet from your door—and I still know next to nothing about you. Well," she added thoughtfully, "only that one moment you can be very cruel, and the next moment very kind."

"Cruel, indeed." Myles Dampier lifted his eyes and demanded of the ceiling, "Why do females interpret being told the truth as cruelty?" The cornflower gaze was deceptively mild as it swept Sabina's blanketed form. "And if you've finished your meal, I suggest you go back to sleep. You look worn out."

Warm with soup, and exhausted by the effort of sitting upright for such a long period, Sabina accepted the advice gratefully. She slid beneath the coarse blanket, her eyes suddenly heavy, and regarded Myles Dampier solemnly. "I don't usually talk so much, you know. It must be because I am alive when I know very well I shouldn't be. What a strange conversation we have had. But then"—she yawned delicately—"I really didn't know what to say to someone who has saved my life."

He stood over the bunk, smiling that inscrutable smile which was half mocking, half serious. "At this stage, 'good night' would be sufficient."

"No, it's not." She felt inclined to argue, even as a pleasant lethargy stole over her, making her aching limbs grow heavy and her eyelids flutter vainly in an attempt to stay open. "I said horrible things to you." She sensed that he was near the door, and she panicked, forcing her eyes open in an effort to prevent him from leaving. "I called you a bear!"

"I forgive you," he soothed.

"I wouldn't. I was r . . . rude. And I'm almost never rude. Except for now. I'm sorry to fall asleep in front of you." She stared at him through her lashes before asking sleepily, "Was there something in the soup?"

"Radishes, by the look of it."

"I mean a sleeping draught. The soup was bitter. I don't mind if there was a draught. I thought I shouldn't be able to sleep for nightmares, and I feel so . . . so *deliciously* weary now. Not like before." She yawned again, and before she gave up the struggle to ward off insensibility, managed to ask coherently, "Do you dream about the *Margaret Rose*, Myles Dampier?"

His answer followed her into oblivion, making her forehead crease in a futile effort to understand.

"No, Miss Grey. I've *lived* with too many nightmares to let them intrude into my sleep."

*   *   *

Smoke and the pungent odor of a dying ship awoke her several hours later. Sabina found herself on her feet, swaying precariously. She flung open the cabin door and confronted the startled gaze of a short, stout man, dressed in blue nankeen and white trousers, a pipe poised in the corner of his open mouth.

It was hastily removed. "Miss Grey. You poor lassie. Are you not well? What's troubling you?"

The calm concern in the man's voice dampened Sabina's panic, and she answered carefully, "Smoke. I smell smoke." She put her hands over her ears and screwed her eyes up fast, like a child blocking out bogeymen and monsters. When she finally reopened them, she found herself being led into a large saloon. The man knocked several charts off a deep armchair and lowered her into it, deftly throwing a rug about her shoulders and arranging it modestly over her unclad form.

"My pipe, lassie, that's all. I should have thought about it before I stood outside your door puffing away like one of Mr. Stephenson's steam contraptions." He paused, and added contritely, "I'm Captain Scully, m'dear. You must tell me if there is anything I can get you."

"Mr. Dampier—where is he?" As soon as the words slipped out, Sabina wished them back. She was behaving like some frightened child calling for its nursemaid. She squared her shoulders, ready to disclaim any necessity for Myles Dampier's presence, but Captain Scully's round face bore such a comic expression of relief not to be called upon to minister to feminine vapors that she held her tongue.

"Mr. Dampier is on deck. I'll fetch him and tell him that you are up and on your feet," The captain eyed her shivering from doubtfully. "In a manner of speaking."

"Please." Pride battled need, and she finally shook her head. "I shall be all right, really I shall. I don't need anyone. I'm just . . ." She raised her head resolutely and continued with a jauntiness she was far from feeling, "Oh! I'm just so wretchedly sorry to be such a nuisance to you."

16

His tone was rallying. "Nuisance? Why, that's no way to talk about a brave lassie like yourself. Plucked from the sea like a real live mermaid. We seldom make a catch like you, m'dear. Now tell me. Is there anything I can get you? Anything at all? You have only to ask."

He smiled like a benevolent gnome in a fairy tale offering her three wishes.

Three wishes.

She considered them dispassionately.

The first, of course, would be to have her father alive and well, sitting beside her, his beloved copy of de Buffon's *Natural History of Birds* open on his lap, drawing her attention to subtle variations in plume and claw and beak. As for the second . . . well, the Marchands would be seated beside him in the saloon, noisy with good fellowship and the sheer pleasure of living.

Good people. People she had loved. And now all that was left to her was . . .

Her third wish. The thing for which she would cheerfully sell her immortal soul.

She turned her head from the captain's benevolent countenance and replied grittily, "I want a bath. And I want to wash my hair in freshwater and soap."

If she had announced that she wanted to take charge of the ship, Captain Scully couldn't have displayed more shock. "A bath. And freshwater for your hair." The pipe bobbed uncertainly in his mouth. "Well, now. I shall have to check the scuttlebutt and see what is left for today. But we had some good falls of rain, and we should be in the Canaries in another week—I'll be taking on more water at Teneriffe. So perhaps a can of freshwater . . . *And* soap. Well, that we most certainly do have." He drew in a determined breath and said heartily, "You may bathe, Miss Grey. Why, you're just like my youngest girl. Insisted on bathing in seawater twice a week."

The thought of immersing her aching body in hot water of any kind was so seductive that she nearly forgot her other desperate desire. She raised her hand self-consciously to the curls brushing her face and neck and

17

added meekly, "I would be very grateful to have a mirror, too, please."

The captain, despite wearing the air of one expected to materialize an entire dressing table, finally produced a small shaving mirror from his locker. He then began to back away toward the door before his guest could demand any more feminine trifles.

"Anything at all," he assured her as he disappeared up the companionway. "Only too happy." Sabina heard the afterhouse door leading onto the deck slam with a relieved finality, and she smiled wryly. Captain Scully's courage obviously did not extend to tending to sick, demanding females. It made her all the more grateful for Myles Dampier's efficient care of her. He was a strange, unfathomable man, she decided, raising the mirror to her face, but she owed him more than she could ever repay.

Her burgeoning thoughts of gratitude were suddenly cut off as she stared at a portrait of the Gorgon Medusa. The blotched face, the cracked lips, the riotous tendrils of hair—they could not possibly belong to her. Dazedly she watched the broken lips part, emitting a shrill scream that echoed alarmingly through the cabin.

Sabina heard the afterhouse door swing open and heavy footsteps swiftly descending the stairs. Myles Dampier swung through the open door of the cabin and then stopped, his taut features relaxing as he took in the significance of the mirror clasped between trembling hands.

"Why," she demanded through gritted teeth, "why didn't you tell me I look like . . . like a scarecrow in a fit!"

He leaned against the door frame, a small smile playing at the corners of his mouth. He was clean-shaven. He was washed and healthy and heartbreakingly handsome, and Sabina decided that she hated him very much.

"Well," she said quaveringly. "Are you just going to stand there and *stare* at me? Haven't you anything to say?"

"Yes." His voice was grave, but the amusement in his face spoke volumes. "I was about to say that now I *know* you are finally on the mend."

"It's all right for you. You don't look a perfect fright.

18

You look"—she struggled for words, finally opting for the most neutral—"shaved!"

"I managed to borrow that mirror from Captain Scully earlier," he explained apologetically.

"I wish I hadn't. I wish I'd remained in blissful ignorance." Sabina stared at the green-eyed madwoman in the mirror and then raised her head with a defiant tilt. "I suppose you think I am terribly vain and shallow to be worrying about my appearance at this moment."

"Not at all," he replied coolly. "I think you are very wise to worry about your one remaining asset."

"My one remaining . . ." She broke off, and sighed with exaggerated patience before continuing aggrievedly, "I guessed I might rely on you for both a total lack of sympathy *and* an obscure reply into the bargain. What on earth are you talking about?"

He replied easily, "Well, obviously you will need all your looks to secure even a passably comfortable life back in England. A husband is not easily hunted without beauty, even in this day and age. No, you are right to be so concerned about your face when it is your entire fortune."

Sabina stared at the nonchalant figure leaning against the door frame and slowly repeated, "Husband . . . hunting." She choked on the final word and discovered that she was very much tempted to use the mirror she clutched as a discus, thrown directly at Myles Dampier's arrogant head. "How dare you suggest . . . I would like to inform you, Mr. Dampier, that I am a great deal more than my face! I'll have you know I am fluent in three languages besides my own, and have a better than average knowledge of botany, geography and Latin. When I return to England, I intend to be a . . . a very superior sort of governess!"

His face was suddenly all ingenuous innocence. "My dear Miss Grey, even from our very short acquaintance I gather that you would be superior at everything you do. However, a future governess really should learn to control her temper. If I'm not mistaken, your teeth are clenched.

And a little more modesty about your accomplishments wouldn't go amiss either."

She stared at him suspiciously, her fury suddenly draining. "You said that deliberately, didn't you? About my . . . faults. Just to make me angry. Why?"

The blue eyes narrowed. "You are very intelligent. And decidedly acute. I hadn't quite realized how much until now." He moved from his post by the door and with a casual movement straddled a wooden chair beside her own, his arms crossed over the back, his chin resting lightly upon his arms as he continued to inspect her with a curiously detached interest that made her feel like one of her father's specimens in a jar of alcohol. He continued affably, "I thought you were about to descend into weeping melancholy, and I infinitely prefer healthy anger. I apologize for my misreading of your character."

"I wouldn't have thought you someone who misread anything. You seem far too sure of your own powers of observation." The remark slipped out, and Sabina was surprised at her frankness. But there was something about Myles Dampier's proximity that seemed to inspire her to say and do things she would normally keep bottled up inside. Even her unconventional life in South America had been lived with all the convention of being an English gentlewoman, expressing conventional thoughts and feelings. But this . . . it was a delicious, heady sort of freedom, possibly arising from their unusual circumstances.

After all, what *do* you say to someone who has saved your life?

The amusement had returned to his face, but his mouth, although curled into a semblance of a smile, was paradoxically hard. "I can assure you, Sabina, that my character judgments in the past have been notoriously inaccurate."

"Well, obviously not *too* inaccurate where I'm concerned." She sighed and risked another glance at the mirror before adding mournfully, "Left on my own, I would have been in tears. I'm obviously vain and silly and shallow, and I never realized it before."

He shook his head, and his smile widened, caught somewhere between bitterness and amusement. He stretched out a long, brown hand and touched her gently on her cheek. "When we reach England I will introduce you to true Vanity. Then, my dear Mermaid, you will realize how very little you resemble it."

My dear Mermaid. The term made something catch in the back of her throat, and caused a delicious melting sensation somewhere in her stomach. Staring up at him, she realized that she had never felt less like a fairy-tale creature in all her life. She was suddenly aware of the physicality of the world she inhabited, of skin on bone and of blood coursing and her heart beating a heavy rhythm like a drummer leading an army into battle. His caress had been a careless one, she realized, much like the stroking of a pet spaniel, but where his fingers had touched her face, the skin was on fire.

I am a very foolish female, she admonished herself, suddenly averting her eyes from the powerful body draped carelessly over the chair. *I'm alone and I'm frightened and this man is strong. And he has cared for me. That's all there is to it. And that's all there should be!* She discreetly withdrew her leg from its proximity to a well-muscled thigh, and said with a fair imitation of an amused laugh, "You are being obscure again. Obscure and completely mysterious!"

"I prefer the word 'discreet.' "

"Well, I prefer the word 'explanation.' "

He grinned and rose from his chair, surveying her muffled form from the advantage of his six-feet-three-inches. "Do you want me to carry you back to your cabin?"

The thought was horrifyingly tempting. "No, I'm staying here to have a bath. Captain Scully will have it set up for me in here where there is more room."

"Ah. And will you be requiring my assistance?"

"No, I will not. Even though you *have* seen me in my shift. I don't know if it is fashionable in New South Wales for ladies to bathe in general company, but I shall cling to the English tradition of privacy!"

21

There was no quick rejoinder to this sally, and a narrowed gaze that had unaccountably hardened met Sabina's look of inquiry. "You've just reminded me that I haven't been back to England in fifteen years." His voice was a curious mixture of bitterness and flippancy. "I'm afraid that I am long unacquainted with the Englishwoman as a species. And the English *gentlewoman* in particular. Tell me, have they changed a great deal in their notions?"

There was no denying the sneer in his voice. Sabina wondered at it, but replied steadily, "Perhaps they bathe in the middle of the street, for all I know. I have no more to report than you. My notions have been living in South America since I was seventeen."

His eyes momentarily widened with real amusement, before the black lashes veiled his thoughts. He was once again the Man on the Raft, Myles Dampier—Enigma. "Yes, I keep forgetting that you are as much a foreigner as myself." His voice was meditative.

"Hardly . . . foreigners. We shall be Home soon."

"Ah, yes. Home," he drawled. "So we shall. And there we will find out how much has changed, and how much remains the same." The sardonic eyebrow quirked upward, and then he looked at her and smiled. It was still very much a piratical smile, gleaming white against the taut, brown face, and once again Sabina felt as though she were being assessed for the slave markets of Morocco. "I shall leave you to enjoy your bath."

The door closed, and Sabina slumped farther into the chair, contemplating her position.

It was undeniably bleak. Over the past few months, she had gradually lost everything she had in the world—her father, her friends, and all her possessions. She had nearly lost her life. Now all that was left to her was a blanket, and a brush and comb that belonged to someone else.

And Myles Dampier, she told herself fiercely. *I have Myles Dampier for my friend. I'm not alone.*

Dear God, I'm not completely alone anymore.

She raised her hands to her face, still covered with its

thin film of grease. She was thankful to feel the tears finally begin to course in hot rivulets down her cheeks—a salty balm, offering her some sort of relief from the terrible ball of emotion lodged near her heart. She was just uncertain whether they were tears of pain or gratitude.

CHAPTER TWO

"The sea roared; and the stormy winds lifted up the waves thereof.

"We were carried up as it were to heaven, and then down again into the deep; our soul melted within us, because of trouble.

"Then we cried unto thee, O Lord."

Captain Scully's broad Devonshire accent was infused with solemn thanksgiving as he read the prayer of deliverance on the main deck to his crew and two passengers. Three days of heavy storms had battered the small brigantine, and more than once Sabina had clung to the side of her bunk convinced that the *Ellen Drury* would meet the same watery fate as the *Margaret Rose*. However, Sunday had miraculously dawned clear of storms, with crisp winds and a benevolent sea, and more than one sailor, forbidden by the good captain to engage her in any conversation lest she be offended by their rough language, had shot her an awkward smile as she hobbled across the deck to join the little band of worshipers. Clasping the woollen blanket that served as her company wardrobe even more tightly around her body, Sabina bowed her head and sent her own silent prayer for both the lives lost at sea and those spared.

Thou didst send forth thy commandment; and the windy storm ceased, and was turned into calm.

Yes, calm at last, and finally a measure of peace after the fear and the sorrow were past. Sabina reflected that it was not only the *Ellen Drury* that had finally sailed into calmer waters. For the past three weeks she had grieved silently for the loss of her friends, until the wound had gradually healed into a nagging ache that bled only during moments of quiet reflection. Like the present. She swayed slightly, her legs still reluctant to hold her for long periods, and felt her arm seized in a viselike grip.

"You shouldn't be out of bed." The words were murmured softly, but Sabina heard the swift undercurrent of anger.

"I'm perfectly all right," she whispered fiercely, disengaging her arm with an impatient action. "And I wanted to be here."

"That's because you have less sense than the monkey." Myles Dampier nodded in the direction of the captain's pet, which chattered amiably above them in the rigging. "In fact," he added critically, "at this moment you both have a similar complexion. Any more so and Scully would be reading the burial service over you."

Involuntarily, Sabina glanced up at the little creature's white-whiskered face, and straightened herself into a ramrod carriage. "I needed to be here," she hissed. "To . . . remember. And to give thanks for our deliverance from the sea."

And, she told herself sternly, *to prove that I can finally stand on my own two feet.*

"I delivered you from the sea, Mermaid. You can thank me by getting back down below until you can walk properly."

She had difficulty catching her breath. "Of all the arrogance! Do you know, Myles Dampier, you are going to be struck down one day!"

A hearty "Amen" from Captain Scully and his crew prevented her from hearing his reply, but the lazy grin that unfurled across the brown features told her he was unrepentant.

"You look remarkably like you did when I beat you at chess the other evening," he murmured down at her, removing her arm from the fold of the blanket and placing it within the crook of his elbow. "And at piquet the night before that. As though nothing but seeing me fall flat on my face could give you any pleasure."

This was so near the truth that a small bubble of laughter was surprised out of her. Despite the gravity of the moment, she was suddenly conscious of a remarkable sense of well-being, and a feeling of exhilaration that was created by much more than the sun beating down on her face and the gentle rhythms of a calm sea. Although she was vividly aware of hard muscle encircling her arm, she relaxed and responded to his teasing tone with a genuine smile. "How very ungallant of you to treat an invalid so. If you were a gentleman, you would let me win once in a while."

"Ah. This is most interesting. Your definition of the term *gentleman* is someone who allows others to cheat."

"Well, a gentleman would not take so much pleasure in winning."

"Mermaid, I always win. And from that I take a *great* deal of pleasure."

His words were light, and his smile vividly white against the dark features, but even so, Sabina was perplexed by his reply. For some reason, his underlying tone reminded her of steel drawn from a scabbard. She wanted to demand an explanation, but Captain Scully, having dismissed his crew, approached them with a beaming smile that changed him from a solemn ship's master into a stout sea cherub.

"My dear Miss Grey, it's good to see you up and about. And on such a beautiful morning, too. Well, the storm

26

clouds are past, and we have seen St. Paul's Rocks in the distance. We should be in the Canaries sometime tomorrow. How will you like to see the mountains above Santa Cruz, eh? Safe harbor at last." He hesitated and added delicately, "Mr. Dampier tells me that you had quite a bout of seasickness during the storm."

Sabina shuddered a little at the thought, remembering her companion's attentions as he held a bowl beneath her head during the worst of the bouts. She had been far too ill to feel any embarrassment at his ministering to her physical needs, and now could only feel gratitude. She replied earnestly, "Yes, I was very ill indeed, but no nurse could have been more attentive than Mr. Dampier."

The captain, obviously relieved at this lack of squeamishness on her part, said shyly, "Then I hope you didn't mind my adding your name to the general prayers at the end. Asking for a complete recovery of your health, you know."

"You . . . you did?"

"You did an excellent thing," Myles Dampier put in smoothly. "Miss Grey was just assuring me how touched she was by your thoughtfulness." His elbow collided gently with her ribcage, and Sabina, startled into good manners, promptly said, "I believe I have never in my life been so overwhelmed by good wishes and good deeds. I shall leave this ship thoroughly spoiled by your kindness."

The captain turned pink with pleasure, and to cover his embarrassment raised his arm and clicked his fingers. The little monkey scampered down the rigging and leapt onto his shoulder, gibbering excitedly. "Jezebel here has grown very fond of you, Miss Grey," he said heartily. "I'm sure she is delighted to see all your bandages finally removed."

Sabina reached out an uncertain hand toward the little creature who grabbed at her fingers and studied them with great interest. However, Jezebel decided that nothing of interest was to be gained there, quickly dropped them, and instead made coquettish overtures toward Myles Dampier, grimacing and chattering to gain his attention. Sabina grinned at this example of feminine capriciousness.

27

"Then she'll be overjoyed to know that not only can I dress and feed myself, but also walk without assistance. *Despite* medical opinion to the contrary."

Her barb was deflected by the movement of one agile dark brow. "If your notion of walking is a step and a stagger, Miss Grey—"

"I can hardly regain my strength if I am cosseted like a baby in my berth!"

Myles Dampier folded his arms across his chest in an arrogant gesture she was quickly beginning to recognize. "Unfortunately, Miss Grey, you don't seem to realize your limitations."

Sabina, all too well aware of her limitations, found herself challenging him with a lift of her chin. "Well, what a pity I'm not like you and have none."

"But how acute of you to recognize that fact. I've seldom met with such perception in a young woman."

"Well, I've seldom encountered such high-handedness in a man!"

Captain Scully, who had listened to this exchange with increasing discomfort, suddenly announced that duty called him to the fo'c'sle deck and hurried away, a reluctant Jezebel clinging to his jacket. Sabina watched him go with gradually dawning horror.

"Oh dear! I drove him away, didn't I?"

Myles Dampier arranged his lean body comfortably against the railing and continued to regard her with amusement. "Do you know, I think you have just cured Scully's infatuation with your beautiful eyes, Mermaid. Are you always this outspoken?"

"I've never spoken to anyone in my life as I speak to you," she said mournfully. "Mama would be mortified if she could hear me. It's as though . . . as though I'm suddenly someone quite different. It's hard to explain . . ." She broke off and, gazing up into his face, asked earnestly, "You aren't offended, are you? You know I don't mean to be rude to you."

"You haven't offended me, Sabina. Far from it. You are entirely . . . delightful."

This admission, made as it was in a low voice, made her chest suddenly tighten and her breathing seem to suspend itself. She raised her eyes shyly to the narrowed gaze transfixing her to the spot. Feeling as though she had been captured in an invisible fishing net, she searched his face for some explanation for her sudden inertia, and then found that her knees were actually buckling beneath her. She gasped aloud as she began to sink to the deck in a graceless bundle of woollen folds, but a swift movement scooped her up into Myles Dampier's arms, where she found herself firmly held against his chest.

"I've never had a woman throw herself at my feet before, Mermaid. A simple apology would have sufficed."

"My legs just won't work," she said breathlessly, conscious that his darkly handsome face was mere inches from her own. She found herself shockingly wishing that she were not wrapped in the cocoon of a thick woollen blanket, so that she might be somehow closer to the strong clasp of his arms.

"Notice that I'm not saying 'told you so.' "

"May I go down to the cabin, please?" she asked in a small voice. Miserably she wondered how much of her collapse was due to the natural exhaustion of an invalid too soon out of bed, and how much was an hysterical response to the physical nearness of a man she was increasingly attracted to. *You are an incredible fool, Sabina Grey*, she told herself severely, and then inhaled sharply as he moved her in his arms, the better to gain a stronger grip on her body.

"I meant that I wanted to walk down," she protested. He ignored her and kicked open the afterhouse door. Ducking beneath the low companionway door, he descended the stairs, stopping at her cabin. Before he could maneuver the door open, she threw her arms about his neck and pushed her foot firmly against the door. "No! Please! I feel like a naughty child being punished. Can't you understand what it's like to be imprisoned for days in a dark cupboard? Please don't make me go back in!"

He hesitated at the alarm in her voice and, turning

29

abruptly, carried her into the captain's cabin, lowering her gently into a sturdy leather chair. He towered above her, his face once more the familiar stone mask that she had learned to dread. "Strangely enough, Sabina, I do understand. I understand all too well. I'm sorry that you can't sit on deck beneath a tarpaulin as you did on the *Margaret Rose*, but there just isn't room."

Sabina shook her head, eager to disclaim any feelings of ill use. She managed a convincing laugh as she said lightly, "No, indeed. I'm sure the crew would be wishing me back on our raft if I insisted on sitting in the middle of the deck like Cleopatra on her barge. But if I may stay for a while in the captain's cabin, I will be as comfortable as if I were back in the ladies' saloon."

The darkness lifted from his face, but she was by no means sure that the polite, expressionless stranger would not stay. She was determined he would not. She lowered her eyes. "I must be a very sad trial to you," she said contritely, peeping through her lashes. "Always complaining about something, instead of acting like a true adventurer. I don't know why you continue to be so kind to me."

"Can't you? Then you aren't as intelligent as I thought." His tone was dry, but she was relieved to detect the hint of a smile behind the cool, azure gaze. His expression was alert, the slight tilt of his head toward her attentive, almost wary; and yet she marveled that, even standing motionless beside her, he exuded a turbulent vitality.

It disturbed her, this physical inequality between them, and she plucked nervously at the blanket still wrapped around her suddenly shivering form. "I sometimes think that you aren't quite human, you know. You don't get sunstroke, you don't get seasick. I wager you never had the usual childhood diseases like measles or mumps. In fact, I have no doubt that you would survive the Black Death were we unfortunate enough to encounter it."

"I have had both the measles and the mumps as a child. But never having encountered the Black Death, we'll leave that open to conjecture." He strode over to the large desk that dominated the captain's cabin and, taking a bottle

and a glass, poured out a large measure. Sabina, too astonished at the image of Myles Dampier as a sickly child,
refrained from pointing out that he was stealing the best
Madeira, and sat blinking at him owlishly. He thrust the
glass at her, and she accepted it mechanically.

She began to talk quickly to cover her sudden confusion. "I'm usually very healthy. Quite revoltingly so, in fact.
In the past five years I've had not even a sniffle, although
there was fever on the ship when we first rounded Cape
Horn, and a dreadful epidemic when we visited Buenos
Aires . . ." She broke off as memory launched a fresh as-
sault on old wounds. "That's why I wasn't overly alarmed
when Papa fell ill in Rio de Janeiro. His health had always
been excellent. We were a little acquainted with the Marchands—through Papa's friends in the Royal Society, you
know—and they summoned a doctor, but . . . it . . . it was
useless." She gulped down a mouthful of wine, determined to swallow her unhappy memories. She added rebelliously, "And now I suppose I won't be able to go into
Santa Cruz when we finally get there. I shall be forced to
stay on the ship."

Myles Dampier regarded her with approval. "Sense at
last, Mermaid. You are completely correct. I have no intention of carrying you about like a Chinese princess. Nor
will Scully arrange to have you borne through the streets
upon a litter."

"But I do have to go!" Sabina fought down the incipient
note of panic in her voice and tried to sound as calm and
responsible as she had in her head when she first decided
to broach the subject of her independence. "It's important. There may be a shipping agent for the *Margaret Rose*
in Teneriffe. Perhaps I can get transport back to England
so I'll not be a burden to either you or Captain Scully any
longer."

"When have you ever been made to feel a burden?" His
voice held a savage quality that made her wince, but she
refused to back down. She squared her shoulders and
transferred her gaze to the bottom of the wineglass she

31

held cradled in her hands before embarking upon a well-practiced speech.

"Be that as it may, the fact is I have no claim on you whatsoever. Captain Scully has been obliged to offer us— me—his help, but that doesn't mean that I shouldn't make some shift to help myself." She drew in a deep breath before continuing grittily, "You saved my life, that's true, but that doesn't necessarily make you responsible for my future well-being. Indeed, you shouldn't be. You can't be. Our . . . unusual . . . circumstances have allowed us a certain freedom of speech and action toward each other that won't be tolerated once we return home to England. You must know that. And my position is precarious enough as it is. If I am to seek a respectable position, I . . . well . . ." Her voice faded away in blushing confusion, and she finally risked a glance at Myles Dampier to see what effect her formal little speech had had upon him.

The stone mask had been replaced by a wide grin.

A less charitable woman would have described it as a smirk.

"You are saying, Miss Grey, that you have been hopelessly compromised by your association with me. A truly well-bred young woman would have preferred to drown rather than spend the night on a raft with a gentleman to whom she was not closely related."

"You make me sound like an absolute idiot," Sabina protested crossly. "Of course I don't mean that at all. But you know that when I return to England, there will be some notoriety. And unless I mean to hire myself out to a traveling fair as the sole survivor of a shipwreck and cannibals, I can't see it working to my benefit. It would be better if I arrived . . . under my own colors, as it were. Now, is there a British consul in Santa Cruz?"

"There is a Spanish governor on the Grand Canary. But I doubt that you'll find him much help in getting back to England. I've told you before, you have no need to worry. I'll make sure you reach England—*uncompromised*—and I'll make sure that you won't starve once you get there."

"I'm not frightened of starving, I don't think." There

was a note of uncertainty in her voice that she strove to suppress. "Mama has a cousin still living. In Bournemouth." With difficulty she conjured up an image of Cousin Sarah's pinched, disapproving face. Sabina had no doubt that her adventures would not endear her to that lady, already scandalized by Sabina's father's determination to explore foreign shores. She added hurriedly, "And there must be one of Papa's friends who could find me a respectable position *somewhere*, despite my misfortunes."

"Ah, yes. We are back to the idea of the Superior Governess."

"It must be thought of! You say that you will help me, and I appreciate that, but . . . but I know almost nothing about you! Apart from your name—and the fact that you had the measles as a child—I know almost nothing at all."

"What do you want to know?" he asked quietly.

"Wh-what?"

"What do you wish to know about me?"

Sabina was rendered slack-jawed by this sudden capitulation. She did not believe it. It was too easy a solution to the mystery that was Myles Dampier.

But even more acute than her surprise was her sudden fear. What on earth *did* she want to know? What else did she need to know, other than that this man who had pulled her from the sea had become her lifeline to everyday existence. She hung her head, feeling suddenly defeated by her own cowardice.

Are you a husband? A father? A lover? A devil? A saint?

It is not important, she told herself fiercely. *We shall be in England within a matter of weeks, and I will be nothing more than a character in an exciting after-dinner story he will tell with the good port. In fact, he'll most probably forget my name altogether and refer to me as the Mermaid, and his audience will smile and wonder what became of me. . . .*

"You trusted me with your life on our raft, Sabina. Why won't you trust me now?"

It was an interesting question, to which she had no answer. Reluctantly she raised her eyes to his, disturbed to see the laconic humor that lingered in the blue depths.

She opened her mouth to demand that he take her concerns seriously when, with impeccable timing, Captain Scully's cheerful countenance appeared around the door frame.

"There you are, Miss Grey. The Peak of Teneriffe is in view, although we are a good hundred miles from shore. You won't want to miss your first sighting of land, I'll be bound."

"Captain Scully," she began, determinedly quelling a slight tremor in her voice. She stopped, flicking an uncertain look at Myles Dampier's suddenly still form. His hands, she noticed, hung clenched at his sides, the brown fingers curled, the knuckles white.

Involuntarily she thought of the lean hand extended toward her through the waves, lashing her to the makeshift raft that plunged and tossed at the mercy of the storm. Washing her, feeding her, holding her . . .

"Captain Scully," she continued evenly, and then paused, holding up her half-finished glass. "I have a confession to make. I have drunk a glass of your good wine. What must you think of me?"

"Why, bless my soul, Miss Grey. What is a man to do in the Canaries if not replenish his stock of wine? We will finish the rest of the bottle in a toast to reaching port so soon after all our tribulations. Shall we drink to safe harbor, then?"

Reluctantly Sabina caught Myles Dampier's gaze. Was that relief she caught there? Or something darker, more bitter . . . more cynical.

She pushed the thought aside and, raising her glass, smiled brilliantly. "Oh, yes, Captain. Let's drink to safe harbor."

The *Ellen Drury* entered the port of Santa Cruz the following morning. Sabina, awed by the brilliant colors of the harbor, and comforted just by the sight of dry land, watched Myles Dampier, Captain Scully, and six of the ship's small crew of nine clamber into the longboat that would take them to the shore.

She realized that this was the first time she had been truly left alone.

On the one hand, she was almost glad of the chance to sit and think without the disturbing presence of Myles Dampier to distract her. On the other, the realization that her future life would be spent with many such idle hours, bereft of people to care for her, reared up at her like a childhood monster. She tried to push such terrors to one side. *After all*, she decided grittily, *there will be something very agreeable about being mistress of my own affairs.*

There would be no one to tell her what to do. Unless, of course, it was a future employer. And then she would be *paid* for being compliant and dutiful.

And no one would ever fuss at her that she sat too long in the sun, or hadn't eaten enough, or tried to read in a weak light. If she wished, she could sit in a draught, or forget to wear sensible shoes on a wet day. And no one would ever comment. Or care.

In this agreeably independent mood, she settled down on a straw-stuffed mattress, laid out on a shady part of the deck for her to enjoy the fresh air. Since Captain Scully's idea of feminine amusement consisted of piles of sewing and mending, she found herself with plenty to do, plying her needle with more vigor than skill, breaking off her labors now and then to admire glimpses of the mountainous peak of Teneriffe through its covering of cloud, and discard any number of unlikely plans for her future existence. After a while, the sunshine, the gentle rhythm of the water, and her own increasing frustration caused her to set her work to one side, and she closed her eyes. When she opened them, not only had the sun shifted position, but a dark shadow loomed over her.

Gasping, she sat up. Myles Dampier leaned back on his heels and regarded her with mild surprise.

"I've never met a woman who sleeps as much as you do, Mermaid."

"What are you doing here? I saw you go ashore with the others."

"That was more than four hours ago. I've managed to

conclude my business and return, as you see."

"Four hours! It just can't be!" Stupidly she pushed a tangle of hair behind her ears, and discreetly struggled with the blanket that had slipped from her shoulders, leaving them bare to the man's gaze. She frowned at the interest on his face, and attempted to turn away from it. "I think you have seen me unclothed quite enough, thank you, Mr. Dampier. If you would have the goodness to look away."

"Ah. I can hear that word 'compromised' again," he murmured, but he turned his head, giving Sabina an excellent view of a strong profile with a small muscle twitching at his mouth. "Tell me when your modesty is satisfied."

No amount of pushing or pulling or wriggling seemed to dislodge the blanket from beneath her body, and she was almost driven to stand up half naked to actually get at the thing. As an impatient exclamation passed her lips, she was startled by a brown paper package tossed into her lap. She stared at Myles Dampier who sat down next to her and leaned back on his elbows, ankles crossed, obviously enjoying her struggles.

"What's this?" she asked suspiciously.

"Open it and find out."

She fumbled with the brown paper and string, eventually freeing the contents. They spilled into her lap in a silken cascade of colors—green, gold, and fiery red, fringed with deepest black. When she had unfolded the shawl to reveal the vivid pattern of flowers and birds, she automatically threw it around her shoulders and rubbed her cheek luxuriously against it.

"It's the most beautiful thing I've ever seen in my life!" She raised a grateful face to her mentor, and then paused, asking uncertainly, "Is this for me?"

"Well, I was going to give it to Scully, but now I believe it might clash with his complexion."

Sabina battled with herself for several seconds before touching it with hesitant fingers; finally she smiled. "Thank you. I know very well you shouldn't have bought it for me, but if you ever think of taking it back, you will have quite a struggle getting it off me."

"I dare say you will say the same thing of these," he said, throwing another package on the straw-stuffed sacks beside her. She looked at him inquiringly before opening it. Since it contained a pair of lace pantaloons, she felt a blush begin to spread across her face to the tips of her ears. The expression in the cerulean eyes was almost angelic as he inquired innocently, "Aren't you going to ask how I guessed your size?"

"I'm going to say thank you once more and leave it at that," Sabina said steadily. She rewrapped the undergarment in the brown paper and laid it to one side as, unbidden, Cousin Sarah of Bournemouth's face appeared in her mind's eye. She pushed the shocked countenance back into the depths from which it had sprung. "And I'm not even going to express my amazement that a man whose purse is somewhere at the bottom of the Atlantic should have been able to go shopping at all. They must use a very strange currency in these islands."

"My name is well known here. I managed to get a letter of credit from one of the merchants," he explained lazily. One long brown finger traced a bird's wing on her shoulder, and Sabina suppressed a shiver at the sensation it aroused. "I also managed to send a letter to my man of business. With luck, and the westerlies, it will get to Plymouth before we do. Our reception should be a great deal warmer than if we arrived unannounced."

Sabina, the lace undergarments burning a hole through their wrappings, had never felt so overwhelmingly shy in his presence before. Fleetingly she wondered if it was because England seemed suddenly closer than it had at any time during their unusual relationship. The intimacies they had shared—her almost complete reliance on Myles Dampier for comfort and companionship—would soon be at an end. Miss Grey, the Superior Governess, would replace Sabina, the castaway. She gave a miserable glance at her exotic shawl, and commented brightly, "How wonderful to be back in England once more. I'm sure I have missed London quite dreadfully. Although it will seem strange to be home without Papa. But then, any home is strange without family, don't you think? Will you be glad to see *your* family once more, Mr. Dampier?"

Sabina was pleased at how adroitly she made her inquiry, although she was fully prepared for him to sidestep it in his usual offhand manner toward any personal question. However, his silence caused her to gaze at him expectantly.

"Whether *they* will be glad to see *me* is debatable," he replied shortly. He rose from his reclining position next to her and abruptly extended his hand. "Come, the sun is too hot for you at this time of day. I'll take you below."

"No. I'm tired of sitting in shadows and dark corners. I want to sit in the sunlight and admire my new shawl."

"Spoken like a true Spanish senorita. Very well. I'm rather tired of shadows myself." He suddenly grinned down at her, his teeth white against the sun-browned face. "Wear it when we dine with Scully in his cabin. He is forgoing the pleasures of Santa Cruz to entertain you in style, you know. The last I saw of him, he was haggling over a barrel of oysters and several specimens of poultry."

"You aren't staying on shore?" she asked, surprised.

"And miss seeing you in your finery? Not for all the wine in the Canaries, Mermaid. Besides, there must be someone to chaperon you and Scully."

"Why do I feel that you have some ulterior motive in mind?"

"Because, Miss Grey, I fear that you are a suspicious, distrustful young woman. What motive would I have in mind other than the joy of your company?"

He spoke with gentle mockery, but the shutters had come down and his eyes were hidden by a thick sweep of lashes. Sabina hunched an impatient shoulder in his direction, and began to nervously plait the fringe of her new shawl. "I wish you wouldn't speak like that. You sound like some awful man-milliner. When you use that . . . that arrogant tone of voice, I don't like you very much."

"I don't like myself very much when I use it, Mermaid,

but unfortunately, it seems to be a part of my character over which I have little control."

"I don't believe there is anything you can't control," she said crossly.

"Go on believing that, my dear. Maybe one day it will be true."

To her complete chagrin, he began to walk away from her. "Why won't you talk of your family?" she asked impulsively, determined to keep him at her side. "Or your life before I met you? We have been friends now for over a month—well, I was asleep for nearly a week of that time, but it still should count!—and yet I know less than nothing about you. But if you asked me about Captain Scully, I could tell you all about his wife and four daughters, *and* his grandchildren. I could even describe his dog!"

"Rest assured, Sabina. I have neither wife nor daughters nor dog to tell you about."

Sabina digested this information with a strange, awkward lurching in her stomach, but she remained unsatisfied. "Nor any idea of what constitutes a proper friendship;" she scoffed.

"That may be because I have so few friends, Mermaid."

"And you aren't likely to *make* any if you are as closed as a tomb! Honestly, it's like traveling with the Sphinx."

"But unlike you, Miss Grey, my purpose in traveling to England is not to make friends."

A cool breeze had begun to blow in from the water, and with it The Stranger had unexpectedly returned, hard-featured, cold-eyed, and so far removed from any human warmth that she shivered with a perverse sympathy. However, this time she refused to be cowed by his sudden withdrawal. She struggled to her feet, allowing the hated blanket to slip unheeded to the deck, firmly drawing her new shawl about her body like protective armor. It was all she needed to tackle the dragon.

"Why won't you tell me anything about yourself? Anything important, that is! Is your history so scandalous? Or am I so unworthy to hear it? Honestly, you'd think I was Pandora at the box, the way you keep yourself shut away from me. And don't think I'm not conscious of the fact that you've found out practically everything there is to know about me. No naturalist could have done better. Not only have I been dissected like some sort of rare tropical plant, but I have a feeling you have already written up all the notes."

The top of her head merely reached his chin, and to do battle she had to tilt her face to look up into his; he was watchful, on guard, as though considering how to deal with an enemy attack. With an impatient sound, she whirled away from him, ready to retreat into her dark little berth below deck.

His voice, cool but composed, stopped her in her tracks.

"My name is Myles Edward Dampier."

She spun around, the folds of her shawl floating out from her body like the plumage of an exotic, caged bird. Her hands were tightly clenched as she stood her ground to listen.

"I am thirty-four years old. I came to the colony of New South Wales some fifteen years ago. I was granted land through the patronage of Governor Macquarie, and I prospered. I bought a ship, which was soon succeeded by other ships. I prospered again. I am returning to England, where I hope I will continue to prosper." He paused, and then continued in a voice made smooth by anger and edged with disdain. "Does that satisfy your insatiable appetite for information, Miss Grey? I wouldn't have thought it, but you seem to be the one who has inherited quite a taste for dissecting things."

He stood tense and angry, contempt etched into every line of his body. She stared at him in horror, unable to recall the last few minutes, wishing that she might do so, yet confused as to the extent of her crime. She strove for some measure of calm, conscious that at any moment, she might burst into tears.

"I see I forgot my mending," she heard herself whisper.

She hurriedly bent down to retrieve the sewing kit and the pile of clothes, determined to hide her face; she was stopped by a firm hand on her arm, hauling her upright so that she was suddenly glaring into Myles Dampier's taut features.

Inches away. Her hands clutching his shoulders, and her body closer to his than even a waltz would permit. Close enough to watch a small muscle contract at the side of whitened lips . . .

"Don't ask me for what I can't give you, Sabina. Take what I can offer, but don't ever ask for more."

His words, spoken in a low growl, frightened and confused her. She tried to step back from the thin, rigid line that was his mouth, but his hands were hard and implacable on her body, drawing her even closer. Panicked, she whimpered and turned her head, squeezing her eyes tightly shut so that she wouldn't have to look into the familiar blue depths and confront the shadows lurking there.

Then she was suddenly free, and she flailed out wildly at the rail. She sagged against it, holding on as if it were a lifeline, and stared miserably into the unshadowed depths of the water, listening to the firm fall of footsteps that carried Myles Dampier down the companionway.

And suddenly Sabina was certain that she knew exactly how Pandora had felt when she opened that box.

CHAPTER THREE

It was nearly twenty-four hours before Sabina saw Myles Dampier again, a feat of avoidance on which she could only congratulate herself, given the cramped conditions on the *Ellen Drury*. She had tried to decline the honor of dining formally with a little sigh and a feeble flutter of her lashes, hoping to convince the captain that she was in hourly danger of expiring.

However, Captain Scully was determined to play host at dinner. Like most masters of seagoing vessels, he led a lonely life, forced as he was to keep a professional distance between himself and his crew. His delight in the company of his two castaways, miraculously plucked from the sea, was therefore entirely unfeigned, and as soon as the *Ellen Drury* put to sea, Sabina found herself seated in state at the great desk, miraculously transformed into a dining table complete with linen and cutlery.

"I purchased a brace of fowl in Santa Cruz, Miss Grey, and we will have figs and mulberries afterwards," Captain Scully informed her cheerfully, taking his place at the head of the table. "A pleasant change from fish and salt-beef, I'll be bound."

"A very pleasant change," she agreed. The fact was, with Myles Dampier lazily sprawled in the chair opposite her, rolling the stem of a wineglass between long brown fingers, she couldn't have cared less if she were served up pieces of boiled rope. She watched the repetitive movement of his hands in reluctant fascination, caught by both their grace and their strength.

Don't ask for what I can't ever give you, he had said.

She crushed her napkin between nervous fingers. Well, at least she had been warned.

She didn't want to eat with him. She didn't even want to look at him. But now she was forced into giving him her polite attention for Captain Scully's sake. And all her father's training in the careful observation of a scientific subject and the aesthetic appreciation of its appearance was obviously going to work against her determination not to be impressed. As the candlelight played over the strong planes and angles of his face, she reluctantly acknowledged that she had never realized that a man could be beautiful.

Not merely handsome, or strong or elegant. No—the terms "almost" and "merely" seemed foreign to Myles Dampier. And the word "handsome" was too . . . tepid. He was beautiful, she decided meditatively, as a portrait of a medieval saint is beautiful, the face honed by suffering to a fine-boned strength. Sabina suddenly remembered the many canvases of Saint Sebastian she had studied in the churches of South America, and the painful combination of purity and pain she detected in that tortured image. One painting in particular had moved her almost to tears—the young man was naked and defenseless, bound to a tree, his torso full of arrows, the dark head fallen forward in terrible suffering. And yet the piercing eyes were raised, not downcast, his arched body threatening to break his bonds and leap impassioned from the frame.

More gladiator than martyr.

More soldier than saint.

In fact, she decided, nervously folding and refolding the napkin in her lap, Myles Dampier was just such a heady mix of spirit and earthiness. So much so that she felt as helpless as if she had been left to flounder alone in the sea. Nothing in her entire life had prepared her for this relationship. How was she expected to react to such a man?

Don't ever ask for more.

Don't worry, Mr. Dampier, she thought rebelliously. *I won't be asking for anything more. When we get back to England I'll go my own way, and that will be the last you need ever see of me. I'd rather eat crumbs at Cousin Sarah's table. I'd rather be a laundry maid than expect anything further from you.* She lifted her chin and nervously adjusted her new shawl.

"Her heart has been completely stolen by you, Mr. Dampier," Sabina heard Captain Scully comment jovially, and she returned her attention to the dinner table with a jolt. "Yes, there is no mistaking the signs of a female in love. I tell you now, sir, I am a jealous man. A very jealous man. What do you have to say about it, eh, Miss Grey? Do you think I have cause to be jealous?"

Sabina's jaw dropped. She stared at both men in complete horror. "I . . . I . . . don't think . . ." Her voice trailed off, and she sent Myles Dampier a silent plea for pity. He responded with a flash of white teeth, and said dryly, "I think you named her aptly, Captain. Jezebel's heart was too easily won over with mere food scraps. You'll have no trouble wooing her back."

"Oh, heavens—the *monkey*." Relief made Sabina's backbone turn to fluid, and she slumped in her seat, a grin spreading across her face. "Of course. Poor little Jezebel."

"Well, that's the first time I've seen you really smile, Miss Grey," the captain cried delightedly. "All the way up to your eyes! Do you know—I have something that will further cheer you. How would you like to see my baked heads, eh? I got them in the South Pacific for less than a guinea each. Why, you won't believe the tattoos on one of 'em. Must have been a ferocious brute in life. I have them wrapped up in the bottom of my sea chest."

"Oh, please! Don't go to any trouble, Captain Scully. Please don't indeed!"

"Ah, well, I daresay you will feel squeamish about them, like my youngest girl," the captain said, obviously philosophical about the aesthetic tastes of women. "She threw one of them into the waters off the Hawaiian Islands. Said either it went overboard or she did. Had to get the ship's boy to dive in and get it. Nearly lost him to a shark."

He leaned over to fill her wineglass, and added with jocular gallantry, "Not that you aren't sight enough to delight any company in your pretty shawl. Santa Cruz is well known for its silk manufacture, you know, Miss Grey, and Mr. Dampier was so determined you should have something fitting for a young lady that right after his business with old Montoya was finished, he set out to find it for you."

He turned to Myles Dampier, the decanter proffered in midair. "Why, it's just occurred to me, sir—I never did ask if you managed to send them letters back to New South Wales or not. The *Circe* was in port, and I know Tom Hudson would have been happy to carry them for you."

Myles Dampier contemplated his wineglass before answering curtly, "Yes, Hudson will deliver them."

"I suppose the loss of the *Margaret Rose* will be a great blow to you," the captain continued. "She was a fine vessel, and no mistake. Four hundred ton, was she not?"

The glass was drained and set firmly on the table. "Four hundred and ninety-three."

"Ah, well. The sea is a fitful mistress, Mr. Dampier, as we who live by her have found to our cost. But when we take her bounty, we must accept her wrath, eh? And as good fortune would have it, the rest of your fleet is as fine as any in the southern oceans. I mind I exchanged letters with the *Goliath* past the Cape one time and thought what a trim vessel she was."

Sabina realized that she had somehow jerked a handful of fringe from her shawl. Stupidly she contemplated the dark strands dangling from her fingers before managing to ask Myles, "Do you mean to tell me that you *owned* the *Margaret Rose?*"

"No, I didn't mean to tell you." His voice was full of a gentle, bitter humor that made her bridle. She raised her eyes to watch him across the table.

"Why not?"

"Because it didn't seem important."

Because you aren't important. He might as well have said the words aloud, so clear was his meaning.

Sabina swallowed and tried to think of something witty and cutting to say, but a sweeping sense of disappointment caused her to abandon all attempts at joining in the conversation. Instead, she listened quietly to the captain's anecdotes about cannibals and pirates in the southern oceans, managing to smile and nod her way through six massacres and a bloody mutiny. When dinner was finished, and the captain had imbibed too much of his new stock of brandy and was beginning to explore his repertoire of sea shanties, Sabina excused herself quietly. She slipped up the stairs, content to stand at the lee rail in the darkness and listen to the creak of timbers and the sounds of the sea against the ship as it made its sure way from the Canaries to England.

She moved along the deck, replying softly to the wary greeting of a young sailor, who promptly disappeared in the direction of the fo'c'sle. Leaning over the side of the vessel, she shivered as the cool breezes ruffled the loose tendrils of hair about her forehead. The sea itself seemed to be lit up by brilliant stars, the breaking waves multiplying them into sheets of bright lights amidst the white foam. Myles Dampier had explained that they weren't really stars fallen into the ocean, but strange sea creatures that gave off a phosphorescent glow. It was a sensible explanation, the sort her father would have given her accompanied by much scientific detail.

But tonight she *wanted* them to be stars.

She wanted there to be mermaids, and selkies, and fairy tales and happy endings.

There's no such thing, of course, the sensible Miss Grey told her crossly. *And there will be nothing waiting for you in England except Cousin Sarah, or some respectable employment. And that's all you should expect. Not stars in the ocean. Not Sir Galahad on a brigantine. He didn't even think enough of you to tell you that he was the owner of the* Margaret Rose. *And yet he listened to you drone on and on about finding an agent in Teneriffe. No. It was too much trouble to have you make demands on him, as you would surely have been entitled to!*

But surely, Sabina thought miserably, *there could have been no ulterior motive for his silence. He saved my life. I owe everything to him. I think . . . I think it was Destiny.*

Destiny, Miss Grey scoffed. *You are a complete fool, aren't you? Stop trying to make it greater than it really is. It isn't love you feel! It's gratitude, mixed with a healthy dose of fear. You always do look for a replacement, whenever you find yourself alone.*

I don't think it's just that, Sabina argued hesitantly. *What about whenever he comes near me? I can't breathe properly. I can't think properly. My pulses race and I start to tremble as though I have a fever. What on earth is that?*

That is too many years spent in hot, Latin countries, came the reply, in what sounded remarkably like Cousin Sarah's voice. *When you return to England you will realize that pulses—like imaginations—should be kept under strict control.*

"When I return to England . . ." She spoke the words out loud, determined to hear them and understand their implications. A month ago, her return to her homeland had seemed the most desirable thing in the world. Now, she didn't care if she spent the rest of her life on the brig.

Dispiritedly she turned from the rail to make her way below. She was stopped by the odor of burning tobacco and heard a casual greeting through the dark. A rough voice replied, and she heard masculine laughter before a cheery "Bid you good night, sir," echoed across the deck.

She stood still, poised for flight, listening to the sudden silence.

"You've been avoiding me, Sabina."

She started as the voice spoke out of the darkness. Myles

Dampier stood by the rail, his body partly obscured by the capstan.

"Are you on watch, Mr. Dampier?" Sabina was pleased that her own voice was steady. She stood, hands politely folded, and watched the cigarillo he had been smoking make a dull arc of light as he threw it into the sea. Now only starlight and moonbeams lit their patch of deck.

"I was on watch this morning. No, I was just contemplating the delights offered by my hammock and wondering if I should retire early."

"You've been sleeping in a *hammock*?"

"Well, Mermaid, you do occupy the only spare cabin on board!"

"But . . . a hammock!" Having had her own experiences with hammocks in several Brazilian inns, she felt a sudden stab of guilt. "And having to sleep with the crew! In that crowded hold! I didn't think . . . I never thought to ask about your . . . your . . ."

"My sleeping arrangements? My dear Miss Grey . . . I would have been shocked if you had shown the least interest." She imagined his grin as he replied cheerfully, "Don't worry about it, Sabina. The rats haven't nibbled at my nose, and the bosun doesn't have to cut me out of it of a morning. And I've yet to arise with 'fat head.' "

"What's that?"

"It's what you get when you sleep in a hold with over a hundred other men. The air becomes so foul, you awake with your tongue swollen to twice its size and the certainty your head is about to explode like a large balloon."

"And to think I've been so ungrateful about my cramped little berth," she said, stricken with guilt. "Really, when you think about it, I've been treated like a princess. I suppose that is why none of the crew will dare speak to me."

"Scully thought it would make life simpler if they had no contact with you. I have no wish to naysay his orders. If you wish conversation, you may make it with me."

"Oh. You have some power, then, aboard this vessel? I don't suppose you own the *Ellen Drury*, too." It was a sly dig, and she made her voice as innocent as possible.

She felt him stiffen beside her. "No, I don't. Her owners are a London syndicate. They deal in sealskins. Sometimes teak."

"Indeed. Well, how nice to know everything about the *Ellen Drury*," she said brightly. "Now I shall let you return to your hammock . . . and your fat head."

His hand shot out from the darkness, preventing her from leaving. "You didn't answer my original statement, Sabina."

"I don't remember what you said," she replied breathlessly. His hand began to caress her wrist, gently and rhythmically, holding her prisoner as surely as iron manacles would have. She wondered how she could suddenly feel so hot on so cool an evening.

"I said you've been avoiding me."

She attempted a careless laugh. "Not at all. I just thought you might have had more than enough of my company. Lately you seem to have found it . . . rather tiresome."

"Not as tiresome as you've clearly found me." He released her and turned toward the sea.

Sabina felt bereft, and wrapped the fingers of her other hand around the skin of her wrist, still warm from his touch. Her pulse was beating erratically, and she was surprised at how calm her voice sounded when she spoke. "Just tell me one thing, Myles Dampier. One thing and I'll leave you alone and never bother you with my vulgar curiosity again."

"Only one thing. What remarkable restraint, Sabina."

"Tell me about your childhood."

"My what?"

"Your childhood."

"Why the devil would you want to hear about that?"

There was no way on earth she could explain her reasons. She wasn't even sure of them herself. Perhaps because the child might be more comprehensible than the man. Or perhaps—just perhaps—because she knew that she had to start somewhere in her understanding of this aloof yet charismatic stranger. Ignoring his astonishment, she let the words tumble out in her eagerness to gain a reply. "Were you happy? Where did you live? What were your parents like? And your family. You must have had family." She added beseechingly, "What harm will it do you to tell me so *little?*"

The silence was so tense, she felt sure she had driven him back into the cold, hard shell he carried like a shield. When he eventually spoke, evenly and quietly, his voice had the same effect upon her as the cracking of a whip upon the silence of the evening. She clenched her hands and drank in each word, like a drunkard given wine.

"My parents were very good, very kind, very . . . loving. I daresay I was as happy as any other child, indulged to a fault and left to run wild as I pleased. And I was . . . wild." He paused, as though a little startled by the information he had just imparted. When he spoke again, his voice was low and tense, almost as though he spoke to himself, and for once it was devoid of the bitter, ironic tone that characterized his speech. "I had little thought as to what the next day would bring. I didn't need to think. I lived on a large estate. I knew it would be mine one day. Rich, rolling acres of farmland by the sea. I always loved the sea, even as a boy. I used to dream of running away and becoming a pirate, sailing the world's oceans and amassing a fortune in stolen gold. Which is, of course, something of an irony when you consider . . . But that's why it seemed only natural that I should go back to it . . . afterwards. Scully is right when he called the sea a fitful mistress, but there's nothing treacherous about her efforts to destroy you. She has all the strength and honesty of a cannonball at your head. An honesty you'll never find on land, Mermaid."

He suddenly exhaled, expelling a deep breath that seemed to shake his entire body, and she watched as his head bowed over his chest in some silent supplication. It was an uncharacteristically defeated gesture, and Sabina was suddenly frightened. She stretched out her hand to touch him, but before she could reach him, he tossed back his head and exclaimed with all his familiar vigor, "God knows, it's given me everything I needed to get back to Lysons Hall."

"Lysons Hall—is that where you lived? It sounds very grand." She sounded shaken and nervous, but the man opposite her seemed too engrossed in his thoughts to notice.

"It isn't. Not what others would call grand. It's too old, and too much a home, to be that. But it will be, my dear. Grand and glorious. I'll make it that way." The old humor returned to his voice as he said smoothly, "There's a legend you know—about a mermaid some illustrious ancestor of mine took home from the sea and married. It seems that she brought good luck to the Dampier family. There's a likeness of her carved somewhere in the house, although it seems to me that my ancestors were remarkably broad-minded to allow great-grandmama to appear in public half naked and wearing a fish's tail."

He paused and added thoughtfully, "When your portrait hangs in the great hall, Mermaid, you might choose to be fully clothed. Although I'd like to see you painted as you were tonight—barefoot, with your shawl loose around your shoulders." His hand reached out and gentle fingers trailed up her arm, pausing only to play carelessly with the loosened curls at her neck. He continued in a strangely thickened voice, "And your hair tousled by ocean breezes. That's how I'll always think of you."

"When *my* portrait hangs in the great hall . . ." Sabina repeated. She swallowed and said, "I'm afraid I don't understand you. I don't think I heard you properly."

"I've known women to turn coy at a proposal of marriage, but *deaf*? My dear Miss Grey—"

"You want to marry me?" Even as she said the words aloud, she felt herself suddenly disconnected from reality, as though the deck, the darkness, the stars—and Myles Dampier—were all part of some improbable dream created by her earlier illness.

Surely less than twenty-four hours ago he had warned her not to expect anything of him, the words brutally

51

branded into her memory. She put her hand to her forehead to check for a return of her fever. It was burning hot, like the rest of her face.

"That is the implication," he said coolly. "Although somewhere I've obviously made myself obscure. Perhaps if I rephrase it for you, you'll sound less as if I made you an indecent proposition. Marry . . . me . . . Miss Grey."

An uncontrollable shiver reassured Sabina that she was in the grip of some dreadful tropical fever, and she pulled the silk folds even more firmly around her body in a futile effort to warm herself. She cursed the darkness that prevented her from trying to read his expression. "No!" She lifted one trembling hand to touch her lips, surprised that the word had shot out of her with the force that it had. "That is . . . I mean . . . you . . . no!"

"Weren't you ever taught to decline marriage proposals a little more graciously, Miss Grey?" Far from sounding crushed by this refusal, his voice held a deep note of amusement. "I thought all young ladies were taught it in the schoolroom. 'I am conscious, sir, of the great honor you do me, etc., etc.' "

"No! I mean—I've never received an offer of marriage. Well, I have, but not from someone I . . . not that it matters a jot, because . . ." She broke off, aware that she was only getting herself into difficulties. Not even during their time on the raft had she felt so . . . so adrift and out of control. "Why do you want to marry me?"

"Why should any man wish to marry?"

"Don't *do* that!"

"Do what?"

"Answer a question with a question! You do it all the time!"

"Do I?" he asked amiably. Even through the darkness, she was conscious of him smiling. Teasing her. Reveling in her confusion. Obviously unable to take her refusal seriously.

"It's because I talked about being compromised, isn't it?" she exclaimed in mortification. "You feel you have to marry me to preserve my honor. You are just being chivalrous."

"Spare me from accusations of chivalry, Mermaid. I'm nobody's knight in shining armor. You might as well know now that I am a completely selfish creature. I'll walk over anybody who stands in the way of what I want."

Could he possibly want me? The question hung in the air like a blade about to descend on her unprotected head.

"But I'm a poor choice of wife," she offered, hoping desperately for a rebuttal. "As you have reminded me, I have no money and no connections—I don't even own the clothes I stand up in! You . . . you could marry anyone!"

"I could, couldn't I?" he agreed coolly. "Being as extremely eligible as I am. However, I have particular reasons for wishing to marry before arriving in England. Since that is less than three weeks away, I don't like my chances of pulling another suitable young woman from the sea."

"Another . . . suitable . . ."

If Sabina had cursed the darkness before, she was now grateful that it hid her round-mouthed expression of shock. Her voice trembled with suppressed emotion as she replied, "Then I wonder you didn't bring a bride with you from New South Wales. I'm sure your cabin was large enough to hold *several.*"

"If I had found a woman with your beauty and breeding, I daresay I might have done so. However, available women are distressingly scarce on the ground in the colonies—any kind of women, unless you are partial to street drabs. One like you would cause a riot amongst the Pure Merinos of Sydney Town."

Her anger finally exploded, gloriously. "How dare you! *Scarce on the ground?* You talk of me as though I'm a sheaf of wheat. Are you making jest of me because I refused to marry you?"

"No, I'm being brutally honest with you, Sabina." His voice was unexpectedly weary, and she jumped as she felt his hands take her shoulders in a strong grip. For a moment she struggled, and then stilled as he spoke gently. "You asked me why I made you an offer of marriage. I told you truthfully. I want a wife. I want one with beauty and intelligence and breeding, who will grace Lysons Hall and add a certain . . . luster to my existence there. I want a woman of quality to fill the role, not some vain, vapid, pea-goose who has neither the courage nor the character to stand up to life's challenges."

When we reach England I will introduce you to true Vanity.

Of course, Vanity was a woman. What else? Was *she* the reason for his secrecy? The reason for the wall he had built around himself like a besieged castle?

Sabina's hands curled into little claws that dug her nails into her palms.

"So," she said tremblingly, "you wish to arrive in England with a souvenir—no, a *trophy!*—of your travels to display to your friends. Weren't there any in Santa Cruz who could add luster to your existence? You could have acquired a wife and had Captain Scully's oysters thrown in for good measure. *And* my shawl!"

The hands on her shoulders tightened their grip. He continued as if she had not spoken, "It's also true that I feel a certain responsibility toward you. Saving your life puts me under an obligation. Marriage seems to be the perfect way to fulfill that obligation. We will both benefit from it. I acquire the wife that I need, while you gain all the security that marriage offers you. You know enough about me to know that I'm wealthy. And before you object that you have no mercenary designs on my fortune, I'll save you the bother by doing it for you. But you can't pretend that marriage to me wouldn't be preferable to a life of dependency and poverty."

She couldn't pretend.

Just as she couldn't pretend that the strength of his hands still resting on her shoulders didn't feel like burning brands scorching the skin beneath the silk shawl. She felt one hand move, and gasped as his fingers gently touched her face. Yearningly she turned her cheek in their direction, only to realize that his hand had moved back to her shoulder, where it suddenly adopted a rhythmic, caressing quality. Sabina closed her eyes and tried to maintain her anger at Myles Dampier's unorthodox methods of proposing.

"And love?" she managed to ask quaveringly.

"Ah, yes. Love. I wondered when we would get around to the word." He sounded amused, although now his hands had deliberately traveled from her shoulders to her back, where their insistent movements caused her to gasp and lean in toward his body. "If you mean do I desire you, yes, I do. I've made no secret of that fact since I first saw you on the *Margaret Rose*. You were standing on deck with the Marchand woman, watching the last of Rio de Janeiro. I had Feeney find out what he could about you, and report back to me. Do you think it was by accident that I found you in the water?" His voice deepened and took on a quiet, subtly hypnotic tone that made her raise her face closer to his in order to hear his words. "When I realized there was no hope for the ship, I searched for you, and found you standing on deck watching those damned lifeboats burning. After you went overboard, and I smashed up what was left of them with an axe, I pushed a section with cork lining after you. *That* was our raft, Mermaid. Divine providence didn't save us. I did. I pulled you out of the sea for a purpose. And when I have a purpose, I generally see it through."

She wanted to ask him what that purpose was, but somehow her vocal cords seemed to have become disconnected from her brain. She could only gape up at him through the darkness. She wanted to see his face. She wanted the sky to light up with fireworks, or the sun to rise at midnight, or even for the man to light another cigarillo, the taper flickering near his eyes so that she could look into them at that moment to determine the truth. His voice seemed to tell her so much about his feelings, possessing a warm, caressing quality that she had never before heard him use—but before she could believe him, she wanted to see the cold, brilliant blue of his eyes glow with a warmth that so far had been missing when he looked at her.

She wanted to be sure he could love her, if not now, then sometime in the future. . . .

"Well?" he prompted gently.

She began to shake. "Ask me tomorrow."

"You'll consider my offer?" Sabina offered no resistance as he used one powerful arm to gather her closer to him while his other hand moved to her face, the fingers stroking her cheek, then moving with butterfly softness over her mouth and eyes, like a blind man, reading every feature. She resisted the temptation to turn her cheek against his hand and, catlike, stroke it over and over again. Somehow she managed to choke out words.

"Yes, I'll consider it."

"Good. In that case, there's something about me I think you should know."

What had he said? Think? Oh, God. Yes, think! Sabina closed her eyes as his fingers moved from their casual exploration of her face and shoulders and he pulled her still closer to him with a fierce, skillful movement that drove out any space between them. Mindlessly she lifted her arms to encircle his neck, the better to accommodate this intimacy, and gasped as his hands reached and stroked her uncorseted ribs, stopping their slow exploration just beneath her breasts. She murmured a feeble protest, and then lifted her face to his as his breath, warm and scented with tobacco, began to mingle with her own. She watched the hard mouth, inches away from hers, hover for an eternity.

"I think you should know, Mermaid, that when I first came to New South Wales, I came as a guest of His Majesty."

"Oh? Do you know the king?" she asked dreamily.

"I wore his livery for five years."

"His livery?"

"I'm an emancipist, Sabina."

She shook her head, uncertain of his meaning, alerted to the significance of his words only by the sudden tension in his body. She tried to keep him close, curling her fingers into the cloth of his coat, but he gently removed them and stepped back from her.

"Fifteen years ago, my dear, I was transported to New South Wales for a term of seven years. I was a convict, Sabina."

When she looked back on Myles Dampier's proposal to her, Sabina realized that he had deliberately chosen both the place and time for it. She was his prisoner in the dark, held hostage to her growing physical attraction to him. He could read her responses as though they were written in a book, and accurately predict how she would react to both his words and his actions.

At the same time, he wore the darkness like an inky cloak, protecting him from her clear-sighted gaze. He had called her intelligent and acute. But she was none of these things in the dark. And not while he held her in his arms.

Later, she sat huddled in her cramped, dark cabin, watching the shadows flickering in the light of the lamp. The shadows filled the small room with fantastic changeable shapes that seemed to act out her fears in grotesque parody. Tigers, lions, dragons—all seemed to lurk in the corners, reminding her of how afraid of the dark she had been as a child. They reminded her of how she had lain shivering in her bed, waiting to be rescued. Like some fairy-tale princess, she always seemed to be waiting to be rescued.

I'm nobody's knight in shining armor, he had said.

I was a convict.

She had drawn back from him, startled at the bleak confession, waiting speechlessly for further explanation. When the silence stretched on for infinite moments, she managed to whisper, "Why?"

"Why what?"

"Why were you a . . . a convict? It must have been a mistake. You aren't a criminal. I know that. Not a criminal."

"Oh, I was much worse than that, my dear. I was a damned young fool."

He still twisted in her grasp like the serpent prince in the old fairy tale. Impossible to capture. Impossible to break the spell. "Is that all you have to say to me?"

"What do you expect? A full confession of my misdeeds complete with a musical interlude and a sermon at the end? I'll save you the trouble, Mermaid. What is that line from Shakespeare? Ah, yes. 'He hath no drowning mark upon him. His complexion is pure gallows.' "

"Why do you always have to be so . . . so cryptic? You stand there and tell me you were transported, and then refuse to say anything about it, except you were a fool! It tells me nothing! Nothing at all!"

"Mermaid, that should tell you everything."

As suddenly as a phantom he left her, and she heard the door to the fo'c'sle creak open and then close with grim finality. She stood in the darkness, abandoned. A voice called out, full of pleading and fear, and she was startled to realize that it was her own. But there was no answer, and she felt her stomach churn violently. She flung herself over the railing in time to be horribly sick. There she remained for some minutes, exhausted and confused, before slowly pulling herself to an upright position, her head reeling, her entire body shaking.

It was not, she reflected as she shakily wiped her mouth on her shawl, the sort of proposal she had dreamed about receiving. She wondered if the bald admission had been some sort of test, an ordeal she was expected to pass in order to gain the prize at the end of it. If so, her shocked reaction might not have been the result he expected. She stumbled back to her cabin, where she watched the shadows and waited for wisdom to settle over her like a heavenly blessing. However, her thoughts remained tumbled and confused. Only her body—a traitor to every principle she had been brought up to revere—refused to look at the situation logically. She could still feel the warmth of the broad chest crushing her unbound breasts beneath the silk shawl, his arms confident and strong about her body, his hands like steel, yet gentle in their subtle exploration. . . .

Myles Dampier was certainly not a saint. He said he had saved her life not out of any chivalrous instincts to preserve human life, but because he wanted her. It had been a coldly calculated act, which even now made small chills travel up and down her spine.

And he could be harsh at times, even brutal in his dealings with others. He had implied as much. He was a self-made man, who had acquired his wealth in a brutal maritime world where the milk of human kindness no doubt rapidly curdled. He had faced the loss of the *Margaret Rose* with a shrug and a pithy expression of regret, concentrating instead on his own survival. And hers.

She rose and began to pace the small room like a caged animal. *And yet,* she argued desperately, *he has always been so kind.* His care of her during her illness, his concern for her well-being—they were not the actions of a criminal. The ship's crew, men not easily impressed by wealth or privilege, seemed to like him well enough. She had noticed his popularity, his easy laughter with the sailors, and his casual acceptance of ship duties that were really no business of his to perform. And Captain Scully had developed a warm friendship with him that seemed based on mutual respect rather than the professional obligations of a ship's master to a shipwrecked passenger.

How could he be a criminal?

What sort of crime *could* a boy of good birth and education have possibly committed?

Forgery? Arson? Theft?

Perhaps a duel. Yes, that could well be the answer. A hotheaded young man and a lady's honor at stake. A misplaced bullet, and his fate was sealed. . . .

A loud rapping at the door had her jumping to her feet and clasping her hand at her throat like the heroine of a novel. She prayed it was the captain, even as she realized it was not. Scully always scraped his fingers uncertainly at her door as though he were afraid of giving offense; this confident rap revealed no such fear. She wasn't even certain that she spoke before it opened, and Myles Dampier entered the cabin. His dark hair was slightly damp, as though he had dipped his head into a bowl of water; the flickering of the lamplight highlighted dark shadows beneath his eyes. He wore a clean jacket, and an air of polite expectancy.

Then he moved toward her, each step as ominous as a tiger advancing on its prey.

"Eight bells have just sounded," he informed her softly. "It's tomorrow, Mermaid. I've come for your answer."

CHAPTER FOUR

Sabina felt a wave of panic engulf her as his tall form displaced the shadows in her cramped quarters. She had expected a reprieve until sunrise at least. She wasn't ready. Never in her life had she felt less ready for anything.

"You expect an answer after deepening the mystery? Won't you at least tell me what your crime was? You owe me that much." Her words dropped like stones into the quiet. She was suddenly conscious of every natural sound on the ship—the creaking of timbers, the thrashing of the waves against wood, the squeaking of the boom's jaws.

The dull thudding of her own heart.

"What would you say if I told you I was a murderer?" His voice was as polite as a courtier's. Once more the thick fringe of lashes hid his eyes from her intent gaze.

"I wouldn't believe you. You aren't capable of murder," she answered resolutely.

The silence that followed her declaration of faith stretched her nerves to the breaking point.

"Perhaps I wasn't when I was nineteen years old. Five years in the lime kilns and salt pans of the Coal River leave you capable of anything." The black lashes swept upward, and the expression in his eyes was fierce and glittering. Sabina had never before seen such passion in a human face, and she found herself shrinking from him. He noted her withdrawal with a sharp, derisive laugh and continued smoothly, "But you are right, my dear. I might as well let you know the worst. I owe you that much. I did kill a man. I struck him down like the murderous, sadistic dog he was. Half of the flesh on my back was on the end of his lash at the time. If I have any regrets about it, it's because I killed him to save my own skin. If I'd acted sooner, I would have saved others, perhaps more deserving than I was. However, I seemed to act solely on instinct in those days. Anything else, and you risked losing either your sanity or your life."

He paused as if to fully appreciate her appalled silence. "But that wasn't the reason for my presence in a penal colony, my dear. No. The crime which saw me shipped into fourteen years of exile was that of abduction." He moved toward the fixed table and adjusted the small lantern suspended from the ceiling bracket. He studied her face with cynical appreciation. "A killer and a kidnapper. Deemed unfit to remain on England's hallowed soil. And that's the man who would be your suitor, Sabina Grey."

His jaw was so taut she thought it might shatter. His tone was soft and self-mocking, but she sensed the world of pain that existed beneath it. Part of her quailed before his words, while another part, the part that recognized the intrinsic humanity of the man who stood before her, immediately sprang to his defense. "It was obviously some terrible mistake. I know it was. And you aren't a convict any longer. You are well known and respected in the colony! They must have recognized that you weren't really a . . . a criminal. You are a gentleman!"

"A gentleman, is it? Now, that title covers a multitude of sins." He smiled bitterly. "You mustn't think that my reprieve came about because of any good behavior on my

62

part—through my *gentlemanly* demeanor. I came to New South Wales as wild and angry as a caged animal. And why not? Up to the age of nineteen I was used to thinking of myself as the center of the universe. You may imagine the shock I received when I found myself deposited in a Thames hulk, and then shipped over ten thousand miles crammed into a ship's hold with three hundred other men—men who had lived on the edge of desperation all their lives. I've no doubt that I behaved rather badly on the whole. But then, to find yourself suddenly in the center of hell takes a little getting used to."

There was no self-pity in his voice, only a matter-of-fact edge that conjured up all the emotions of a spirited boy wrested from his home and sent on a nightmare journey into penal servitude. Sabina wrapped her arms about her body in an effort to protect herself from the horror his words evoked. She tried to imagine herself in such a position and could not. Every instinct told her that he spoke the truth, but even so, she felt that he was holding something back, despite the raw emotion of his confession.

"You said you were transported because you . . . you . . ."

"I was charged with abduction. Not any ordinary abduction, of course. Like the young gentleman I was, I abducted an heiress, Mermaid. In England, where heiresses are a protected commodity, that is like trying to run off with the crown jewels. An attractive proposition at the time, but the penalty outweighs the rewards. Now, if I had only chosen to abscond with a milkmaid . . ."

"Were you guilty?"

"Oh, yes, my dear," he answered pleasantly. "As guilty as hell."

As hell. The word seemed to haunt his vocabulary. Sabina tried to study his face, but he had turned the lantern so that he was part of the shadows. "Will you tell me about it?"

"No."

"Why not?"

"Why not? Because, my dear—why, because it is a tale told by an idiot, full of sound and fury. That's why. It's all in the past, and has no bearing on the present."

"But you still expect me to marry you?"

"Why not? You have nothing to fear from me. I only prey on overseers and heiresses."

A wave of healthy anger flooded over her and she suddenly surged toward him like a small tidal wave. "Stop it!" she shouted, hitting her fists futilely against his chest. "How dare you speak to me so! Is it because I have nothing—*am nothing*—that you treat me like this? Do you think you own me just because you saved my life? Is that all I am to you? *Flotsam!*"

He was genuinely surprised by her attack—she saw that in the reluctant grin that slowly unfurled and the way he positioned his arms at her sides, not touching her but protectively hovering, as though to prevent a naughty child from hurting herself during a tantrum. Her fists made little impression on his broad, muscular chest.

"Don't laugh at me!" she fumed.

"I'm not laughing. I'm just wondering if every man on this ship is now aware that I'm in your cabin in the early hours of the morning."

"I don't care! I'm past caring about anything! I don't care if you abducted the Princess Charlotte! I don't care if they transported you for a hundred years! You . . . you can go to blazes for all I care!" To her embarrassment, she realized that she had begun to cry, the tears slipping down her cheeks in molten rivulets. She felt her wrists suddenly seized as he roughly pulled her against his body, the amusement wiped clean from his face.

"Stop crying, Sabina. I don't respond well to women's tears."

"I don't either. But I can't help it. And if you don't like it, you can go away."

"Can I?" he murmured softly. "I wonder."

The shawl had slipped to the floor, and she felt his hands slowly slide up her bare arms, stopping only to caress the soft flesh just beneath her shoulders with a gentle circular movement that shot something like an electric current through her body. She inhaled sharply and raised her eyes to his, only to find them hooded, guarded. Her own, she had no doubt, would reflect the wild confusion that she felt. She tried to pull back from him, but somehow a powerful thigh thrust against the folds of her skirts prevented her withdrawal; off balance, she leaned against its strength, and in doing so gave him the advantage. She tumbled against his chest, her breasts, untrammeled by corsets and covered only by an almost transparent layer of chemise, crushed against the thin cotton of his shirt. The heat of his body burned her like a branding iron, and she murmured a protest that turned out to be his name.

"I like to hear you say my name. You never do say it, Mermaid."

"Myles." She breathed it like a prayer, uncertain, questioning.

She heard his indrawn breath and felt his fingers tighten convulsively on her arms. Slowly he pulled her still closer until his body felt like an addition to her own, and his breath was warm and ragged against her face. Then her arms were free and she unconsciously wrapped them about his shoulders, struggling to get closer still. It seemed she could not get close enough no matter how hard she strained against him, and when his lips descended upon hers, it was a physical relief to feel his breath mingling with hers. Now she could taste him, she realized with astonishment, and offered no resistance when his mouth skillfully pushed past her lips. The touch of his tongue, so unexpected, should have shocked her, but his invasion raised little more than a surprised murmur. If she was tempted to pull back at that moment, his hand at the back of her head prevented her, his fingers entwined in the thickness of her curls.

A small, sensible voice advised her to retreat, but as her tongue hesitantly moved to meet his, she realized that any glimmer of sense had little competition from the rising desire flooding her body like a warm spring. An uncertain movement of her hands against his cheek seemed to open a floodgate in Myles Dampier, and his lips pulled against hers with a new ferocity, his tongue no longer teasing hers into response but thrusting into her compliant mouth with renewed ardor. Slowly, methodically, his hands slid from her shoulders to her back and ribs, and then moved possessively over the soft flesh of her breasts. She started guiltily at this new intimacy, and managed to murmur an incoherent protest, but it was stifled beneath the expertise of his mouth.

In reply, she closed her eyes and arched against him with an abandoned passion that seemed to drive Myles Dampier into further action. With his mouth still locked onto hers, he stooped and put his arm beneath her knees, sweeping her into his arms. He took one short stride toward the narrow bunk and laid her down on it, breaking contact with her swollen lips, only to press hot kisses into the base of her throat. Her eyes flew open as she felt his weight settle against her, and she shuddered with pleasure, lifting her hands to smooth back the dark locks that fell over his forehead. Sabina was filled with a heady sense of power over this man, a power that combined tenderness with passion, and made her realize that she would never have the strength to deny him anything. His mouth moved to the top of her bosom, parting the remainder of lace that clung there, and she moaned softly and closed her eyes.

Anything. He had only to ask.

He turned his head against the soft flesh, one hand moving to cup her breast. "Marry me, Sabina," he whispered, and mindlessly she moved her head from side to side in agreement.

"Yes." The word was barely a breath.

"Tomorrow. On deck. Scully will marry us."

"Yes." Ecstatically she opened her eyes and looked up into his face.

What she saw there chilled her to the bone.

Sapphire eyes, darkened with unmistakable desire. Watchful. Calculating. Unmistakably assessing her every response.

Like an insect pinned to a canvas, ready for the scientist's dissecting knife.

With a swift, humiliated movement, Sabina buried her face in the pillow. She felt him suddenly tense and lie motionless above her, his hands stilled, the only movement in the cabin the gentle rolling and pitching of the ship. Then he groaned and turned his head away, his breathing tortured. She raised herself up to watch him as he swung his legs over the bunk, pulling himself upright, his back eloquent of his struggle for composure. When he finally turned to speak to her, his eyes glittered with a terrible self-mockery.

"I told you I was no gentleman, Mermaid. You may now add vile seducer to my list of vices."

It was almost too painful for her to speak. But she had to know. "I could forgive your wanting to seduce me," she said carefully. "I'd understand it. It would be human. Natural. But what happened just now . . ." She paused, uncertain how to voice her fears. "It wasn't real, was it? Was it all just . . . a pretense? To make me marry you?"

His reply shattered any hopes that she was wrong. "I'm sorry Sabina. I truly am. But I thought you needed . . . convincing." He paused and rubbed his jaw meditatively, shooting her a look that was half apology, half cool appraisal. "It just . . . got out of hand. You have a tendency to underrate your personal attractions, Mermaid. I assure you, I wasn't totally in control just now."

I wasn't totally in control. The words seemed to echo mockingly in her ears. She had never been so totally out of control in her entire twenty-two years.

"Well, I was certainly almost *convinced*, wasn't I?" She was proud that her voice was so steady. "It seems that I'm more vulnerable to seduction than I ever realized. I must certainly watch myself in future, or I will end up like one of the poor girls in a ballad sheet." She paused and added with quiet dignity, "I'd like you to go now. It's come as something of a shock to know that I can behave like a common street drab. I'm going to have to think on this new development."

His face darkened. "Don't lie there and blame yourself for what just happened, Sabina," he said grimly. "Yours was a perfectly human response. God knows I calculated that response. You aren't made of stone."

"I know that." She levered herself onto one elbow and looked directly at him. "But are you? Are you made of stone?"

The silence lengthened until it was almost unbearable. Then he turned as if to leave the cabin. She stopped him, her voice full of sweet venom.

"Is this how you abducted your heiress, Myles Dampier?"

He stood motionless for several seconds, then stooped to retrieve her silk shawl from where it had slipped to the ground during his lovemaking. He turned its exotic beauty over and over in his hands before replying easily, "No. She was infinitely less difficult to *convince* than you are, Miss Grey." He threw the garment onto the bunk and allowed an insolent gaze to roam her half-naked body.

Sabina, suddenly aware of the abandoned display of legs and bosom that she presented, tugged at her skirts and crossed her hands across her breasts in a belated attempt at modesty. Myles Dampier smiled and added admiringly, "By the way, I think you should change your plans of becoming a governess. With your . . . talents, Miss Grey, you have all the makings of a highly successful courtesan. Under the right tutelage, you would set half of Europe ablaze."

As a parting shot, it was fairly successful in depriving her of the ability to reply. Sabina, stifling the urge to call out to him, stared at the empty doorway as she battled with rage and misery and a deep hurt that felt like a knife wound to her heart. She wanted to once more bury her head in the pillow and pretend that the evening's events had never happened.

Little hope of that, she realized miserably, with her lips still swollen and tender from his kisses, and her skin still on fire wherever his hands had touched her.

Moaning, she raised herself awkwardly onto her elbows

and saw the silk shawl lying in a heap at her feet, an un-welcome reminder of the man who had given it to her. She wanted to take it and crush it between her hands, flinging its insolent beauty over the side of the ship. Re-luctantly she reached out for it, letting the feel of cool silk slip between her fingers before carefully folding it and placing it by her pillow. She climbed from her berth and pulled the blanket from the bed, throwing it around her shoulders to protect her from the sudden chill of the night.

And realized, with an aching clarity, that love was not the sweet and tender emotion promoted by the poets and three-volume novels. It could be bitter and painful and grueling, totally beyond reason and common sense. And the object of that love could be as remote and incompre-hensible as the heavens themselves.

I love him, she thought dazedly. *God help me, I love Myles Dampier. I don't care if he has killed ten men and abducted a hundred heiresses. I'd still love him.*

Sabina noticed that her whole body was shaking, al-though whether from shock or cold she couldn't decide. She wrapped her arms about her body and attempted to calm herself as she had during the height of the storm, by reciting large slabs of Latin learned at her father's knee. "Atoms are exceedingly small; they are indestructi-ble and they are ceaselessly in motion . . ." When this had no obvious effect, she sat down on the bunk and tried to assess the situation as coolly and rationally as a scientist.

She was in love with Myles Dampier.

Well, of course she was. It was as inevitable as a math-ematical equation. He was handsome, magnetic, and had saved her life. *Gratitude and admiration plus physical attrac-tion equals romantic passion.*

It was all so obvious that she didn't quite understand why she felt so miserably confused.

She knew he didn't love her. His strange rules of hon-esty had prevented him from pretending he did, and for that she was remarkably grateful. To have thought otherwise and then one day learn the truth would have been a humiliation she could not have borne.

He had said he wanted her. Even now the thought of this bold admission had the power to make her grow hot and cold, and her heart to pound faster in her breast. She told herself fiercely that she was behaving no better than the light o'love he had accused her of resembling. Her behavior had been wanton and immodest; it was clear that unless she was safely married to Myles Dampier, she would turn into a complete demimondaine, leading a life of champagne, expensive jewels, and open carriage rides through Hyde Park in order to market her assets to the bored aristocrats who frequented it for just such transactions.

Sabina Grey, Ladybird.

Sabina's lips twitched at the humor of this extravagant picture. Myles Dampier, she knew, would appreciate it as well, adding his own well-placed suggestions to savor the full ridiculousness of the idea. He never seemed to be shocked by anything she said or did. Instead, he always encouraged her to say and do exactly as she wanted, allowing her a delicious freedom she had never before experienced. Unconsciously, she had searched for just such an exhilarating liberty all her life, and for the past three weeks had reveled in it.

"But I sent him away," she said aloud, panic choking her voice. Despite the fact that he could hardly leave the brig, and she would almost certainly see him sometime that day, Sabina wrenched the cabin door open and flew up the companionway stairs, stealing onto the deck just as dawn was breaking. She startled a young sailor, who in that mysterious ritual common to all ships was throwing buckets of water on the deck.

"Mr. Dampier! Where is he, please?"

The sailor stared openmouthed at her, then jerked his head in the direction of the fo'c'sle. Sabina's shoulders sagged as she realized that she could hardly enter the living quarters of the ship's crew, no matter how urgently she needed to find Myles Dampier. She turned despondently to return to her own berth, but the boy's voice stopped her.

"Not down there, miss. Near the binnacle box." He jerked his head again, this time in the direction of the topmast, and Sabina's eyes flew heavenward, expecting to find her quarry hanging from the rigging.

"No, miss!" Forgetting his captain's orders, the boy took her by the arm and turned her around to face the bow of the brig. The dark head visible past the roof of the after-house faced the sea. Flashing the young sailor a grateful smile, Sabina hurried toward her goal, ignoring the pitching and heaving of the deck beneath her bare feet, and the high waves that threatened to drench her.

Myles Dampier stood at the helm, his legs braced and his hands firm upon the great wheel, but he noted her presence with a brusque command: "Go down below, Sabina. This is not the place for you."

"What are you doing? You haven't slept yet."

"I don't need any more than three or four hours. But thank you for your concern."

The chilly formality of his manner was so unexpected that she almost turned tail and fled back to the safety of her cabin. However, she managed to mentally square her shoulders and stand her ground, despite the rolling seas. "I wanted to talk to you," she began uncertainly, and then jumped as a voice above her called out, *"Hard alee!"* Myles Dampier turned the wheel to follow the ship's head, and then above them there was a great noise as the sails snapped and blocks banged. A cry of *"Mainsail haul!"* echoed through the commotion of bellying sails, and the ship came round with a great lurch that made Sabina, barefoot on a slippery deck, grasp out at the nearest stable object.

"Keep your balance, Mermaid. I don't want to have to haul you out of the water today."

She found herself clutching at his coat with both hands, while one leg had somehow hooked around his. She hung from him like a monkey from a tree, staring up into his grinning face.

"You won't mind if I hang on to the wheel?" he murmured softly. "As much as I'd prefer to hold on to you, I think it might be better for the ship."

She straightened herself with difficulty, releasing him with exaggerated care and testing her balance. Miraculously, she found she could stand unaided, and launched into a tangled speech whose rhythm seemed to keep pace with the movement of the vessel. "I want to say I'm sorry. I'm not sure about what—in fact, I know you were in the wrong, so I shouldn't be apologizing at all but I am, and I want you to know that."

"Apology accepted. Now get below before you get a drenching."

"In case you haven't noticed, I'm already drenched. Can't you give the wheel to someone else and talk to me?"

"I just took it. I needed something to keep my mind occupied. That and sufficient amounts of cold water."

She shook her head, not understanding the significance of this remark. "You aren't very gracious," she said tightly.

"Well, well, Mermaid. I've learned a great deal about my character this morning. I'll seduce virtuous young women to get my own way. And I'm not very gracious. I wonder what other remarkable discoveries I'll make about myself today?"

"What about the fact that you are entirely ruthless?"

"Ah. That was already common knowledge, Sabina. It seems a ruthless streak runs in my family."

"Well, marriage seems to run in mine. I must marry one day, and considering my circumstances and . . . and what I owe you . . ." Her voice trailed away. For her pride's sake, she wanted to pretend that she was marrying him for purely practical reasons, but an innate honesty prevented her from carrying her speech any further. She swallowed and asked bluntly, "Do you . . . do you still want to marry me?"

"Yes." That was it. One word, baldly stated.

She swallowed at his lack of enthusiasm, and said with a pathetic attempt at dignity, "Very well, then. You had better make the arrangements with Captain Scully."

"Scully already knows."

"Scully already . . . Do you mean to tell me that you *knew* I would agree to marry you?"

"Let's just say I was . . . gambling on the possibility."

Sabina realized that she was staring at him open-mouthed. "I don't know what is worse, Myles Dampier—your despicable honesty or your overwhelming arrogance."

"Why, Miss Grey. Just when I thought you had run out of character traits to surprise me with." His grin was dazzlingly white.

Sabina ignored this sally and continued grittily, "Before we do marry, however, there are things we should discuss."

"Such as?"

"Well . . . things! Marriages aren't just thrown together at a moment's notice, you know. It takes weeks, sometimes months. Surely we need to speak of . . ." She faded into confusion, having very little idea of any particular matters their marriage would raise. She was of age. She had no family. There were no settlements to be made. There could hardly be any impediments. "I'm sorry," she said, shaking her head ruefully, "but I have absolutely no idea what I'm talking about. I was thinking of banns to be read and . . . and attendants and flowers. It's all so foolish, I know, but after all, I've never been married before."

Sabina expected an amiable acknowledgment of this naïve statement, or one of his quick, ironic replies. Instead, he preserved a grim silence that immediately aroused her suspicions. She noted the whitened knuckles gripping the wheel and said faintly, "But you have been, haven't you?"

"Relieve your mind that you will be marrying a bigamist, Sabina. The marriage was annulled fifteen long years ago."

Another wave brought a shower of cold water across the bow, but Sabina barely noticed. She looked at the man who stood braced at the wheel, his black hair ruffled by the wind, his shirt, soaked through, clinging to the hard-muscled chest. He was an image of power and certainty, not adolescent, star-crossed love. "Was it . . . your heiress?" she asked slowly.

"Not mine for very long."

"I see." Such a foolish expression, she decided as soon as she said the words. She didn't see anything at all, except the hard, shuttered look that had descended over his face. "Is there anything else I should know?"

"I've told you the rest. I am legally a bachelor, and you a spinster. Scully will perform the ceremony as supreme authority on this ship. When we reach England, we will do so as husband and wife." He added brusquely, "Stop acting as though this is some sort of Fleet marriage I am proposing. Not only will you be mistress of Lysons Hall, Sabina, but you will also have my very substantial fortune at your fingertips. You will have carriages and silks and furs enough to make any woman happy."

"Oh! And you think furs and silks and . . . and things will make me happy?"

"If they do not, then you will be unhappy in considerable comfort."

The equanimity of this reply made her want to stamp her foot. The fact that both feet were almost numb with cold brought her to a sense of her surroundings. The blanket was soaked, and her hair was plastered to her head. She had no doubt that she looked like a drowned rat, not a radiant bride-to-be. And her teeth were beginning to chatter. "I'm going below," she announced grandly. "If you wish to speak to me, I'll be in my cabin."

"Good. And get some sleep while you can. There are storms up ahead. You'll soon be tossed about like a rag doll in a nursery."

There seemed nothing left to say. Shivering, Sabina turned and left him at the wheel. As she carefully made her way back to her cabin, she sincerely hoped that Myles Dampier's dour prediction was not a prophecy about her decision.

Whenever Sabina as a romantic schoolgirl had dreamed of her wedding day, it had rarely borne any resemblance to the actual ceremony performed on the damp deck of the *Ellen Drury*.

Two more days of storms had left the ship at the mercy of huge seas and howling winds. The calm that settled over the ocean with the return of fair breezes and blue skies had seemed to call for a celebration of some sort. Sabina crawled out of her cabin limp and exhausted, unable to offer any argument to Myles Dampier's insistence that the marriage take place that morning. Instead, she found herself garbed in her "best"—Miss Scully's calico skirts, a borrowed shirt, and the captain's knitted slippers—a present from his wife—liberally stuffed with paper so that they might stay on her feet. Her silk shawl served as the only touch of beauty in her wedding attire, and Sabina clutched at its folds with all the desperation of a drowning woman.

"Well, well, Miss Grey," Captain Scully huffed nervously as he stood on the deck before a shuffling group of interested sailors. "Happy the bride the sun shines on, as they say." He smiled encouragingly and waved the Order of Service at her. "I've been prepared to commit men's bodies to the deep for the past few days. I never thought it would be a marriage service I'd be conducting this morning."

From the suddenly solemn look on his face, Sabina realized that the captain was making little differentiation between the two. She made a small panicked movement, only to feel her arm grasped and held by the man standing at her side. Uncertainly she looked up into his face, and was calmed a little by the resolution she saw there.

"Nervous, Mermaid?" he murmured. His hands gentled, feeling less like iron manacles, and she attempted a smile.

"A little," she admitted. "Are you?"

"No." He seemed amused by the question. "Do I look nervous?"

He looked anything but. Casually attired in a blue jacket and white trousers, with a kerchief carelessly knotted under his shirt collar, he looked both confident and relaxed. She searched for a word that would adequately describe her groom's demeanor and could come up with only one: complacent—like the cat who'd licked the cream from the bowl. Sabina wanted to believe that it was because he had finally found the wife he had long searched for—a helpmate, with whom he could build a new life in England, wiping out the stains of his past unhappiness.

I will be a good wife. We will be happy, she told herself fiercely as she stood blinking up into the morning sunlight.

He will love me in time.

And then Captain Scully cleared his voice and began the ceremony, and unexpectedly, her mind ceased to think at all. Dimly Sabina heard Myles Dampier's deep voice recite the words in response to the captain, and then she was prodded into making her own feeble response.

"I will." Somehow, on her lips the words became a question.

She threw up her head in sudden panic, one hand on Myles Dampier's shoulder, only to be held captive by an intent blue gleam that seemed to demand her total capitulation. There was no reassuring smile, no comfort to be offered. Instead, her hand was seized in his, and he solemnly made his pledge in a strong, steady tone.

"I, Myles Edward, take thee, Sabina Charlotte, to my wedded wife, to have and to hold, from this day forward, for better, for worse, for richer, for poorer, in sickness and in health, to love and to cherish until death us do part; and thereto I give thee my troth."

The strength of his hand somehow seemed to be the only thing that kept her standing. Distantly she heard someone well schooled by the captain automatically repeating these words, the voice trembling a little as they reached the climax, which was lost anyway in the creaking of timbers and the sudden bellying of sheets in the wind. She felt a band being slipped onto her finger, and awoke from her stupor to watch a lean, brown hand hold the ring firmly in place.

She studied it with detached interest. It was a signet ring, bearing a small crest, and much too large for the ring finger of her left hand. Sabina was about to point this out with calm reasonableness, but Myles Dampier's voice once more deprived her of her ability to think rationally, much less speak. "With this ring I thee wed, with my body I thee worship, and with all my worldly goods I thee endow . . ."

Sabina shuddered and drew in a deep breath. She didn't need Scully's final blessing or the snapping of the book covers to tell her that the ceremony was at an end. Nor the cheerful congratulations of the sailors who nodded their bare heads respectfully in her direction, and shook her groom's hand to affirm that she and Myles Dampier were now husband and wife.

Captain Scully cleared his throat and saluted her shyly, adding his congratulations, saying, "Well, Mrs. Dampier. I've seen my fair share of death on this ship, and my very own grandchild born below, and now a marriage on the quarter deck. Might I say, no bride could have been prettier. Nor one more radiant . . ." Here the captain's reverence for the truth caused him to blush and hastily amend, "Er . . . well, *prettier*, in all events. Much happiness to you in the future, ma'am."

She blinked at this formal address, and fought a rising sense of excitement. For better or for worse, she was married to this enigmatic stranger standing at her side.

She hadn't been able to look at him since she had made her first vow. Now she shyly did so, and was surprised by the emotions that flickered across the austere angles of his face. It was not joy, nor pleasure, nor eagerness that glittered from beneath the dark lashes, nor any of the usual emotions a bridegroom might feel on his wedding day. Instead, she sensed a cool satisfaction—a contained self-congratulation that seemed to exclude her altogether.

Her apprehension must have been apparent, because he bent over her and asked softly, "You aren't sorry, are you?"

"I'm not sure," she admitted, incurably truthful. She felt hot, fervent tears unexpectedly rise, and immediately put her hand to her head, hoping to stem them before they fell. How dreadful to cry on your wedding day all because you realize you are foolishly, hopelessly in love with your groom. The entire ship would think she was mad. She continued shakily, "I think the captain must practice mesmerism, because I still feel as though I'm in some sort of a dream. The whole ceremony was . . . a reverie. Any moment now and I shall awake to find myself back in my berth on the *Margaret Rose*. And you . . . *you* will turn out to be the mysterious man in the opposite cabin, only you will be a fat, middle-aged tea merchant with a wife in Putney and twelve children. And that will be a very good thing, too!"

As her voice rose, Myles suddenly placed his tall body between her and the little assembly who must have watched in pleasure as bride and groom created a romantic tableau in a corner of the deck, his hands hard on her shoulders, her head leaning trustingly against his shoulder. Captain Scully cleared his throat for a final time, and then barked orders that had the crew flying to their various duties.

Myles Dampier smiled down tenderly at his bride. "I trust this isn't hysteria, Mrs. Dampier. I'd hate to have to dump you in the water barrel within the first five minutes of married life."

Sabina wiped her eyes on her shawl, resisting the urge to blow her nose quite thoroughly. Instead she sniffed, and said sadly, "You know what I mean. You always do know what I mean. I don't have to explain anything to you, do I? You . . . you *understand* me! And I hate that just about worse than anything. If I'd remembered that, I wouldn't have married you at all!"

"Look at me, Sabina."

"But I don't want to be understood!"

"Congratulations, Mermaid. You've certainly achieved your goal. Now, quiet down and look at me."

Reluctantly she looked up into the familiar features gazing down at her unsmilingly. There were the same dark winged brows, the same arrogant, high-bridged nose, the same mouth that could be white-lipped with anger one moment and curled with teasing laughter the next. But to Sabina, it was suddenly a different face altogether from the one she had known. This was the man she loved. She bent her head, and began to twist the ring that hung far too loosely on her finger.

"Are these merely bridal nerves, or do you honestly regret becoming the wife of an ex-convict?"

The question was so unexpected that she flung her head up, her loose curls whipping in the breeze. "No!" she finally managed to choke out. "Oh, no!" Unconsciously she lifted her hand and touched his cheek, determined to stroke away the strained expression that lingered there. "You know it isn't that, Myles! Any woman would be proud to be your wife. I am. How can you think it would be that?"

"Contrary to your accusations of my omniscience, my dear, I find you are as much of an enigma as any woman I have ever met." He softened his words with a wry smile and, taking her hand from his cheek, brought it softly against his mouth.

His lips were warm against the soft flesh of her palm, and the spear of desire that suddenly pierced her shocked Sabina. She wondered if his taunts about her appetites weren't more than mere teasing, but some secret masculine recognition of her desires. All at once she felt foolish and vulnerable and wicked and very unsure of herself. She gently pulled herself away with a genteel murmur that she hoped would bring him—and her!—to a sense of propriety. "Mr. Dampier. Please. We are on public display."

"Mrs. Dampier, as the bridal couple we are expected to bill and coo in quiet corners. In fact, I believe it is mandatory." The blue eyes were alight with laughter, and all tension had finally vanished from his features. He looked happy, and strong and confident, and Sabina, wiping away the residue of her tears, was suddenly overwhelmed by the fact that she could make him look this way.

She asked impulsively, laying her hand on his arm, "We will be happy, won't we, Myles? It will turn out well."

Myles carefully tucked her hand into the crook of his arm, drawing her to his side. They began to stroll about the upper deck, at present diplomatically deserted by the crew. "I intend it to turn out very well indeed. I have a feeling you will become the Dampiers' luck, Mermaid. Like my dear great-great-grandmama."

"What sort of luck did she bring?"

"A treasure haul of sunken riches, to begin with. And legend has it that she presented her lord with seven times seven sons, each more handsome and gifted than the last." He paused and added modestly, "I, of course, am descended from the forty-ninth son." He quirked one dark eyebrow at her suddenly crestfallen expression. "It's all right Sabina. One or two sons will be sufficient. You won't find me unreasonable in that respect."

She blushed rosily. "I wasn't thinking about that at all! It was . . . it was the mention of treasure."

"And I thought you beyond mere avarice. Well, if you think I can drape you with pirate booty, my dear, I have to confess that it disappeared long ago. I'm afraid the forty-nine sons, like most Dampier men, must have been expensive items to keep."

"I wish I had something to give you, that's all. Some sort of dowry. But there's nothing. My father sold his library years ago, and we lived on that and a small income which ceased when he died. For the rest, we lived on patronage, and the goodwill of our friends. Papa always expected me to marry well, but he could never quite see his way to looking into the practicalities of settlements and the like."

Myles smiled lazily, and began to sing. " 'My face is my fortune, sir, she said.' Didn't I say that your beauty would eventually be your dowry?"

"You said a lot of things. Mostly to make me angry, I think."

"Mrs. Dampier, Mrs. Dampier, I don't hear a proper respect in your voice when you speak to me. Was I deceived by your meek and obedient manner before our marriage?"

Sabina stopped and reluctantly withdrew her hand from the warmth of his arm. She looked up at him with renewed seriousness, unwilling to lose his gentle teasing but determined to understand his motives for sweeping her so hastily into matrimony. "Just tell me this, Myles Dampier. Did you marry me because—and I understand I sound like a . . . a complete *mushroom* for even asking this question—but did you marry me for my looks?"

Myles Dampier's arms went around her, drawing her close. His eyes, the color of cornflowers in sunlight, were unclouded as he confronted her gaze. "No, Sabina. I can honestly say, you are much more valuable to me than that."

His words filled her with a sudden inexplicable sense of well-being. Even her body felt so light she feared it might blow away in the breeze. She rested against him and promised fervently, "I will be a good wife, Myles Dampier."

He took her chin gently in one hand. "I have no doubts on that score, Mermaid. And now, if you will permit me, I have a bride to kiss."

His lips descended with unbearable languor, finally resting on hers with a feather-light touch. He withdrew slightly, and then pressed against her mouth once more, parting, touching, and then finally lingering with renewed ardor, until she found herself clinging to him, trembling, her lips parted with longing. His arms tightened, and finally he kissed her with such incredible tenderness that it seemed to unstop the tears that welled behind her tautly held control. When he finally raised his head, his smile was slightly crooked as he wiped away the moisture from her face with a gentle movement of his thumbs.

"Go downstairs now, Mrs. Dampier. Scully is waiting to toast us in his cabin with his best Madeira. *Curse him.*"

The rest of Sabina's wedding day was spent alone in the fastness of the captain's armchair, a copy of one of Sir Walter Scott's romances open on her lap. A problem with the pumps had called all hands into action until the carpenter could deal with it, and a crewman's fall from the rigging had smashed a collarbone and thrown the deck into confusion. Her offers of assistance being firmly dis-

81

missed, she waited patiently beside the novel and a dwindling pile of sewing, listening to the sounding of bells and the constant movements of man and ship. At one point, Jezebel had provided her with some company, but since the little creature tended to sulk quietly in a corner when kept indoors, Sabina turned her out into the fresh air. She was soon glad to hear footsteps in the companionway.

Myles Dampier entered carrying a small pile of possessions, which he placed in the captain's chest. As he knelt down, he said over his shoulder, "I'll get the rest of your things and move them in here. Scully is happy to relinquish his cabin for the rest of the voyage as long as he has use of it during the day."

"The captain's cabin—he's giving it up?"

"Well, we can hardly both fit into your bunk, my dear. Even Scully thought it would make a poor place for a honeymoon."

The significance of his words swept over her like a wave of warm lava.

"We are to sleep in the captain's bed—together!"

He straightened at the unexpected panic in her voice, and slowly appraised her with narrowed eyes. "Yes. Together, Mrs. Dampier. That's the general idea of a honeymoon."

"Of course. Of course it is. I wasn't thinking." Which was a complete lie. She had thought a great deal. She was the daughter of a naturalist. The mysteries of procreation held very few mysteries for her, and she could hardly say, after the intimacies she had already shared with Myles Dampier, that she believed the marriage would be in name only. But the thought of giving herself to him without love filled her with a deep sadness that she could hardly begin to explain—even to herself.

"I thought I had made it plain to you, Sabina. I want this to be a marriage in fact. I want sons to inherit all that I've regained. And that, you may be surprised to learn, often involves sharing the same bed."

She felt her cheeks burn as she fought for a measure of control. No one could have been more surprised than she at her hysterical schoolgirl response. "I'm not a child, Myles Dampier. I know very well . . . that is, I'm prepared to do my duty."

He emitted a sharp, mirthless laugh. "*Duty*. Lord, Sabina, I want a wife in my bed, not some sort of virgin martyr. And here I was willing to wager that there wasn't a cold bone in your body." She watched him drag one distracted hand through the dark curls, and then a slow grin spread across his face. "Damned if I'm not hoist upon my own petard, Mermaid."

"Myles! Please, I said I would . . . that is . . ."

"I'll sleep on the floor tonight, if you don't mind. Even my pride might take a few dents if I had to return to the fo'c'sle on my wedding night." He sounded more resigned than annoyed, but Sabina was horrified by the idea.

"Oh, Myles. Not on the floor!"

"Don't worry. It won't be the first time I've slept on the floor. Not necessarily in the same set of circumstances, of course."

"But I said that I'm quite willing to . . . Damn it all, Myles Dampier! You aren't listening to me! I said I'm willing to consummate the marriage."

Sabina realized that her voice had risen to a shout. A startled flurry of footsteps sounded outside the door, and then stampeded up the companionway stairs. However, she was beyond embarrassment at this point, merely reflecting rather bitterly that Captain Scully must find them an exceedingly strange couple.

She looked helplessly at her new husband, who stood with folded arms, one elegant eyebrow quirked in a look of wicked amusement.

"As delightful as that offer is, I'm going to have to decline. While it's not the wedding night I had imagined . . . in all fairness, I understand that I am still very much a stranger to you."

A stranger. Sabina lowered her eyes, silently acknowledging the truth of his words, torn between her desire to be in his arms and her even stronger need for his love. When she became his wife in every sense of the word, it would be an act of complete need, not expediency on one hand and duty on the other.

"You aren't angry, are you?"

"No, I'm not angry." He suddenly reached over and took her chin gently between forefinger and thumb, raising her flushed face so that she looked directly into his. The expression in the cornflower eyes was deceptively mild, the grimace he made only slightly self-mocking. "But I am very, very patient in getting what I want, Mermaid." He released her and moved toward the door.

"Where are you going?"

He paused at her anxious inquiry and, turning, delivered a formal bow of exquisite grace and courtesy.

"To help man the pumps, Mrs. Dampier. Something tells me I'll need lots of physical activity over the next few days."

CHAPTER FIVE

The pumps had stopped.

Sabina sat up in bed still half asleep, uncertain as to whether the leaking had ceased or if the ship was actually sinking. She rubbed her eyes and then chuckled, throwing back the bedclothes, her feet sliding onto a floor that no longer pitched or rolled. Two short strides took her to the casement. She flung the window open and joyfully inhaled the pungent odors offered by a London inn yard. Resting her chin on one hand, she propped her elbow on the grimy sill and took in the confusion below her.

Being on dry land was still something of a novelty. Perhaps it was because of the speed with which she had been bundled from the *Ellen Drury* and into a closed carriage, barely having time to bid a reluctant farewell to Captain Scully, that she had found it difficult to get her land legs. She pitched and rolled with the motions of the sea many hours after she was deposited in a comfortable Plymouth inn, her rags stripped away by a clucking chambermaid and replaced by a plain but respectable round gown.

She had bathed in hot, scented water. She had eaten food that had never been to sea.

And she had smiled sweetly when Myles Dampier requested separate chambers of the landlord, explaining with unnecessary detail that this was due to his wife's terrible habit of snoring.

"We shan't be here long," he had said, the ready laughter in his eyes more pronounced than ever. "I have business to conclude in London before we go into Norfolk."

London. Agreeing wholeheartedly with Dr. Johnson's statement that only those tired of life could tire of that city, Sabina, snuggled under a rug and with a hot brick at her feet, had settled into the chaise that would take them there feeling as though it were an enchanted coach.

The Bull and Mouth, their chosen hostelry in Piccadilly, was not a restful place. A large coaching inn, vehicles rumbled in and out of its courtyard day and night, and even in one of the "best" bedchambers on the third story, sleep was often impossible. It was a measure of her exhaustion after their late arrival from Plymouth the previous night that she had slept like the dead. Now she turned from the window as a slight tap on the door signaled the arrival of a smiling maidservant who entered bearing hot water and the cheerful news that breakfast awaited her in the private dining room.

"Is my . . . husband waiting for me?" She shyly stumbled over the word, conscious of the separate bedchambers.

"Oh, no, ma'am. Mr. Dampier went out earlier. He asked that you not be disturbed." The girl's voice held a hint of reverence, as though the request had come from a being superior to the rest of humankind. "Mr. Dampier said to tell you that he would be back after he had concluded his business."

Stifling her disappointment at this news, Sabina thanked the girl and waited for the door to close before shrugging herself out of the nightdress she had hastily acquired in Plymouth. After hurried ablutions, she climbed into the petticoats and gown she had been given secondhand. Of good quality, the gown was a sensible round-necked dress several seasons out of date, its waist too high to follow current fashion trends. But it was clean and serviceable and didn't hang from her in tatters. And the joy she felt in putting on stockings and shoes was something she knew would not fade for some time.

The dining room, however, was not as private as she had expected. She entered to find her husband's man of business awaiting her pleasure at the breakfast table. Mr. Marney, a small, gimlet-eyed man who looked as though he had been bleached, bowed deeply and smiled. Sabina had taken an instant dislike to the man on their first meeting on board the *Ellen Drury*, distrustful of his small, thin hands and the cold assessment of his pale eyes, but she adjusted her features into a civil greeting.

Mr. Marney's smile widened. "My dear Mrs. Dampier, how very *rested* you look. I hope that you will allow me to offer my services this morning. Your husband has requested that I escort you to Bond Street to make some purchases for your wardrobe."

Sabina was torn between delight at the prospect of new clothes and the grim necessity of Mr. Marney's company. She smiled sweetly in return. "That won't be required, thank you. I am London born and bred, sir, and quite capable of finding my own way to Bond Street."

Mr. Marney's thin eyebrows rose. "Unaccompanied? My dear Mrs. Dampier, I don't think your husband would approve of that."

"Since he isn't here to ask, I won't know, will I? But if you are concerned that I may need help to carry my boxes, I'll hire a hackney. That way I can visit both Grafton Street and Burlington Arcade. I do hope all those splendid shops haven't disappeared in the five years I've been out of the country."

The man's smile stretched like rubber. "I have taken the liberty of engaging a personal maid for you, Mrs. Dampier, along with the other domestics necessary for your new home. Since my own company seems so . . . *distasteful* to you, shall we say, you might wish to wait for her arrival. After all, *a lady of quality* should not be abroad by herself.

It will leave you open to all kinds of insult." His tone was an insult in itself.

"Well, I was never insulted when I was *not* a lady of quality!" Sabina heard the querulous note in her voice and didn't like hearing it. She decided to give in on this one small point of independence, and tried to alter her manner. "Oh, very well. I will wait for the girl to arrive and she can lend me both consequence and respectability. And now, Mr. Marney, if you don't mind, I am famished. I believe there must be eggs under one of those chafing dishes and I mean to have at them."

Her voice carried a polite dismissal. However, far from looking happy at her capitulation, the man seemed annoyed. Stepping back, he put his hands together and rested his chin on the pointed fingertips, his pale eyes running over her with a barely concealed insolence. He said bluntly, "You know, you aren't at all what I expected. I knew you would be beautiful. But I didn't anticipate that you would have a mind of your own."

"I beg your pardon." She stared him down, a dish lid poised in her hand.

Marney's smile was now at its widest, showing little sharp white teeth. "When your husband told me he had married, I expected something more . . . pliable. But you are out of the common way. Yes, indeed. Something very much out of the common way." His tongue darted across his lips like a small, hungry lizard. "Trust Myles Dampier to fall on his feet, even in that respect. Well, I've no doubt you will cost him a pretty penny. But, m'dear, I should warn you that you must dance to his tune if you are to remain comfortable. I learnt that lesson a long time ago. Accept what he gives you, and don't question anything."

Sabina felt her mouth gape open in surprise. It was more than just the horrible familiarity in his voice that left her feeling shocked and shaken. His words seemed to be a terrible parody of Myles's own warning to her on the *Ellen Drury*.

"I'm afraid I don't understand you," she said coldly.

"Don't you? Well, I've no doubt you soon will. By then

you might be happy to endure my company for an hour or two. Remember, Mrs. Dampier, I know where the bodies are buried."

Mr. Marney, obviously sensitive to an effective last line, made his exit on this interesting turn of phrase, leaving Sabina to stare blindly at a dish of kidneys.

His words, hateful and offensive as they were, seemed to be a warning of some kind.

But about what?

She was inclined to write the incident off as the spite of a mean-tempered man piqued because she so obviously showed disdain for his company. Yet at the back of her mind, a niggling little doubt took hold and soon blossomed into a full-fledged anxiety. Myles Dampier was still very much a mystery to her. Was he hiding something from her? Something much darker than he had led her to believe?

A very unbridelike question surfaced in her mind.

Who was the man she had married?

Unsettled, Sabina left her breakfast untouched, returning to her bedchamber where she sat stiffly at the window watching the constant flow of traffic in and out of the courtyard, and waited for her husband's return. She didn't have long to wait. She heard the door to his chamber close, and then a forceful knock had her springing to her feet to wrench open her door.

Myles Dampier stood at the threshold examining her critically. Sabina's eyes widened at the transformation in his own appearance. If he had been an attractive figure in "slops," he was now a man to command attention in any sphere of society. The pale green frock coat stretched across his broad shoulders without a wrinkle, and the tight-fitting breeches of nankeen displayed shapely legs. His neckcloth, fashionably checked, had replaced the carelessly tied kerchief, and his gleaming hessians were a far cry from the rough leather shoes of shipboard life. He looked suddenly taller, and infinitely more remote. Sabina pulled at the neck of her plain gown, feeling like a peahen under the scrutiny of a peacock.

"I thought you would be out shopping," he said bluntly. He slapped his leather gloves against his thigh in a gesture of impatience and moved into the middle of the room, where he stood scowling at her. "Told Marney to take you."

"I dislike Mr. Marney," she said passionately. "I dislike him intensely."

"So do I. But you'll find him very useful on occasion."

"If I ever have any bodies to bury?"

Her tart reply caught him up short, and his eyes narrowed suspiciously. "I don't understand you."

"What a delightful change!" She whirled over to the shabby dressing table, where she made a great play of patting down her neatly braided hair. An impassioned explanation trembled on her lips, but she paused, assuring herself that Marney's insolence was only a temporary state of affairs. Within a few days she would—with any luck—never see the man again. "Oh, it doesn't matter. A private joke, that's all." She caught his questioning gaze in the mirror and burst out, "But it seems I am now such a flower of gentility that I may not walk the streets on my own."

"If that is all Marney said to you, I am surprised it put you into such a snit. I hope you didn't expect to wander down Bond Street without an escort."

"You talk as though it is full of cannibals!"

"Worse. Bond Street beaux. And, my dear wife, before this argument gets too heated, I might point out that what was perfectly suitable for Miss Grey is not acceptable behavior in Mrs. Dampier." He added blandly, "I might have been in the colonies for the last fifteen years, Sabina, but I don't believe that conventions have changed that much."

Feeling as though she were fighting a losing battle, she gave in with a careless shrug. "And I thought you quite ignorant about the rules governing the behavior of English gentlewomen. I had no idea I would be marrying such a high stickler. You put Cousin Sarah to shame."

He held out a hand, his face fighting a grin. "Not even comparisons to Cousin Sarah of Bournemouth will move me. Come. Let's call a truce. I will take you to whichever mantua-maker you have your heart set on visiting. More importantly, I will bring a wallet full of banknotes and a purse full of guineas."

"In that case, I hope you don't think I intend to visit only *one* shop."

"Buy whatever you want, Mermaid. Gowns, bonnets— all the fripperies you need. I can't have the new mistress of Lysons Hall labeled a dowd. I want you to do me credit."

There was nothing disturbing in the words themselves, but Sabina felt her heart sinking a little. The clothes were obviously not for her pleasure, but for his credit. She admonished herself for her foolish qualms, reflecting that no man of consequence could wish his wife to wear cast-off clothing. And yet, the thought that she was to be outfitted purely for display took away much of the promised pleasure.

"Have you breakfasted?" he asked abruptly. "You seem a little pale."

"No. I . . . didn't feel like it. I was tired."

"In that case, if you are very good, we may take our midday meal at a respectable chophouse."

"At a . . ." She looked at him closely. "You are jesting, of course." But she wasn't certain.

"Well, I've bespoken a light luncheon at the Clarendon Hotel, if that would please you more."

His teasing half-smile made her own smile radiant in response. She gathered up her cloak, suddenly light-hearted at the idea of a day spent in his company. Dismissing luncheon at one of the most exclusive hotels in London with a toss of her head, she replied severely, "It would serve you right if I demanded you take me to a disreputable chophouse."

"We might be reduced to that if the morning's shopping is successful."

The morning was extremely successful. Sabina was able to purchase several gowns at a modish establishment, which seemed determined to satisfy even the most unreasonable demands of such an elegant and openhanded customer as Mr. Dampier of Lysons Hall. Promenade dresses, dinner dresses, evening dresses, morning dresses, walking dresses, carriage dresses—Sabina's head whirled as lengths of materials and patterns were thrown at her and over her. Her plain, round gown was swiftly removed by a pursed-mouthed assistant, never to be seen again. Instead Sabina floated from the premises in a dress of sea-green silk, festooned with ribbons of the same color. The full sleeves and fluted muslin collar were such a revelation that she had to stop herself from stroking them to register their existence. A milliner's shop on Regent Street supplied a silk bonnet of exactly the same color, veiled with a curtain of blond lace, while stockings, gloves, handkerchiefs, and slippers were purchased at the Opera House Arcade.

"I'm afraid I've been like a woman starved of pretty things," she said guiltily when they finally settled into the hackney carriage that was to take them to Albemarle Street. She adjusted one of the bandboxes that held her new treasures. "For someone who hasn't had a new gown in five years, all this finery is rather overwhelming. I don't know how I can wait till the other dresses are made up." She looked appreciatively at her gown. "If you only knew how wonderful it is to have something of my own again. And something so delightfully modish."

"You look beautiful, Mermaid. The color of the sea was a perfect choice. Nothing could become you better."

His voice had a husky quality that made her skin feel as though it had suddenly taken on a life of its own. Her eyes were irresistibly drawn to his, the blue depths darkening with an emotion that caused her heart to skip a beat.

"I believe the choice was yours," she said uncertainly.

"Was it? Then I chose well. Tell me, Mermaid. Have you ever been kissed in a carriage?" His question was an unexpected caress.

It should have made her retreat against the window in

girlish confusion. Instead, she found herself lifting her chin and replying, "Yes. I have."

Her blunt reply surprised a shout of laughter from her husband. "I might have known someone would beat me to that privilege. Which dauntless swain accomplished the feat?"

"He was my father's assistant. He drew seashells and butterflies for me. I was fifteen, and he kissed me while Papa was climbing from the carriage."

"An enterprising young man. And tell me, how did he perform this daring deed? Did he lean over you—like this—or did he take hold of you, tenderly of course, so not to frighten you—like this?"

"I don't remember. But I'm quite certain I didn't do this." She marveled at how calm she sounded as she slid her arm around his neck and raised her face to his, her lips parted tremulously. His mouth descended with a devastating gentleness, slanting softly across her lips, teasing her into a response, and then hardening as he gathered her close to him. He smelled of fresh soap and leather, a heady masculine scent that made her bold in her exploration of his firm jaw. She tore her mouth from his and nuzzled the base of his ear, moving her lips softly across his freshly shaven skin. Her boldness caused him to stifle a groan, and he gripped her waist with hard, insistent hands.

"We can either continue on to the Clarendon or we can go back to the inn, Sabina. To my bedchamber." His voice was not quite steady.

She realized that, more than anything in the world at this moment, she wanted to be back at the inn. But even as she leaned submissively into his shoulder, Marney's words rose up in her memory like a snake's head, spewing venom.

Accept what he gives you, and don't question anything.

You'll cost him a pretty penny.

A cold chill ran up her spine. She released her hold on his jacket and slid miserably back into her seat, caution overriding passion.

"I . . . I think I'd like to take luncheon," she faltered.

The silence within the carriage was suddenly so thick that she was almost frightened to breathe. Myles sat stiffly, his eyes glittering with some strong unexpressed emotion; then he sighed and leaned against the squabs, a crooked smile flickering over his face.

"My dear, you are a torture that not even New South Wales could devise."

She hung her head, wanting to apologize but uncertain what to say. Explanation seemed impossible under the circumstances, particularly as she had acted like a shameless hussy, practically throwing herself into her husband's arms. How could she explain her fears to him when she herself was one quivering mass of confusion?

Unexpectedly, his hand reached out and touched her face with the delicacy of a butterfly wing.

"Don't look so tragic, Mermaid," he murmured. "Perhaps it's for the best, after all. I need a cool head over the next couple of days while I attend to business. You are proving something of an unforeseen distraction."

Sabina fought against a sense of ill usage at this description. "I see. I wouldn't want to be that. Just what sort of business are you attending to?"

"Nothing clandestine, if that's what you are thinking."

"Is it a secret?" She made a great play of smoothing out the creases in her new gloves.

"Not at all. Just not important. This morning I had business with my bank. Marney hired servants, while I purchased a traveling carriage and several horses. I intend to keep my own horses on the roads from now on. All blood-cattle. I presume you ride. I found you a very pretty mare at Tattersalls. I'll send it ahead with the servants and the chaise bearing our baggage."

"When do we go to Lysons Hall?"

"As soon as all the preparations are ready. Until then, we stay in London. You'll need more clothes if you are to take your rightful place in Norfolk society. You'll have to order a riding habit from Stultz. And you may wish to choose some pieces of jewelry." He added in satisfied tones, "When we arrive, my dear, it won't be as ragtag gypsies."

"So we will go when I am fit to be presented as your wife. Perfumed and painted, and elegantly gowned like some sort of porcelain doll."

"Do you object to looking like a rich man's wife, Sabina?" The fringe of black lashes shielded his eyes from her gaze.

"No, but I object to being hoisted to your mast, like your own private battle colors."

This time the lashes flew upward, revealing the blue depths lit with an unmistakable interest. "You have a definite way of expressing yourself, wife, that would cross a blind man's eyes. What the devil do you mean by that?"

What did she mean by it? She had absolutely no idea. But she plunged into a heartfelt explanation anyway.

"Only that we could have traveled straight from Plymouth to Lysons Hall if you were serious about making it your home. We didn't need to come here at all. It seems your business in London is to adopt all the trappings of wealth that you possibly can, so that you can dazzle everyone. You hide me—us!—in a coaching inn until we can burst onto society in all our glory. I am garbed like a duchess, while you hire smart London servants rather than local ones. You order a fine new carriage, which, I hazard, will bear a crest emblazoned on the door, and you buy your own horses instead of hiring them post!"

"These are crimes indeed, ma'am. What else am I charged with, Your Worship?"

"I daresay you have hired postilions and outriders, too!"

His face was stiff with an unexpected hauteur. "Of course. And since it's likely that we may be traveling separately, a courier as well. Mrs. Dampier of Lysons Hall does not travel into Norfolk as Miss Grey of Rio de Janeiro would travel into Norfolk."

"But our journey threatens to be as resplendent as a Roman triumph. It's preposterous and . . . and vulgar!"

"You would have preferred to arrive by mail coach, looking like a chambermaid?" he inquired softly. "And yet I seem to remember promising a girl who gladly wore a silk shawl over her rags that I wouldn't let her arrive home like a beggar. I must apologize for my ostentatious display of wealth, Sabina. But, in my defense—as you have so rightly pointed out—I am no longer a gentleman. Merely a vulgar emancipist, attempting to claw my way back into respectability."

She was shocked into speechlessness both by his words and by the controlled anger resonating in his voice.

So caught up had she been in her own uncertainties, she had forgotten all about the demons of his past, and the effect that fifteen years in exile might have had upon him. Somewhere in that suit of armor he wore over his emotions there was a point of vulnerability—invisible, yet accessible—and it made her suddenly conscious of her ability to wound him.

And it made all her reservations about her place in his scheme of things appear remarkably petty.

"Oh, Myles. I'm so sorry." She didn't try to hide the misery in her voice. "I didn't think. Of course you would wish to return to your home as . . . as a conquering hero. And you will! That wasn't what I was concerned about. It's just that . . . while I appreciate all the fine things you are giving me, I don't want to be treated as some sort of simpering idiot who will be well satisfied in life with a new carriage and a silk gown."

I don't want to dance to your tune if it's a loveless melody.

She watched the tension suddenly drain from his body, and he stretched, catlike, against his seat. An unsettling smile unfurled across his dark features.

"This proves to be an even more interesting morning than I had first imagined. Tell me, my dear, what *will* you be satisfied with?"

"Your friendship," she replied steadily. *Liar,* she told herself softly, but she resisted the urge to cross her fingers and instead looked into his face with every indication of sincerity.

"My friendship." He spoke the word as though it were strange and new to his vocabulary. She watched his lips twist painfully. "I've told you before, Sabina, that I seem to be remarkably bad at friendship."

"And yet you've been my friend." She smiled tremulously and put her hand on his arm, letting it rest there despite the fact that he looked down at it as though an insect had settled on his sleeve. "You've been my good friend ever since you pulled me out of the ocean."

"My dear, allow me one good deed without turning me into a saint."

"That's something I would never mistake you for."

"Then don't mistake me for your friend, Sabina. Because I tell you now that I'm not, and never will be."

His words were gently spoken, but they were as effective as a saber slash. She tried to think of some witty, cutting reply that would hide her concern at this admission, but she couldn't find the words. Then her heart suddenly felt too big for her breast, rising to lodge firmly in her throat. She was certain that she was going to burst into great, ragged sobs, but she also knew that the tears would never be able to get past that terrible blockage.

"Sabina."

She ignored her name, concentrating instead on the passing panorama of London streets outside the carriage window.

"Look at me, Mermaid."

She obeyed, turning toward him with the reluctant fascination of a bird cornered by a snake.

"Be that as it may, my sweet, *we are all that the other has.* Whatever happens, wherever we go, remember that."

Her lips quivered, and she put one gloved finger to her cheek just in time to catch a stray tear coursing down her face. She studied the drop of moisture with frowning concentration, and then found her wrist seized in a strong brown clasp. Myles Dampier softly placed her raised fingertip against his lips, his eyes fixed unwaveringly on her face.

"Don't ever let me make you cry," he said quietly. "You are too strong for that, Sabina. I'm depending on it."

His words seemed like a cruel mockery. She wasn't

strong at all. She felt utterly destroyed, his curiously tender gesture nearly proving her undoing. She shifted miserably, one part of her longing to fling herself from the carriage, the other determined to sit beside her husband in stiff dignity, ignoring the tall body sprawled beside her on the seat, one long leg only inches from her own.

"I'm not hungry," she suddenly announced.

"You will be when we get there. I won't have you refusing food every time we have a disagreement."

"I want to go back to the inn."

"Oh? You aren't reconsidering my earlier offer, are you?"

She said through gritted teeth, "I should very much like to hit you."

"Go ahead. I promise not to hit back, if that's what you're worried about."

"I wouldn't put it past you to strike a woman." She cringed at her own petulance.

"Yes, my dear, I am every kind of a fiend." Myles stared straight ahead, the self-mockery in his voice all too bitterly apparent. "I strangle kittens and pull the wings off flies. I abduct innocent heiresses and leer at strange young women on the promenade deck of sailing ships. In short, I am a monster. But one thing of which I will not be accused is starving my wife to death. Now, my dear Mrs. Dampier, it will either be the Clarendon or a chophouse in Cranbourne Alley. Take your pick. We have just turned onto Albemarle Street."

Sabina sat silently fiddling with one of the ribbons of her new gown. She inspected the lace cuffs with trembling lips before admitting resentfully: "You always make me feel such a fool whenever we quarrel. I try to remember what it was about and end up deciding I must have made it all up. But I know I didn't."

"We are both fools when we quarrel, Sabina. Come, cry peace with me. I promise I will attempt to keep my animal lusts under control, and you will eat a decent luncheon to please me. And," he added swiftly before she could argue with him, "if your Puritan soul is not too much offended by the suggestion, we will attend the theater tonight as amicably as brother and sister."

It was a low blow.

"The theater." Sabina found herself wavering. "I've never been to the theater in my life."

"I'm sure that Madame must have supplied you with an evening gown amongst all those other items."

Sabina's eyes traveled to a large box where her most exciting purchase lay nestled in tissue paper. "Yes," she admitted, adding unhappily, "It's blue, with silver ribbons."

"Wear it tonight," Myles cajoled.

"I'm still angry. You are still treating me as though all I am is some sort of pretty pet, to be pampered and admired. I want to be treated as your wife."

"A wife. Now, what a novel idea. I believe I have made several suggestions as to how that might be accomplished. Please let me know when you are willing to be treated as a wife."

His tone had lost none of its restored good humor, but his meaning was undeniably clear. Sabina suddenly gave up the struggle to resist his wishes, leaning wearily against the squabs as the carriage pulled up outside the august portals of the Clarendon Hotel.

After all, what was she fighting against? The vague warnings of a venomous little man with a large chip on his shoulder? Her husband's cold-blooded determination to turn her into a trophy to his own success? Or her own terrible sense of loneliness, and the fear that she would be forever trapped in a marriage where love was one-sided?

She watched Myles climb from the carriage and then lean toward her, holding out a demanding hand. The challenge in his eyes was unmistakable.

"Well, Mrs. Dampier?"

Mrs. Dampier. It was said without irony. She could be grateful for that much at least.

And perhaps, after all, half a glass was better than an empty one.

Deliberately she placed her elegantly gloved fingers in his. "If I am to attend the theater, Mr. Dampier," she said steadily, "I will need a silk cloak. I saw one trimmed in ermine that I particularly liked in Regent Street. And I hope you won't turn suddenly into a regular lickpenny when you are given the bill."

Sabina wore her new cloak to Drury Lane, settling into the handsome box with the sad reflection that she could not possibly have a Puritan soul, so great was her excitement at her present surroundings. The streets outside the theater were, she well knew, ill-lit breeding grounds of vice and crime, but inside the playhouse itself with its gilt furnishings, its colonnades and heavy velvet curtains, it seemed that every stratum of society was represented, from the pickpockets and prostitutes who hovered in the vestibule and lobbies, to the young bloods and ornaments of society who filled the private boxes. The play had not yet begun, and she was treated to the delights of seeing and being seen by what seemed to be half of London. She touched her hair a little self-consciously, wondering if the rather severe upsweep of tresses and loose braids that she had adopted were very much out of place amongst the heads of large, loose curls and feathers, so obviously the season's fashion.

"Do I look all right?" she asked anxiously. "There was not enough time for my new maid to curl my hair properly."

Myles Dampier, sprawled elegantly in the gilt chair beside her, raised an eyeglass and gave her a lingering appraisal. "You are possibly the most beautiful woman in the room." It was said not as a compliment but as a cold matter of fact.

She felt ridiculously downcast by the statement. "Thank you, but a simple 'You look very nice' was all I was after. My hair seems to be most unfashionably dressed, you see. I've only just realized it. Perhaps I need to have it cut."

"I won't allow it."

His tone was so pleasantly agreeable that it took Sabina several seconds to comprehend what he had said. She stared at him outraged, wishing that he didn't look quite so handsome in a tight-fitting dress coat of black superfine wool, his chin sunk carelessly into the snowy white folds of his cravat, his long trouser-clad legs languidly disposed in front of him. It was nothing more than a front. Myles Dampier, she thought furiously, was as languid as a coiled snake.

"You won't allow it." She carefully enunciated each word. "And how am I expected to react to that?"

"Knowing you as I do, Sabina, you will most probably shave your head and wear a wig. But I hope you don't. Your hair . . . gives me great pleasure."

There was a deep, honeyed note in his voice that made her snap open her fan and make a play of cooling her suddenly burning face. She changed the subject with a brittle laugh. "I heard in the lobby that the view from the new private boxes was worse than anything. And yet it's like suddenly being transported among the gods. Those women down there—the ones who seem remarkably underdressed and are so very affectionate toward the young gentlemen. Are they the famous *impures*?"

Myles grinned. "You sound like a seasoned theater butterfly already, Mrs. Dampier. You must understand that the play is the last thing you are here to observe."

"Well, it will have to be good indeed to be half as interesting."

"I agree. And if we stay the full five hours we might have the pleasure of the king's arrival in the royal box. Or of watching the pit break out into a riot during the after-play. Like life, London theater is unpredictable and rarely dull."

There was a note in Myles's voice that she had rarely heard before. She looked at him uncertainly, nonplussed to catch him smiling with something that seemed like very real affection into the seething mass of humanity that made up the pit.

"You have missed it, haven't you?" She was startled by the revelation. Somehow it brought home, more keenly than anything else he had ever said, the tragedy of exile.

"I beg your pardon?"

"Did you go to the theater a great deal before . . . you left England?"

He hesitated and averted his face, so that she could study him only in profile. "I was one of those young bucks you see down there, Mermaid," he admitted slowly. "I ogled the beauties in the audience and attempted assignations with the opera dancers. I played cards during the performance, and drummed my heels if my favorite was not on stage. Oh, yes, during my first year on the Town, I was an ardent patron of the arts." He suddenly turned to face her, adding with bitter wit, "That was before I enacted my own small drama. The hapless hero, removed from the arms of the heroine, is sent into exile. End of act one. He returns, a sadder but a wiser man. Curtain falls. And what follows is a jolly farce." He showed his teeth in a smile that left his eyes two chips of ice. "Don't look so downcast, Sabina. If we had wished to see a great tragedy, we would have gone to Covent Garden. Tonight is all about comedy."

"I'm sorry," she whispered. "Everything I seem to say is wrong."

Myles sat rigidly beside her, all pretense at elegant boredom having disappeared from the tense set of his broad shoulders and the inflexible line of his jaw. From her line of vision, he looked as though he sat on the edge of a precipice, staring down into a great darkness.

"I'm sorry too," he finally said. "It's unpardonable of me to take out my bad temper on you, Mermaid. I shouldn't wonder if you were wishing me to the very devil."

She waved her fan again and looked straight ahead. "The most surprising thing of all is that I don't."

After this exchange unfolding in their box, the drama on stage seemed somewhat tame. It wasn't until the curtain went down on the first act that she realized they had become the center of some attention. People seemed to be pointing and whispering, some bolder souls even raising their quizzing glasses the better to study them. Nervously Sabina touched her hair, wishing she had insisted that the curling irons be heated properly.

It wasn't long before a hesitant knock sounded on the box door and a gentleman entered. He was a tall, rather watery-eyed man who, after throwing Sabina a curious glance, made an elegant bow, and then extended a hesitant hand toward Myles.

"I am quite certain—forgive me if I am wrong! But I know I can't possibly be mistaken! Lord, I nearly fell into the pit when I looked across and saw you. Dampier, old fellow! Is it really you? I heard you were dead!"

Myles got up from his chair and shook the extended hand, smiling coolly at this effusion. "I was . . . lately resurrected, Cedric. In truth, I have but recently returned to England." A measure of warmth suddenly lit up his face, and he added with quiet sincerity, "It's good to see you again."

The man reddened, and said with some difficulty, "I am glad of it, Myles. It has been . . . what? Ten? Twelve years since I last saw you?"

"Almost fifteen. Cedric, allow me to present you to my wife. Sabina, this is an old school friend of mine, Cedric Carstairs. His family were our neighbors in Norfolk."

Sabina held out her hand and smiled with real pleasure. "How do you do, sir? I am delighted to be introduced to one of my husband's *friends*. I have met so few." She emphasized the word, deriving pleasure from Myles's raised brow and the slight crease beside his mouth.

Mr. Carstairs took her hand with obvious astonishment, bowing low. His eyes darted nervously to Myles before he said with simple earnestness, "Mrs. Dampier. A great honor, ma'am." He straightened, and turned once more to his friend, his air that of a man who is quite possibly out of his depth but decides to dive into the water anyway. "This is a night for surprises. You look so well, Myles—in spite of everything. And married into the bargain! I am, too. I believe you might be acquainted. She was Miss Harriet Purefoy, you know. Well, well. This is beyond anything. I know there will be a great deal of astonishment in several quarters. I suppose . . . I suppose you have recently heard from Richard, then?"

The strained silence that suddenly possessed the box was an odd mixture of embarrassment and frost. All about her, Sabina heard the dull roar of voices, gossiping, arguing, in some cases raucously singing—and yet she could listen to nothing but the painful stillness that hung over the three of them.

"No," Myles said slowly. "You suppose wrongly, Cedric. I have yet to hear from Richard."

Mr. Carstairs began to babble. "Of course, he must be at Curstone. Doesn't like Town. Never did. Particularly at this time of year. You might not know it—of course you wouldn't, having been . . . er, out of the country for so long, but he sold the house in Brook Street after your uncle's death." Cedric's voice trailed off as he met his friend's implacable stare, and he hazarded feebly, "Dash it all, Myles. I don't want to put my foot in it. I suppose you *knew* your uncle died."

"I was kept . . . informed."

"Ah, yes. Informed. Excellent. Well . . ." He obviously cast around for a safer topic and offered desperately, "You will be astonished to know that Lysons Hall is sold at last. To some East India nabob, by all accounts. Bought it all, lock, stock and barrel. Good thing, too, for the place was badly run down by some fool of a tenant. Richard is well rid of it." He trailed off, and catching his friend's expression, added, "Just thought you might want to know. In case it's a shock."

"I doubt if the shock will be mine. I bought it, Cedric. Lysons Hall belongs to me."

Mr. Carstairs's mouth fell open, and he stumbled back with a dramatic flourish that wouldn't have looked out of place on the stage. "You! Good God, Myles. You don't mean . . . you don't mean to return to Norfolk. You must be mad!"

The familiar piratical smile darkened her husband's features, while his eyes were narrowed to hard blue slits of light. He couldn't have looked any more dangerous if he had suddenly drawn a sword.

"That's a point many people have debated over the past fifteen years, Cedric. I'm still uncertain what the eventual verdict will be."

Mr. Carstairs began to look hunted. "Look, old fellow. The curtain is about to go up, and I must get back to my box. My wife is waiting—the devil to pay if I don't get back. But if you give me your direction I shall call on you. I would . . . I would be happy to renew our connection." He turned to Sabina and made an elegant salute, then blushed and said, "Delighted, Mrs. Dampier. Hope to meet you again. Er . . . my wife *would* call on you, but I am afraid her health is very delicate at the moment. Visits of any kind could be . . . fatal."

Sabina looked across to the box directly opposite their own. A rather peevish-looking lady quickly averted her face and sat ramrod straight, staring at the curtained stage with the air of an offended duchess. Slowly, Sabina's eyes roamed the other fashionable boxes, and she realized that she and Myles were being regarded with not only curiosity but also a hostility that was almost palpable. Fans were raised, eyeglasses dropped, heads deliberately turned away. Sabina felt her face flame with a sudden fierce, protective anger, and she unconsciously lifted her chin.

"How tiresome for her, Mr. Carstairs," Sabina said composedly. "In any case, it would not be possible. My husband and I mean to go into Norfolk within the next few days. Perhaps we will meet there."

"Oh, Lord," said Mr. Carstairs unhappily, and after bestowing a sickly smile, he slipped from the box.

Myles resettled himself in his chair and stared moodily at the stage, his knuckles showing white as he curled his hands into fists. After drawing in a great shuddering breath, he turned toward Sabina and said gently, "This is how it will be from now on, Mermaid. I'm sorry. I should have understood that there would be no fatted calf for

105

this prodigal. Or for my wife. In my extreme selfishness, I have made you an outcast like myself."

The bitterness in his voice made her want to burst into tears.

Instead she replied steadily, "As a scientist's daughter, I was never *in* society, so I can hardly say that being ignored by it will ever upset me." She tried very hard to attempt a careless laugh, but it faltered as she studied her husband's hard mask. She seriously contemplated removing her shoe and throwing it at the woman in the opposite box. "I have a feeling I wouldn't have much admired Mrs. Carstairs, anyway. Nor the rest of those who sneer at you."

"Perhaps." The ghost of a smile pulled at the corners of his mouth. "But how much more satisfying to despise those with whom we are on talking terms, as compared to those with whom we are not."

Sabina was suddenly frightened. Myles's strength seemed almost sapped by this meeting with his childhood friend, like a Samson shorn of his locks. She looked helplessly at the taut profile of this man who had carved out a successful life in one of the harshest terrains on earth; who had risen from virtual slavery to build a maritime empire; and who had fought the sea not only for his own life but for hers as well—and she felt sick to her stomach.

She reached out to touch his hand. It was a natural gesture of comfort, but she was surprised when he flinched at the movement, pulling away for a split second before he faltered and gathered her gloved fingers in his. She clung to his hand, somehow frightened that even at this point he would withdraw from her.

"What do we care what they think?" she demanded passionately. "*They* didn't survive a shipwreck. They haven't sailed around Cape Horn. They've never seen a whale rising off the starboard bow, or stood shouting into a gale. And they wouldn't know a baked head from a baked goose."

For several long moments Myles stared at her, and then he threw his head back and laughed uproariously, the gesture drawing murmurs from those who still watched them with interest. He grinned at her, pure, natural amusement displacing the anger.

"By God, you are right, Mermaid. I managed to stare down the disdain of the Pure Merinos of Sydney Town. And they could give the royal family lessons in exclusiveness. So why I allowed myself to be blue-deviled by this insipid, lackluster crowd I have no notion." The dark head bent over her raised hand, and even through the fabric of her glove she felt the warm pressure of his lips on her hand. He raised his eyes to hers, his expression so warm with gratitude that it took her breath away. "Thank you."

"If I knew what a Pure Merino was, I might appreciate your victory a little better," she said shakily.

"A Pure Merino, my dear Mrs. Dampier, is a free settler in the colony of New South Wales—someone who arrived there of their own free will. The dull, the dutiful, the eager, and the ugly—they all have one distinct advantage over the convicts and the emancipists. They have no criminal background."

She immediately pounced on the word. "And neither do you have a criminal background. Those who know you best *must* know that. Don't you think your friend Mr. Carstairs realizes it?" She lowered her head and said forlornly, "I liked him, but I admit—I envy him. He hasn't seen you for nearly fifteen years, and yet he seems to know everything about you and your affairs."

"We went fishing together as boys," he explained, a half-smile on his face.

"If I promise to go fishing with you, might I not find out who Richard is?"

There was a noise from the stage that seemed to threaten the resumption of the drama. Myles straightened in his seat. "And just as I was admiring your iron self-control. Can you wait until the end of the play to satisfy your curiosity?"

"No."

"Very well. As much as I resent leaving those assembled here to think they have scored a victory over us, I believe we have provided enough comic relief. I suggest we leave before the farce begins. But I warn you now, if I am to tell you the whole, I will need brandy. And lots of it."

He gathered her cloak from the back of her chair in a theatrical gesture that made them the center of attention once again. Handsome and aloof, he stood at the front of the box, his eyeglass raised at just the right angle for his glance to sweep the auditorium with a magnificent arrogance. He was possibly the most riveting sight Sabina had ever seen, a sardonic sneer slowly curling his lip, his eyes brilliantly contemptuous. Even if the curtain had risen at that point, it was doubtful that the stage would have commanded any attention at all, as almost every eye seemed to be fixed on her husband's tall form. Then the glass fell, and, tucking her hand into his arm, Myles Dampier deliberately turned his back and led her from the box.

They were followed by a murmur that rose to the very rafters.

"I'm so sorry our evening was ruined," she murmured softly as they made their way through the lobby.

"Indeed, my dear? I thought it went very well. Very well indeed."

Sabina was stunned, uncertain for a moment if she had heard him properly.

His words could have been mistaken for sheer bravado. Or comfort. Or denial. But Sabina, descending the stairs beside her husband, was suddenly—*blindingly*—certain that their excursion to the theater, far from being staged for her pleasure, had taken place as some sort of calculated social experiment.

Unnerved by the suspicion, she stumbled slightly on a step, gripping his arm with a desperation born of shock. That would, she reasoned, explain the prominence of their box and their very public display. It might also be an explanation for the air of suppressed excitement she had detected beneath her husband's relaxed demeanor. Myles Dampier, far from walking innocently into social ostracism, had flaunted himself deliberately, gauging the reaction with a scientist's careful objectivity. *Extending a challenge.*

But a challenge to whom?

She clasped her gloved hands together and sent him a searching glance, horrified to see a deep satisfaction glowing in his handsome features. If he had, for one dark moment, unexpectedly found himself vulnerable, that moment had passed as quickly as it had arrived. He looked more thoughtful than crushed.

It was all a sham, she realized miserably. His need for her strength, her support, her reassurance—it had been as artificial as the drama enacted on the stage.

When they returned to their rooms at the inn, Sabina found her new maid, Maria, dutifully if wearily waiting to divest her of her finery. She sent the girl to bed and, after pausing to elegantly arrange the silk shawl she had worn on the *Ellen Drury* over her elbows, left her bedchamber to knock quietly at the door of the private parlor. A brusque reply led her into the room; she closed the door and leaned her back warily against it, uncertain of what she would learn.

Myles was in the process of draining a glass of brandy. He looked at her from under brows that drew together in a fierce frown.

"For God's sake, Sabina, you look like one of Bluebeard's wives."

"Strangely enough, I feel like one of them. The one who discovered the bodies in the cupboard, presumably."

"There are few corpses in my cupboard, Mermaid. As yet."

"Who is Richard?" she asked bluntly.

" 'Who is Richard, what is he, that all our swains commend him,' " he quoted contemptuously. "He is, my dear Sabina, my cousin—Sir Richard Dampier of Curstone Abbey, Norfolk. Also formerly of Brook Street. I knew that, of course. You see, I bought the house a year ago. As Cedric explained, Richard was never fond of town life. I doubt if he will miss it."

"Your cousin!"

"You seem surprised to find I have such respectable

109

connections, Sabina." He refilled his glass, examining the contents briefly before tossing it down in a single movement. He drew his hand deliberately across his mouth. "Yes, my dear, you would be hard-pressed to find any man with a more respectable family than I."

"You sound bitter toward him. Do you blame him for what happened to you?"

"Not at all. I blame my own wild, youthful impetuosity. Even at nineteen my reputation in the district wasn't of the best. It seemed to be a hereditary failing. After my mother's death, my father, God rest his soul, went through all of his own money, and the little that was left of hers as well. Lysons Hall was heavily mortgaged, my father was slowly drinking himself to death, and I was tumbling from one scrape into another. No wonder my uncle looked upon the both of us as though we were the eighth plague of Egypt."

"And he would be Sir Richard's father, I suppose. No, don't stop to explain," Sabina said impatiently. "You'll only seize the chance to tell me nothing at all. What does he have to do with your transportation?"

"Transportation." He seemed much struck by the word and rolled it on his tongue as if learning a new language. "What a charming euphemism, Mermaid. It sounds like a journey to Tunbridge Wells, doesn't it? Of course, we old lags like to talk of being 'boated.' 'When were you boated?' we'd say. 'What were you boated for?' But I digress . . . what did you ask me about? Ah, yes, my amiable uncle, Sir John Dampier. He did not approve of my father or myself." He held his glass between careless fingers, rotating the stem as he brooded into the dregs. "Of course, drinking, wenching, and gambling away one's inheritance is not a crime in this country. If it were, England would be empty, and New South Wales well populated. Luckily for dear Uncle John, I was so obliging as to provide him with a misdemeanor he could capitalize on."

"Your heiress." Sabina, who had been holding her breath, was startled to find she had said the word aloud.

He raised his head slightly, and a savage smile lit his

face. "Unlike Bluebeard's wife, Sabina, you have shown remarkable patience in the face of my little mystery. My heiress—exactly. Let's call her ... Juliet, shall we? A young and charming Juliet to my besotted Romeo. I loved her, and was loved in return. My suit was hopeless, and so we eloped. If you try to imagine the scenario using every time-worn cliché, you would have our little escapade in a nutshell. Fainting heroine, stalwart hero, hired carriage, horses steaming, a breakneck chase along the road at midnight—it was all so romantic that even now I wonder if it was all quite real."

His cruel self-mockery made her wince. "What happened?" she whispered.

The glass snapped with a sickening crunch. Startled, Myles prised open his fingers to reveal a well of blood beginning to pour down his hand. Sabina exclaimed in horror and moved toward him, grasping his hand and removing a large sliver of glass from his palm. "Your handkerchief! Give it to me."

His free hand searched, and presented it to her with a flourish and a sheepish grin. The expression of terrible, bitter anger had gone, replaced by a certain amount of caution.

"There you go, my ministering angel. Bind my wounds if you can."

"I'd like to *inflict* wounds, Myles Dampier. How could you be so careless?"

"I'm sorry," he said meekly. He watched her mop up the blood rather inexpertly, the familiar crooked smile curving his mouth, and then he flinched as Sabina leaned up to pull at the ends of his white neckcloth. "What the devil ... ? I take it garroting is a new medical technique to stop blood flow in a patient."

"I'm going to use this as a bandage. Stop being a baby, Myles, and help me remove it. Take off your jacket, too."

He rolled his eyes in mock exasperation. "The first time the lady insists I shed my clothing for her ..." But he struggled out of both the neckcloth and jacket, and sat down in his shirtsleeves while she knelt on the floor and finished her bandaging. She felt strangely vulnerable kneeling at his feet, and waited for some biting quip, but he sat still and regarded her with quiet interest.

"I'll need to put an ointment on that or it will fester," she said doubtfully, leaning back on her heels. "I will ask Maria for one tomorrow morning. She seems a very sensible, obliging girl. And I'm afraid I am not so efficient a nurse as you proved to be."

His free hand reached out to touch her face. Startled, she looked up into stormy blue eyes. Their expression, strangely enough, was a curious mixture of watchfulness and regret.

"I'm sorry," he said simply.

Her heart seemed to be turning over and over in her breast, but she heard herself asking coolly, "Sorry? For abusing an innocent glass?"

"No, Mermaid. For dragging you into something you may well live to regret."

For the rest of the night his words reverberated in her brain, like the poetry of a half-forgotten song, impossible to understand and yet impossible to forget. It was the stuff of nightmares.

CHAPTER SIX

The monkey arrived the same day that the street urchin Gammon made his entrance into her life, and although at first Sabina felt that their addition to the household was something of a mixed blessing, she was grateful for the distraction they provided.

During the week that followed the revelations after their visit to Drury Lane, Myles challenged the usual conventions of married life by becoming even more of a mystery, withdrawing into a remote condescension that set her teeth on edge. The moment of closeness they had shared in the theater box, his moment of vulnerability when she had knelt at his feet to bind his wound . . . they might never have occurred at all. She wondered if he regretted confiding as much of his past as he had, regardless of the fact that as his wife she had every right to know. At all events, the shutters, politely inflexible, were now firmly in place.

And to add insult to injury, Mr. Marney had fallen into the habit of making morning calls.

"He's here again, ma'am," Maria announced in long-suffering tones. "What shall I do?"

Sabina put down the letters she was writing to some of her father's old friends at the Royal Society and pulled a face. "I had better see him. This is one of the drawbacks of living in a public inn—I have no butler to gainsay admission."

"That wouldn't stop him. Thinks he's the King of France, does Mr. Marney. Do you want me to sit with you, ma'am?"

"No, but make an appearance before the required half hour is up. Invent some excuse."

Maria rolled her eyes. "Then I'd better say the inn's on fire. Nothing else will get him out."

Mr. Marney inched furtively into the room and sat on the edge of a chair, refusing all offers of refreshment. He seemed content to sit and stare at her, his eyes narrowed into slits, his lizard tongue making little forays over his lips. Sabina, resisting the urge to reach out and swat him with something, schooled her features into a mask of cool hauteur.

"What brings you here this morning, Mr. Marney?" Not even the Queen of France, she decided delightedly, could have produced that note of complete disinterest.

Marney, however, was far from quashed. "I thought you might wish to drive out with me and watch the demolition of Clarendon House. It was the king's home when he was regent, you know. It is the most diverting sight. I believe the south section is to go this week. And what with Mr. Dampier so busy in Brook Street, I felt sure you must be bored. . . ."

Sabina's polite refusal died on her lips as she found her interest suddenly caught. She said sharply, "Brook Street? Is that the house Mr. Dampier purchased from his cousin, Sir Richard?"

Mr. Marney permitted himself a genteel snort. "*Purchased* is a very elegant word for the transaction, Mrs. Dampier. Let's just say that I helped him acquire it. House, furnishings, pictures—the lot. It was the same with Lysons

Hall. He was adamant that no other properties in England would satisfy him. Particularly bent on getting his own way is Mr. Dampier. Not always easy unless you have the knowledge and experience to make it happen."

Sabina awoke to the fact that she was actually leaning forward in her chair, mouth agape, eyes wide, hanging on to every poisonous word. She straightened abruptly and tried to recover her previous poise. "You speak as though there was something dishonest in the way it was done."

Mr. Marney raised scant, pale brows. "Mrs. Dampier," he said in shocked accents, "only fools need be dishonest in business. A wise man merely seizes opportunities as they present themselves. Let's just say that Sir Richard, as desperate as he was, might have thought twice if he had known who was so interested in buying the properties." He continued smoothly, studying a loose thread on the back of his gloves. "I fancy he will be surprised to find his cousin at Lysons Hall. In fact, I have no doubt the entire neighborhood will be diverted. Considering their history."

Considering their history. What history?

Sabina drew in a deep breath as moral outrage battled with vulgar curiosity. There was no doubt that this repellent little man was not averse to telling her things she could not prise from her husband were she to strap him to the rack. But just as she was about to find out how low she could truly sink, Maria created a diversion by appearing at the door and announcing in tragic tones, "A monkey has arrived, ma'am. What would you like me to do with it?"

As an excuse to get rid of a morning visitor, this was as unexpected as it was original. One look at Maria's face, however, convinced Sabina that the monkey was no figment of her maid's imagination. She rose with a startled exclamation, and a grinning boot boy staggered into the parlor bearing a large wicker cage.

"This come for you, ma'am," the boy announced in a voice of congratulation. "Wiv a letter."

Bemused, Sabina took the letter and broke the seal. "It's from Captain Scully!" she exclaimed, scanning the sheets. "Why, of course! This is poor little Jezebel. He says she is a belated wedding present. How . . . how thoughtful of him." She turned to Mr. Marney and bestowed a gracious smile. "As you can see, sir, I'm quite unable to accompany you on your delightful expedition. I have to . . . to settle the monkey, and write a letter of thanks to Captain Scully."

Mr. Marney had been staring at the chattering little creature with undisguised loathing, but at the captain's name, his head jerked up and he asked tightly, "That is the name of the ship's master who rescued you? Scully?"

"Yes. He also presided over our marriage, so I feel I have most shamefully neglected him. I must write a letter *immediately*. I can waste no time," she added with meaning.

The gimlet stare turned toward her with unusual intensity.

"You were married aboard ship? By the ship's captain?" At her nodded assent, his smile slowly stretched into a slit revealing pointed teeth. "Then I must not keep you from your letter, Mrs. Dampier. Or from the new addition to your household."

He bowed sketchily and left the room. Maria, who had stood sentinel at the door, sniffed and muttered something under her breath. She sent the boot boy scurrying with a jerk of the head and the promise of a penny, and then turned to her mistress to say flatly, "I hope that looking after wild animals is not part of my duties, ma'am. Dogs I'm partial to. But not jungle beasts."

Sabina shook her head ruefully and crouched down beside the cage. She could heartily sympathize with her maid's sentiments, and was a little bewildered by the gift. She had thought the captain was sincerely attached to his pet. Jezebel expressed her own feelings about this surprising turn of events by chattering angrily in the corner, ignoring all efforts to coax her out of the cage. "No, Maria. It won't be part of your duties. But whatever am I to do with her? I'm sure the captain meant it kindly, but it wasn't my intention to arrive at Lysons Hall with a menagerie in tow."

The maid's face was impassive as she replied tartly, "Well, if you'll pardon the impertinence, ma'am, you already have a fox in the household."

Sabina looked up, shocked. "I don't know what you mean, Maria. Is something troubling you?" Over the past week she had been very happy with the young woman's brisk efficiency, but she could see that something more than Jezebel's arrival had upset her.

"It's that man, Mrs. Dampier. That Mr. Marney." Maria's face twisted with hesitation before she finally burst out, "He keeps asking me to go with him to watch the public hangings! I say no, but it does no good. His eyes glaze over and he's ever so insistent. Fair gives me the creeps, he does!"

"Oh, Maria." Sabina was a good deal shocked, and not a little sickened. "I shall speak to Mr. Dampier about this at once. I'm sure he'll take Mr. Marney to task about his . . . his unwelcome attentions to us—you!"

"I'm not used to being in an unregulated household, ma'am. Monkeys and such. I took this position because I believed I'd be working in a gentleman's house."

"And so you shall be," Sabina soothed, resisting the urge to cross her fingers behind her back. "Fetch me my bonnet and cloak, and I will find Mr. Dampier. If Mr. Marney doesn't slink away from us—you!—with his tail between his legs, then I will want to know the reason why."

On this crusading note, Sabina set forth, pausing only to promote an excited boot boy to the role of monkey keeper.

However, it dawned on her sometime during the short carriage ride to Brook Street that she was by no means certain of a cordial reception when she arrived. Not, she told herself severely, that it was in any way improper to seek out her husband. Particularly when their small, eccentric household was in danger of dissolution. Of course, she *could* have sent a servant with a message rather than choose to arrive on his—their!—doorstep unannounced. But Myles had never intimated by even a raised eyebrow that she was unwelcome there.

Or welcome.

When the carriage finally pulled up, she was met by a scene of elegant chaos. Carriers loaded quantities of dark, old-fashioned furniture onto the back of a wagon, and from the vestibule she could detect a small army of servants scurrying to do the bidding of some domestic general. Uncertainly she checked the number on the brass plate with that scrawled on a crumpled piece of paper, confirming that this was indeed the Town residence of Sir Richard Dampier.

Myles Dampier's house, now.

She alighted without waiting for assistance and ran lightly up the steps, pausing at the entrance to inform an astonished footman that she was Mrs. Dampier. The man's eyes bulged in surprise; whether or not he was willing to take her at her word, she was never to find out. An ominous crash from the street diverted his attention long enough for her to slip past him into the house.

The entrance was full of light, invited in, it seemed, by fanlights and soaring columns that pulled the eye to a domed ceiling supported by a regiment of Roman busts. The tiled floor stretched toward an iron staircase whose balusters were fashioned in the shape of lyres—a hundred delicate lyres leading heavenward past recessed statues of Greek gods and goddesses, mounting in increasing grandeur toward the upper levels of the house. Everything seemed to be gold and ivory—the urns, the plasterwork, the mirrors, even the fireplace so unexpectedly set at the far end of the vestibule for the warm reception of . . . whom?

Not for Mrs. Myles Dampier, obviously.

There were no other servants in sight, and drawing her courage firmly about herself, she began to mount the staircase, marveling at the absence of the usual ancestral portraits on the walls. It was, she knew, the custom of most noble or well-connected families to adorn their reception areas with the length and proof of their lineage. Unless, of course, she reflected wryly as she paused to examine a half-naked Aphrodite, the Dampiers were convinced they were descended from Mount Olympus.

The second floor was deserted. Her hard-heeled boots made a soft thunking sound on the polished floors that caused her to grit her teeth and begin to walk on her toes. She felt like a housebreaker, not the mistress of a fashionable London house. Resolutely she rocked on her heels, and taking a determined breath entered one of the withdrawing rooms leading from the head of the staircase. What she discovered caused her to expel her breath with a cry of pleasure.

It was an intensely feminine room. None but a woman's hand could have chosen the muted tones of gold and rose, or decorated the walls with plump cherubs and copious baskets of flowers. Most of the furniture was covered in dust sheets, suggesting that the room had been unoccupied for some time; only a few delicate pieces were visible, the sheets deliberately discarded on the floor, as though someone had been in the room, searching for something. She followed the trail with her eyes; they widened when she noticed the harp that stood on a raised dais in a corner of the room. Its gilded beauty drew her hesitantly toward it, and she gently drew her fingers across the strings. They immediately sprang to life, the sound of untutored notes breaking the perfect silence of the room.

Sabina started guiltily, feeling much as she would if she had laughed out loud in church. Irreverence! Yes, that was the emotion she struggled to describe. Because the room was undoubtedly a shrine, she somehow felt that her presence was a kind of affront.

But to whom?

She turned to leave, and was suddenly caught and held by the limpid brilliance of wide, blue eyes. They were set beneath a riot of silver gilt curls, tumbling carelessly over bare white shoulders. One delicate hand rested on the arm of a sofa; the other supported the alabaster face in a classical attitude.

Sabina drew in a deep breath. Here was the goddess for whom this shrine had been created. A woman—no! a girl, charmingly innocent in her youth—was dressed in the fashion of a previous decade; the simple white muslin gown revealed a great deal more flesh than was currently acceptable. And yet there was nothing provocative in the slim figure reclining against the ornate gold sofa, a soft cashmere shawl draped over her hips. She had been depicted as Flora, goddess of spring, rather than as Aphrodite. And either the painter had been in love with his subject, leading to a certain amount of artistic license, or this was possibly the most beautiful woman Sabina had ever seen.

Sabina, capturing a glance of herself in an ornate gold mirror on the wall opposite the painting, regretted the charming Florentine hat and checked gown which, only that morning, had seemed so desirably modish. By no stretch of the imagination did she resemble a classical goddess.

The sound of heavy footsteps approaching made her tense, and she swung around to face the door. Myles Dampier strode into the room, dispelling whatever ghosts lingered in the corners. He stopped abruptly as he caught sight of her.

"It's you," he said blankly, and lifted an uncertain hand to his eyes, rubbing them slightly as though to clear his vision.

He was, Sabina realized with shock, completely disheveled. Not even on the *Ellen Drury*—in the middle of a storm!—had she seen the dark curls so thoroughly tousled, as though he had been continually dragging his hands through his hair. He was in his shirtsleeves, rolled up to the elbow, and his neckcloth, usually so meticulously arranged, was seriously awry. But it was not only the disarray of his clothing that made her wary. There was a careless glitter in the beautiful eyes that she had never seen before.

And the faint, smoky aroma of brandy clung to him like a tantalizing perfume.

In the short time she had known him, her husband had rarely consumed more than a glass or two of claret. Surprise made her voice sharper than she intended. "Yes, it's me. Why? Is there any reason I shouldn't be here?" She felt more like an intruder than ever.

"Of course you should," Myles said coolly. He had recovered some of his usual control, and sauntered toward her. "It's just that when the footman told me the mistress had arrived . . ." He broke off and grinned ruefully. "You have a habit of surprising me, Mermaid. I wanted the place to be ready to receive you before you came here."

"It's charming," she replied stiffly. "I can't imagine how it could be more ready than it is now."

He began to pace the room like a wild animal marking out its territory. He shot at her over his shoulder, "My grandfather built this house over half a century ago, Sabina. There are certain items that are no longer . . . desirable. I wanted to dispose of them before you came."

His tone was bland, his expression guarded, and she felt a familiar surge of anger at his distance.

"I see." Putting one finger to her chin, she tipped her head in elaborate study of the portrait and said sweetly, "And *this*, I take it, is your grandmother."

One dark eyebrow flew up. "Do you think you have finally entered Bluebeard's den, Mermaid?"

"Perhaps. Who is she?"

"That, my dear, is the present Lady Dampier. My cousin Richard's wife."

"She must be very beautiful."

"Very beautiful indeed. The painting barely does her justice."

There was no admiration in his voice. In fact, there was no expression at all. His eyes were hooded, and a tense whiteness had appeared at the edges of his mouth, as though his lips were compressed with some strong emotion.

Disapproval? Dislike?

She could no longer tolerate the woman's bright gaze and turned from it abruptly, determined to force some response from her husband.

"But how interesting, Myles. You appear to have bought

the house with all the personal effects intact. Ornaments, books, portraits . . . does Sir Richard no longer have any use for them?" She lifted a dust sheet and examined a china shepherdess, running a hesitant finger over its delicate contours before picking it up to examine it more closely. She wondered what Myles would do if she flung it at the beautiful, smiling face on the wall. Would he be angry? Or would he merely laugh?

She decided not to risk the laughter. It would be more than she could possibly bear at this moment. She carefully put the little figure back beneath the sheet, and turned to find him regarding her with the familiar amusement that was as effective as a wall in keeping her at arm's length. It was almost as though he could read her mind. She blurted out, "Did you do something illegal?"

"No, Mermaid. I did not do something illegal. I did something illegal once, and didn't like the consequences. Now—if you had asked me if I did something *immoral* . . ."

"Myles! I'm serious! I want to know!"

He grinned down at her, unrepentant, the blue eyes suddenly clear of shadows. Unexpectedly, one brown hand expertly untied the ribbons of her hat, pulling it free from her head, while the fingers of the other reached up to capture her chin in a gentle grip. It didn't need to be strong to hold her still. She couldn't have moved if the floor had collapsed beneath her. She closed her eyes and thought desperately, *I'm flesh and blood. Not paint and canvas. I have that advantage, at least.*

If it was an advantage. She felt one long finger follow the contours of her mouth, and she was shocked at her urge to open her lips and meet its progress with her tongue. She gasped at her own wantonness, and her eyes flew open. His were no longer amused; instead they smoldered down at her, his breathing suddenly shallow and uneven. Warm, brandy-scented, inviting. *But at least he was breathing.* Her own breath seemed caught somewhere between her chest and her throat, hardening into a huge lump that prevented her from swallowing.

"Myles . . ." His name was meant to be a censure, a gentle rebuff, but even to her own ears it emerged as half question, half invitation. He answered both by bending his head and softly possessing her lips, offering her more questions, more confusion . . . and clarifying things she had hardly dared ask herself. In one swift, eloquent movement she found herself pulled into his arms, his breath softly feathering across her face. She thought he said something to her in a low, rasping voice, but the words were lost against her lips as his tongue burned deep within her mouth, expertly flaming her body until it bent toward his like a young aspen in the wind—taut yet pliant, ready to break at any moment if the force were too great. Her hands, flat against the broad warmth of his chest, moved slowly and hesitantly upward to encircle his neck. She was momentarily checked when he dragged his lips from hers and with a violent tug removed his cravat, and then bent his head to press hot, slow kisses against the line of her chin. Sabina felt herself balancing on that fine knife edge between control and abandonment; she leaned back against the strength of the arm that held her, and closed her eyes. That way she could imagine that it was love glowing in the dark face above hers, not a mere satisfaction of the senses. Even when she felt herself pushed inexorably downward onto a shrouded sofa, she kept her lids tightly shut, refusing to open them. It didn't matter that she was a mere convenience, a trophy wife pulled out of the sea.

Then his free hand made a foray causing her to gasp and involuntarily her eyes flew open . . . only to see that this time her husband was not looking down at her with the cool calculation of a scientist. This time he was not looking at her at all. Instead, his eyes were raised to meet the painted gaze that mocked her foolishness with gentle irony.

A knife wound could not have hurt her more.

"No!" She pushed him from her with a furious movement that was as forceful as it was unexpected. Unprepared for her response, Myles staggered upright, and stood over her for several seconds, his chest heaving raggedly, his expression anything but cool or calculated.

"For God's sake, Sabina!" He was angry, and it didn't surprise her. But it didn't frighten her, either.

"I'm sorry," she lied faintly, and raised one hand to her face, surprised to find that her hand was shaking violently. She examined it with unconcealed concern, amazed at the effect that Myles had on her. Dear God, she was wearing *gloves*, and the touch of the man had still burned through to her palms like molten lead. If she hadn't opened her eyes . . . if he hadn't been so intent on the woman in the portrait . . . The realization made her temper flare gloriously, and she found herself shouting, "No, I'm damned if I'll say I'm sorry! I'm not sorry. This was all your fault!"

"My fault, is it, Mrs. Dampier? And how does your behaving like all twelve foolish virgins rolled into one come to be my fault?"

For so obviously wanting another woman. For proving that I'm not enough. She drew in a deep breath and said through clenched teeth, "For trying to seduce me in your cousin's drawing room as if I were a . . . a chambermaid."

"This is *my* house, and you are *my* wife, not a chambermaid. You might want to remember that!"

"That's right! Everything belongs to you, doesn't it? The *Margaret Rose*, Lysons Hall, this house . . . even the clothes I'm wearing. How dare I prefer to keep them on if you want me out of them?"

"Sabina . . ." His mouth suddenly twitched, and the angry glare faded from his eyes, but she stubbornly ignored any sign that battle was being averted. She launched a fresh attack, giving vent to all the frustration and loneliness of the past few weeks.

"I suppose that's why you come here day after day. Just so you can stand here and *own* this house to your heart's content!"

"Mermaid—"

"Well, you might as well understand that you don't own me! If I'm not mistaken, there was a law passed that made slavery illegal!"

"Sabina—"

"And you might as well know right now that I hate this place! It's like a . . . a charnel house, full of old memories and old bones." She drew in a deep breath as she paused to reflect that it was here that the bodies were probably buried. Bodies of beauties with blond hair and porcelain skin. She resumed passionately, "I hate it! I tell you, I hate it!"

"I hate it too, Sabina. God knows I hate this house."

He had moved from her sight to lean against the ornate mantelpiece and flung the words over his shoulder like a final volley. They caught her unawares, and she felt her mouth drop open.

"Then why? Why do you want it so badly?"

"I bought it because my grandfather built it, Sabina." His voice was soft, and the cornflower gaze seemed to bore into her like twin blue icicles. "Because my esteemed Uncle John *owned* it. Because my father and I were never any more than unwelcome guests in its hallowed halls."

She wanted to understand him more than anything on earth. Desperately drawing on every skill her father had ever taught her, she studied him as he continued to lean nonchalantly against the fireplace, his eyes once more fixed on the cold, naked hearth rather than on either herself or the silver beauty who reclined in golden splendor above him. The handsome face had assumed a mask of rare arrogance she had seldom seen before; it sat oddly with the unkempt appearance he presented. He was obviously dressed for riding, but his shirt was loosened, his neckcloth discarded on the floor, the dark hair disordered across the high forehead—and this time not only by his own hand, she realized with the birth of a blush staining her cheeks. She had seen Myles Dampier in rags and sailor's slops, yet never until now had she seen him so . . . she struggled for the words . . . so bedraggled. So out of control.

So bitterly beyond her comprehension.

"Is it because Sir John Dampier was Richard's father that you dislike him so?" She struggled to keep her voice calm, to dampen the sense of pity that threatened to spill over. She wondered what he would do if she went to him and laid her head against his shoulder and smoothed the hair back into some semblance of order. The thought was so horrifyingly appealing that she launched into a rapid speech. "I suppose I can understand that there would be some resentment against Sir Richard on your part. After all, he inherited the title and had so much, while you . . . you spent so much of your life in exile. Is that it, Myles? Is that why you seem to hate him? Is that why you have set out to acquire everything he owned?"

In reply, her husband left his post by the fireplace and deliberately moved to where the great harp stood in a corner of the room. He should have been an incongruous sight in contrast to the elegant luxury of the instrument— his tall, lean body spoke of action and anarchy rather than refined drawing-room manners. And yet . . . there was a natural grace about all of the man's movements that convinced her he was no stranger to music.

She watched him lean his chin against the edge of the harp, softly blowing on the strings, producing a gentle sound that echoed ominously in the silence of the shrouded room. "I spent two short but decidedly interesting London seasons here in this house," he continued quietly, as if she had never spoken. "Uncle John allowed me to stay here under sufferance, most probably in the forlorn hope that I would either find a respectable career or at best, a respectable alliance with a suitable young woman. He seemed to labor under the belief that a virtuous female would have a beneficial influence on my character." He shot her a look that was suddenly pure mischief. "What do you think about that theory, Mermaid?"

"I think," she said with a valiant effort at composure, "that Uncle John was regrettably optimistic."

Myles grinned and continued amiably, "Oh, but this virtuous female would possess a comfortable income so that he could finally wash his hands of me. My father was an invalid, you see—brought on by his own excesses, it is true—and my uncle professed a responsibility toward me as head of the house. But . . . he did not like me. Not that I can blame him. I was, in his own words, a *hell-raiser*."

His thumb moved across the strings in a loud, discordant note that twisted his lips into a grimly satisfied smile. Suddenly he straightened, and Sabina was amazed at the subtle cruelty lingering at the corners of his mouth. It was as if he were reliving all the slights and disappointments of his youth in this cold, beautiful room. And then his expression changed as his gaze, unbearably scornful, bored directly into hers.

"Sister Anne, Sister Anne. Come and I will introduce you to Bluebeard's family." He seized her hand in a steel grip and pulled her from the room, ignoring her cry of protest.

"You are hurting me," she said untruthfully, dragging her feet.

His response was to sweep her up into his arms and, despite her protests, carry her across the landing into an adjacent room.

Whatever she had expected, it was not the respectable sobriety of a library, lined with bookshelves and furnished with the shabby comfort of a gentleman's retreat. A large desk bore the evidence of Myles's journey into the brandy bottle; a half-empty decanter and a single glass sat atop a pile of discarded papers and charts. He ignored those that were scattered on the floor, crunching across them as if they were fallen leaves, and deposited her in front of a dead fireplace. She swayed slightly, grasping at the mantelpiece to steady herself, and wordlessly followed her husband's gaze toward the portrait hanging above it.

"Since you are so interested in meeting my family, my dear, I will now introduce you to Sir John Dampier, my esteemed uncle."

Sabina stared, and found her hands fluttering to her mouth with unfeigned astonishment. Whatever else she had expected from Sir John Dampier, she had not expected the startling similarity between him and his nephew. Although the portrait was of a haughtily elegant

127

young man painted sometime during the last century, the striking face and form were almost a mirror image of the man who stood beside her, arms folded, legs braced, a look of indescribable contempt etched into his hard features.

Could this have been Myles in his youth? Proud, confident, at ease with the world and his place in it? Myles before his exile into hell?

Almost as though he had read her mind, he uttered softly, "It's Lucifer before the Fall, isn't it? As proud as a king, and as full of the milk of human kindness as a Borgia."

She shivered slightly and turned away from the painted gaze. The hateful tone in his voice sickened her. "Is that what Richard looks like?" she asked faintly.

"No. Cousin Richard is as fair as a lily. But like Uncle John, he is polite to the point of pain, as charming as a debutante, and appears to possess all the seven deadly virtues. You will undoubtedly admire him."

"And Lady Dampier? Will I admire Lady Dampier?" It took every ounce of her courage to ask the question.

"Speaking of lilies . . ." he murmured. He turned his gaze from his uncle's portrait and smiled at her. She decided that if a tiger could smile, he would look just like her husband at this moment: amused at his own power, lightly contemptuous of his victims and their feeble attempts to defend themselves. "Oh, yes, Mermaid. How could you not? She is a sweet, delightful creature, the lovely Sylvia. I am sure that upon meeting, you will become firm friends of the bosom. Although, if you don't mind me saying so, you undoubtedly win out over her in that respect."

She ignored the deliberate crudity, asking tightly, "She was your heiress, wasn't she? The woman in the portrait—she is Juliet."

During the tense silence that followed, his smile did not falter. If anything, it widened, becoming piratical, mocking, deepening to a sneer as he spoke. "How clever you are, Mrs. Dampier. I really do keep forgetting that fact."

There was nothing clever about it, she thought bleakly. She had known from almost the first moment of entering the room upstairs. The woman in the portrait was the kind who would make men commit any kind of foolishness, forget any kind of restraint.

More to the point, she would be a difficult woman to forget, even after fifteen years. For some men, it might prove impossible to ever forget her.

Sabina felt as if the room were falling in on her, books and portraits threatening to spiral about her head like a child's spinning toy. With a startled gasp, she picked up her skirts and ran out the door, turning sharply so that she could scuttle inelegantly down the ornate staircase, two steps at a time. Dimly she heard her name called, but she was too intent on escape to pay any attention; it was not until she had pushed past a startled footman and pounded down the front steps that she became aware of what she was doing. Gasping, she turned clumsily and sank against an iron railing, clutching at it as though it were a lifeline in a storm, her chest heaving with the exertion.

Strong fingers clamped about her wrist, and she found herself staring up into her husband's stormy face.

"What the devil do you think you are doing? You could have broken your neck bolting down the stairs like that!"

"I'm going home!" She made a futile effort to free herself, but his hands were steel manacles. Then, despite the fact that they were in the middle of the street, he released her suddenly, only to grasp her by the shoulders and shake her, his face fierce with suppressed fury.

"We don't *have* a home, Sabina," he said roughly, "We live in a public hostelry! *This* is your home. It will be your home whenever we come to London."

She shook her head miserably. Couldn't he understand that she could never set foot in this place again? The ghosts that haunted its rooms were angry, friendless ghosts, and she and Myles would never know any peace there.

Looking up into Myles's hard, unyielding face, she

knew that she had never felt so powerless in her entire life. Not even as she watched her father struggle for breath in a dark corner of a foreign inn; not even when she had found herself dragged down into the watery darkness of the ocean depths—no, not even then had she felt such a *drowning* sensation, such a feeling of complete helplessness in the face of something she could not control.

She sought some kind of refuge in anger. She drew in a shaking breath, and managed to say in a low voice, "Take your hands off me, you drunken oaf!"

She was amazed to discover that it worked. Wordlessly he released her and stood looking down at her, his expression cold and inflexible. "You are out in the street without a hat, Mrs. Dampier," he said finally, and turned to walk back into the house. Back to his ghosts, and to his hatred, and to the beautiful, silent harp sitting alone in its darkened corner.

Sabina knew she couldn't let him go back in there to face his memories alone. Somehow she had to save him from them.

"Myles!" The wild urgency in her voice stopped him at the threshold of the house. An obsequious manservant held the door open, his eyes goggling at the spectacle of master and mistress so obviously in the middle of a very public argument. Sabina ignored him as she flew up the steps and laid her hand uncertainly on his arm. "Please, Myles. Take me away from here. Anywhere. Anywhere there are people and noise. But, for God's sake, don't go in there."

He studied her hand impassively. She half expected him to shake it off, but instead he put his own over it and tightened his fingers about it. She almost sagged in relief at this sign of concord, and tears sprang unbidden to her eyes. "Please," she insisted.

"I can hardly leave the house in my shirtsleeves, Mermaid. You'll have to wait a few minutes until I find my coat." He didn't relinquish her hand. Instead he slowly drew her arm into the crook of his own and escorted her into the vestibule. She went reluctantly, their footsteps echoing eerily in the splendid silence of the hall. When she faltered at the foot of the stairs, he raised one dark eyebrow and remarked dryly, "I can assure you, Sabina. There are no monsters up there waiting to pounce."

They have already pounced, she thought sadly, but she merely shook her head. "Fetch my hat, Myles. I'll wait down here."

He released her and began to mount the stairs, and then paused, before turning to look down at her. The dark lashes shielded whatever emotion he might have felt, but she noticed that he held his shoulders stiffly and his hands had curled into two taut fists. "I spent my twentieth birthday in the lime pits of the Coal River settlement," he said pleasantly. "My back and hands were burnt raw, and I had twenty lashes to look forward to the next day. That night I dreamed I stood where I am now, and I was master of this house. Now this is the reality, and the past is merely the nightmare. And nothing can prevent me from making every dream I ever dreamed come true. In my own way, Mermaid."

Which, she decided as she watched him disappear from view, was a nightmare in itself.

Myles dismissed the carriage and sent his horse back to the inn, leaving Sabina in no doubt that they had left their servants at both London establishments with a great deal to talk about. She was pensive as they walked the streets, seemingly as respectable a couple as any they passed on their silent journey. Myles stalked slightly ahead; his efforts to take her arm were politely but firmly shaken off. She wanted an opportunity to think clearly, and that meant preventing all physical contact with the man.

Sylvia. That was her name. Not Juliet, but the heroine of a Shakespearean poem. "Who is Sylvia, what is she, that all our swains commend her?" Sabina wrinkled her forehead as she tried to remember where she had heard that misquoted recently. She hummed the rhythm in an effort to remember, conjuring up further fragments of the poem. "Is she kind as she is fair? For beauty lives with kindness . . ."

Was Sylvia Dampier kind? Somehow Sabina doubted it. Was it *kind* to watch a lover sent into exile for her sake, and then quietly and discreetly marry his wealthy cousin? Sabina's lip curled in contempt at this display of poor-spirited betrayal. Now, if it had been *she* who was in that situation, she knew she would have literally followed him to the ends of the earth, waiting until they were free to be together.

And to make matters worse, Myles had not been merely her lover!

Sabina's steps faltered slightly as that fact suddenly reared up and spat in her face. Somehow she had failed to register that he had actually been, however briefly, her husband at the time! The beautiful Sylvia had been as legally Myles Dampier's wife as she herself was now!

"What the devil is the matter with you? Why are you dragging behind so? Are you tired? You did insist on walking, you know." Myles Dampier's voice, irritable and not a little frustrated, penetrated through the sudden shock that had stopped her dead in her tracks, her mouth agape and her eyes staring blindly. "If you want to take a hackney back to the inn, just say so."

She recovered quickly, and stood staring up at him with renewed awe. There was little left of the unkempt figure she had found in Brook Street. Top booted, green coat smoothed to an immaculate fit, his cravat intricately tied, he looked the very picture of an elegant London gentleman. Only the expression in those remarkable, intolerant eyes remained stormy and bleak.

She drew in a deep breath and exhaled the words, "I wonder how far the ends of the earth actually is, Myles. Would you know?"

"By the look of you, I'd say about as far as Piccadilly, Mermaid."

She shook her head. "I'm not really tired. Let's walk on."

He raised his brows but said nothing, falling into step

beside her, shortening his stride to suit her slower pace.

And then her brow cleared as she suddenly thought that Lady Dampier, for all her beauty, would no longer be so very young. Perhaps she was no longer the woman in the portrait. Perhaps she had grown very fat—a matron with a brood of children and three chins. Or perhaps she was gray-haired and round-shouldered. After all, fifteen years was a very long time. . . .

"Did you really kill a man?" The question seemed to come from nowhere, and Sabina, startled to hear it spoken aloud, was astonished to find that she had asked it.

Was that because it was easier than asking about the woman in the portrait? Because the answer hardly concerned her anymore?

Myles stopped abruptly, causing a large man in a greatcoat to toss him a nervous glance and dart past him with a muffled apology.

"You choose the most unusual topics to begin a conversation, Mermaid." His voice was almost lazy with patience. "Do you really want to discuss my past misdemeanors all the way to the Bull and Mouth?"

She blushed deeply, recollecting the press of people that even now streamed past them. They had left the quiet streets of Mayfair sometime earlier, their grim-faced expedition taking them farther into the chaotic jumble of London's commercial district in the west, where rich man, pauper, merchant, and housewife jostled at their elbows. It was not, perhaps, the best place to indulge in intimate dialogue with one's husband.

"I'm sorry," she stammered. "I don't know where that came from. It just sort of . . . popped out."

"You might want to prevent that from popping out in front of Cedric Carstairs when we meet him next. He is the local magistrate. I might just find myself on the next transport heading for New South Wales."

"Myles!"

He grinned and took her suddenly limp arm with graceful gallantry. "I was joking," he said softly as they slowly began to stroll along the street. "It couldn't be proved then, and it can't be proved now."

"But . . . are you sorry?"

"That I told you, Mermaid? More than you can know."

She sighed, knowing that she would get nothing more out of him while he was in this mood. "I'm sure he deserved it," she said by way of a peace offering. "I know you wouldn't harm anyone unless they had done great wrong." She paused as she seized the opportunity to squeeze his arm, adding desperately, "In fact, I don't think you could harm anyone under *any* circumstances. You are much too good a person to do that."

Myles Damper lifted his eyes to the heavens and muttered something under his breath. She was about to demand a translation when she suddenly felt her knees knocked from under her; a strong arm shot out to steady her, and by the time she was placed firmly on her feet, Myles had his other arm firmly clamped about the throat of a bundle of dirty rags.

Kicking its legs feebly, it yelped and rolled desperate eyes in her direction.

"It seems," Myles said calmly, relaxing his arm so that the bundle could drag in a gasping breath, "that I have nabbed a natty lad. Well, my rogue, it will be ruffles rather than a rum bung for you."

"I ain't a rogue, honest, guv'nor! Don't know nuffink abaht it!" Like a tortoise emerging from its shell, a dirty blond head rose up from the filthy wrappings, and a clear hazel gaze, deeply set in a face little more than nine or ten years old, stared up at his captor with convincing innocence. "I fell against the gentry mort, so I swear!"

Myles removed his arm to grasp the boy by the scruff of his coat. He shook him and growled, "Honest? Why you mealy-mouthed maw wallop! A bung nipper like you wouldn't know the meaning of the word. What rookery did you slither from? Little Barbary, by the sound of you! You are out of your own country here in the west."

The boy's neck screwed around in sudden alarm as he took nervous stock of his captor. " 'Ere! You're a swell cove. 'Ow come you talk flash patter?" He stared and demanded hoarsely, "You ain't a prig, are you?"

Sabina, who had listened to the exchange between her husband and the child with increasing confusion, made a rapid decision. If the boy *was* a pickpocket, he was a very inexpert one. She flourished her reticule and exclaimed heatedly, "It doesn't matter, Myles. He's only a boy. Let him go, before a crowd gathers. I still have my purse, and he's had a fright."

"A fright, is it? He'll have more than a fright when he's dancing on air." But he released the boy with a shove that sent the slight body spinning onto the road. Myles added a short but vicious diatribe in a language utterly foreign to her. The boy paled beneath his dirt and scrambled to his feet, disappearing around the corner with an adroitness that more than made up for his earlier clumsiness.

"What did you say to him?" she demanded.

"I merely gave him some good advice that might save him from a long sea voyage spent in chains." He stared thoughtfully in the direction the boy had fled, adding quietly, "He's too old for that lay. Too large and too slow. Whoever uses him as their cat's-paw must know that. In a few years he'll graduate to housebreaking or highway robbery and he'll find himself swinging on the gibbet."

"But he's only a little boy! It's terrible, Myles."

"Yes, it's terrible, Mermaid. Perhaps not so terrible as the dark rat hole he has no doubt returned to in Wapping or St. Giles. Or the cell he'll find in Newgate prison." His voice was bitter, and as she watched the unchecked play of emotions across his face, she understood that he was reliving his own dark places.

Myles Dampier, gentleman, spoke the secret language of London's criminal world because he had come to know it intimately. Its thieves and murderers had been his companions during the horrors of his imprisonment in the Thames hulks, and the long, torturous journey to the penal settlement of Sydney. And then the living hell of life as a convict.

Sabina realized that he had never intended to hand the

boy over to the authorities. It would have been a betrayal, not justice.

She placed her hand hesitantly on his arm in an attempt to communicate a sympathy so profound that the words dried up in her throat. Instead she made a small, incoherent sound at the back of her throat that drew the brilliance of his blue gaze down upon her. His eyes narrowed, and then the dark lashes curtained whatever thoughts might be lingering there. He drew his lips into a painful semblance of a smile and drawled lazily, "Don't look so tragic, my dear." One long brown finger casually flicked her nose. "You really must learn to control that jealous streak of yours. While I am fluent in thieves' cant, you are proficient in five languages, are you not? That makes you undoubtedly superior."

She withdrew her hand, feeling as though he had doused her with cold water. "It would take all five to tell you just what I think of you, Myles Dampier."

"You usually do very well in English." He turned abruptly from her and resumed his stride down the street, leaving her to scuttle along in his wake.

An unwelcome thought suddenly occurred to her, driving away all the other unwelcome thoughts of the morning. She called out a little breathlessly, "Speaking of gibbets, Myles, I have to talk to you about Mr. Marney."

He didn't break his stride, merely tossing back at her, "What about Marney?"

"He's making unwanted advances to Maria."

Myles checked slightly and asked impatiently, "Who the devil is Maria?"

"Maria is my abigail. And one I wish to keep. Mr. Marney is quite pressing in his attentions toward her."

"Tell her to tell him to go to the devil."

"I would if I thought he would go there!"

Myles stopped abruptly and swung around to face her. They had turned into the middle of a crowded street, and, Londoner-like, people pushed carelessly past her, shoving her against his body like the waves of some great sea. Almost reluctantly, he stretched out a hand to hold her steady. It was an impersonal gesture, and this time there was no warmth in his face, no pretense of a smile. His eyes were as brittle as blue glass.

"Marney is useful to me, Sabina. I have no intention of getting rid of him just because his manners displease you and your maid. Is that understood?"

She didn't understand. There was far too much she didn't understand, but because she was suddenly weary from the revelations of the morning, and because her feet hurt, and she was very much afraid that she was in love with a man who was obviously determined to destroy himself if necessary in some futile attempt to avenge past wrongs, she merely closed her eyes and nodded.

"Sabina!" He shook her slightly, and she opened her eyes. He was watching her warily. "Is this some sort of feminine ploy to get your own way? You look as though you are about to faint on me."

"If I thought fainting would get rid of Mr. Marney, I would have collapsed days ago," she said truthfully. "I suspect that I'm merely . . . overwhelmed." She made a futile little gesture with her hands, and her head drooped in defeat.

Myles swore beneath his breath and summoned a passing hackney, ignoring her protests as he easily picked her up and deposited her inside as if she were a doll. As she steadied herself against the squabs, she wearily listened to the instructions he hurled at the driver.

Back to the inn, she thought despondently. Not home. Myles was right in that respect. But that meant she had no home in London now. And never before had the great city seemed so cold and friendless.

She waited until the door of the carriage was pulled shut and then leaned out of the window, knocking her hat askew. Righting the brim, she tried to keep the pleading note out of her voice, but it crept in all the same. "Please, Myles, you will come with me, won't you?"

"No. I have more business to attend to, Mermaid. I'm sorry." He paused and added softly, "And I apologize for dragging you around the streets at a link-boy's pace. I keep forgetting you are mere flesh and blood." He smiled crookedly as his hand touched her cheek in a gesture as brief as it was unloverlike. Then he barked out an instruction and the carriage moved off.

Sabina collapsed against the seat with a small moan, the skin on her cheek still tingling. "Forget, do you? Well, I wish *I* could, Mr. Myles Dampier!"

CHAPTER SEVEN

Myles was sober when he arrived back at the inn later that evening. Sober, and as immaculate as if he had just stepped from the hands of a valet, a cold preoccupation replacing his usual carelessly amused greeting. Sabina, who realized she had been reading a highly improbable gothic romance upside down for the last hour, welcomed him with a mixture of relief and apprehension.

"Have you dined?" she asked, stumbling to her feet.

Myles, in the act of stripping off his greatcoat and gloves, smiled a little sourly at the anxiety in her voice. "What a charmingly domestic question, Mermaid. Very . . . wifely. Thank you, yes. I am in no imminent danger of starvation."

She could feel the welcome drain from her face. Swallowing, she fought the desire to throw the book at his head, instead resuming her place in the chair and turning the pages right side up. "I am very glad to hear it. I would hate it if the dinner hours I tend to keep inconvenienced you in any way."

"Sabina, I want you to go on to Lysons Hall without me."

The words—low, determined, and totally unexpected—seemed to hang in the air like the dialogue balloon of a political cartoon. They were the emotional equivalent of a physical thrust. The book tumbled to the floor from fingers that were suddenly nerveless. "You want me to go away?"

The blue eyes were a curious mixture of understanding and intolerance, curtained all too suddenly by the sweep of black lashes.

"It will make things simpler, my dear," he explained gently. "I dined with Cedric Carstairs this evening, and he has prevailed upon his sister, Lucilla, to call upon you in Norfolk. Her husband was my friend once, and, it seems, still thinks kindly of me. They suggested it might be easier if you are introduced to the neighborhood . . . without me. Once you are accepted, my presence might be more easily tolerated."

"Tolerated! Accepted! Myles, I told you I don't care what your neighbors or . . . or society think about me!"

"But I do!" he replied harshly. He restlessly picked up the gloves from the table where he had discarded them, turning them over and over in his hands as if examining the seams for a flaw. "I didn't marry to have my wife treated like a leper. You will be mistress of Lysons Hall, and, God willing, mother to the next baronet. Do you think I came ten thousand miles to see everything ruined because of a few stiff-necked fools who will only follow where others lead?" He clenched his fists, his eyes still riveted to the gloves that were now nothing more than a ball of crushed leather in his fingers. He flung them on the table and spun round to face her, his stance rigid and distinctly threatening. "Don't fight me on this, Sabina. I promise you that you won't win."

Fight? She realized that she could barely draw breath, let alone stand up to him in any way. One devastating phrase was still echoing in her ears like the beat of a battle drum.

"So I'm to be the mother of the next baronet, am I?" She choked the words out with difficulty, her gaze transfixed by the mangled gloves. To her suddenly shocked mind, the empty fingers were curled up like claws—sharp, grasping claws, ripping at any dreams she might be foolish enough to harbor. Inhaling deeply, she managed to say carefully, "I knew there were any number of reasons why you married me, but I didn't realize I was specially chosen as . . . as aristocratic breeding stock."

"I made no secret of the fact that I want children, Sabina. I told you at the outset, this will be a normal marriage!"

"Normal!" She choked back a small, bitter laugh. Suddenly she couldn't bear to look at him—not at the hard, beautiful face or at the muscular body. "I take it, then, that Sir Richard's marriage has proved . . . barren."

The silence before he replied would have been a mere second's duration, but to her taut nerves it seemed to last for an eternity. "In fifteen years there has been no sign of a child. I am, despite everything that has happened, legally heir to the title." He added pleasantly, "As my son will one day be."

"And if our marriage proves childless? If I can't give you a son?"

"There has to be a real marriage first, Sabina, before we can worry about that eventuality."

She realized that the battle drum's thudding was actually the dull, blind beat of her own heart. Except that, confusingly, her heart seemed to be lodged somewhere in the middle of her throat, preventing the words that wanted to spill out of her. She heard her name spoken, but still she could not look at him, and she merely shook her head, desperately holding back tears.

"I once told you not to expect too much of me, Mermaid."

His voice was so soft that she wondered if she had actually heard the words spoken, but when she reluctantly raised her eyes to his face, it was as impassive as stone. Not by the single movement of a muscle did he seem to regret anything he had said—only the martial set of his body suggested that he was implacable in his wishes. She exhaled the breath that she seemed to have been holding since his entrance into the parlor, and said dully, "Very well. I'll go to Lysons Hall without you. As soon as you wish. In fact, the sooner the better."

His reply was brisk and unemotional, although she wondered if she hadn't detected a flicker of relief in the depths of his expression. "Good. I'll engage a courier. Marney will see to the rest of the servants who will travel with you. Lucilla Carstairs—Lady Vantry as she is now— will make sure that everything is in readiness. She will be—almost—your nearest neighbor."

"Who will accept me and tolerate you as the future heirs to the baronetcy," she said bitterly. "With such dizzying heights in front of me, I had better begin my preparations immediately."

She marched toward the door, only to be stopped by the plaintive calling of her name. She spun around on her heel, desperate for some small sign of accord, some gesture of tenderness. He was smiling now, the thin, mobile mouth quirked in an infuriating mixture of satisfaction and amusement, those remarkable eyes darkened by an emotion too hard, too illusory to be affection.

"Yes?" she demanded breathlessly.

"Take the damned monkey with you."

The chariot purchased for Mrs. Myles Dampier of Lysons Hall was of the very best quality, complete with a sword case and an ornate crest painted on the doors. Four matched grays (the owner's own horses), two postilions, two liveried outriders, two grooms, and a courier, hired to deal with such unfortunate necessities as tollgates and landlords, completed the lavish cavalcade. The horses had been changed at a posting inn, replaced by another perfectly matched four, also belonging to the Dampier stable. Two carriages, which contained the lady's luggage, several servants, her personal maid, and a very angry monkey in a wicker basket, had gone on ahead.

Sabina, who found that she could be as seasick on land as she ever was in the middle of the ocean, heaved a great sigh of relief when they reached the final posting inn. She listened to the clatter of wheels on cobblestone as if it were the sweetest music, swinging the door wide before either groom could leap down from his precarious position on the platform at the back of the chaise. She waited with ill-concealed impatience while the steps were put into place, and staggered down them with all the dignity of a drunken woman.

Mr. Charles, the courier, all respectful efficiency, removed his hat and offered her escort into the private parlor where he said she would enjoy a delicious meal.

"Mr. Charles," she said firmly, "I would enjoy stale bread and water as long as I don't have to eat it on wheels."

The man smiled broadly, obviously glad to impart happy news. "Not long now ma'am. You will be at Lysons Hall in less than two hours."

"Two hours!"

She tried to remember that she had promised to play the part of the dignified Mrs. Dampier of Lysons Hall and reeled thankfully into the inn. She found her maid and the monkey already ensconced in a chair in the private parlor reserved for them. Her heart lurched as she observed Maria's thunderous face.

"Poor Maria. Has Jezebel been a sad trial for you?" she asked, removing her bonnet and gloves. "I should have had her in my own carriage, but I'm afraid she goes into fits when she has to sit with me for long periods of time."

Maria looked as though she were about to go into a fit of her own, but she struggled to keep her voice respectful. "It's not the monkey I object to traveling with ma'am. Well, I do, but she minds her language at least. No, it's the boy I object to sitting with, and I don't mind telling you so. I've never met such a hell-born babe in all my life! Begging your pardon, Mrs. Dampier."

"What boy?"

"The one you told to sit in the coach with all the baggage."

"I told . . ." She stared blankly at her maid, trying to remember issuing orders to any boys to sit in carriages. "Maria, I don't know what you are talking about. I assure you I never told any boys to . . . Where is he?"

"Stuffing his face with pork pie in the taproom."

Sabina had already moved to the door, intent on solving the mystery, when it opened and Mr. Charles entered holding a tattered figure by the shoulder of an old coat several sizes too big. The same hazel eyes that had peered from the pickpocket's rags peeped over the collar.

"You! What . . . what are you doing here?"

Mr. Charles cleared his throat and explained diplomatically, "It seems that Mr. Dampier hired him as a stable boy, ma'am. At least that's what he says. The other servants found him hiding in the boot of the second baggage coach and made him sit with your maid, as there was no room inside. Perhaps you would know best"—here he paused delicately—"if Mr. Dampier was likely to do such a thing."

I would know best! The irony of the words was not lost on her as she regarded the boy with a feeling of total helplessness. He seemed to dangle somewhere in the folds of the coat like a small, malnourished puppet, his eyes wide, his mouth wisely closed until he took stock of his surroundings and the likelihood of being given over to the nearest magistrate.

Was it likely that Myles Dampier would pluck an urchin off the streets of London and transport him to the stables of Lysons Hall?

Just as likely as marrying a woman he had pulled from the sea and making her mistress of Lysons Hall.

She looked at the child and felt her heart turn over in her breast. There was a ridiculous dignity about his efforts to hold himself straight within the heavy folds of the coat. The small, dirty fingers, just visible within the frayed cuffs, were curled into two taut fists. She cleared her throat and tried to speak with all the gravity of an experienced chatelaine dealing with a crisis within her household. "Please let him go, Mr. Charles. I'll speak to him. Has he been fed? Oh, yes, Maria told me." She put her hand briefly to her forehead and fought back the craven wish that Myles were here to handle the situation. After all, she was now the mistress of a large estate. Both Mr. Charles and Maria were obviously awaiting her decision, as people would await all her future decisions about . . . pickpockets and such. She fixed the boy with a stern eye and asked in a fair imitation of Myles's abrupt manner, "What is your name, boy?"

The child had pulled himself once more, tortoiselike, into the folds of the coat. His reply was muffled against the dirty shawl wrapped about the collar, and Sabina repeated dazedly, "Salmon?"

"Gammon!"

"Is that your name?" she asked helplessly. Or was she being sworn at by a creature from whom she would gather in her skirts in order to avoid if she passed him in the streets.

"Yus." The hazel eyes were wary, but there was a certain adult swagger about the boy that made her lips twitch involuntarily. He definitely reminded her of someone.

"And you say that Mr. Dampier said you were to work in the stables?"

"Yus." He paused and offered slyly, "I follered him, missus—just sociable like, 'cos he talked like a rogue and looked like a swell. He guv me a yeller boy and said as how I should find work with prancers, rather than go on the prad lay."

Sabina rolled a desperate eye toward Mr. Charles who coughed and translated self-consciously, "It seems Mr. Dampier gave the boy a guinea and suggested he look for work with horses. Rather than steal from them."

"That . . . that is very commendable, Gammon. However, I am sure Mr. Dampier didn't mean that you were to steal away in the boot of our carriage. Or work in *his* stables."

The boy straightened, causing the thin young neck to appear over the folds of his coat. He looked unbearably vulnerable, like a drenched kitten peering over the edge of a bucket. "But the guv'nor said I could." There was a note of desperation in his voice now, replacing the cocky arrogance that seemed to be an integral part of his character. " 'E said I didn't have to end up in Newgate or New Souf Wales. And he guv me a yeller boy for nuffink!"

He seemed close to tears, and Sabina, touched by his desperation, made a decision that immediately settled her stomach.

"He shall have to come with us to Lysons Hall and wait for Mr. Dampier to arrive. We certainly can't abandon him on the road."

Maria glared at her mistress. "I'm not sharing a carriage with him, Mrs. Dampier. Not if you were to say I have to go back to London if I don't."

"Both the boy and the monkey will sit in my chaise, Maria, since it hurts your consequence to travel with them." She struggled with her temper, determined to keep calm. "And now, if you will all excuse me, I believe I have a luncheon awaiting me. Mr. Charles, if you will be so good as to leave the boy here, I shall endeavor to shake some of the dust from my clothes and appear presentable. No, Maria, I don't need you. You may also attend to your own repast. I shall manage very well on my own."

Chastened by her mistress's sharp tone, Maria meekly left the room, leaving Mr. Charles to hesitate at the door. "Mrs. Dampier, I doubt if the boy means you any harm, but we have no way of knowing if he of a vicious character or not. At the very least, his language may cause you distress."

Sabina glanced at the thin, hunched figure and dismissed the courier with a wry smile. "Mr. Charles, since I barely understand one word in three that the boy utters, I think I might be safe from distress." He withdrew, leaving her alone with the boy, who drew a grimy hand across his face and sniffed audibly. Sabina automatically searched her reticule for a handkerchief and handed it to him.

He looked at it suspiciously. "Wassis?"

"Use it on your face . . . er, Gammon. You must know what a handkerchief is for."

He looked insulted. "Course I do. It's a nose wipe! I seen *'undreds* of them."

"Well, then, this is for you to use." Seeing his look of surprise, she assured him, "You may keep it, if you like."

Gammon stared at the delicate piece of fabric and then carefully folded it, stowing it away in the cavernous depths of his coat with a quickness of hand that spoke a great deal about his professionalism. The large hazel eyes then turned toward her, speculation rife within their depths.

"You belong to him, don't you? Not old chortle-face out there"—he jerked his head in the direction of the closed door—"but Mr. Dampier. You're his missus, right?"

"Right," she agreed gravely. "I am Mrs. Dampier, Gammon."

"Then why aren't you with him? Why are you travelin' with that geezer?"

Sabina was startled by the question. She floundered for several seconds before finding refuge in dignity. "That is none of your affair, Gammon. In fact, I should be the one asking the questions." She watched the boy's neck contract warily as he made a small ball of his body. Apparently, questions were usually accompanied by some sort of physical unpleasantness. She drew in a deep breath and picked up a piece of bread which she proceeded to casually butter. "Don't you have a family you should be with, Gammon? Won't they be worried?"

The boy's eyes were riveted on the bread. "Naw. I'm an orphing."

Even more casually, Sabina handed the boy the slice. His gaze widened, and he lunged at it with the abandon of a half-starved dog. "But don't you have someone you live with?" she asked gently. "Someone who takes care of you?"

"Olmuttererockins," Gammon said, his mouth full of bread. He swallowed and repeated obligingly, "Ol' Mother 'Awkins. She keeps a doss 'ouse in St. Giles. I lives there when I 'as the money for the night."

"How old are you, Gammon?" Sabina's voice was sharper than she had intended, but the discovery that the child lived virtually alone on the streets shocked her. She had no idea why. Before her adventures on the other side of the world, she had lived all her life in London, and was well aware of the existence of its seamier side. She had just never been so close to one of the doyens of this shadowy world—close enough to notice that his clear hazel eyes seemed to hold a weary knowledge of the world that no child should be expected to own.

Gammon swallowed the last of the bread and narrowed his eyes. "Six," he announced defiantly.

"Six! Oh, Gammon, surely you are mistaken about that. You must be at least ten years old."

"Six!" he repeated stubbornly, and fell onto another piece of bread with all the delicacy of a wolf in a sheep pen.

"Well, I suppose it doesn't matter how old you are." She sighed and regarded him ruefully. "You can come with me to Lysons Hall, Gammon, and we'll wait until Mr. Dampier arrives before we make any decisions." She caught the haunted look in the child's eyes and added gently, "I'm sure we can find a place for you there. Perhaps until then"—she stopped and bit her lip, casting around for some duty that would occupy him—"until then . . . you could . . . you could look after Jezebel." She rose and crossed over to the corner where Jezebel sat dejectedly in her cage. "Look, Gammon," she said warmly. "I wonder if you have ever seen a monkey before."

The expression that dawned on the boy's face was almost comical in its eagerness. "I thought it was stuffed, missus! Like the one in the King's Tavern."

"Oh, no, she's all too real. Would you like to see her?"

The boy nodded and, obviously forgetting his hunger, slid off the seat and padded over to the cage, his movements stiff and clumsy in the oversized coat and shoes. He stared at the little animal, who began to preen coquettishly. One spiderish hand peeped between the bars and was gently taken between grimy fingers.

It was, Sabina observed with a small sigh of relief, love at first sight.

"You can be my monkey keeper, Gammon. You shall sit in my carriage and talk to her. Should you like that?"

Gammon nodded enthusiastically. "I'll take care of 'er, missus. And then you'll tell his nibs I done a good job, won't you?" The thin face was suddenly raised to hers beseechingly, his gaze no longer a hundred years old but that of an uncertain child. "You'll tell 'im, won't you?"

And she realized, with a sickening lurch of her stomach, that the boy was as desperate for Myles Dampier's approval as she was.

She said gently, "I'll tell him, Gammon. And now you can begin your duties and take Jezebel outside for some fresh air. Don't let her out of the cage, however. But you can feed her with a little bag of nuts Maria keeps in her pockets."

"That mort don't like me," Gammon announced cheerfully. "Said I was born to be 'anged."

"It doesn't matter if she likes you or not, Gammon. Go and ask for them, and then sit outside in the yard until it's time for us to leave."

Gammon shot her a grin, and despite the fact that the cage was only a little smaller than he was, managed to walk from the room as jauntily as his oversized clothes would allow. Sabina, turning back to her luncheon, noticed that two more slices of bread were unaccountably missing from the table, along with some jellied eggs, and she stifled a laugh.

Somehow she doubted that he would bother to *ask* Maria for the contents of her pockets.

Since Mr. Charles had had the forethought to bespeak a bedchamber as well as the private parlor for Sabina's use, she took advantage of its somewhat faded mirror to try to repair some of the ravages of nearly two days on the road. Maria, obviously determined to win her way back into her mistress's regard, hovered at the door, and was finally allowed to tidy the elaborate labyrinth of braids that Sabina had adopted in deference to the latest fashion in hairstyles. At last, feeling rested and sufficiently human to once again resume her journey, she dismissed her maid with a smile and, throwing her traveling cloak of wool and ermine around her shoulders, descended the stairs, determined to climb back into the carriage without a word of complaint.

She was stopped by the landlord, who hovered at the foot of the stairs, his face agog with excitement.

"Begging your pardon, Mrs. Dampier, but there is a gentleman in the parlor desirous of a word with you." He nervously flapped the large leather apron covering his ample stomach and, much to her surprise, leaned forward to whisper conspiratorially, "I think you'll find the gentleman is related to you, ma'am."

She felt her body go suddenly limp, supported, it seemed, only by whalebone and the stiffened folds of her traveling dress. She was clutching the railing so tightly that her nails dug into the hard wood, and she prised her hand away with an incoherent murmur. Pushing past the startled host, she flung open the parlor door.

And stopped. Her husband's name died on her lips as she found herself confronting a perfect stranger.

A tall, fair-haired man stood facing the fireplace, but at the suddenness of her entrance he swung around nervously, his eyes widening with a combination of surprise and admiration. Automatically he extended an uncertain hand, and then, seeing her hesitation, withdrew it abruptly, clasping it behind his back.

He cleared his throat. "You must forgive me, ma'am, for my intrusion, but Trout—the landlord, you understand—informs me that you are Mrs. Dampier of . . . of Lysons Hall."

Disappointment replaced shock, washing over her in a great cold wave, but she managed to incline her head graciously, the formal gesture leaving her time to collect her wits and find her voice. "I am Mrs. Dampier. But I'm afraid you have the advantage, sir. I don't believe we have ever met."

"No, we have not," the man assured her hastily. He seemed ill at ease, his aristocratic features rather pale, but his gaze sought hers with a determined honesty. "But I wanted to seize this opportunity—bad manners, I know, to make myself known under the circumstances—the thing is, I often stop here for refreshment on my way back to the Abbey, and I saw the crest on your carriage. Gave me a start, I can tell you. Should have talked to your man—Charles, isn't it?—but Trout said you are about to leave." He stopped, obviously exasperated with his own rambling, and ran his fingers through carefully ordered locks in a gesture that was heart-stopping in its familiarity. His eyes were the exact color of cornflowers, wide and candid, unmarked by shadows. He added with a rueful shake of his head, "Lord, I feel like one of those chaps on the tightrope in a traveling troupe. I hope very much I don't . . . tumble to the ground here."

"You are Sir Richard Dampier, aren't you?"

It was not a brilliant deduction on her part. His resemblance to Myles was remarkable, despite the obvious differences in coloring and manner. Richard Dampier's frank, open countenance radiated a warmth and sense of goodwill that would have wilted under the darkness of his cousin's shadow.

He was spring to Myles's winter.

She took a step back to study him, registering his very real dismay at her obvious retreat. So this elegant country gentleman was her husband's mortal enemy. The man who had married his Juliet, and inherited the family title and lands while Myles became little more than human cargo.

This man was Myles's prey.

The thought made her stomach churn. She had been prepared to face an ogre, and instead confronted a very ordinary man, mouthing ordinary civilities to cover up the painful uncertainty lurking in his gaze. Attractive, certainly. It seemed to be a family trait, and no doubt his willowy grace and courtly manners made him popular with the ladies of the neighborhood. But to Sabina, he so obviously lacked the irrepressible life force that burned through his cousin like molten iron in a blacksmith's forge.

Sunlight to shadow. Safe harbor to dangerous shoals.

What was it Myles had once said to her? That she would no doubt like Sir Richard very much.

Well, once again, Myles was right. She did.

She smiled warmly, her reservation dropping away from her like a discarded cloak. "For my part, I must apologize for my entry. What a hoyden you must think me. But I thought you were . . . someone else."

"Myles." The man exhaled the name, his brow furrowing as he clasped and unclasped his hands behind his back. "I . . . wasn't certain if Myles . . . your husband was traveling with you or not."

"No," she confessed reluctantly. "He wanted me to precede him." She lowered her eyes, and then, seized by a fierce desire to make someone in the Dampier family say more than they hinted at, raised them resolutely. "He is uncertain of his reception in the neighborhood, you see, and wished me to meet with as little prejudice as possible. He is convinced that that will only be accomplished by my coming here without him. And you must know that Myles . . . well, even after all these years, he is *very* fond of getting his own way."

Sir Richard ignored the last part of her speech, seizing on one word. He pulled up a small stool and perched beside her chair, saying impulsively, "Prejudice? No indeed! How could there be after all these years? You cannot imagine how happy I will be . . . *we* will be to see him home once more. And married! It is above all things wonderful! I hope . . . I want . . . but you see, my wife is something of an invalid and cannot call upon you. However, I trust that *you* will call as soon as you are settled in the neighborhood."

Sabina's spirits had begun to soar, but as his last words sank in, she felt herself retreating from the ingenuous goodwill in the handsome face. "Thank you, Sir Richard. But that might not be possible." The memory of the disdainful women in the opposite box at the opera caused her to add bitterly, "I have already encountered invalid wives who are unable to call upon me. It does not inspire me to offer friendship where it is not wanted."

"No! You are mistaken." His sincerity was all too apparent, and she was alarmed to notice that the long white hands that rested on the arm of her chair were actually shaking. Uncertainly her eyes flew to his, and what she saw there convinced her that here was a worthy ally in her struggle to restore peace to her husband's turbulent life. He continued, "When Sylvia learned that Myles was back in England, *and* had brought a wife with him, she was most insistent that I make some attempt to heal a breach that . . . that was never of my making. You must believe me. I would not have made so bold as to accost you— unannounced—in a public inn if it were not so."

And there, she realized, lay the yawning chasm between the cousins' characters. Myles would have been so bold as to accost her *anywhere* convenient to him. In fact, she had no doubt that by now she would be in *his* carriage on her way to . . . the Abbey, did he say?

Her mouth quirked at the thought. "I'm sorry, Sir Richard. You must think me very thin-skinned. Please inform Lady Dampier that I will be pleased to call on her as soon as I am able. In fact, I will be *delighted* to do so."

He rose from his position by her chair, his face beaming with a simple pleasure that Sabina found difficult to resist. "It is very good of you, Mrs. Dampier. And if you find yourself in need of anything, I am less than two miles away at the Abbey—Curstone Abbey is its formal name, but in the neighborhood we are known as the Abbey and . . . and the Hall. Yes, there have always been Dampiers at the Hall. Well, well, it is as things once were many years ago, only . . . only better."

This was as it should be, she thought, encouraged by his optimism. Of course, everything would go well once Myles met his cousin and saw that the enemy of his imagination was a flesh-and-blood man, who proffered the hand of friendship. "I'm glad," she admitted a little shyly,

HOLLY COOK

rising from her chair. "No matter what has transpired in the past, I should like to see Myles at peace with his family."

"So should I!" Sir Richard exclaimed. He took hold of her gloved fingers in an impulsive gesture. "We were good friends in our youth, you know, Mrs. Dampier, and despite . . . events, I should like us to be friends once more. But I am keeping you from resuming your journey. We will meet again soon, and then we will have a great deal to talk about. A common inn is no place to begin our friendship."

A discreet cough from the doorway startled them, and she pulled her fingers from Sir Richard's light grip. Mr. Charles, his face impassive, examined the baronet from head to toe, and then turned to Sabina, asking politely, "Is everything in order, Mrs. Dampier? I've sent the other carriage ahead. However, if you wish to delay your leave . . ."

"Everything is *indeed* in order, Mr. Charles," she replied happily. "Sir Richard Dampier will escort me to my carriage." The courier's eyebrows shot up, but he merely bowed again and diplomatically removed himself from the room, leaving Sir Richard to comment ruefully, "I see your man suspects me of being some sort of tavern knight. It brings home to me just how shameless my behavior in approaching you was, Mrs. Dampier."

"I must have been out of the country for a very long time if you rank your behavior as *shameless*." She smiled up at him and added impulsively, "Will you not call me Sabina? After all, we are cousins, are we not? And, I sincerely hope, soon to be friends, as well as neighbors."

His face lit up, leaving her to reflect rather wryly that the Dampier men—any of them!—were rather too attractive for their own good. He offered his arm with all the grace of a seasoned courtier and escorted her from the inn. Once in the yard, Sir Richard bent his head so that the fair curls brushed across his forehead, and ceremonially kissed her hand, before walking her to her carriage and handing her into it with exquisite care. She settled

154

Join the Historical Romance Book Club
and GET 4 FREE* BOOKS NOW!

A $23.96 Value!

Yes! I want to subscribe to the
Historical Romance Book Club.

Please send me my **4 FREE* BOOKS.** I have enclosed $2.00 for shipping/handling. Each month I'll receive the four newest Historical Romance selections to preview for 1O days. If I decide to keep them, I will pay the Special Members Only discounted price of just $4.24 each, a total of $16.96, plus $2.00 shipping/handling ($23.55 US in Canada). This is a **SAVINGS OF AT LEAST $5.00** off the bookstore price. There is no minimum number of books I must buy, and I may cancel the program at any time. In any case, the **4 FREE* BOOKS** are mine to keep.

*In Canada, add $5.00 shipping/handling per order
for the first shipment. For all future shipments to
Canada, the cost of membership is $23.55 US,
which includes shipping and handling.
(All payments must be made in US dollars.)

NAME: _____

ADDRESS: _____

CITY: _____ STATE: _____

COUNTRY: _____ ZIP: _____

TELEPHONE: _____

E-MAIL: _____

SIGNATURE: _____

down in her seat, prepared to bid him a formal goodbye, only to find a small, grimy body leaning determinedly over hers to look out the window.

" 'Ere! You keep your lips to yoursel', my buck. This is Mr. Dampier's missus! Not some rum doxy! Gawn with ye!" There was an explosion of surprise outside the carriage, and, apparently satisfied, Gammon collapsed into his seat beside her. He shot a thoughtful glance at his new mistress. "You ought to be careful 'oo you talk to in taverns, missus. What sort o' thatch-gallows was that, taking liberties with you?"

Sabina felt her mouth working and desperately tried to keep it prim. As the carriage began to move, she resisted the opportunity to look out the window and observe the results of Gammon's fierce protection. Instead she drew in a deep breath and said with a fair effort at calm, "That, Gammon, was Mr. Dampier's cousin. He is a baronet."

"A barrow-net? Never heard of 'em. I know a few barrow *men*. But," he added wisely, "I guess that gentry cove don't own a barrow."

She would *not* laugh at the boy. She would not. It would be too cruel . . . he wouldn't understand. . . .

She lifted her hands to her face and tried to stop her shoulders from shaking.

"If you're gonna start bawling," she heard Gammon say severely, "you'd better get your nose wipe out! If you ain't got one, you can use mine."

Sabina, struggling for some sort of composure, realized that the next two hours would be either delightfully long or unbearably short.

The horse was in its death throes, the thrashing hooves suspended in midair as the lion on its back carelessly ripped out its throat. This tableau was only initially less violent than the dying gladiator who seemed to be captured in a state of eternal astonishment at the huge sword protruding from his naked chest.

The Dampiers, Sabina noted, had a refreshingly simple solution to the problem of unwelcome guests. As the carriage made its elegant journey down the drive of the estate, she counted the number of marble statues that depicted horrid death.

"It seems," she mused aloud, "that the family motto must be 'I will destroy.' Now, why aren't I surprised by that?"

Gammon had been hanging openmouthed out the opposite window, but at the sound of her voice he slumped into his seat, knocking Jezebel's cage so that the animal chattered in protest. "Mr. Dampier must be as rich as the king!" he exclaimed. "You say 'e owns all them trees." The boy inhaled ecstatically. "Fancy owning a tree!" He paused and sniffed experimentally, then put his head to one side, adding, "But there's a funny smell, missus."

Sabina, who had already planned and mentally executed a bath for her grubby companion, suggested faintly, "Perhaps you aren't used to all this fresh air, Gammon. Trees and grass and flowers smell different from the streets of London."

"I know that! But this don't smell like no tree." He was like a puzzled animal, his head making small, darting movements as he sniffed excitedly. Sabina was amused to notice that she was doing the same thing, trying to locate the source of Gammon's aroma. When the explanation suddenly occurred to her, she half rose in her seat, craning to see past the parklike scenery.

"The sea! Oh, Gammon. We are only a mile or two from the sea. That's what you smell!"

"Well, 'ang me by the heels and call me a Scotsman! The sea! I ain't never seen it afore!"

"You will, Gammon." She felt an unlooked-for excitement suddenly surge through her body, wiping away the exhaustion and nervousness that had been her constant companions on the journey from London. "The sea is wonderful! It's wide and deep and blue—or green or gray or sometimes black, and sometimes dreadful and unforgiving, but at other times it's so beautiful it makes you want to cry for no reason at all." She caught the boy's skeptical look and laughed, feeling happier and more optimistic than she had for some time. "Well, perhaps not. But I guarantee that you will never see anything more breathtaking in your life."

"If it's so good, why don't everyone want to be a sailor? I seen 'em running from the press gangs."

"I suppose because people don't want to be sent away from their homes and their families," she replied absently, craning her neck to catch a view of the house through the army of trees. "They may not see them for years and years."

"Like Mr. Dampier? Like when he got sent to Botany Bay?"

Sabina's head swiveled around so quickly that she felt a muscle catch in her neck. "How on earth . . . ! Where did you hear that, Gammon?"

The hazel eyes were a study in innocence. "In the coach with the others after they dug me out of the basket. They said as 'e was a convict come back to cause trouble for those as shipped 'im out. They said he's as rich as a king 'cause 'e dug up diamonds and rubies in New Souf Wales, and you married 'im 'cause 'e saved you from cannibubbles."

"Saved me from what?" Sabina asked faintly, fascinated by this new version of her husband's history.

"You know—people what eats people!"

"Oh, *cannibals!*" She looked down into the boy's shining eyes, and hesitated, before admitting softly, "But they weren't very big cannibals, Gammon. And there couldn't have been more than . . . oh, twenty or thirty of them."

Gammon gave a blissful sigh and sank against the shiny leather seat, his mind obviously somewhere where men dug up rubies like turnips and heroes wrested maidens from the cooking pots of cannibals. Sabina resisted the desire to smooth a straggle of fair hair back from his enraptured face and turned resolutely toward the window. She let out a gasp that caused the boy to sit up at once, every faculty alert.

"Gawdblimey!!"

Sabina wasn't quite sure if she or Gammon had uttered

the word. The carriage had reached a wide stone bridge, where the trees suddenly parted, and what had been half-caught glimpses of red brick and roof materialized into a magical building that was half citadel, half Jacobean fortress, its turrets and spiraling chimneys competing with each other for domination over the landscape.

"Is that it? Is that Mr. Dampier's 'ouse?"

House indeed. It seemed that somewhere in his fond description of Lysons Hall, Myles had neglected to tell her that it was a cross between a medieval castle and Hampton Court. It filled the horizon like a small city. She swallowed, wondering rather desperately if Cinderella-turned-princess had ever experienced an unbidden cowardly desire for her ashes and her broom and her fireplace.

"Yes, Gammon. It's Lysons Hall. Our new home."

Home. She almost choked on the word that conjured up the coziness of the rooms she had shared with her father, or her cramped quarters on the *Ellen Drury*. Not the stone acreage that loomed closer with each passing minute.

Gammon found nothing in its appearance to cause dismay. He seemed pleased that Lysons Hall was worthy of Myles's status as demigod. "It's better than the king's palace! It's better than anything!"

Of course, it wasn't. As it came closer into view, she could see the signs of decay and neglect that made it seem more than ever like the sleeping castle in a fairy tale. Ivy covered most of the upper levels, while many of the windows were darkened or broken. Some of the high chimneys had all too obviously toppled, and the hands of the clock tower were missing. But still the house wore its three hundred odd years with an impressive dignity that no amount of deterioration could erase.

By the time the carriage swept into the stone courtyard and stopped before a wide gatehouse tower, even Gammon was speechless. Sabina, thankful for small mercies, waited until the carriage door was open and the steps lowered before giving her hand to Mr. Charles, who, having safely delivered her to her destination, was full of brisk efficiency as he helped her alight.

"Home at last, Mrs. Dampier." He smiled and suggested kindly, "You might want to send the boy and the monkey to the kitchens until you are settled. Your maid has been directed to your chamber, and Mrs. Ferris, the house-keeper, is awaiting your instructions."

Home at last, she thought bleakly, examining the huge medieval door and what looked suspiciously like arrow slits above it. Through a smaller door open within the huge portal, she could see a lineup of servants in the courtyard beyond, ready to greet their new mistress. Her heart sank at the thought. It should, she thought bitterly, have been Myles who welcomed her to her new home, not a servant with nice manners. It should have been Myles who offered her escort as she ran the domestic gauntlet.

Why the devil wasn't he here?

After all, wasn't this house his Holy Grail? The culmination of fifteen years of suffering and striving?

Hadn't he married her to make her its final adornment?

She stood motionless, fighting the desire to climb back into the chaise and order its return to London, until an insistent tugging at her skirts roused her from her stupor.

"It looks like the entrance to Newgate," Gammon hissed. Jezebel's cage was clasped protectively in his arms as he squinted into the courtyard beyond. "You be careful, missus."

Sabina stared into anxious hazel eyes and felt some of her terror begin to recede. Put into perspective, she was now the mistress of this great house, not some common interloper arriving under false pretenses. Myles Dampier had made her its chatelaine, and it was now her respon-sibility not to be a mere ornament, but to look after its inhabitants, Gammon included. If she was to make any-thing of her marriage, she could accomplish that much.

"My instructions," she murmured thoughtfully, and paused to weigh her options before continuing determinedly, "my instructions, Mr. Charles, are to have the boy washed, the monkey fed, and both delivered to my rooms. If Maria squeaks, have her thrown into the dungeons. I take it there are dungeons?"

"I believe they are now referred to as wine cellars, ma'am."

"In that case," Sabina said stoutly, placing her hand on his proffered arm, "I shall *undoubtedly* have need of them before the end of the evening."

Despite her misgivings, Sabina's first night at Lysons Hall passed without incident. The housekeeper, Mrs. Ferris, an amiable, respectful woman who had presided over the household during the previous tenant's occupancy, revealed by neither look nor gesture that she found it odd that a bride of less than a month should be deposited alone in her husband's country residence. The rest of the household seemed to have been specially imported from London, and if there were whispers below stairs about their master's scandalous past, these seemed to center on his remarkable prowess with cannibals.

Lysons Hall, she realized disgustedly, had been swept clean with a new broom. It was *not* the place where she would discover the truth about Myles's past, despite the fact that it was big enough to hide an army of skeletons. That is, if they chose to hide. As she walked through the great hall with its walls bearing the antlers of long-dead stags and the shields of long-dead warriors, she began to wish that she were not quite so addicted to gothic novels.

That evening, she dined in solitary splendor beneath a high vaulted roof of wooden beams, blackened by the smoke of medieval feasts when knights and ladies had sat at long wooden benches and thrown scraps to the dogs groveling in the rushes on the floor. She felt rather foolish to be seated at a table that could have hosted the entire court of Camelot, attended by two silent footmen who anticipated her every move. When she abruptly stood up, causing one of them to make a futile dive for her chair, she realized that she had absolutely no idea of where to go or what to do next.

At least Myles could have provided her with a map!

She looked at one of the footmen who shifted nervously beneath his powdered wig. Should she ask him where she should go? Or should she sweep grandly from the room and pray that somehow she didn't get lost between here and her bedchamber? She was still debating the merits of each action when the door opened and Mrs. Ferris entered bearing an expensive brass lamp that glowed brightly and smokelessly in comparison to the spluttering candles and dimming lusters that lit the huge chamber.

"I've brought you some more light, ma'am, you not being familiar with the house as I am. I've had a fire made up in the Tapestry Room if you would like to sit there." The woman smiled as Sabina expelled a relieved sigh, then went on, "It's a pretty room, made up for a lady. Mr. Dampier gave orders to have it ready for you."

Did he now? "Mr. Dampier must have a very loud voice to be heard all the way from London." In response to the housekeeper's perplexed frown, she added wryly, "Thank you, Mrs. Ferris. I am somewhat . . . disoriented. This is a very large house."

"It is indeed, ma'am," Mrs. Ferris said with simple pride, leading her mistress from the dining room into a darkened corridor where shadows leapt from the light cast by the lamp's steady progress. "We are bigger than Curstone Abbey, for all it's said to be so grand. Of course it's not as old as the Hall. Mr. Dampier's grandfather came back from the Grand Tour and decided he wanted to live in something like Holkham. You know, ma'am, with lots of Greek gods and grottoes and temples and such-like nonsense. Myself, I prefer the Hall. We may be short of water closets, Mrs. Dampier, but we burn wax candles, not tallow, *and* the chimneys don't smoke, whatever they say at the Abbey."

Sabina could only murmur incoherently at this information, and wordlessly followed the other woman into what turned out to be a charming sitting room, with modern furnishings and a delightful fire glowing seductively in the ancient fireplace. She was drawn to it like a grateful moth, determined to keep the shadows at bay; she was stopped, her hands still automatically outstretched, by the sight of the carvings in the ancient wood.

A mermaid, her tail twisted improbably, held up a comb and a mirror as she stared contemptuously out at the room from above the bright flames.

Sabina's startled intake of breath alerted Mrs. Ferris, who was hovering to make sure that her claims of smokeless chimneys were substantiated. "Is there anything wrong, ma'am?"

"There's a mermaid." Sabina extended a faltering hand and, despite the heat, softly traced the carving. It was very old, and hardly a thing of beauty, blackened as it was by years of smoke and neglect. And yet there *she* was, just as Myles had told her, her breasts bare, her thin smile beguiling, her hair exotically disheveled.

Mrs. Ferris gave a relieved snort. "Oh, that's the sea wife, ma'am. She's part of an old family legend. Not that I ever served the family, you understand, only coming here when Mr. Bradshaw leased the house from Sir Richard. But I like old stories. Just imagine, ma'am, only a century ago the sea was almost a mile closer to the house than it is now. Practically on our doorstep, so I suppose it's only natural there was talk of sea monsters and mermaids. You'll find her on the family crest—the old one in the banqueting hall. I do believe she's the ancestress of all the Dampiers."

So this was Great-grandmama Dampier, taken from the sea to marry a long-dead lord of the manor. Sabina tipped her head to one side to study her, and decided that the distinctive arrogance of the twisting figure with its upraised arms and self-satisfied features was fairly unmistakable.

"Do you think she's an emblem of good luck, Mrs. Ferris?"

"So they say. But I think she looks a right hussy, begging your pardon, ma'am."

Sabina gave a little ripple of laughter, surprising herself with the sudden lightening of her spirits. And while she ached at the memory of a deep, dark voice caressing her with the name, another part of her joyfully registered the fact that she might just possibly belong here. Here, amidst all the decaying splendor of an old house that sat waiting for a family to give it back life.

After all, she and Great-grandmama had a great deal in common.

The thought, as whimsical as it was, made her suddenly brave. Her gaze still fixed on the fireplace, she said lightly, "I couldn't agree more, Mrs. Ferris. She looks like a most particular hussy." She drew in a determined breath, and exhaled slowly before turning to face the housekeeper with more authority than she had felt since climbing into her carriage in the courtyard of the Bull and Mouth. "I have a great deal to learn about both Lysons Hall and the Dampier family, Mrs. Ferris. I shall look forward to our tour of the house tomorrow."

She was surprised at the easy dismissal in her voice, although Mrs. Ferris obviously found nothing amiss, merely smiling and dropping a small curtsy.

"At your convenience, ma'am." The housekeeper paused, and inquired respectfully, "But before I leave you, Mrs. Dampier, may I ask what you want done with the boy?"

Sabina's jaw dropped slightly as she realized guiltily that for the past few hours all thought of "the boy" had been banished from her mind. "Oh, Lord! Gammon! I can't believe I forgot. . . . Is he all right?"

"Well, he's been bathed, as you ordered, ma'am, although not without incident. He had to be held down, and he bit one of the younger footmen." She took pity on Sabina's horrified expression and added comfortably, "Luckily, James has a large family of young brothers at home and promptly bit him back. There seems to be some sort of mutual respect between them now. And I've discovered that the boy can be quite biddable if you tell him that Mr. Dampier wouldn't like him doing something or

163

another. He's fallen asleep in the servants' quarters, and the monkey refuses to leave him."

"Mrs. Ferris," Sabina said feelingly, "I have an idea it should be *your* image on the family crest in the banqueting hall."

The housekeeper blushed rosily, curtsying more deeply to cover her embarrassment at the compliment. She picked up the lamp, and then paused at the door, her face half hidden in shadows. "If you will excuse my impertinence, Mrs. Dampier, but . . . I am very glad that you have come. Mr. Bradshaw was a bachelor, you see, and had no thought of anything beyond his horses. And before that . . . we aren't to talk of that, I know, and you'll find I don't stand for gossip below stairs. But this is a fine house, for a fine family, and I hope that it will be a very happy one for you in the future."

Sabina watched the door close, sincerely moved by the woman's unexpected benediction. Mrs. Ferris was right. It was a fine house. Sabrina knew she would come to love it as passionately as she hated the coldly elegant town house in Brook Street, with its golden harp and its golden goddess. She had been a stranger in that house, while here . . . she moved closer to the fire, drawn once again to the carved figure that seemed to leap out at her from the dark oak mantelpiece.

A mirror for fertility, a comb for entanglement. She knew their significance from her father's interest in the legends of the seas and the lands they had explored together. Curiously enough, mermaids were far too often creatures of infamy, luring sailors to their doom, more monster than fairy-tale creature. And yet the Dampiers, with their close bonds to the sea, had chosen to honor one in their family mythology. Why? she wondered. Was it to establish good relations with those very sea demons? Or had marriage with the sea wife of legend arisen from sheer masculine bravado? After all, it said a lot for the potency of a man who could tame a dangerous siren into a devoted wife and mother.

Or was it just plain old Dampier common sense used

164

in a very practical way. *When there's a problem, marry it.*

Her fingers trembled slightly as she once more traced the lines of the hand mirror held high above the figure's head. It was this symbol that disturbed her more than anything else, carved deeply into the wood like a small, secret derision of her hopes and fears. *I made no secret of the fact that I want children,* he had said.

So did she. She pulled back her hand, shivering suddenly although she stood in an arc of warmth and firelight. Despondently she stared into the flames and admitted what she had been afraid to admit before, even to herself. It had been too bold a thought, too frightening, too glorious . . . too *married.* One day, she wanted to bear Myles Dampier's children. She wanted them to be born and grow up in this house where he had shared a happy childhood with loving parents. Where the eager, loving boy had existed long before the ruthless, bitter man.

But she would not bear them as child-sacrifices to his desire for revenge. And certainly not to begin a new dynasty built on hate.

Or worse, built on arid convenience and indifference.

CHAPTER EIGHT

Cedric Carstairs's sister made good her promise to call, and within a few days of her arrival, Sabina had the dubious pleasure of receiving Lady Vantry for a genteel half hour of tea and pleasantries. She was a year or two younger than Myles, whippet thin, with restless hands and eyes. Her features, jutting out sharply beneath a purple turban festooned with feathers, were distinctly harder than those of her good-natured brother; at the moment they were alight with barely suppressed curiosity.

"As an old friend of the family, I feel sure you will forgive me a natural inquisitiveness." She hesitated before asking delicately, "Did you meet Myles in . . . er . . . the colonies, Mrs. Dampier?"

Sabina paused in the act of pouring tea and coolly considered recounting the cannibal story. "No, Lady Vantry," she said, regretfully dismissing the idea. "We met on board a ship that was bringing us both back to England. My father died in South America and I was returning to . . . to live with my cousin in Bournemouth." She felt sorry

166

for the lie, but decided that Cousin Sarah's remote existence provided her with a respectability that a potential governess, however superior, just didn't possess.

"Oh." Lady Vantry seemed disappointed with the commonplace explanation. "I thought . . . but then," she broke off with a little laugh and sighed, her hands fluttering over the tea things, "of course, one should never believe half of what one hears. People so often tend to exaggerate, don't they?"

"Indeed they do." Sabina steadily lifted a cup to her lips. She had no intention of sharing the story of her rescue from the sea with this woman, or anyone else, for that matter. They would turn both the tragedy and the miracle of it all into a trite little romance to be gossiped about over just such a tea table as this.

And that, she could not bear.

"We are a very small world here, and we find that we depend upon each other for society," Her Ladyship pursued discreetly. The feathers bobbed fiercely up and down, as if corroborating her statement. "There are no more than ten or twelve families who *matter*, although we may sit down to dinner with a good deal more during the hunting season. That begs a question. Do you ride, Mrs. Dampier?"

Sabina, who had once managed to sit on a mule for four days from São Paulo to Rio de Janiero, declared stoutly, "Yes indeed. There's nothing I like so much as riding. Unfortunately, my delicate constitution does not always permit me to indulge. Particularly during the hunting season."

Her Ladyship's eyes narrowed, and Sabina realized that her flippant tone had been a mistake. Lucilla Vantry was not a fool. And no doubt she was trying to be kind in her own way, but it was a condescending kindness that Sabina found she resented. If Myles's *acceptance*—and she felt her teeth beginning to clench at the word—if it hinged upon the approval of ten or twelve families who mattered, then it was likely not worth the having.

She must have looked as mutinous as she felt, for Lady

167

Vantry suddenly abandoned her *grande dame* air and leaned forward to place a hand on her arm.

"Mrs. Dampier, there is no need for us to play a game. You understand that Myles is in a difficult position. He has chosen to return to Lysons Hall in a manner which has set tongues wagging for fifty miles." Her expression softened slightly, and a smile flickered over the severe lips. "Those who remember him as a boy—a little wild, a little reckless perhaps, but full of laughter and charm—those people will remember the . . . the *unjust* circumstances and welcome him back with pleasure. Others will only remember the scandal. They must be won over . . . with time and patience."

Sabina looked down thoughtfully at the gloved hand and then raised her eyes and looked into her visitor's face. There was a curious mixture of warning and understanding in those pointed features, and it made her bold enough to ask impulsively, "What was he like? Before he . . . left England."

Her visitor hesitated, and then shrugged, as if bowing to the inevitable. Her face softened as she remembered the nineteen-year-old Myles. "He was a lovable young rogue who understood the gift of friendship—handsome, sweet-natured, and as wild as a March hare. But kind, always kind. I've never seen him bully or hurt anything or anyone in his life. His uncle—Sir John, you know—despaired of him, but his father let him go his own way, practically unchecked. He led Cedric and Richard into a series of scrapes, which wasn't easy, given that they were both quiet, steady young men. But he always made sure he got them out of trouble just as quickly." She drew in a deep breath and confessed, "As young as I was, I was more than a little in love with him."

The smile trembling at the corner of Sabina's mouth was threatened by the tears she felt pooling in her eyes. She said brightly, "He seems to have had the terrible power of invoking strong feelings of one kind or another in people, doesn't he? You say he had the gift of friendship. Then I only wish he had had more friends."

Lady Vantry rose to her feet, obviously unwilling to discuss the past in any more detail. Her voice was a mixture of severity and understanding. "Myles has friends *now*, Sabina, and that is what matters. I, for one, will do all I can to see him reestablished in the neighborhood, and I am not without influence. May I call you Sabina, my dear? Such a pretty name. It suits you. And it's well you are a beauty, my dear. It's always an advantage in a successful hostess. I believe Myles intends to turn the Hall into a showpiece? Yes? That's a wise move on his part. The invitations will flood in out of sheer curiosity at first, if nothing else. But you must be careful in all that you do and say."

Sabina gaped up at her visitor in surprise. "Invitations? But I understood we were to be pariahs! That's why Myles stays in London. So that I can slowly *ingratiate* myself with the neighborhood without his corrupting presence."

"Does he indeed?" Lady Vantry shook her head in mock sorrow. "I did wonder. That sounds like something Cedric would serve up. How very foolish men can be. But then again . . . perhaps sending you ahead as the advance guard does have its merits. The Myles Dampier I remember had little interest in ingratiating himself with anyone. He was honest to the point of rudeness, and cared little for what people thought of him. I can't believe he has changed that much."

A sudden knife turned in Sabina's heart. In these things, no. But in so much else . . .

She stood up, and across the tea table asked the question that had been burning on her lips for the past twenty minutes. "Do you know Sylvia Dampier?"

"Of course. Since childhood."

"What is she like?" *Beautiful? Faithless?* She already knew these things. What she wanted to really know was . . .

"An invalid." The word was stretched out, as though Her Ladyship was deeply amused by its connotation. "And unlike you, my dear, not only in the hunting season." Lucilla Vantry let Sabina digest this small rebuke, and then continued kindly, "I understand why you ask. You must not be jealous of her, Sabina. The past is the past, and it is well for all of us to forget it as best we can."

"I can hardly forget what I have never experienced, Lady Vantry," she said quietly. "I just want to *understand*, so that I can help Myles forget."

"Was it a love match? Is Myles in love with you?"

The question was so unexpected, so breathtakingly brazen, that Sabina suddenly felt her knees buckle under her, and she collapsed back into her elegant satin chair. She stared at the woman in sheer astonishment, her cheeks staining a brilliant pink.

"Why . . . why do you ask?" she managed to say feebly.

Lady Vantry's face was a polite mask, but to Sabina it seemed that a satisfied gleam momentarily lit up the pale eyes. "Because a clever woman can make a man do anything she wants him to. And if he loves her, she has unlimited power. Think about that, my dear, before you meet Lady Dampier. And now I really must take my leave." She held out her hand like a departing queen and added kindly, "When you know me a little better Sabina, you might trust me with more of your own story. I gather the child you arrived with is not Myles's bastard?"

Despite her shock at the woman's frankness, Sabina's lips quirked. If she hadn't known better, she would have sworn the woman was Myles's sister, not the diplomatic Cedric's. She had made the initial mistake of underestimating Lucilla Vantry, something she would not do in the future.

"Gammon? Is that what they think?" she replied evenly. "No. Even Myles is not godlike enough to have fathered him all the way from New South Wales. No. He is the result of . . . a charitable impulse."

As I am. The words hung suspended in the room like an invisible glass chandelier, ready to collapse and shatter the already fragile hold she had on her emotions. Lady Vantry seemed to sense this, for she gathered her things and forbade Sabina to see her from the room.

However, she paused at the door, asking curtly, "Will you come to dinner next week? I should like to introduce you to some of your neighbors." She added flatly, "Sir Richard and Lady Dampier seldom leave the Abbey after dark. Sylvia has an aversion to being abroad at night."

Sabina heard herself assent unsteadily, and then her visitor, like the ghost at the banquet, was suddenly gone, leaving her shaken and confused, and no more the wiser about Myles or Richard or Sylvia Dampier than she had been in the first place.

She needed to clear her head. Still unused to ringing for servants to wait upon her every whim, she made her way to her chamber to fetch her cloak and walking shoes and, once there, managed to waste a good ten minutes staring out her window at the breathtaking vista spread out before her. The gardens, Mrs. Ferris told her, had once been the pride of the entire county, but under the tenancy of the mythical Mr. Bradshaw they had gradually decayed into ruin. They had been one of the first things to be restored when Myles acquired the house more than a year ago, and the aspect of rolling green lawn, formal flower beds, ponds, and stone bridges was a delightful one.

But it was the thought of the sea only a few miles behind the house that beckoned to her rather than the manicured parkland or the desolate fenlands beyond, and she found herself leaving the house like a furtive housemaid, breaking into a run as soon as she reached the edges of the park. She spread her arms out as she ran down the side of a hill, suddenly enraptured by the feeling of her cloak billowing behind her and her hair tousled by the breeze, relishing a sense of complete freedom that she hadn't felt since standing on the decks of the *Ellen Drury*.

And, released from the shadows that filled every corner of the house, she began to think, ideas and plans tumbling over in her mind.

A clever woman can make a man do anything she wants him to.

She wanted her husband to love her. Was she clever enough for that? Maybe if she met his expectations as Mrs. Dampier of Lysons Hall. If she became a brilliant hostess.

If she presented him with a son. If . . . if . . . if . . .

If he didn't inhabit his own dark world of loss and revenge, scorning all efforts to escape it. After all, how could you make a man love you whose entire energy was directed toward hating?

Her breath caught in her throat, and she stopped suddenly on the top of a rise, flinging herself around to get a better look at the Hall. Seen from this distance, the ravages of time were concealed. It looked somehow . . . bereft. Yes, that was the word she sought—all longing and loneliness, like an abandoned fairy-tale castle waiting for the return of its questing knight.

Perhaps it was because this impression was so strong that it seemed the most natural thing in the world to turn around and find him astride a horse on the next rise, one hand lifted to his eyes as if closing a visor.

He was coatless and bareheaded, the breeze lifting the dark hair across his forehead like the wing of a raven. The horse suddenly whipped its head to one side, moving nervously, and was easily checked by a light gesture. Myles handled the animal gently, but with a casual mastery that was more effective than force, and the beast meekly plodded toward her with the docility of a plow horse rather than the high-strung movements of the thoroughbred it was.

She had been dreading this moment. Not because she hadn't been longing for his arrival like some infatuated schoolgirl, but because she knew she would have to school her features into an expression of indifferent pleasure, rather than expose the great surge of joy that had her blood singing and her body shaking like an aspen tree.

She realized she was moving awkwardly toward him up the slight rise, as if walking were suddenly unnatural to her. One foot after the other, her hands held rigidly at her sides like a soldier . . .

"Mermaid."

She closed her eyes. One word. Nothing else. Not a greeting, nor a sentiment, nor even a polite inquiry after her health. Only the one word that stripped every piece of skin from her body and left her feeling so vulnerable that her clothing seemed to slowly choke her and even the very air hurt.

When she opened her eyes she found he was smiling, the slow, arrogant, vivid smile that could change so readily from a predatory wariness into real amusement. The laughter was there now, hidden behind the furl of dark lashes. She felt the brilliance of his gaze shred what little composure she had left, and she sought refuge in an anger that was out of all proportion to the crime.

"You didn't tell me you were coming! Why are you here? I thought you wouldn't be here for weeks!" Her voice very nearly broke on the last word, but an iron self-control saved her from an embarrassing stumble. "Why the sudden change of plans? Don't you trust me to fly the flag of the Dampier armada, Myles? Have you come to make sure that I acquit myself adequately as your wife?"

"You really are an innocent, Sabina. You've left yourself wide open to all sorts of biting wit with that last remark," he said smoothly. He dismounted with a single graceful movement and stood stroking the horse's neck while she struggled to pull herself together. But he had never played fair in the past, and she shouldn't have expected him to do so now. He barely allowed her to regain her breath before he leveled the full impact of his smile at her. Lazily, languorously, he murmured, "I thought you might be glad to see me, Mermaid."

"Of course I'm glad," she stammered. "Only . . . only I wasn't expecting you so soon. And not like this. Did you ride all the way from London?"

Myles shot her a thoughtful glance before taking the reins and leading the horse to the top of the rise. He was suddenly isolated from her, as if standing on an island of memories and thoughts, his legs braced, his arms hanging lightly at his sides, surveying the vista spread out before him with cool detachment. Only the clenched fingers revealed the cauldron of emotions bubbling inside him. "No," he said finally. "I stopped at the inn and decided to ride the rest of the way. I wanted to be on my own when I saw all this again."

So she was once more an intruder in his world. Internally, she curled up into a little tight ball. "I'm sorry. Of course. I'll go."

The whiplike quality of his voice stopped her. "I didn't mean you. You are where you should be. I realized that as soon as I saw you coming toward me from the park." He turned to smile, but it did nothing to dispel the winter from his eyes. They were as hard and brilliant as sapphires, and his expression so self-satisfied that she expected him to begin to purr at any minute. Just as a leopard might regard the bloodied body of its prey.

"Myles Dampier triumphant." She murmured the words almost inaudibly, but he caught them, and a ghost of the old self-derision returned to his expression.

"It's been fifteen years since I last saw this place, Sabina. Let me have my moment of triumph." He mounted his horse and then stretched out his hand, his eyes once more alive with laughter, his manner imperious. "Come, Queen of Sheba. Ride with me."

Automatically responding to the command in his voice, she held out her hand and was effortlessly lifted up before him, his arm clamped about her waist to steady her. It was an awkward seat, but she was conscious only of the warmth of his body at her back, of the ironlike grip that held her to him, of the warm breath that stirred the hair at the base of her neck. She closed her eyes and prayed that she hadn't just made a very grave mistake.

"We will look like a couple of gypsies entering the courtyard," she said a little unsteadily.

"Do you care?"

"No, but you did. Isn't that the reason I arrived here like the Queen of Sheba? We even fought over it. After all your careful plans to establish our *consequence*, I find it a little strange."

"There is an old saying in this part of the world, Sabina. 'Rich men have no faults.' Perhaps I want to find out how much our consequence can survive."

She ignored the cynicism of his tone, and, seduced by the warmth of his hold, she finally relaxed against his body, snuggling her head beneath his chin. She heard a sudden indrawn breath, and despite her precarious seat, twisted to look at him curiously.

"Am I making you uncomfortable?"

"For the last two months, Mermaid." He grinned as her forehead creased in confusion, and added softly, "Turn around before I do something that will shock the horse."

She continued to regard him warily, before twisting in her seat to peer over the horse's head. "Well, this must be the first time you've worried about shocking *anyone*."

"As you reminded me, I have my consequence to think of now I am returned to Norfolk.

"Talking of consequence," she said for the sake of something to say, "Lady Vantry called to see me not an hour past."

"I know. I saw her carriage arrive."

Sabina looked down at the arm that held her securely to him. He had rolled up his sleeves, and she idly noted the hairs on the muscular forearm, and the light touch of the long brown fingers on the reins. There was a series of small scars just above his wrist that she had never noticed before. Probably because she had never been this close to him before. Not relaxed, and quietly alone together. She wanted to reach out and touch the scars, ask about them, but her courage failed her and instead she inquired coolly, "How long have you been here?"

"A few hours."

"And you never thought to call? Or were you too busy being master of all you surveyed?"

"Something like that, Mermaid. I see your tongue has lost none of its pertness."

"I met Sir Richard Dampier."

She didn't know why she blurted it out like that. The horse plunged slightly, its head tossing alarmingly, and then it was still.

"So Charles told me." His voice was calm, almost sweetly so, and Sabina cursed the fact that she could not see his face without twisting herself into a knot. "Did you like him? I feel sure that you did."

"Very much so. He is a proper gentleman. He felt the awkwardness of the situation, but was brave enough to . . . to take the bull by the horns." She waited nervously for a reply to this statement, adding abruptly, "He wants a reconciliation, Myles. If you could only meet him and judge for yourself how sorry he is for . . . everything in the past. I could tell that he feels dreadfully for what you went through, although it's hardly his fault that he inherited a fortune while you were stripped of yours. And . . . and if he happened to fall in love with . . . with your Juliet, well, it's not always possible to fall in love by a set of rules, you know. You can't always choose who you will love and who you won't. And I'm sorry to say, but Lady Dampier doesn't sound like the sort of person who would follow *anyone* to the ends of the earth."

The silence that followed this outburst was broken only by the sound of hoof upon earth. Finally Sabina could stand no more.

"Myles!"

"What did you say, Mermaid? I'm sorry. You must forgive me, but I was so taken with the image of the impeccable Richard confronting a horned bull that I lost the rest of it."

"Why did you come back here if you did not wish to see him again?"

"Of course I wish to see him again, my dear. In fact, there is nothing I want more than to meet my esteemed cousin again. What is the quote I am thinking of? 'To mourn a mischief that is past and gone, is the next way to draw new mischief on'?"

She did not need to see his face to recognize the lethal combination of sugar and poison in his voice.

"You are impossible," she said tiredly. To pursue the topic would get her little results other than the barbed end of Myles's wit. In an attempt to shock him out of his complacency, she demanded, "Did you know that your base-born son is in residence at the Hall?"

"Ah, yes. The street urchin from St. Giles." He sounded far from shocked, adding in a good-humored tone, "He seems to have followed me home like a stray mongrel. Charles told me about him."

"Mr. Charles seems to have told you a great deal. I didn't realize I would be traveling with your *spy.*" She regretted the waspish tone in her voice, but the idea that the courier had presented her husband with a report on everything that had transpired on the journey was galling. "I don't want to send Gammon back, Myles. It would be too cruel. I want to find a place for him here at the Hall."

"As you wish," he replied easily. "Although you may want to count the silver periodically."

"Oh, he won't steal from you. He seems to think you are some sort of demigod with all sorts of divine powers." She was careful to inject just the slightest note of incredulity into her voice.

"Out of the mouth of babes. What a very perceptive child. How old is he? Does he know?"

"Well, he insists he is six, but he is obviously older."

"That, my dear Sabina, is because the official hanging age is seven. I've no doubt young . . . Gammon, is it? . . . has been six at least these four or five years to stave off the threat of the gallows."

This time she did squirm around to face him, making sure that he was not indulging in some horrible joke. But the sculptured features were hard and humorless, his mouth a grim line against the tanned skin. "Do you mean to tell me that they hang seven-year-old children?" she demanded.

"By the time they are spewed out of Newgate or the hulks, they are usually eight or nine. But most often their youth is a ticket to New South Wales instead." He stared down into her shocked face, his own suddenly softening. "I'm sorry. I should have made up some pleasant fairy tale. But I can't protect you from the entire world, Mermaid."

"I didn't know! Myles, someone should do something! How wrong that is!"

"Someone intends to try, Sabina. When my own . . . affairs are settled, I mean to try."

His voice assumed the bland tone she had come to recognize as a no trespassing sign, but his arm automatically tightened to secure her more firmly to his body. She turned her head, conscious once more of their surroundings. The Hall house loomed up at them through the trees of the park, the physical decay clearly evident.

The horse faltered in its steady walk, throwing its handsome head up several times as if in disapproval at what he saw. Sabina felt the tautening of Myles's tall body, and she stiffened in sympathy.

"You won't be too disappointed, will you?" she asked urgently. It was suddenly important that he wasn't. This, she understood, was his real homecoming. Not finally reaching English shores, or walking the streets of London, or even riding the fen lands of Norfolk. But this—returning to the home of his childhood, where his family had laid down myth and tradition and history that stretched back hundreds of years. He was silent during their approach, and Sabina was sensitive to this need, merely placing her hand over the one that encircled her waist. He started, and then relaxed, pulling her even tighter; she wanted to believe that the feel of his lips on the curls just above her ear was intentional, not merely a result of their close proximity and the rhythmic movement of the horse.

"No. I won't be disappointed," he said finally, adding softly, "angry, delighted, maddened . . . but rarely, I think, disappointed," and they cantered into the great stone courtyard.

The news that the master had arrived at Lysons Hall spread through the house like a grass fire. Those servants whose duties kept them in the quiet underbelly of domestic life made some excuse to catch a glimpse of him; those whose duties kept them directly in his path wished it were not so.

He spent at least the first half hour striding from room

to room, his face darkened with anger. He slashed a riding whip against his fashionably tasseled Hessian boots, his sleeves pushed up to his elbows, his dark curls disheveled from the furious combing of his fingers through his hair.

Even an excited Gammon had taken one look at his hero and made himself scarce, scattering to the nether regions below stairs. Sabina was the only one who watched his frantic pacing unmoved. But she suddenly understood some of the restless drive and passion that had built Myles Dampier a maritime empire. And why some men might have cause to fear him.

"Damn that fool Bradshaw! I wouldn't lease him a pigsty! And I see that my fond cousin Richard didn't give a damn whether or not the east wing ceiling stays up or falls to the floor!" He kicked a balustrade viciously.

"It's no use yelling about it," Sabina said spiritedly. "Neither Mr. Bradshaw nor your cousin can hear you, although I'm sure everyone else within a mile radius can do so!"

Ironically, she decided to put a stop to his tirade in a set of rooms that had once been used as a nursery. The bare floors were scarred and pitted, the walls as abused as those of a fallen citadel. Sabina was inclined to think that this was the result of generations of children at play, but Myles, who no doubt remembered the Hall through a rose-colored mist almost two decades old, took slight at every blemish and disfigurement. However, her words seemed to give him pause, and she watched some of the tension drain from the powerful body. He pushed back a stray lock of hair from his forehead, his expression still unremittingly grim.

"I'm sorry, Sabina. But damn it to hell! I didn't imagine it would be this bad."

"It's not. It's shabby and neglected, not ruined. And no amount of swearing will make it better than it is. Stop acting the part of the Robber King and . . . and try to behave!"

He stopped and stared at her as if seeing her for the

first time in hours. One dark eyebrow quirked in comic disbelief at her tone.

"Why, Mrs. Dampier, you sound exactly like my old governess." A wide piratical grin suddenly unfurled across his face, dispelling the anger. "If I remember, she was small like you, dark, and not . . . unattractive. And in every way, superior."

Sabina covered her relief at this change in his humor by making a small curtsy and saying lightly, "*Merci du compliment*, Mr. Dampier. You remind me that I most probably missed my calling in life."

"Not at all, Mermaid." His voice was suddenly like thickened honey, slowly and sweetly pouring over her. "I thought we had sorted all that out on the *Ellen Drury*. Your calling in life is to fill this room with children. My children."

He moved toward her with the speed of a predator, lithely and easily, his hands at her waist, his dark face only inches from her own. She had not expected that half elegant, half wild body to be so close to hers, demanding a response to the touch of his fingers as they slid in a long, controlled movement down the stiffened material of her gown, crushing it in his hands, gathering her in to meet him.

Not now. Not in the middle of inspecting his beloved Hall, not in the middle of the afternoon, and definitely *not* in the middle of an abandoned nursery. His attempts at seduction had always been about power and persuasion and possession, not simple need. Or love. Or even procreation. And now . . .

She just didn't care.

She watched with an almost detached interest as her hands moved to his chest, where her fingers began to play with the fine lawn of his open shirt, pushing aside the material so that she could tease out the dark hair beneath it. She heard him expel a ragged breath. One brown hand imprisoned her own in a crushing grip, while the other jerked her chin up so that she stared into the blue eyes. There was no calculation there, no cool attempt at manipulation. Instead they were dark with hunger and invitation, and they traveled over her face and body with a possessiveness that made her feel as if the floor had fallen away beneath her. Or possibly, like the east wing, the roof had collapsed on top of her. Either way, the simple act of inhaling seemed an impossibility.

Dear God, she wanted to be with him so much. In every way.

"You want to begin filling the room now?" she finally whispered.

"Now. Here. On the moon. Anywhere. I want you, Mermaid." She watched his eyes roam over her face and travel down her body, and she felt as if it had been painted with fire. "Just looking at you makes me feel I've never properly looked at a woman before. God knows I never wanted anyone as much as I want you at this moment."

What about Sylvia?

She wanted to say to say the words, but somehow her tongue seemed to cleave to the roof of her mouth, and then he moved her hand slowly across the hardness of his chest, burning her flesh like a brand onto his. And suddenly it didn't matter.

I want you. Not "I love you." But it might be enough. It might just have to be enough.

Tentatively she reached up on tiptoe to place her lips softly against his. His head jerked back in surprise, then lowered swiftly so that their mouths met in a silent joining that made her entire body ache with a sudden undefined need. She pulled her hands from his grip, only to throw them around his neck, and his mouth ground against hers in a movement that was half fierce, half tender.

Closer. She needed to be closer still.

As if in answer to her unspoken desire, his hands went to her hips, pulling her body along the length of his own, then slowly lifting her so that she was pressed urgently against the hardness of his need, her arms still encircling his neck, her mouth moving from his, to the strong line of his jaw, to the base of his neck, where a small pulse beat like a rapid tattoo.

"Damn this new fashion for full skirts," he groaned against her ear. "Take them off."

"Not here." She didn't quite know where those cautious words came from. Certainly not from her traitorous body, which would have instantly shed its skin upon the floor if he had asked her to. "Not here, Myles. Please."

"Unless we can get to a room with a bed in the next few minutes, Sabina, it's going to be here."

She shook her head helplessly. "I don't think I can move. My legs won't work."

He grinned down at her, his face dark with desire, his eyes glittering with a possessive triumph that slid down her body like warm, sweet honey. "Spoken like a true mermaid, my sweet."

He swept her up from the floor in a movement that was as swift as it was efficient, and sent the door crashing open, striding from the room with ruthless haste. It was a noisy seduction, the quick tread of his boots echoing down the uncarpeted hall, his breathing labored, not with exertion but with passion. A passion *she* had ignited. It was not a golden ghost but she, Sabina Grey, who was making this strong, enigmatic man act like a besotted lover. She reveled in her power, tightening her hold about his neck and brushing her lips against the hard angle of his jaw, tasting the salty flavor of his skin on the tip of her tongue. He didn't falter, but his stride lengthened, and disdaining the stairs, he turned sharply into a bedchamber, kicking the door closed and depositing her on the threadbare covers with a gentleness that was all the more unexpected given the evidence of his impatient desire.

She raised herself on her elbows, laughter and desire mingling together in her voice, as he put one knee on the bed to steady himself and began unbuttoning her tight-fitting bodice with expert fingers.

"There are twelve buttons on each sleeve, as well, Myles. If I had known you were so proficient at this, I would never have hired Maria."

"You could talk under water," he said through gritted teeth. The thin material gave way under his hands, and her corseted flesh was exposed to his searing gaze. Gently he touched the top of one white breast, and his breath, expelled in a ragged explosion dragged from the depths of his chest, wiped away any lingering amusement.

Sabina had never been so vibrantly aware of her own body before.

Until this moment, it had merely been something to be clothed, and fed, and kept clean and warm; it walked and talked and appeared to give people pleasure to look at. Now she was aware of every inch of her own skin, burning and tingling under the blue brilliance of his gaze; of bone and muscle and blood and the slow, even beating of her heart.

She had never felt so . . . so *raw*.

Unconsciously she moved, arching herself toward him in unspoken invitation, and then lowered herself to the bed, her eyes fixed on the wild, passionate face hovering above her.

He was poised on the edge of the bed, one knee still on the cover. Then he slid his body so that he was crouched before her, once more the predator, his eyes stripping her of the gown and petticoats that weighed her down like a sea anchor. He placed his hands on the lace chemise just beneath her breasts and using his thumbs began to softly stroke the rounded softness still hidden within.

Her back rose from the bed in surprise.

"What did you just do?" she gasped.

He smiled, a sensuous, primitive smile that made the breath catch in the back of her throat, and then his hand spread over one hardening nipple, pushing down the lace until her breast was exposed to his burning gaze.

"Do you like it? Do you like me touching you, Mermaid?"

She murmured her pleasure, a fire spreading from her breast to her thighs like a cooling river of lava, and waited for his practiced hand to continue its slow, torturous caresses. He gently kneaded the other breast until the nipple hardened beneath his fingers, and then, apparently

183

satisfied, bent his head until his breath was only a heart-beat away from the pink bud. He blew softly, and she gasped at the uncontrolled ripple of sensation.

"Myles . . ." She breathed his name like a prayer, and the face he raised to hers was that of a fallen angel, the blue eyes at once innocent and blazing. Half saint, half devil, and thoroughly human . . .

"What is it, Mermaid?"

"Nothing. Nothing at all."

"Nothing, is it? Then I mustn't be doing it right."

And this time he lowered his mouth to her breast, his tongue making hot darting forays that caused her hands to curl into small talons and bury themselves in the dark luxury of his hair.

"Myles!"

There was a demand in her voice that he instinctively responded to, his hands moving to her arms, anchoring them to the bed while his tall body adjusted itself to her writhing form.

"Tell me you want me, Sabina. Tell me you want me as much as I want you. Tell me now."

"I . . ." She couldn't speak, could only look up into the dark, beautiful face beseechingly, her head moving from side to side as she fought to confirm and yet deny the unfamiliar sensations that made her weak with yearning.

He smiled, a slow, satisfied smile, and lowered his head, his mouth meeting hers in a kiss that was unexpectedly tender, his lips nibbling her, his tongue delicate in its gentle probing. He released her arms, and unthinkingly she wrapped them around him, feeling the tempered steel of the muscles beneath his shirt and the heat that ema-nated from his body like a blacksmith's forge. He contin-ued to nuzzle at her, exploring the corners of her mouth, teasing her lips until she opened them, and his tongue flickered in, probing and tasting until it met hers in an elemental rhythm that promised a completion beyond anything she had ever experienced before.

Saint and devil. Salvation and damnation. Everything was being offered to her on this shabby bed in a disused chamber of a decaying house. Everything in the world had shrunk to the size of the bed, to their two bodies, suddenly entwined, her petticoats bunched up about her thighs as he began a thorough exploration of her hips and buttocks, easing his hand into the silken recesses of her pantaloons.

Slowly, expertly, he touched her, and the roof collapsed on top of her once more, this time throwing her into a vortex that seemed to consist of darkness and shattering light. She shook with sensation after sensation, crying out against the prison of his mouth.

Myles turned his face against hers, his eyes drugged with passion as he watched the ecstasy rake through her pliant body.

"Be my wife, Mermaid. Tell me you are ready to be my wife." It was not a plea. The demand was all too evident beneath the hoarseness.

"I love you, Myles," she said quietly.

And all at once the world stopped.

His body froze, locked in an attitude that reminded her of the dying gladiator beside the carriageway.

When he finally moved, it was to swing his legs over the side of the bed, his back turned away from her, his posture such a complete rejection that she put her fist to her mouth to jam back the whimper she felt rising in her throat.

"Myles." She stretched out her hand, but he sat motionless and silent. Only the ragged rise and fall of his chest indicated that he was moved in any way by what had just occurred. She struggled into a sitting position, mindful of that first encounter so many weeks ago on the *Ellen Drury*. But surely it was all changed. Her rejection of him, his manipulation. They were man and wife now. And, God help her, she loved him.

"Myles. What have I done? Please tell me. Don't turn away from me like this. Whatever happened . . . I'm sorry."

Was he disgusted at her wantonness? Should she have lain pliant and still beneath him, her face screwed up in abhorrence? Perhaps that was what he expected from a wife.

He stood up and walked to the door. For one terrible moment, Sabina thought he would open it and leave her, stripping her of any shred of dignity she might have left. But he didn't. Instead he spread his arms wide like an injured eagle, clutching at the door frame, his head bowed, his broad shoulders taut as if expecting a rain of blows.

He looked like a man tied to a whipping post.

His voice, when he spoke, came from a thousand miles away. "It's not what you've done, Mermaid. It's what *I've* done. God rot my soul for the selfish bastard I am. I'm the one who's sorry. More than you can know."

She shook her head, trying to understand his descent into self-loathing. The misery welled up inside her and threatened to overflow in hot, scalding tears.

"It's because I said I loved you, isn't it? That was my mistake. But you must have known I did. Why else would I have married you in the first place? Why would I be on this bed with you if I didn't love you, Myles?"

He turned to look at her, his face a granite mask. The brown skin seemed tightly stretched over the clean, spare angles of jaw and brow, giving his features a hard, shuttered appearance. His eyes, which only minutes before had seared her with their ardor, were now remotely crystalline in their indifference.

The Stranger had returned. She could not bear to look at him.

She shifted awkwardly, realizing that once again she lay in front of Myles Dampier in a pose of wanton abandonment, her skirts bunched up around her legs, her bodice wide open, her hair tumbling around her shoulders like a common hedge drab. And at this moment, that was exactly what she felt like. She began to button up the tight-fitting bodice of her gown with trembling fingers; her hands were shaking like an old palsied woman, and she bit back a small sob at her incompetence.

Long fingers brushed hers away, and she was too ex-

hausted to resist, leaning listlessly against the pillows, her
eyes shut tightly in an effort to close out his image, while
he leaned over her and rebuttoned them with damning
efficiency. He straightened and remarked coolly, "It's getting late, Sabina. I want to see the rest of the Hall before
dark. I take it you won't wish to accompany me."

His colorless tone suddenly whipped her into anger,
and she opened her eyes to glare up into the cold, handsome face.

"You'd like that, wouldn't you, Myles Dampier? You'd
like me to go and sulk in my room while you go off and
play Lord of the Manor, stewing in your own misery!"

One sardonic eyebrow flew up. "Perhaps you are right,
Sabina. But perhaps after this little farce, I deserve to . . .
er . . . stew."

"Don't you dare leave this room!"

"Is that a threat, Mrs. Dampier? Do I detect an 'or else'
somewhere in that command?"

She shook her head, trying to deflect the knife wound
of his contempt. "No, Myles. I don't seem to be very good
at ultimatums. I haven't your experience in issuing them.
But I think I deserve some explanation after what . . .
nearly . . . happened. I'm your wife! Isn't this what you
wanted? Lysons Hall, a wife, children . . . and all the normal, ordinary, beautiful things that you lost so many years
ago." He was silent, his mouth a thin, forbidding line in
a face that had suddenly paled beneath the tan, and she
continued ruthlessly, "Did you think I would give you children without love? Did you expect me to live without love?
Without normal human affection? You said you wanted a
normal marriage. Isn't love part of a normal marriage?
Love and *trust?*"

She pounded her fists on the bed, then slid from its
grimy covers to confront him, her fingers still curled into
her palms like a small prizefighter. She had expected him
to show anger at her words, using his biting wit to engage
swords with her; instead he appeared suddenly bleached,
his eyes narrowed into brilliant blue slits, his face a death
mask of the man she loved.

When he spoke, it was as if she were listening to a ghost.

"Trust, Sabina? You expect me to give you trust? Even though I once warned you not to expect anything from me? Well, why not? You are everything you appear to be, aren't you, my sweet? Honest, gallant, fierce in your protection for those you love . . . I daresay there isn't a dissembling bone in your body. Do you want to hear about trust, little Pandora? I see from the way you wrinkle your brow so charmingly that you do. Then I'll tell you about it."

She took a step backward, groping for the poster of the bed. It was something—anything!—to hang on to, but she remained silent, dully pressing her cheek into the carved wood, relishing the discomfort. It would anchor her to reality, a reality that was fast slipping into the realm of nightmare.

Myles watched her, a curious pity spreading over his features, before turning away to examine the chimney-piece.

"I trusted once before, Mermaid. I trusted where I loved. People I . . . loved. That trust landed me in hell." He paused and added grimly, "I understand why a soldier will often bear no rancor toward his enemy after a war is over. It's because they are faceless strangers to each other. A stranger plunging a bayonet into you is a lot less hateful than a friend, my dear."

"Please, Myles. I can't . . . I have no power over that." Wearily she turned her head from side to side, bleeding inside from the pain in his voice. "I can't do anything about the past, and neither can you. Please let it be."

"You want to know why I can't let go of the past, Sabina?" His voice was mellow, beautiful, like thick, dark honey. He had used the same voice when he made love to her. Now it sounded like an obscenity, a paean to revenge. "There's a line from Shakespeare that I used to repeat over and over when I was at the penal colony of King's Town, digging coal and carrying lime until my back blistered and burst. 'What's past is prologue.' I thought of that when I prepared my return to England, planning how I would deal with the people who had betrayed my trust. You think I'm obsessed? Perhaps I am. It's what saved me, Sabina. It saved my sanity and it saved my life." He looked at her directly, and a crooked grin suddenly broke across the stark lines of the mask. He added with a dark semblance of humor, "As worthless a commodity as my life may be, *love* didn't get me out of there in one piece. Hate did."

The silence in the room stretched until Sabina thought she would scream with the pain of it. But she was unable to move a muscle.

Instead she clung to the bedpost and watched the man she loved plunge back into the darkness of his past. She could not reach him.

"Myles . . ." She said his name once more, and her voice, brittle as glass, seemed to shatter the unnatural stillness.

He lifted his head, the rawness of his stare stripping her of the last protective layer.

"It wasn't my uncle who betrayed me, Sabina," he said softly. "Oh, he certainly participated. He used every bit of influence he had to make sure I was safely got out of the way. And he didn't have to dirty his fine, white hands with the details. The Crown did it for him, so that he could sleep the sleep of the just every night for the rest of his hypocritical, self-satisfied life. But *his* isn't the real betrayal, Sabina. I always knew he would do me an injury if he could. He made no secret of that fact."

He left his position by the fireplace and moved to where she clung to the bedpost. She didn't flinch as one elegant finger traced the tears that were streaming down her cheeks. She hadn't even been aware of them, and now stood helplessly as she watched him lift his finger to his mouth, tasting the saltiness with a wry lift of his lips.

"Don't cry, Mermaid. None of us are worth it, you know. I'm certainly not. And neither is your admired Richard. You see, he was the only one I trusted with our secret—the secret that Sylvia and I meant to elope that night. My cousin and best friend. Who else would I trust? He even lent me the money for the carriage. Of course, I didn't realize at the time he looked on that as a clever investment in the future. He betrayed us, and then stood by and let them convict me without so much as lifting a finger in my defense. I couldn't understand it at the time—why he didn't come to see me, why my father turned purple every time I mentioned his name. I thought Uncle John might have forbidden it. Richard was always a dutiful son, even if it meant treachery toward his friends. And then I learned that he was in love with Sylvia, himself." He drew in a deep shuddering breath, and leaned his forehead wearily against hers, so that the warmth of his words feathered the curls about her face. "I was rotting in a hulk on the Thames some three months later, when that information was relayed to me. By then, nothing came as a surprise."

"Don't," she whispered, and pushed him away. It was a futile gesture, and his hands moved out to grasp her arms, pulling her away from her crutch and into his arms. It was a dreadful parody of the way he had held her such a short time before. This time the passion in his face was distorted and ugly. She closed her eyes so that she could block it out.

"You can't believe that a gentleman could find himself in such circumstances, can you, my dear? With all of the cheerful corruption of our noble British justice system, I could have bought my way out, couldn't I? Or at least enjoyed privileges that the scum of the earth were not entitled to? My uncle made sure I disappeared into pitch-black darkness. If he had to grease a palm or two, he made sure it happened. In the end, he secured an heiress for his son, and rid himself of both a brother and a nephew who were stains on the peerless name of Dampier. And Richard found that a little treachery could be a fine thing."

There was so much revulsion, so much contempt in his voice that she knew the answer to a question that had been fluttering at the edges of her mind for weeks.

"Is that why you flaunted yourself at the opera? To

make sure the whole world knew you had returned? To create a scandal? To shame the Dampiers?"

"You always do learn quickly, don't you, Sabina? Yes. Something like that."

She was past shock now. The tears cascaded unchecked down her face. She was astonished at how calmly she could ask, "Why me? If you wanted to drag the family name through the mud, why not marry some doxy from the stews? Why marry me, when you could as easily have given me a bag of guineas and sent me on my way? Why fret about whether or not I am received by your neighbors? I don't understand!" Her voice cracked with hurt, and she dug her nails into her palms to stop herself from dragging them down the lean, angry planes of his face.

His words were cudgel blows.

"I told you why. I'll create my own dynasty, Sabina. On my own terms. Not society's. My sons won't be cringing, whining sycophants, manipulated by a pack of puling idiots. You could make this the center of society. You have everything a great hostess needs—beauty, breeding, and intelligence. The fact that your birth is humble need not worry you or anyone else. There's not a woman in England could hold a candle to you if you set your mind to it."

"Except one."

His eyes narrowed. He didn't pretend to misunderstand. He released her, and she felt herself sinking to the ground like a wounded animal, her legs entirely useless.

"She is nothing to me now."

"Nothing? You wear her memory like armor! Whether you love her or hate her, Myles Dampier, she is as much a part of your life as she ever was! While I . . . I have no place. It is I who have *nothing!*"

The admission caught in her throat, and she felt that she was choking on some heavy lump that wouldn't move. She put her face to her hands, and then the lump disappeared in a noisy burst of weeping that doubled her over the pool of crushed skirts and, when it was past, left her weak and gasping.

He was still there when she finally raised her face from her hands. He stood and watched her like a palace sentinel, expressionless, unmoved. Only the clenched hands and the set of his taut shoulders indicated that he was in any way affected by her misery.

"What do you plan to do?" She pushed back the damp curls from her face, her voice that of an old woman.

"Destroy Richard Dampier."

"How?"

She tried to struggle to her feet, her petticoats impeding her already jerky movements. Myles knelt down to help, but she shook off his hand, withdrawing from him like a kicked dog. He straightened and observed her quietly for several seconds before answering.

"If you have some vague idea of preventing it, Sabina, disabuse yourself of the notion now. Marney has been an efficient tool. You were right not to trust him. He would skin a flea to make a rug and sell it to his own mother. But in matters of . . . finance he has no peer. Richard Dampier is a ruined man. Within a year or two, Curstone Abbey will be mine."

"What do you plan to do with it?"

"Pull it down brick by brick." His tone was pleasant, even congenial.

She had given up trying to get to her feet. She sat where she was, feeling like a broken marionette whose strings had been cut.

Myles had been right. There were some things that would have been better undiscovered. Poor Pandora. And poor Sabina, finding out too late that ignorance was bliss. She raised her face to where he loomed over her, all his elegant male beauty and wild grace suddenly more dangerous to her than it had ever been before.

"I knew you were consumed with hate, but I didn't understand that it had turned you into a monster."

"Can you love a monster, Sabina?"

"No," she lied.

"Good. Then we have made some progress today."

She was still on the floor long after the door had quietly closed.

CHAPTER NINE

Myles's method of dealing with the tempest in the disused bedchamber was to continue with life as if it had never happened. He treated her with the distant courtesy that she was owed as Mrs. Dampier of Lysons Hall, politely smiling down the length of the dinner table at her and listening pleasantly when she had anything to say to him.

He was elegant, civil, and kind. Exactly the type of husband she had once dreamed of marrying. And she was terrified that she would remain married for life to this courteous stranger.

Dazedly she responded in kind, avoiding his physical presence as much as she could, which, in a house the size of the Hall, was mercifully easy. And if at night his footsteps lingered in front of her bedchamber before stomping off in the direction of his own, she was usually able to stuff a pillow over her head until she was sure he was gone.

So she was surprised when he appeared one morning at breakfast dressed for riding in a tight green jacket that set off the breadth of his shoulders to perfection. His neckcloth was starched and intricately folded, his tasseled boots polished to a fashionable gloss.

He acknowledged her raised eyebrows with a grin. "The joys of employing a valet, Mermaid. Seton weeps tears of blood if I attempt to shrug myself into a jacket without his assistance."

"You look every inch the English country gentleman, Mr. Dampier," she said dryly, spearing a kipper with her fork. She observed it with unaccustomed concentration, asking disinterestedly, "Are you riding this morning?"

"I want you to come with me."

The kipper was returned untouched to her plate. "I don't ride," she said coldly.

"You told me you did."

"No. *You* told me I did. I don't remember ever mentioning it."

"Then I'll teach you. I know you have a riding habit— I settled the bill for it. Go put it on."

"I don't want . . ." She stopped before she could complete the sentence, acknowledging to herself that she actually *did* want. She wanted very much.

"Thank you. I accept. But are you going to be able to teach me from a distance of five yards? That's about as near as you've come to me in the last week."

"I'll wear gloves. And I'll keep my eyes closed," he said dryly. "I'll meet you in the inner courtyard in twenty minutes."

She lowered her head, ashamed of the tears that suddenly pooled in her eyes. "I've missed you," she finally admitted, but when she raised her head, the room was empty.

And breakfast, congealing on her plate, was suddenly very unappealing. She stumbled up the stairs, careful not to take them two at a time in her unnatural haste and fought back her growing excitement. But it finally bubbled over when Maria helped her into the riding habit of dark gray wool and placed her hat jauntily over one eye, fixing it with pins. It was a delightful affair of felt and

194

feathers, and Sabina couldn't help feeling that if she didn't end up sprawled on the ground somewhere, she would make a very good showing of fashionable horsemanship. And she would not be the brown hen to Myles's magnificence!

She stopped long enough to give a slice of apple to Jezebel, who, no doubt belatedly realizing her importance as the mistress's pet, had lately forsaken the kitchens and taken up residence in her rooms. Sabina touched the little creature with a gentle finger and murmured, "Do you sometimes wish to be back on the *Ellen Drury*?"

"Beg pardon, ma'am?"

"I was speaking to the monkey."

"Sorry I'm sure," Maria said curtly, but there was a look in her glance that went beyond surly. If Sabina didn't know better, she would have described it as concern.

"It's all right, Maria. I'm not losing my mind," she said frankly.

"No, ma'am. It's just that those are the first words I've heard you say to *anybody* in days." And her maid collected a bundle of petticoats from the bed and disappeared into the dressing room, trailing a cloud of injured feelings.

Sabina was tempted to call after her and hotly remonstrate, but an innate honesty stilled her. It was true. For the past few days she had been withdrawn and remote, brushing past Gammon with a distant smile and a few kind words, repulsing Mrs. Ferris's attempts to involve her in domestic issues, and penning a polite refusal to dine with the Vantrys. She bit her lip as the enormity of her behavior sank in.

She was behaving like the wilting heroine of a three-volume novel rather than the mistress of a large estate.

She studied her image candidly in the long mirror and tried to look at herself as Myles must see her. Regular features, brown hair, green eyes . . . all very ordinary, really, when everything was said and done. What was it about her, then, that had set her husband alight like a powder keg, ready to explode at her slightest touch?

What was it that had caused him to abandon her in the

middle of the bed like an importuning doxy?

An unflattering mixture of humiliation and confusion stared out at her from glittering eyes. She raised an uncertain hand to her cheek. Had she looked like that in the bedroom? Was that the face that had confronted Myles?

No wonder he had thought himself a monster.

She closed her eyes, fighting back the pain that threatened to resurface. At least he no longer avoided her like a leprous house guest. He had made the first move toward some sort of reconciliation. Today—this morning—she would find out the answers to all her questions. And, God willing, today she would finally understand.

A footman stopped her before she could leave the Great Hall for the inner courtyard.

"Begging your pardon, ma'am, but Mr. Dampier requests that you come to the library. You have a visitor."

She stifled a vexed exclamation, disappointed that her time alone with her husband would be delayed, and yet, at the same time, filled with a natural curiosity. Who on earth would be calling on the Pariah Dampiers so early in the morning?

She waited until the footman flung open the library doors, collecting the long train of her habit in one gloved hand before she swept elegantly into the room. And once there, stood frozen in shock.

Her husband's visitor was none other than Sir Richard Dampier.

He stood as he had at their first meeting, his hands nervously held behind his back, his face a picture of indecision. Yet there was a certain courageous determination painted on his pale features which, after her first stunned reaction, drew her reluctant admiration.

Treacherous he may be, but he was not a coward.

It would have taken a fair amount of boldness to face his cousin in his own lair. Particularly as Myles, resplendent in his elegant riding clothes, his whip held tautly in his gloved hands, was the very representation of male strength and vibrancy. If she had entered the room as a stranger, she would have sworn that *Richard* was the returned prodigal, doubtful of his position in polite society.

Of course, Myles held the floor. He could not have stage-managed it any better to suit his purposes. His cousin was somehow backed against the fireplace between the great oak desk and a settee, cornered like a deer. Myles's face, however, was a study in amiability. Only the bright luminosity of the cornflower eyes warned Sabina that every emotion had been placed under powerful control.

"My love," Myles purred. He took her by the arm and drew her into the warm circle of his smile, announcing happily, "We have unexpected company. Unexpected, but most welcome. You must allow me to present to you my cousin, Sir Richard Dampier. Richard, this is my wife, Sabina."

"Mrs. Dampier and I have already met," Richard said frankly, bowing over her outstretched hand. "I . . . I was just explaining to your husband why I have taken the liberty of calling on you, Mrs. Dampier. I know I should have merely left my card, but it seemed such . . . such a *cold* thing to do, under the circumstances." Eyes the familiar color of bluebells and sapphires stared beseechingly into hers. "When you didn't call, I thought . . . of course it is a presumption on my part, but when I heard that Myles had returned . . ." he drew a deep breath and finished bravely, "whatever my reception, I knew I must make the first move." He dropped her hand and turned awkwardly to his cousin, adding, "This has been difficult for both of us . . . all of us, I should say. I understand that there will be a certain amount of embarrassment attached to our first meeting. . . ."

"My God, Ricky! You sound as though you swallowed a damned missal!" The exclamation seemed to be an unconscious one, but its effect was the same as an arrow bolt.

Sir Richard gaped at his cousin, and then started forward, his hand extended with a boyish eagerness that touched Sabina's heart. "I'm sorry, Myles. I don't . . . I don't know what to say. All I can do is stand here and babble."

" 'Welcome home' might be a start." Myles's tone was deceptively mild.

"You must know that you are! Lord, I've thought about this moment so many times. I even rehearsed everything I was going to say, but . . ." Richard stopped, a fugitive smile appearing. "It's been such a long time."

"Fifteen years, Ricky. Fifteen years . . . and three months."

The silence that met Myles's words seemed to stretch into infinity. Sabina, watching the faces of the two men, made a small movement to leave, but her husband's hand tightened around her arm like a vise, holding her prisoner. She studied his stormy profile, noting the hard set of his jaw and the sweep of dark lashes that disguised his expression.

He was reliving it all, she realized in growing horror. Everything. Right now. Right before his cousin's innocent, boyish gaze. She didn't understand how the baronet couldn't see it . . . and couldn't sense his cousin's pain. To her it was as palpable as her own heartbeat.

Sabina tensed, ready to break the long, painful silence with an incoherent plea, but Richard suddenly spoke, his voice hoarse with lost years. "You know I'm sorry for what happened." And then, as if realizing the insufficiency of his words, he asked tightly, "Would you have come back if my father were still alive?"

"Oh, yes. I still would have come back." Soft words, wearing a scorpion's tail. "This is my home, after all. It always was, no matter what ends of the earth I happened to be at."

Sir Richard seemed to be a drowning man, his mouth moving nervously. "Yes, it is," he declared stoutly. "I never thought of it as anything else. I'm sorry it's in such a state of disrepair. My father leased it to Thomas Bradshaw after . . . after your father died." He said with some difficulty, "The rumor was that he used the family portraits for target practice. I hope it wasn't true."

"Oh, it was true, all right. Luckily, Bradshaw couldn't hit a cow at three paces. I'm still digging bullets out of walls." Myles turned to a sideboard, his good humor apparently restored. "Will you take a glass of Madeira with me, Ricky? To celebrate my homecoming. Ah, but I forget. You don't drink before noon, do you?"

"I'll make an exception this time." Richard accepted a glass with pleasure and had raised it halfway to his lips when his host asked solicitously, "And how is Sylvia?"

The dark liquid slopped over the rim, and Richard jumped back with a dismayed exclamation. "Clumsy! How very clumsy!"

Sabina wrenched her arm from Myles's hold and went to their guest, taking the glass from his loosened grasp and extracting a handkerchief from her sleeve to blot up some of the wine spilled on his jacket.

Myles Dampier looked like the cat who had stolen the cream. She wanted to throw something at his smug, handsome face.

"You must not mind, Sir Richard. Anything spilled on this floor can only be an improvement." She cast her husband a darkling glance and then turned to smile up into his cousin's blanched features. "Neither Myles nor I have lived in England for some years now. It's always difficult to return and pick up where one left off, isn't it? Myself, I find it difficult to understand the English notion of hospitality when I compare it to the Latin countries. If we were in Brazil, for instance, we would beg you to stay for both luncheon and dinner, convince you to spend the night with us, and then send you away with a suckling pig tucked under your arm!"

Sir Richard goggled down at her, clearly grateful, but seemingly confused by this suggestion. "No! Really, Mrs. Dampier—Sabina!—I don't need a—"

A loud shout of genuine laughter made the two heads turn toward Myles in surprise. He had relaxed against the sideboard, his arms crossed, his legs braced, the brown face alight with amusement untouched by shadows.

"Don't worry, Ricky. My wife is not about to load you

down with livestock. She is attempting to put me in my place—in a roundabout sort of way. She is teaching me the first rule of hospitality. *Don't torture one's guests.*"

Sir Richard's confusion seemed to deepen for a moment, and then his brow cleared. "Oh, it was a *joke.* I'm sorry to be so slow. As you can tell, Myles always left me behind in such things." He smiled at Sabina, his pinched countenance softening. "I really came to keep you to your word, Mrs. Dampier. My wife is eager to meet you. That is the purpose of my morning visit. I want you to dine with us on Thursday evening."

"Why wait so long? What about tonight?" Myles interjected coolly. He unwrapped his long body from its position on the sideboard and stood up, bearing down on his wife and cousin, so that they formed a tight triangle in the middle of the floor. "I find that I, too, am eager to . . . reconcile. As you say, it has been far too long already."

"But . . . but I was going to ask the Vantrys and the Allingtons. And there are so many who wish to—"

"Oh, no, Ricky. Not yet. I have a strange desire to dine completely *en famille.* It will be . . . a Dampier celebration."

Sabina was aware that Myles had taken complete control of the situation. He was not embarrassed. He was not at a loss for words. Like the snake and the rabbit, he made subtle suggestions while his mesmerized victim followed course.

"That is far too little notice!" she said firmly. "I am certain Lady Dampier will be wishing us to the devil."

Richard was eager to refute this suggestion. "No! Of course, she will be only too delighted . . . and if you don't mind taking us as you find us . . ."

"I wasn't expecting the fatted calf, Ricky." Myles's voice was touched with a dark humor that made the hairs lift on the back of Sabina's neck. "A cold collation will suffice. Believe me, I have dined on much worse."

There seemed little to say after that. Richard Dampier took his leave with a quiet courtesy that brought a blush of mortification to Sabina's cheeks. Myles, however, seemed thoroughly unaffected by his cousin's dignified exit. He stared thoughtfully at the closed door and stood tapping his whip lightly into the palm of his hand.

When she was sure that their visitor's footsteps had echoed beyond the Great Hall, she swung around to face him, her anger kept in check only by the greatest effort of will. Myles had taken a book from the shelves and ripped it in two. His expression was mild, but he threw the ruined volume onto the desk with a gesture of contempt.

"So much for Plutarch and the Roman Republic. I suppose I'm lucky Bradshaw didn't use the paper to wipe his . . ."

"That," she said through clenched teeth, "was unfair."

He raised one eyebrow. "Unfair? I thought I was more than fair. If this was several years ago, he wouldn't have left this room with his throat intact."

"He came to offer you his friendship!"

"And I offered him wine and refrained from killing him where he stood!"

"I wish you would be serious!"

"My dear, I am being serious."

He wasn't. He was being impossible. His eyes glittered, and his mouth was quirked in a dark, secret smile that made her blood run cold.

He was beautiful and he was lethal. For the past fifteen years he had carved out a life for himself in a land where greed and cruelty and the sting of the lash had reigned supreme. And yet, he had not only survived in that place—an indulged, gently born youth who had never before encountered hardship—he had prospered. She kept forgetting that. It took both great physical and mental strength to have conquered life there. The scars it had left on him were doubtless deeper than mere flesh.

He had once admitted to killing a man.

It had not been a boast. It had been a confession painfully wrung from him when she had pushed him back into the darkness of his past. And now she feared that he was ready to do battle with that darkness.

She wondered if this time it would prove an uneven match.

"Where are you going?"

His voice checked her in mid stride across the room. She answered briefly, without turning around, "To my room."

"I thought I was going to teach you to ride."

She swung around to face him, surprising something in his face that made her stop and raise her hands to her lips in an involuntary movement.

If she didn't know better, she would have sworn that there was some sort of entreaty in those remarkable eyes. A pleading which left her feeling shaken and vulnerable.

It was simply ridiculous. Myles Dampier never pleaded for anything. He just took. He manipulated, and he controlled like a field marshal in battle, with nothing and no one to oppose him. There was only one thing he said he wanted which he wasn't able to have . . . and if he only knew, *that* could all too easily be taken. All he had to do was hold out his hand and ask.

She wondered what he would do if she went to him now.

"I don't . . ." She broke off the lie before it left her lips. Who on earth would she be punishing if she went to her room?

She fought for control, her hands clasped in front of her, her eyes lowered to the floor. She wondered how long it would be before she felt as demure as she no doubt looked. "Very well," she said finally. "I want to learn to ride."

"Good." His voice was suddenly brisk and businesslike. "I've had them bring around a mare I purchased from Bradshaw. The man is a fool, but he knows good horseflesh when he sees it."

She couldn't resist the opportunity. "Everybody, you know," she said a little desperately, "has some redeeming feature. No matter how badly they have acted in the past."

He sauntered toward her, a grin of pure devilment spreading across his face. He stopped only inches away, closer to her than he had been in days. A gentle finger traced down the side of her face, trailing fire, and it was only a great effort of will that stopped her from chasing after his hand with her burning cheek.

"I thought we had agreed, Mermaid, that I have very few redeeming features."

"But what if . . . what if . . ." Her voice trailed off, and she cursed her inability to put a warning into words. She had never felt more helpless in her life. What could she say to stop the man she loved from destroying himself before her very eyes? And destroying other innocents alongside him. "What if you think that you don't *have* a choice and then you end up doing something you might regret for the rest of your life?"

"I've already done something I regret, Mermaid. And I find that I can live with it . . . quite adequately."

Sabina's riding lesson commenced in the great inner courtyard next to the stables and attracted a gallery of onlookers all eager to offer their advice. Curtis, the head groom, dismissed the lowliest stable boys back to their duties, allowing Gammon the honor of remaining only because of the gossip surrounding the boy's parentage, and a desire to curry favor with his sharp-tongued employer.

Sabina regarded her horse with misgivings.

"It's taller than a mule," she said nervously.

Gammon, who proudly held the reins, regarded her with disappointment. "It's only fourteen hands high, missus. It's a littl'un."

"Well, they must be very big hands," she replied stoutly. She looked at her beautiful riding habit and had visions of herself lying muddy and broken on the ground. She turned to Myles and said politely, "I've changed my mind. I don't want to ride today."

"Get on, Sabina." His voice was patient, but something about the set of his body told her he was not in the mood for feminine vapors. "I won't let anything happen to you."

"It's not *you* I'm going to be riding," she said querulously, and then, hearing a muffled gasp of laughter from the waiting grooms, blushed a fiery red as the full impact of her double entendre hit home. "That is . . . I mean . . . it's all very well for you to be brave about it, you aren't . . ."

He watched her lose her struggle with dignity and sighed tolerantly. "Are you going to stand there and dig yourself in deeper, Sabina, or are you going to get on the horse?"

"I suppose I'll get on the horse."

Somewhat subdued, she stood with her hand resting lightly on the saddle, half attending to the list of instructions he issued to her, and then suddenly found herself physically lifted from her feet and placed onto the mare.

The horse turned its head and regarded her with as much surprise as Sabina did Myles. "Thank you. But you distinctly told me—in that charming way you have—that I would have to learn to mount without any assistance at all—sidesaddle or not!"

He wore his devil-angel smile, all injured innocence. "It's your first time, Mermaid. Everyone needs some guidance the first time. Anyway," he added softly, "I wanted to see if your waist is as small as it appears in that habit."

Her eyes narrowed as she sensed a trap. "And what was the verdict?"

"Tight lacing."

"Go away," she said succinctly.

Laughing, he did, but only to take the reins of her horse and lead it around the large stone courtyard. He watched her adjust her leg around the crutch and grasp tightly at the pommel, before he issued a series of curt instructions that had her sitting at a right angle to the horse's shoulders, and relaxed enough to lift her head and observe her surroundings. Then he handed the reins to Gammon and mounted his own horse with an enviably lithe movement.

"Gammon will lead you around the yard a little longer, until you are comfortable. Then I'll take the reins."

"You always do," she muttered, before giving the urchin a conspiratorial smile. Gammon, puffed up with self-importance, led her gently round and round the medieval enclosure where once knights on horseback had no doubt trained in just such a manner. The boy looked well fed and happy, and much, much cleaner than when he'd climbed out of the boot of her baggage coach. He was, she noticed with a start of surprise, quite a handsome child, his fair hair brushed into a riot of gold curls, the hazel eyes clear and shining.

"Why has Jezebel deserted you, Gammon?" she asked impulsively. "Doesn't she love you anymore?"

The boy's face fell. "She won't come to the stables, missus. The 'orses make her nervous."

"I understand how she feels."

Gammon didn't respond to this poor-spirited statement, merely rolling his eyes so that Sabina giggled helplessly. She was still smiling when Myles rode over to where her horse was patiently circling.

"I'm glad to see you in a good mood, Mrs. Dampier. Give me the reins, Gammon. I'll take charge now."

"Don't I get to take my own reins?"

"When I'm satisfied you know what to do with them."

"Are we talking about riding?" she demanded impishly.

"You seem to be in a remarkably playful mood, Mrs. Dampier. An hour ago I could have sworn you wanted to cut my throat."

"That was an hour ago, Mr. Dampier. I am now in the fresh air, wearing an outrageously expensive riding habit that should tip you into bankruptcy, and," she finished triumphantly, "I'm not riding a mule."

"You aren't riding anything yet. You are merely being led in circles. When we move out into the park you might find it a little more daunting."

"I might. But at least I'm willing to try." She fixed her eyes to his face and declared bravely, "I'm not afraid of letting go of past fears and . . . and taking up a new challenge. And I'm not afraid of giving in to something that might be totally beyond my control! Just because I'm afraid I can't handle the consequences!"

"Are we talking about riding?" he asked.

"What else?" she asked haughtily.

He snorted, and pulled his horse's head about, issuing

brusque orders to the grooms. Sabina followed Myles's roan gelding through the imposing stone gateway and out into the grounds. She found the swaying, somnolent gait of her horse a different experience from the jerky rhythm of a mule, and suddenly relaxed, determined to enjoy this new sensation.

The only thing vexing her was her view of her husband's back.

Not that it was an unpleasant view, but it had not been part of her plan to admire it for the next few hours. He was, as usual, as hatless as a gypsy, the dark curls ruffled by the wind into a wild disorder. He sat in the saddle with an easy self-assurance that made her more suddenly confident in her own skills.

"I think you exaggerated the riding part. This is called walking, isn't it," she called out.

He glanced over his shoulder and grinned.

"You have to walk before you can ride, Mermaid. This is the learning part."

"Oh. And what exactly am I learning? How to be seasick on land?"

He stopped, and her mare, drawing alongside and finding herself in handsome equine company, threw her head coquettishly and danced a little. Sabina, who had listened to her riding instructor more closely than she would have admitted, managed to right herself and controlled the animal with a dexterity that surprised her.

"Very good," Myles approved. "With a little more practice you'll be Diana, the huntress."

She clutched nervously at her hat. "I don't feel very goddesslike at the moment," she admitted, and then confessed in a rush, "I don't think I'm ever really going to enjoy riding. Oh, I'll do it, because everyone seems to expect me to—*especially* Lady Vantry—and I want you to be proud of me. But, honestly, Myles, I think . . . I think it will always make me a little frightened."

This admission had well and truly caught his attention. He regarded her thoughtfully through narrowed eyes before finally saying, "You have too much courage to be frightened by a mere horse, Sabina. In fact, I would have said you aren't afraid of anything."

"Me!" She was too surprised to be grammatical. "Why, that's ridiculous! I'm frightened of hundreds of things! You heard me when I found a spider in my work box. The servants thought I was being murdered." Suddenly curious, she turned a limpid gaze on her husband. "But you, Myles Dampier? Are you frightened of anything? Shipwreck? Storms? Pirates? Lucilla Vantry?"

"Snakes," he answered promptly.

"Really?" She was delighted to have learned some new fact about him, however spurious, and asked eagerly. "Like *Eunectes murinus*? The anaconda? They can swallow an entire deer at one sitting, you know. Papa dissected one once in South America, and it was perfectly true. A little *digested*, of course, but quite whole. There are stories of it swallowing people, but I think that is just a myth. At all events, we never came across an example of it happening, so it's no use speculating, is it?" She noticed her husband's shoulders shaking slightly, his jaw set like a man determined not to laugh, and she demanded crossly, "What? What have I said?"

"Not a thing that you shouldn't have, Mermaid. In fact, I suggest you save that charming little anecdote for dinner this evening. I've no doubt our host will appreciate it."

"Oh. Of course. I had forgotten about dinner this evening."

She had indeed. The sheer joy of being in Myles's company in such a thoroughly uncomplicated setting had wiped most of the morning's events from her mind. She was sorry to be reminded, but decided to seize the chance to prepare herself.

"What will you do at dinner tonight?"

There was a cynical twist to his lips as he answered gravely, "Dine, I suppose, and drink inferior wine. What do you expect me to do, Sabina? Challenge Richard to a duel? Carry his wife away and ravish her?"

"Oh. Is that something you want to do?"

"My dear," he drawled. "I'm having enough trouble ravishing my own wife, let alone anyone else's."

She sucked in a startled breath, as shocked as if he had leaned over and slapped her. She examined him for any sign of resentment, but he was wearing his St. Sebastian air, the blue eyes almost angelic in their virtue.

If the comment was designed to render her silent, it didn't succeed. "Talking about swallowing people whole, I like your cousin very much."

"That doesn't surprise me. For all his mealy-mouthed ways, he has a knack of ingratiating himself with women. The same way curly-haired curates and bishops do."

"He's glad you are back. God help him."

"Which shows he is a bigger fool than I took him for."

"People are always fools if they don't think as you do, aren't they?"

"Fools or Tories, my sweet."

"You are impossible!"

"You have to remember, Sabina," he said quietly, "that I once liked him, too. Very much."

She didn't want to pity him at this moment. She wanted to pity Richard Dampier and his wife. And herself. She gritted her teeth and, releasing one hand from the pommel, stretched it out to him. "I want to handle my own reins, please."

"I'm sure you do," he said dryly. "Whether you are capable or not is another matter."

"Let's find out, shall we?" she said sweetly. She watched as he looped the reins over the mare's docile head and she took them uncertainly. Her eyes flickered from her own shaky hands to his, so confidently holding his reins.

"You do make it look so easy," she confessed sadly, and then nearly leapt from her saddle as one large gloved hand suddenly covered her own. Her head jerked up, and she stared into eyes that were free of all pretense. There was desire there, naked, hungry desire, and something else that she could only read as anger. She tried to draw back, but his grip on her hand tightened.

"So do you, Mermaid. You make everything look so damnably simple. And it's not. It never was."

His voice was hollow, like the last echo from a shout of pain.

Sabina lowered her eyes and sat quietly on her horse, waiting, feeling the restless movements of the little mare, but unable to do anything about checking them. She drew in a shaky breath.

"This is ridiculous," she said finally, after her heart had ceased pounding and her breathing had returned to normal. "We can't go on like this, dancing around the reality of my feelings for you." She gathered enough courage to raise her eyes and look into his dark face. "I love you, Myles Dampier. You know it. It obviously disturbs you, but I can't help that. I also can't help the fact that you don't love me. But I can accept it. I can live with it . . . because I have to. What I can't accept is being a party to some grandiose plan to wreak vengeance on anyone who has ever wronged you!"

She added desperately, "That is the action of a weak man, Myles. And you aren't weak. If you were, I wouldn't be alive today! We wouldn't be here at Lysons Hall! You would be moldering away in a penal colony, and I would be at the bottom of the Atlantic Ocean! Please, for the sake of any chance that our marriage might have, give up this plan of yours to ruin your cousin!"

Despite the fact that a small, cynical smile twisted his lips, his eyes were blank and his face had hardened, all life removed from it, like some living travesty of a marble bust. She waited for him to speak, straining toward him.

" ' 'Tis safest in matrimony to begin with a little aversion,' " he quoted softly. "I should have remembered that at the outset, Mermaid, and now I wonder if it's too late."

"I intend to stop you!" The words were torn from her, a child's bravado, born of hurt and anger.

"You can't, Sabina. No one can. Not even myself."

She suddenly felt drained of life. His reply had been almost regretful, as though he now had no power over the Furies he had released. His revenge, it seemed, had assumed a life of its own, set on its inexorable course, taking all her dreams with it.

"I don't know who you are anymore," she whispered.

"Perhaps you never did, my dear." His voice was remarkably gentle, and as deadly as a saber slash. "You made up a hero in your own head, Sabina, and decided to fall in love with him out of gratitude and loneliness. Don't think I don't understand what loneliness can make you do. I do. When I dragged you up by the hair, spitting out half an ocean, it was inevitable that you would turn me into some romantic figure. I knew it, and I used it for my own ends. I made peace with what little conscience I had left, by telling myself you would be better off with me than set adrift in the same cold world that would condemn Gammon to the gallows for stealing a roll of cloth."

He smiled bitterly and then looked down at his hands. He seemed to note, with the same surprise that she did, that they still covered hers. He withdrew them, and she swayed in the saddle while he continued ruthlessly, "I thought you would accept every material thing I gave you, and live in your own comfortable wife-world like every other man's wife I've known. Demanding nothing, because you had everything you wanted."

His words were knife thrusts. She struggled against the pain they inflicted and demanded hoarsely, "Did you think so little of me?"

"I didn't want to think," he said frankly. "I couldn't think. Every time I looked at you, I wanted to take you so much, it was a wonder that damned ship didn't go up in flames like the *Margaret Rose*. I still do. I wish to whatever gods are listening that I didn't. But I do."

Seduction.

She had heard the word before, but this was the first time she had fully understood its meaning.

Now, looking into Myles's beautiful, bitter, unflinching face, she knew. *This* was seduction. This desire to yield completely, no matter the consequences. To say to her husband, *I don't care. Take me on any terms you like. Destroy Richard Dampier. Burn down his house and set up his wife as your mistress if you like. Throw me the scraps. I don't really care, but for God's sake, want me enough so that I don't have to think.*

"I can't ride any farther," she croaked, feeling the mare move restlessly beneath her. "I want to go back."

"I was taking you to the sea. I promised you I would, remember?"

"I wish to God you had never taken me out of it!"

It was a petulant statement, and she regretted it as soon as the words flew from her mouth. But it had the desired effect, and they rode back to the Hall in tense silence.

Once she reached her bedchamber, her thin-lipped brevity caused Maria to scuttle from the room, all her natural pertness dying on her lips. Then Sabina began to remove her riding habit herself, pulling at buttons until it slipped down to her feet in an avalanche of superfine wool. She stepped over it and kicked it into a corner with uncharacteristic anger, stripping off her boots and the obligatory breeches she wore beneath the habit, in case her modesty was compromised by a tumble to the ground. The little beaver hat with its modest, feathered crown followed suit, and she stood in the middle of the room clad only in a thin chemise, cleansed of the morning's outing and shivering despite the fire that had been lit in the grate against the day's chill.

She was drowning.

And there was no sight of rescue. Not this time.

She wrapped her arms about her body in a desperate effort to retain some sort of warmth, and tried to think.

She couldn't stay here any longer. She couldn't remain and watch the man she loved turn into a marauder, destroying lives because it fitted some twisted idea of justice. But where could she go?

She thought briefly of Lucilla Vantry, and then dismissed the idea. They were barely acquainted, but something told her that Lady Vantry would regard her flight as a bride's temper tantrum and send her home. Cousin Sarah would no doubt tell her about a wife's sacred duty to her husband, and add something about making one's bed and lying in it. But the only other person she knew in England was her husband's intended victim.

She tried to conjure up a vision of Richard's polite features as she begged him to help her leave Myles. It was enough to make her laugh, a little coughing laugh that ended in a shuddering sob. She put her hands to her face and began to rock with misery.

She didn't hear the door open softly.

Or just as softly close the world out.

"Sabina?"

She lifted her head to find him standing there, his hands hanging by his sides, palms turned toward her in a curiously vulnerable gesture that made her catch her breath.

But there was nothing vulnerable about the dark cauldron of his eyes.

Someone else seemed to wear her body as it walked slowly toward him, her hips swinging in an invitation that was as unconscious and as natural as breathing. She stopped in front of him, swaying slightly, her arms crossed under her breasts, aware of and relishing the fact that the modest movement only lifted the soft flesh to his gaze.

"Get out," she whispered, and then wound her arms around his neck, throwing back her head in a sudden agony of need. "I don't want you here."

"I know," he whispered. He didn't touch her, and she clung to him like a smoldering piece of clothing. Then Myles's hands closed on her waist, claiming her delicately, supporting her weight, his fingers spreading in two wide, searing arcs just beneath her breasts.

It was sweet agony, like being suspended over a fire. She closed her eyes, willing those long thumbs to move upward, to stroke her breasts and once more make their peaks hard to his touch. His hold tightened as she moved mindlessly against him, and then he let her slip to the floor inch by leisurely inch, her body sliding against his, until she settled with her cheek against the wild thudding of his heart, her hands grasping at his shoulders for support.

She turned so that she could look up at him.

His face was a study in torment, his jaw held so rigidly she felt that if she touched it he would crack wide open.

She raised herself and turned her lips into the vulnerable area at the base of his throat, opening her mouth slightly to let the tip of her tongue taste the exposed flesh. His hands suddenly jerked to her hips, restraining her, holding her against him, the movement sending waves of fire right through her body.

"I don't want—" he said jerkily.

"I don't give a damn what you want, Myles Dampier," she said clearly, and pulled his head down to her mouth.

It set off an explosion.

His lips descended on hers with the swooping accuracy of an eagle, moving slowly, filling the recesses of her mouth with deep, tongue-stroking kisses, demanding, taking—*giving!*—with a ferocity that only made her press herself closer into him, her mouth imitating every skillful advance. He seemed to consume her in a way she hadn't thought possible, daring her to meet him in a mindless combat in which they both emerged victorious. Just when she thought she would burst with longing, his lips suddenly gentled, tugging and nibbling, before he moved his head and began to press hot, moist kisses along the fragile line of jaw just beneath her ear.

She moaned her pleasure, but she would not let him escape, greedily seeking his mouth once more, demanding that he fill her with fierce, darting movements, which her hands mimicked in small circles against his chest. Beneath the fine fabric, she felt his muscles tauten, and his breath was expelled in a ragged sound that was neither a laugh nor a groan but something caught between the two.

Not merely touching but caressing, his hands traveled over her hips, seeking out the bare skin under the lace of her short chemise. She whimpered into his mouth as hard palms trailed fire along the smoothness of her hips and buttocks, and he lifted her higher so that she could feel the strong, masculine demands of his passion.

"Myles . . ." she whispered, suddenly alarmed.

"Don't talk, Mermaid," he growled. "Don't let's say a word."

He was right. Words had always separated them.

And right now she wanted to be closer to him than she had ever been to any other human being. Without words. Without thought.

He stepped back from her suddenly, and she made an anxious movement toward him. He smiled, a lazy, languorous smile that would have made her blush right down to her pantaloons if she were wearing any. Seemingly satisfied, his eyes slid up and down her body; then his fingers went to the ribbons of her chemise, untying them with an effortlessness that made her wonder how many times he had looked at a woman in that same possessive, heart-stopping manner, and then undressed her with a methodical, maddening deliberation that made her want to lift her head and scream in frustration.

He wouldn't let her struggle out of the chemise. Instead he stilled her arms with a gesture, and then dragged the material down her body with excruciating care, lingering in curves, meticulously following every contour of breast and hip, thigh and leg. The sensation of his warm hands sliding the silk of her underwear against her skin was probably the most sensuous thing she had ever felt in her life. She watched the dark head lower and then bow as he knelt on the ground before her, like a knight paying court, while the silk chemise pooled about her feet. She automatically stepped out of it, so that she was clad only in her stockings.

She expected him to rise and face her, but he remained kneeling, his eyes uplifted, feasting on her nakedness, until he chose to concentrate on one white thigh, placing his hands around the soft flesh and gently peeling off the stocking until he could place her foot tenderly in one hand and remove it. Sabina closed her eyes and rested her hands on his shoulders, swaying slightly as the process was torturously repeated, sending little shudders of delight through her body, all the more powerful for their delicate frequency.

Silent, so silent, except for her own wild breathing.

Her own startled cry shattered the quiet. Myles had

leaned into her and placed his mouth into the soft inner curve of her thigh.

She shook her head in mute appeal, and he smiled his devil-saint smile, casually placing his lips just above the dark triangle of hair. She jolted and then shuddered deeply, but kept still, whimpering slightly as he trailed his tongue upward over her stomach, stopping at the delicately sensitive flesh beneath her breasts.

She was in an agony of waiting, suspended in a desperate rapture as he turned his hard cheek over and over against her softness, his lips exploring the deep valley with excruciating patience. Her hands were entwined in the thick curls of his hair, pulling his mouth closer to her body as she leaned into him; she let go as his arms abruptly wrapped around her body and she was lifted up toward him, helpless, naked, her face for once on a level with his, so that his eyes, glittering, exultant, stared into her own.

But only for a moment. He strode over to her bed and knelt down on its edge, balancing her lightly on his knee, one arm pinning her tightly to his body while the other adroitly stripped back the thick brocade of covers.

His smile was one of complete, triumphant masculinity as he laid her down gently on the cool white sheets. His hands tangled for a moment in her hair as she stared up at him, and then she closed her eyes, feeling as though the sight of that dark, passion-filled face would break every nerve in her body that wasn't already on end, screaming for some undefined fulfillment she could only guess at.

"Look at me, Sabina." His words startled her. Somehow she had expected that what took place would do so in silence. She listened to his voice as if she were drugged, only half attending, her mind solely registering the fact that his hand continued to caress her cheek, her jaw, her lips with fingertips dipped in fire. "If this continues . . . if I don't leave this room now . . . you become my wife in every possible way. And, Sabina . . . I will never let you go."

"Don't go, Myles . . . don't go," she managed to whisper.

His face changed, and for a single, fleeting moment he looked uncertain, but it was all too rapidly replaced by hunger.

"Then God grant me patience, Mermaid. For both our sakes."

He loosened his neckcloth, unwinding it with a muttered oath that set her laughing at his intolerant haste. He tore himself free of his shirt, and then turned around to remove his boots, suddenly exposing the broad expanse of his back to her gaze.

She gasped, the sound lost in the dull thud of first one and then the other boot on the floor, but when he twisted around, he caught the fading look of horror in her face.

"Myles! Oh, my God. Your back!"

It was crisscrossed with a series of deep, ugly scars.

She struggled up from the pillow to reach out a hand to touch him, but he flinched, and she drew back wordlessly.

"Do they repulse you?"

"No." She shook her head so that the brown tresses caught in her mouth and eyes, and he automatically leaned over her and pushed them back with one tender brush of his thumb. "They don't repulse me, Myles." He was silent, still, staring at her through narrowed eyes that managed to take in everything—her nakedness, her passion, her need for him. She added, a little wildly, "Do I look repulsed, Myles Dampier?"

"You look like a goddess." He stood up and removed his breeches with controlled haste, his eyes suddenly aflame with unexpected laughter as he quoted unsteadily, " 'She is Venus when she smiles. But she's Juno when she walks, And Minerva when she talks.' Who will you be in bed, Mermaid?"

"Your wife," she whispered, and held out her arms.

He came to her, as supple as a panther, his hands stroking her body to ease the tension of taut muscles, and she forgot everything except the searing of his flesh against hers, and the pleasure gathering deep inside her with every new touch of his hands, his lips, and his tongue. She wasn't quite sure what drove her, serpentlike, to move against him with increasing hunger, but she was blindly reaching out for something—something that licked at her core like blue flame, making her strive blindly toward an unknown climax.

Heavy-lidded, he smiled down at her, his breathing ragged. "You don't make this easy for me, Mermaid. I want you to find as much pleasure in this as I will."

"I do Myles, I do. I . . . oh, my God!"

The cry was torn from her lips as she felt his hand move intimately between her legs, and she bucked uncontrollably at the sensations bursting through her in a wave of pleasure, so unexpected and so unfamiliar that she heard a great sob burst from her lips.

He froze, every muscle corded, and asked tightly, "Did I hurt you?"

"No. It's just . . . the stars shattered again."

"I might hurt you, Mermaid. The first time . . ."

She didn't answer. She couldn't. Instead she laid her hands against his chest and curled her fingers in the dark hair, before smoothing them over his shoulders, where she clung to him trustingly.

She was more vulnerable before this man than she had ever been in her life. He shifted between her legs, gently moving one thigh outward, and then his hand gently, teasingly stroked her, moving against the point of her desire, until she was drenched with an intense, flaming heat and her hips arched toward him with desperate enticement.

His hips were between her thighs, poised, taut, and then slowly he moved over her, making her gasp at the heated invasion. She closed her eyes, suddenly frightened, while her body, obeying a primal urge, pushed against him in a primitive rhythm that was both rejection and invitation.

"Mermaid? Open your eyes. I want to see if I'm hurting you." His voice was so hoarse as to be almost unrecognizable, and her eyes widened so that they stared up into his—two dark pools of pleasure in a face twisted with the effort to control his passion.

She moved her hips.

He inched farther into her until, seemingly satisfied, he thrust into the tight core of her resistance. Whatever pain she felt was lost in the pleasure of watching his body, like some pagan god, move above her, his gaze concentrated upon hers as though she were the very center of his existence. Then he carefully threaded his fingers through hers and, leaning over, took her mouth in a long, lingering kiss, before his hips began to rock against hers in a fierce, drumming beat that made her gasp and move against him mindlessly, clenching her body around him with a wild, desperate dance of fiery thrusts and release.

It was primitive and dark, this rhythm, and beyond anything she had ever experienced—ever imagined, or ever dreamed of.

She had certainly never felt that she was going to shatter into a million fragile, exquisite pieces, each one made up of skin and blood and fire.

She looked into the dark, sweat-licked face that panted above her, his expression one of such pain that she wondered if he felt the hurt he warned her of. Feeling almost disembodied by heat and desire, she watched him disentangle one hand from hers, moving it to where they were one body joined, and touch her.

And with a cry she shattered, wave after wave of pleasure pulsing through her body, arching her even closer to his thrusting hips. He caught her and held her, driving into her body in a final act of possession that seemed to touch some spring deep within him, so that he shuddered and shouted, and fell against her, a scarred gladiator, brought down by passion.

Later, she lay beside him in a tangle of sheets while one large hand stroked her breast as though it were some exquisite pet. She lifted her head, languorous with love and satisfaction, and looked at him, her own hand unconsciously traveling over the pale skin of his hip. She let her fingers trail down toward the thick hair half covered by a sheet, only to have them caught and held in a warning grip.

The blue eyes glittered in amused admonition.

"Don't start what you don't intend to finish, Mermaid."

She laughed, amazed at the confidence that surged through her like a warm tonic. "I was just curious, that's all," she said teasingly, and then rolled on her back, deliberately taking the sheets with her, casting him a glance that was pure mischief.

He was unperturbed, stretching out beside her like a cat, his hand propping up his head as he studied her through a curtain of dark lashes.

"You really are the most curious mixture of innocence and seduction I've ever come across, Mermaid. If I didn't know better, I'd think I accidentally dragged some sea siren up by the hair, while the real girl sank to the bottom of the ocean."

She turned her face toward him, marveling at the grace and strength of his naked body, his passions now reined in, but simmering, she knew all too well, just below the surface.

" 'With this body, I thee worship,' " she quoted softly. "Do you know, I never understood that phrase until this moment. I didn't know that that's what it truly could be . . . worship. Did you, Myles? Did it ever occur to you?"

"No. It never occurred to me." He suddenly arose and swung himself agilely from the bed, gathering the clothes discarded on the floor. She watched him climb into his breeches, buttoning them with intense concentration, before he shrugged himself into his shirt and padded barefoot toward the door.

Panic suddenly seized her, and she struggled to her elbows.

"Myles! Where are you going?"

He stopped, his back to the bed, his voice even. "Going? Have you forgotten that we are to dine tonight at Curstone Abby?" He turned around to face her, every trace of the tender lover of the past few hours stripped away. In his place, the Stranger had returned, his face a sardonic mask. "As delightful as the afternoon has been, my dear, we have little time left for further dalliance."

Dalliance. A foolish word for an experience that had left her changed forever. He had been right. She belonged to him now, as she had never belonged to another living being. As she never would belong. She had given him her heart and her body and her soul. And now he smiled at her as if she had been a flirtatious housemaid with whom he exchanged a few stolen kisses.

She suddenly felt naked and ashamed, dragging the sheets up over her breasts and curling into a small ball. "But surely," she heard herself quaver, "that's all in the past now. There's no need to go—not tonight. It's all different. It's all changed."

"Changed?" There was nothing saintly in his beauty now, his mouth twisted into a dark, bitter smile, his eyes as hard as sapphires. He was suddenly all tormented devil, angry at the world and its gods, determined to lash out and cause pain. "My dear, nothing has changed. As remarkable as you are in bed, Sabina—and I am delighted that my earlier predictions proved true—your performance was hardly enough to melt my cold heart and fill me with the milk of human kindness."

In the silence that followed, she could hear her own regular breath and her heart beating, but that was all. She didn't want to move, or make a sound.

That way she wouldn't have to acknowledge the words that thrust right through her like the blade of a knife.

"Sabina." His voice was harsh, imperative.

"Why?" she finally asked. "Why?"

He understood her, just as he always seemed to do.

"For my son, Sabina. For the next baronet."

There was nothing anybody could ever do to really hurt her after this moment, she realized. The knife blade twisting in her heart was painful enough to make her double over, and she put her head on her knees, dragging in deep, tortured breaths that didn't quite seem able to slip past the enormous blockage in her throat.

"Don't enact a tragedy, Sabina. This isn't the stage for it."

He had opened the door, and when she raised her eyes he seemed to be bathed in light, like some fallen angel whose visitation to the earth had delivered chaos and grief.

"Get out," she said softly.

"You will come tonight, Sabina. You have the courage to do it." He paused and added mildly, "Perhaps you will work out a way to save my cousin from my evil clutches."

The door closed, and she sat shivering in a tight ball of misery. She didn't know how long she sat there, until a tentative knock sounded and Maria put her head around the door. The maid's quick eyes took in the rumpled sheets and her mistress's nakedness, and she faltered a moment before bustling in and briskly informing Sabina that her bath was drawn.

Sabina pushed the hair out of her eyes and wearily raised her head.

"What?" she asked dazedly.

"Your bath is ready, ma'am. You *are* dining at Curstone Abbey tonight, aren't you?"

Sabina looked at her maid, meeting the girl's steady gaze.

She didn't want to dine anywhere. She wanted to draw the bed curtains and hide under the covers in the dark, like a wounded animal gone to earth.

She wanted to curl up and die. . . .

"I want . . ." She faltered and cleared her throat.

Don't ask me for what I can't give you.

Devil take you, Myles Dampier, she thought bitterly. *I want so little.*

She exhaled a shuddering breath and straightened her shoulders, climbing from the bed with an enormous effort of will that left her swaying slightly on her feet. "I want to wear the blue-green silk, Maria," she said flatly. "And dress my hair differently. I want to look different tonight."

Maria scurried off to do her bidding, and Sabina turned

to face the mirror, shocked at the sight of her own naked body.

It was strange that she could look the same when she felt so utterly alien.

And Myles? Had it all really meant nothing to him? Had their making love really not touched him?

Or was there now merely one more scar that he carried?

CHAPTER TEN

The silence in the carriage rattling toward Curstone Abby was the kind that most probably existed the split second before the guillotine blade descended. Except that this silence endured, stretching out nerve ends until Sabina felt like screaming.

She couldn't break that silence and Myles obviously wouldn't, maintaining an air of chilling aristocratic hauteur that was as effective as a suit of armor. He had complimented her on her looks, her choice of gown, and made a polite observation on the balminess of the evening. Now he sat in contemplation, his chin sunk into his neckcloth, his profile in the flickering of the carriage lamp a study in marble.

Anyway, what could they say to each other that hadn't already been said? What use was it to go over and over old ground?

Instead Sabina repetitively practiced a conversation between them in her head that more than occupied the half-hour drive from Lysons Hall.

I love you, Myles Dampier. You may find that a trifle inconvenient, but if you want to know the truth, so do I. I wanted to fall in love with someone who would give me warmth, and laughter, and sympathy. I thought I had found that in you, but you deceived me. You deliberately made me love you, and now you pretend that it's all my own fault.

She imagined the twisting of that thinly chiseled mouth and heard his reply in the grinding of the carriage wheels against the road.

You knew what kind of man I was when I married you. You had your choice then. Don't deceive yourself into thinking that I forced you into this counterfeit. You know as well as I do that if you had refused me I would have made sure you were taken care of once we were back in England. I wouldn't have abandoned you. I owed you that much for having saved your life. But no, you were so confident that you could shape me into the man of your imagination that you set out to redeem me. Well, redemption didn't come in your bed, Sabina. I have fifteen years of hatred and broken pride built up inside me, festering like an open wound. It will take more than the use of your body to satisfy me.

The voice in her head sounded so lifelike that she emitted a small gasping sound, securing her husband's attention. One dark eyebrow arched devilishly.

"Are you all right?"

"No. Of course I'm not all right."

There was more silence, and then in a viciously reasonable voice he said, "It's your own fault, Sabina. I warned you not to expect too much. I thought you were sensible enough to understand that I meant it."

Her lips quivered, and she raised a shaking hand to still them. This was so much like her imagined conversation that she immediately charged in where she had left off, flinging herself around so that she could watch the muscles of his jaw tighten like rope.

"What will tonight accomplish, Myles? Can you tell me that? What will happen after you see her again? Will it get any better, or will it be worse? What if you discover that you still love her after all these years? Will you make her

224

the innocent victim in your plans to ruin your cousin? Is that what your love does?"

She had spoken in one long rush that left her breathless. She paused to draw in more air, but before she could continue her tirade, he spoke softly, cutting her off.

"I don't know."

"What?"

"You asked what would happen after I see her again. I answered you truthfully. I don't know."

Truth, she decided miserably, had a lot to answer for. "Do you love her?"

"If I did, you wouldn't be in this carriage with me, Sabina. She would. And to hell with the consequences."

The Dampier family motto, of course. *To hell with the consequences.*

"I think," she said tightly, "I would like to kill you."

"It's been tried."

"Obviously not often enough."

He chuckled softly, enraging her to such a point that she cast around for some method to hurt him as much as she had been hurt. Through the darkness beyond the glass window, the lights of the Abbey were distantly discernible, beckoning to her like the walls of Jericho, and she decided that she had finally found that method.

"Do you know, Myles Dampier," she said smoothly, "I've suddenly realized why you believe that you are entitled to have Curstone Abby for your very own. You are so obviously your uncle's spiritual heir, aren't you? I hadn't realized that . . . until now. Neither of you really care who you destroy along the way. As long as your own ruthless ambitions are served, you don't care about anything. Your Uncle John would be so proud of his protégé."

As soon as the words left her mouth, she wished them unsaid, suddenly nauseated by her own cruelty. But to her extreme disappointment, he didn't reply, and she was left to smolder in silence until the carriage drew up at the entrance. Myles sprang out, scorning the use of the steps, and kept silent sentinel until she was handed out by a liveried footman and stood safely on the gravel outside the great horseshoe staircase.

The house, magnificently Palladian with its domes and its classical niches sporting Mars and Venus on either side of the door, was illuminated like a fairy-tale palace, and Sabina acknowledged that the hundreds of burning candles in the lower rooms had probably been lit in their honor.

Whether or not it was an instinctive response to the darkness that Myles brought with him, she didn't know.

She drew in a deep breath as her husband gave her his arm. Laying her gloved hand lightly on the taut muscles, she climbed the steps, her heart drumming so loudly she was positive Myles would hear it and make some cynical comment. But he kept his face still, his expression glacial as they entered the great marble hall and were bowed into the drawing room by an obsequious servant, who closed the doors on what Sabina could only describe as a frozen tableau from a play.

Whether a tragedy or a farce, she was yet to discover.

Richard Dampier, impeccable in evening dress, stood in one corner of the room, his hands characteristically clenched behind his back, his expression half welcoming, half fearful. Even in his own domain, he seemed somehow uneasy, as though always expecting blows and unkindness from everyone he met. She put her head to one side, puzzled by it, making a mental note to discover its cause if she could.

However, it was the woman reclining on a sofa in the middle of the room who caught and held Sabina's attention.

Myles had been right, Sabina decided. The portrait in Brook Street *didn't* do her justice. No artist could ever possibly capture the elusive nature of Sylvia Dampier's loveliness. She seemed to be made out of gilt and filigree, her complexion alabaster pure, her blue eyes large and luminous. The ice-blue gown she wore was filmy with lace as delicate as dewdrops, and she trailed the wispy gauze of a scarf over arms that were held out toward them with trembling intensity.

She was a fairy princess in a fairy-tale setting, welcoming back her long-lost knight.

"Myles," Sylvia breathed, her velvety voice warm and husky. "Dear Myles. You are come back. After all these years, you are home again."

Sabina closed her eyes. Was this what Myles had been thinking about when he had attempted to make love to her beneath the portrait? Had he thought about those slender, milky arms entwined about his neck?

Myles Dampier sauntered toward the reclining woman, his entire body a languid, elegant greeting, and bowed low over her hand.

"Sylvia. How well you look. You don't seem to have changed at all."

He uttered the commonplace words in a flat, emotionless voice and stared down at her through half-closed lids, before turning to beckon Sabina to his side. She moved falteringly and stood beside the sofa, feeling unaccountably like an impertinent housemaid about to be reprimanded. But Sylvia Dampier's magnificent eyes were fixed solely on the man who, for those few, brief hours so many years ago, had once been her husband.

The thought twisted in Sabina's heart like a piece of cold steel.

"Oh, but I have changed, Myles. And very much so, since you went away. I am not at all well." Her voice was full of cobwebs and dust. "You must ask Richard if you do not believe me. I suffer so. No one knows how I suffer, Myles." She caught sight of Sabina and suddenly extended one jeweled hand toward her, the ghost of a smile flickering over pale lips. "Mrs. Dampier. How happy I am that you are here. You must forgive me for not rising. It will take all my strength to sit with you at the dinner table, you know. Usually I dine in my room, but I knew I must make an effort to welcome you. However, the most simple effort positively *exhausts* me."

Richard started forward, unnaturally pale but determined to play the host now that the awkwardness of initial introductions seemed to be over.

"Now, my love, you must not tire yourself out too quickly. Our guests have come to see you." His tone of voice, affectionate but firm, was better suited to a fractious child than a wife. But she was unperturbed, shooting him a fond glance.

"No," she agreed happily. "I must conserve my strength. As soon as Richard told me you were coming, I knew I must not do anything naughty. You are so lucky to have your health, Mrs. Dampier. How . . . how *robust* you look."

Sabina suddenly felt as feminine as a prizefighter under the force of those limpid eyes.

"Indeed I'm not. I've had the most awful cold," she said defensively.

"Yes, Lysons Hall must be so dreadfully drafty, my dear. It would have been a death sentence if I had ever lived there." Sylvia Dampier broke off, her eyes widening as she understood the significance of what she had just said. "But it was not to be, was it? And that is what we are all standing here thinking. It was not to be. But it doesn't matter now, because Myles is home, and he has brought his wife with him, and we may all be comfortable again." And she plucked at her gauzy wrap and smiled serenely on them all.

The room, Sabina thought, was about as comfortable as the condemned cell in Newgate Prison. She sat down on a gilt chair beside her hostess and smiled tightly as she cast about for some unsensational topic of conversation.

"Norfolk," she said politely, "is very beautiful, Lady Dampier. And your grounds appear delightful."

"Do they?" Sylvia replied vaguely. "I seldom leave the house now, Mrs. Dampier, so I must take your word for it. May I call you Sabina? Such a pretty name. Who was your father?"

The question was so incongruous that Sabina stared uncomprehendingly at her hostess, before understanding that she was being subjected to the inevitable inquisition.

"My father was an ornithologist. He was a member of the Royal Society."

"Oh. Is that like being a Methodist?"

"An ornithologist studies birds, Lady Dampier. He was a naturalist, with an interest in plants and animals and . . . birds."

"I like birds," Her Ladyship whispered softly, and then the incredible eyes glided over Sabina in a painstaking, unblinking appraisal. "Myles rescued you from cannibals in the Pacific Ocean, I believe."

Sabina sighed, thoroughly tired of cannibals by now. "He rescued me from drowning in the Atlantic Ocean, Lady Dampier." At least telling the truth would put off any further stories being told to the incredulous. "He pulled me from the water after our ship caught fire, and kept me afloat until we were rescued by a passing brigantine."

"So very romantic. And so very like Myles. Everything he ever did was imbued with . . . romance. And you are so young and lovely. I have always wondered what sort of woman Myles would eventually choose to be his wife—his real wife, that is. We were in love once, did you know?"

Richard moved from his place by the fire as though he were shot from a cannon. "My love," he said desperately, "this is hardly the time or place."

"But it's true!" she countered in surprise. "We none of us have lost our memories, you know, Ricky. It's bound to be talked of, now that Myles is living at Lysons Hall again." She turned to Sabina, her exquisite features creased with amusement. "Myles and I eloped together when we were nothing more than children. It was so exciting and romantic, like something out of a poem. Or a very sad ballad. You know—the type that ends with everyone weeping over a grave and singing 'hey nonny nonny'! But Sir John—he was my guardian at the time, you know—Sir John found out and brought me back less than an hour after we were married, and they sent Myles away. I cried and cried, but he didn't come back, and so I married Richard. And as Uncle John said I would, I became

Lady Dampier, which has been most agreeable. But *you* must not mind being plain Mrs. Dampier, my dear, and sitting down the table from me, and not taking precedence when we go in to dinner. Indeed you must not, for we are very informal tonight."

Sabina couldn't meet her husband's eye, although she sensed his presence somewhere behind her. Sylvia Dampier's artless ramblings had lowered the temperature of the room by several degrees, and Sabina wondered what significance lay beneath them. Surely the woman wasn't fool enough to think that Myles had come to effect a reconciliation, or that her reminiscences were in any way amusing to those who listened to them. She studied her closely, noticing for the first time the dilated pupils in those lustrous eyes, and the stertorous breathing.

Sabina straightened in her chair and cast an incredulous glance at Richard Dampier. He was specter-pale, a thin shimmer of sweat beading his forehead, while his eyes darted nervously from his wife to his guests.

Surely the exquisite Sylvia wasn't *drunk!*

It was Myles who seemed to save the situation, advancing to the sofa and taking the invalid's hand. His face was unreadable, but the curve of his body over hers suggested that here, at least, some pity might eventually be found.

Please, Sabina prayed, *let it be pity.*

"I am sure that Sabina has no dispute with precedence, Sylvia. And now, will you not play for us before dinner? I remember . . . I remember how very fond you were of music."

Her face lit up with pleasure, but then faded just as suddenly, leaving her looking far older. "I don't play anymore. I'm not well enough." She looked up at Sabina and added mournfully, "I once had a harp, Mrs. Dampier. It was the most beautiful harp in the world. I used to play it. But it doesn't belong to me now. It is . . . somewhere else, and Richard says I may not have another. But that doesn't matter, because I want my own harp, not someone else's."

Her voice faded into a whisper, and Sabina jumped to

her feet as sympathy for the woman surged through her.

"I will play," she announced, desperate to put an end to Sylvia Dampier's frank speeches. "I'm sadly out of practice, but I would be pleased to play for you."

Richard Dampier dived toward the pianoforte before she could move, wrenching open the lid and shuffling a wad of music sheets at her. He gave her a look of profound gratitude, murmuring as she seated herself, "Thank you. Thank you so much. She is usually . . . much better than this. It was the excitement. It proved too much for her . . . nerves."

"I wouldn't thank me until *after* you have heard me play," she murmured back, and was startled to hear the man chuckle in her ear. He was still chuckling and guffawing long after he moved away from the pianoforte, drawing a long, thoughtful look from Myles.

There must, she thought sadly, *be a distinct lack of laughter at the Abbey.*

She flexed her fingers and began to play. She was, as she had admitted, sadly out of practice. There were few instruments in the jungles of South America. But she had always played well, and now, with an urgency born of desperation, acquitted herself adequately. At all events, Sylvia Dampier's loose tongue was finally stilled, and all the room's savage beasts temporarily soothed.

She played until dinner was announced, rising with a profound sense of relief. Lady Dampier, who seemed to have conserved all her energy for this moment, rose unsteadily to her feet, claiming Myles's arm. Sir Richard, ever the polite host, offered his own to Sabina, and they made a grimly formal little procession to the dining room.

She was horrified to discover that it was the state dining room, rather than a more intimate setting. She was seated next to Sir Richard at an interminable table which bore an elaborate centerpiece depicting an unfortunate creature being trampled by a porcelain elephant. Myles, who sat on Sylvia's left, caught Sabina's eye and leaned over to murmur, "Perhaps that anaconda story will not be out of place."

She fixed a brilliant smile on her face and did her best to pretend that her hostess was not drunk, and that her husband was not plotting his host's imminent financial ruin. Myles, however, looked strangely relaxed, his eyes busily roaming the walls of bewigged and beribboned ancestors who stared down at them with arrogant Dampier disdain.

"I see that you have made very few changes since your father's death, Ricky," he commented blandly. "The first baronet watches us eat as usual. It's a pity he had himself painted as Mars. Those naked knees of his always had a tendency to put me off my food."

"Yes, well . . . I . . . you know how I am, Myles. I was always a creature of habit. I like things to stay the same. And you? Will you be making changes at the Hall?"

"If you mean will I make repairs, most certainly. But I also mean to rebuild. The east wing, for example. I have a mind to modernize, and install my family there."

"Your family . . ." Richard blanched and glanced at his wife. "Do you mean . . . are you . . . ?"

"Oh, come, Ricky. That is an indelicate subject for the dinner table surely."

Sabina, who had fixed her attention on the bowl of soup placed deftly in front of her, snapped her head up so quickly that a stray curl flew into her open mouth. She brushed it aside, meeting Myles's eyes. They were all too quickly curtained from her gaze, but she understood the implication.

She was supposedly with child.

Clever Mrs. Dampier was about to fill the nurseries of Lysons Hall, like some accomplished brood mare, while the baronet and his wife remained pathetically childless.

She counted slowly while she put her spoon down, trying to catch his eye, but he merely turned his head and remarked softly, "I am planning to build a ballroom, Sylvia. I remember how you loved to dance. You must let me lead you out when we hold our first ball."

"If," Sabina interjected smoothly, "we are acknowledged

by our neighbors by then. It will be a poor ball with only the four of us in attendance."

Myles fixed his eyes on hers, the blue depths shining with a curious flame. He continued to regard her steadily as he asked, "What say you, Ricky? Will we continue as pariahs, do you think, shunned by the entire county?"

"No." Richard was eager to disabuse his cousin, twisting in his seat the better to face him. "There can be no danger of that. Oh, perhaps a *few* sticklers, and people who are new . . . but you aren't a boy anymore, Myles. You have friends now. Powerful friends."

"And money, Ricky. There is no more powerful friend. I learned that very early in my life."

There was a painful silence after this declaration, broken only when Sylvia sighed, "I love to dance. But I don't dance very often now. It's my health, you know, which prevents me. But now that you are back, Myles, perhaps I may dance again." She leaned across the table and asked Sabina conspiratorially, "Do you dance, my dear? I hope you do. Myles taught me to waltz, you know. Uncle John was very cross, because it was thought very fast then. But Myles taught me to waltz in the garden by the little fountain. Do you remember? Do you remember when we waltzed?"

She was like an eager child, demanding that he remember. Sabina felt her hands begin to tremble in her lap out of sheer pity for the wreck of a woman Sylvia Dampier had become. For all her great beauty, she was one of the most pitiable creatures she had ever met—part woman, part child, part . . . drunkard! No wonder Lucilla Vantry had told her not to envy Sylvia. If only she had warned her of what to expect!

"I remember," Myles acknowledged gently, and Sylvia, who had been excitedly leaning forward in her chair, relaxed with a contented sigh, laying her sliver-gilt head on the high back of the chair, a warm smile spreading over her delicate features.

"I thought you would," she murmured, and then, without further ado, appeared to drift off to sleep before their very eyes.

Richard's chair scraped as he struggled to his feet, and he placed an experimental hand on his wife. She didn't respond, and he bent down to gather up her legs, swinging her into his arms in a single confident movement, his slender form disguising hidden strength. "You must excuse us," he apologized formally, as though it were an everyday occurrence for the hostess to fall asleep at the dinner table. "She is worn out by . . . excitement. I thought it might be too much for her, but she insisted. Please, don't rise. I shan't be gone long."

They watched him exit with his fair burden; then Myles dismissed a wooden-faced footman with a slight movement of his head.

"Leave us." He waited until the servant slid unobtrusively from the room, and then rose and walked around to the chair vacated by his host. He sat down and leaned back, locking his hands behind his head, his expression profoundly thoughtful.

"What are you doing, Myles? Trying the chair out for size?" Sabina's voice was sweet. "Isn't it best to wait until the corpse is cold? Richard could be back any minute."

"He has to stagger up three flights of stairs to reach the main apartments, Mermaid. And as sylphlike as she looks, Sylvia can be a dead weight. I know that from experience. I doubt if he will be back in time for the third course." He unthreaded his hands and reached down to take a roll from a plate, crumbling it between long fingers. She reached out and placed her own hand over them, so that the bread dropped to the table, and he suddenly grew still.

It was the first time she had really touched him since they were together in her bedroom—less than four or five hours ago, when he had broken her heart in two.

Strange how it seemed so long ago.

She pulled back, returning her trembling fingers to her lap, where she proceeded to mangle a linen napkin.

"This is dreadful, Myles. You can't go through with it.

How much more miserable do you want Richard Dampier to be? His wife is . . . is an *inebriate.*"

"She wasn't drunk," he said calmly. "I've seen it too often for there to be any mistake about it. The lovely Lady Dampier is an opium eater."

"A what?"

"Opium, Sabina. Surely you know what that is."

"Of course, I do. But how—"

"Laudanum, of course. Opium dissolved in alcohol." His voice was cold, as though the fact held no interest for him beyond a scientific one. "I daresay she started taking it for her damned imaginary megrims, and now finds herself unable—or unwilling—to stop."

"That's terrible! What can we do?"

"Do?" He sounded amused. She wanted to reach over and hit him. "If Richard were a man instead of merely a *gentleman,* he'd have done something about it by now."

Her growing anger forced her to her feet. Once there, she unaccountably began to shake, as if suddenly afflicted with the ague. She could not stop, and found herself leaning into the table for support. They had just never seemed quite real before, his plans for revenge. The individuals involved had been like the characters in a novel, not flesh-and-blood humans. She had felt sympathy, even feared for them, but now that she had finally witnessed the effects of Myles's vengeance on real people, she was appalled.

"Don't you feel any pity for them, Myles Dampier? Is your mind so twisted that you can sit there and merely gloat at their misery? Your cousin is teetering on the brink of ruin and his wife has lost her mind! Don't you feel anything for *her,* at least? She is an innocent in all this!"

"Don't lay Sylvia's plight at my door!" He glowered up at her from under straight dark brows, the skin suddenly stretched too tightly over the bones of his face. "Do you think it would take mere months to turn her from the girl I knew into . . . *that*? She has obviously been addicted for years." He stood up so suddenly that the chair went crashing unheeded to the floor and they faced each other across the table like armed combatants. "No, my dear," he said, grinding out the words contemptuously. "That particular misfortune can be laid firmly at the door of that weak, spineless fool you seem to admire so much. He's to blame! Sylvia Woodhaven was no mere beautiful doll to be put upon a shelf and admired. She was spirited and vibrant, and nobody's fool. It's quite clear that fifteen years of marriage to a sneaking, treacherous cur has turned her into what she is!"

"You blame him? But he loves her!" she cried, aghast. "And Lord knows I *understand* how completely helpless you feel when you watch someone you love destroying themselves without any help from you!"

"Love? My God, Sabina. You use that word pretty freely, don't you?" he sneered. His face was as arrogant as a devil's, drained of all human emotion. "You use it like a blanket excuse for all crimes. Lust, greed, ambition . . . Richard Dampier doesn't love Sylvia! He never did. She is his shining trophy, his golden dome of achievement. Do you know he was almost frightened of her when we were boys? She lived in this house as his father's ward, and he could barely bring himself to address more than a dozen words to her."

"Loving someone and being frightened of them aren't mutually exclusive!" she shouted.

He was rendered immobile by her words, as startled as if she had reached over and slapped him. The silence that followed made her insides curl with dread, and she closed her eyes, only the hard reality of the table beneath her hands giving her support. Why on earth didn't she keep her mouth shut? Why was she so determined to prod at the sleeping tiger until he turned on her?

When he spoke, his voice was lifeless. "Do I frighten you, Sabina?"

"Yes." She opened her eyes to find that he had moved away from the table and stood in the middle of the great dining room, his hands clasped behind his back in a gesture so reminiscent of his cousin that she gaped at him. "Yes," she added more loudly, "you do."

He turned his head and studied her as if assessing a complete stranger.

"It's ironic, isn't it?" he said finally. "That those who should fear me don't, and the one person who shouldn't, does so? I never wanted that to happen, Sabina. I swear to God that was the last thing I wanted."

She had an overwhelming sense of his isolation as he stood there in the middle of that magnificent room, beneath his ancestors' mocking regard, caught in the grip of the deep, scarring memories of past betrayals. She left the table and ran to him, half expecting to be repulsed, but she felt herself suddenly lifted from the floor as her arms snaked around his neck, and she pressed her mouth to his with a searching, aching intensity.

His lips, warm and welcoming, slanted across hers, first gently caressing and then deepening into something dark and fierce. Their tongues began a rhythmic duel that made her whimper with her furious need of this man. She pulled her mouth away, whispering something against his jaw, and she felt her body slide down the length of his, crushing her beautiful, expensive gown against her in a manner that was pure delight.

She laid her cheek against his chest, and then slowly drew her hands down from his shoulders, feeling the muscles bunching beneath the fine fabric of his coat as she did so.

"Look up at me, Sabina." His voice was raw, and she obediently raised her eyes to his.

She saw desire there, but also a terrible self-loathing that had her blindly reaching for his hand. Capturing it, she lifted it to her lips and pressed a fervent benediction into his palm. He stilled, and the severe lines of his face seemed to soften, before he caught her chin gently in his fingers and tenderly caressed the line of her jaw.

She turned her face into his hand like a cat, and then whispered, "I want to go home, Myles. Please. Now."

"Home? Is that what it is to you, Mermaid?" There was a vibration in his voice that she had never heard before, and in answer she raised her hand to follow the chiseled lines of his face, seeking, like a blind woman, to find the man beneath the mask. "If we go home now, it will be to my bed. Is that what you want?"

"It's what I want," she replied shakily, and her hand fell to her side, her fingers dangling uselessly.

She had surrendered.

Finally he would have her on his terms.

From now on, she would not speak of love, or a future built on friendship and forgiveness.

To stay in his arms, to be a part of his world, she would enter the darkness and become a part of it.

And she knew that when tomorrow came he would work her into his empire of bitterness and destruction. But tonight that didn't matter. Nothing mattered except that she loved this man with all her heart. She loved his darkness and his light, his weakness and his strength. She loved him so completely that not even his total rejection of that love could make it flawed.

He led her from the room, calling to an astonished footman to fetch their carriage, leaving the evening's meal to grow cold on the Dampiers' long, elegant dining table.

They took no leave of their host. Sabina reasoned that Richard would no doubt be grateful for their departure. She spared a moment's thought for him and his foolish, ailing wife, and then shrugged the pair ruthlessly from her mind. Myles was right. Sylvia's misfortune was none of their concern. If the woman was foolish enough to crave something that was clearly no good for her, she deserved everything she got.

It was a pity that her own particular craving was more potent than anything that came out of a bottle.

CHAPTER ELEVEN

Myles folded his tall frame into the carriage and issued curt orders to the coachman. The carriage jolted into life, trundling down the driveway of the Abbey with a painful finality.

"Are you sure you know what you are doing?" His voice was darkly seductive as he took hold of her hands, threading his fingers through hers and lifting them to his lips. "If you give in to me, now, my sweet, you acquiesce in all my plans. You promise not to interfere. No more futile attempts at my redemption. No more talk of love and romantic dreams. You accept what happens. You take your place in society as my wife. You live in the expectation that either I or our son will live to be the next baronet." He dropped her hands and slid his own along her arms, massaging the bare flesh at the top of her shoulders. "In short, Sabina, you stop fighting me."

And Sabina finally understood what Eve had been up against.

In the flickering lantern light, she stared into his fallen-angel face, the shadows deepening its planes and angles as he sat half in light and half in darkness. *This is how Milton must have imagined his Lucifer*, she decided wearily. *Son of the morning, the most beautiful of all the angels, sinful with pride and sick with a terrible desire for vengeance.*

She closed her eyes and asked softly, "Is it 'Better to reign in Hell than serve in Heaven,' Myles?"

His hands stilled, and one sardonic eyebrow rose in mute inquiry.

"I seem to have caught your habit of reciting at inopportune times," she explained almost tearfully.

"If you can remember your poetry, then I'm obviously doing something wrong."

He pulled her onto him in a movement that was swift and unexpected. Then he pushed up her skirts and moved her thigh so that she was straddling him, her hands grasping at his coat, her eyes wide with shock.

"Myles!"

"You seemed to find riding sidesaddle so damned awkward," he said thickly.

She shook her head, even as her whole body moved yearningly against him. "There is a driver up front and two footmen behind us," she hissed. "What will they think?"

He grinned the lazy, mocking grin she had not caught sight of since the *Ellen Drury*, and her heart turned over in her breast. He began to undo the small buttons of her silk bodice and replied evenly, "They will think I am a very lucky man, and my reputation in the region will soar. By the way, have I remarked before on what a delightful fashion all these buttons down the front of women's gowns are?"

"This is wrong," she whispered without much conviction.

"Is it?" The bodice came apart in his hands, and he softly moved the material with his thumbs, leaning in to place his mouth on one fabric-covered breast, his tongue making lazy circles that had her gasping for air.

Instinctively she arched up and lowered herself nearer

to the strong evidence of his desire, reveling in the sensation of the hard-muscled thighs that supported her own. Her actions dragged his hands from where they had supported her waist, to her hips, and he pulled them closer to him, his breathing hoarse and deep. A quick fumbling movement and she felt his hard flesh against the entrance to her tight, pulsing core. The small slit in her pantaloons offered no resistance to his heated entry.

She rose onto him and mindlessly settled herself as if she had been taught the movement by a master, rocking tentatively toward him as he thrust into her, his aroused male flesh no longer an invasion but a perfect union of pulsing bodies.

He was hard and full, and she whimpered at the driving motion of his hips, moving hungrily, wanting more of him, reveling in the expression on his face. He wasn't in control any longer, his eyes fixed almost hypnotically on hers, the muscles in his neck held taut like a mizzen rope in a storm. But then, neither was she in control, almost weeping with her need to attain the completion that seemed just beyond her reach.

She felt wild and wonderful, on the brink of an extraordinary release that had everything to do with the wild, pulsing pleasure gripping her body, expanding her world. Myles was a skillful teacher, showing her with each movement of his body what to do, guiding her hips with his hands, teasing her, touching her, letting her ride him into glorious freedom.

That liberation came to her like an arrow of flame, raking through her in a hot, unstoppable rush, and she cried out his name in ecstasy, before she felt his own shattering release in a great shout that seemed to rock the entire carriage. She slid down onto him, panting and spent, only to find herself wrapped in his arms, pulled close to him in an intimacy more startling than that which their bodies had just shared.

When the world finally stopped tilting, she found her head propped under his chin, the regular rise and fall of his chest lifting her cheek in a comforting rhythm. She moved within his arms, conscious once again of the swaying of the carriage and the prosaic nature of her surroundings.

She lifted her head and surprised a gleam of amusement in his eyes as he looked down at her.

"What are you thinking?" she asked shyly.

"That I might have missed being the first to kiss you in a carriage, but I believe I've made my mark."

"I might have known you would be insufferable about it. In fact, I believe you've made several marks. I'm feeling rather battered . . . to say the least."

He frowned and sat up, holding her away from him, his hands clasped viselike about her arms. He examined her closely. "Damn me for being a thoughtless, rutting fool, Sabina. Did I hurt you?"

"No. No, Myles." She shook her head and smiled at him. "You didn't hurt me." She wanted to say *You made me touch the sky and fall back to earth again*, but she wasn't sure she could tolerate that unbearably knowing smile.

He released her, but only to do up her bodice with deft fingers. She put her head to one side as she watched him, smiling a little at his air of concentration, like a small boy fulfilling a task he thought might well be beyond him.

"Why, that's who he looks like! He looks just like you!" she exclaimed suddenly.

His task completed, he produced a comb from his pocket and proceeded to run it through her tousled curls. "Who?" he asked disinterestedly.

"Gammon, of course. Oh, not in coloring, but in features and mannerisms. The way he has of staring at you until he gets the answer he wants, whether it's right or wrong. The stubbornness, the tendency to make judgments and stick to them . . . even that trick with his eyebrows! No wonder everyone thinks he's your son."

"I hope *everyone* realizes that if he was, he wouldn't be working in my stables."

"I . . . I suppose they do." She waited for several seconds before she ventured, "He is such a very bright little boy. He's always asking questions, and it's so sad that he hasn't had any formal teaching. I don't suppose we could provide him with . . . with some sort of schooling. Just a little."

"Of course. He can read Shakespeare while he's mucking out the stables. Or if he ever returns to his former profession, he can quote Latin epigrams as he robs his victims."

"There is no need to be sarcastic, Myles Dampier. I'm not suggesting that you adopt him!"

Myles closed his eyes and mouthed something she couldn't understand. When he opened them again, his voice was calmly measured. "You do know, Sabina, that if I took that unprecedented step, everyone would be convinced he was my bastard."

"Do you mind what other people think?"

"There hasn't been a day in my life that I have minded what people thought of me. I was worried about you."

"If I had ever minded what people thought about me, I'd be sitting in Bournemouth with Cousin Sarah. Not making love with my husband in our carriage, only four miles from the nearest marital bed!"

Slowly his shoulders began to shake, and then he threw his head back and laughed, a sound of pure, unaffected amusement that lifted the shadows from his face. "Mermaid, Mermaid. I should have known better than to have worked that one on you. Very well. I'll refrain from putting his name down for Eton, but I'll make some arrangements for him. But you do realize it will make him a figure of jealousy for some of the other servants."

"I'll handle that," she said firmly. "That will be my job." She was surprised at the confidence in her own voice. She was even more surprised at how happy the thought of returning home to Lysons Hall made her, even after the sensuous magic of their carriage ride through the night.

Home.

It was surely one of the sweetest words in the English language. No wonder Myles had struggled so long and so hard to come back here. She understood that it was not only bitterness and hatred that had strengthened his resolve to return. She could see it in the simple pride he wore when he supervised some building improvement, or inspected the planting of the gardens. She had seen it in his face when he first rode to the top of the rise and surveyed his ruined castle. Even then, it had been beautiful to him.

"How did you come to return?"

He glanced down at her sharply, as if her impulsive question had caught him by surprise.

He replied slowly, "I had waited long enough. I was certainly rich enough by then. My . . . employees in England were merely waiting for my instructions when they approached Richard to buy both the house in Brook Street and the Hall. Naturally, he was delighted to sell at the price I offered."

"I see." She didn't really, and she tried to make things clearer in her mind. "Why didn't your uncle inherit Lysons Hall from your grandfather? He inherited everything else, didn't he? Wasn't it entailed?"

"No. They broke the entail when my great-grandfather was alive. A messy legal business, but it ensured that my father gained possession of the Hall."

She frowned, still trying to understand. "And lost it again?"

"I loved my father, but he was a weak man." Myles's voice softened, and he sounded as though the words were quoted from a well-read book, spoken without thought or emotion. "He seemed to give up on the world after my mother died. Without her, he had no real reason to live. I came home from school to watch him drink himself into an early grave. Although I probably helped finish him off." He continued harshly, "The last time I saw him I was in prison. He said to me, in that soft, slurred drunkard voice, 'Are those shackles really necessary, my boy?' and left. I never saw him again."

The pain in his voice was still raw. Sabina couldn't help from putting trembling fingers over his mouth to stop the agony. Startled, he looked down at her, as though he had forgotten she was there, and then pulled her back into his arms, laying his chin on the top of her head.

She listened to the quiet thumping of his heartbeat, audible even over the noise of the wheels and the steady gait of horses' hooves.

"You don't have to say any more," she said softly.

His chest moved against her ear in a grunt of amused skepticism.

"We might as well get the inquisition over and done with, Sabina. I might not be so forthcoming with all my dark secrets another day."

"Bluebeard," she murmured.

"No wives, Mermaid."

She found herself studying his coat with great interest, smoothing her hand repeatedly over the collar. "But there were women," she said in a small voice.

"Yes, there were one or two." Her hand faltered, and he gathered it into his own, adding harshly, "They came to me for their own survival, Mermaid, and I kept them because of need. They benefited, and so did I. An honest, sensible arrangement, my dear. No one sits pining for my return on the other side of the world."

She had leave to doubt that, but she concentrated instead on *honest* and *sensible*. Two words that could hardly be applied to their own relationship. The thought made her brighten, and she happily dismissed his former women into a pit of oblivion.

"So, how did you make your wealth? You never told me. I always imagined piracy or something of the sort."

"You would. But it was far more prosaic than that. A governor arrived in the colony who believed that convicts were human beings, not animals, and that once your time was over, you deserved a chance to make a new life." The edges of his hard mouth softened slightly as he continued, "By some miracle, Governor Macquarie got a letter from one of the few friends I had left in England, and sent for me. They found me in the mines at King's Town, tunneling under the sea to cut coal. The governor didn't believe in waste, he said, and the colony needed my skills." Myles gave a sharp snort of laughter, full of derision for the boy he had been. "That was the first time anyone thought I had any skills apart from gaming and wenching. He put me to work at Government House, and when my term was finished, granted me some land. I turned my hand at farming—unsuccessfully—until I turned up a nugget of gold the size of a man's fist."

"Gold!" Sabina's jaw dropped. "Myles . . . you found gold on your land."

"I found it, and was promptly bribed with enough money to buy my first ship, just to keep it quiet." He smiled down at her disbelief. "Use your common sense, Mermaid. What do you think would happen to a penal colony in the grip of gold fever? The government realized the chaos it would cause, and paid me to keep quiet. So, my dear, my fortune was built, not on honest labor and the sweat of my own brow, but on blackmail and deception."

He didn't seem particularly ashamed of the fact, and she said dryly, "Well, I have no doubt that your ancestors didn't make theirs by being kind to widows and orphans."

"No, I believe a fair amount of ravishing and plunder went on."

"Well, with forty-nine sons to keep in Dampier style—"

"As well as voracious Dampier wives."

"Am I? Am I voracious?"

His arms tightened around her, his voice suddenly thickening. "We shall have to find out, shan't we?"

She closed her eyes in excited anticipation, and then the wheels beat a sharp, rattling tattoo that shook the carriage. The change of surface indicated that they had reached the bricked entrance to the Hall.

Sabina struggled from the warmth of his arms and sat against the seat. "We're back!"

He sighed. "So we are. What excellent timing."

"Myles, do I look like . . ."

"Someone who has been made love to in a closed carriage? Yes."

"Why do I always end up looking a mess while you look . . . groomed?" she demanded mournfully.

"We can, of course, change that."

He swooped on her, fixing his mouth to hers, kissing her with a breathless precision that made her almost forget the fact that at any moment the door would swing open and a goggling footman would witness their mutual ardor. Without pulling his lips from hers, he took her hands and placed them on either side of his head, then deepened his kiss, stroking the inside of her mouth with a skill that had her fingers curling and spreading into the dark thatch of his hair.

When he finally tore his mouth away from her, his eyes, glittering by the light of the carriage lantern, were innocently questioning.

"Do I look . . . er . . . groomed now?"

"No," she laughed breathlessly, attempting to smooth back one tousled black curl. "You look thoroughly kissed."

The carriage jerked to a halt. He leaned over and flicked her nose with a careless finger.

"Not thoroughly enough. But we'll discuss that later, wife."

A liveried footman held the door open, his eyes averted from his openly disheveled master and mistress, gloveless, hatless, and laughing like children as they climbed from the carriage. Sabina tried to shake her skirts into some semblance of order and then, taking her husband's arm, sailed through the Gothic entrance and into the Great Hall, her heart light.

James, the young footman who no doubt still bore the marks of Gammon's teeth in his arm, bowed and cleared his throat.

"Mr. Marney is just arrived, sir. I've shown him into the library."

"Has he, now? Then take some brandy in, and tell him I will be with him shortly."

James hurried away to do his master's bidding, leaving Sabina to stare at her husband as if he had just sprouted horns and a tail. When she finally found her voice, she was dismayed to hear it tremble.

"Marney is here? Myles, no! Not here. Please."

His eyes narrowed, and he stood very still. "I'm afraid I don't understand you, my dear."

He understood her, she realized sickeningly. He understood her all too well. His face, which only moments before had been warm with laughter, was now as severely formal as a death mask. Right before her eyes, he had withdrawn into that tight little world of vengeance where she could not reach him.

"Send him away," she pleaded, her voice low and desperate. She was afraid to touch him, afraid he might shatter in her hands like the marble statue he resembled. "Please send him away. We don't need him here. I don't want him here."

"But I've sent for him, Sabina." He was quietly reasonable, as if soothing a hysterical child. "We have business to discuss. It would seem very odd if I sent him away just because my wife does not care for his manner."

"I don't care for what he *represents*. Myles, please. He's like some awful dark shadow peering over our shoulders. I thought we wouldn't need him anymore!"

"But you agreed, my dear, that you would no longer interfere."

Desperately she tried to think back to what had taken place during the carriage ride. Had her own treacherous body tricked her into agreeing to submit to his plans? She shook her head, unconsciously rejecting the idea, and backed away from him, step by painful step.

"That wasn't an agreement to become your . . . your acolyte in hate, Myles Dampier. That was love!"

"That was *lust*, Sabina. Glorious, healthy lust between a man and a woman." He walked toward her, his lips tightening as she took another step away from him. "I chose you because of your beauty and your intelligence. Try to use a little of the latter now."

And then she was no longer afraid. She was suddenly, magnificently angry.

She looked around the Great Hall for something to hurl at him, her eyes fixing on a display of battle-axes arranged on the wall in the shape of a great cross. If only she could reach one of them . . .

He followed the direction of her gaze, and his mouth quirked in a bitter smile.

"Better men than you have tried something like that, my dear."

"Go to hell, Myles Dampier." Her voice shook with the ferocity of her fury. "Go to hell and . . . and take that creeping, crawling *creature* of yours with you. Damn you because you're too frightened to think that there is any hope of salvation in the world! I hope you both burn!"

She swung around on the last word and ran across the expanse of floor and up the great staircase as if pursued by imps. Only when she reached the top, before disappearing along the gallery, did she pause and turn around to see what effect her exit had had upon her husband.

He was no longer there.

The Great Hall, with its shields, and stag heads, and medieval armory, was deserted.

Myles had taken her at her word.

She didn't sleep that night. She couldn't—tossing and turning until the bed was a pitiable parody of the state it had been in after she shared it with Myles.

It had been stripped and the sheets crisply replaced, all evidence of the breaking of her maidenhead and the first joyous union with her husband gone. Just as if it had never taken place.

But what if Myles had fulfilled his mission? What if his gentle hints to Richard Dampier and his wife had been more than just the final twist of the rack?

What if she really was with child?

How did one know? When did one know?

She could talk knowledgeably about the gestation of the Indian elephant and the nesting habits of the red-beaked parrot, but human pregnancy was still something of a mystery to her.

Whom could she ask? Mrs. Ferris? Maria? Lady Vantry? Myles?

She struggled to her elbows as the tightness across her chest intensified to an unbearable degree, and she let out a sound that was half sob, half strangled gasp for air.

She had failed. Miserably. She had tried to fight Myles, and had ended up becoming nothing but a pawn in his monstrous game with the Dampiers. She had been so sure she could win, step by step, little by little, the depth of her love dragging him out of the sea of hatred and deception that surrounded him.

She collapsed against the pillows and tried to sort through the jumble of images and sounds in her head. Was this what had happened to Sylvia Dampier? Had she, too, lain awake at night trying to put the world back together like the pieces of a giant puzzle? No wonder the poor woman had resorted to laudanum, in the forlorn hope that it would somehow make the world and all its pieces fit together neatly and tidily.

She was too tortured to sleep, and slipped from beneath the covers, dragging a wrap over her nightgown and re-kindling her candle. She stood swaying a little before deciding that she needed some air, and made her way to the casement where Maria, convinced that night air was poisonous to the lungs, had wedged the window shut.

Sabina placed her candle on the sill and threw the window wide, inhaling deep breaths that went some way toward dispelling the terrible tightness in her chest. She knelt on the little seat and turned her burning cheek into the glass, peering down into the darkness of the great, gray courtyard.

A man stood there alone in a pale puddle of moonlight.

She could not see who it was from that distance, but she had a strong impression that he stared up at her window. Instinctively she backed away, but then a second instinct, deeply primal, drew her back, and she knelt on the seat again, placing both hands on either side of the window, leaning forward so that she was visible by the flickering flame of her single candle. She let her hair tumble forward over her breast and continued to kneel there until the figure finally turned away and walked into the shadows.

Sabina slid back into a kneeling position on the window seat, trembling so much that she had to wrap her arms around herself to stop from falling. Then she blew out her candle and went back to bed, sleep claiming her before she had time to rearrange her mental jigsaw.

The next morning, Maria, who disapproved of breakfast in bed as a matter of course, nevertheless tried to coax her mistress into partaking for once.

"You look like you haven't had a wink of sleep, ma'am. There are great circles under your eyes."

"Thank you, Maria. I have a mirror, and I've already looked into it. And I don't need help tying my own stockings, either. Will you bring me the sea-green morning gown? The one"—she swallowed suddenly—"the one with all the buttons down the front of the bodice."

Maria fixed Sabina's hair as elaborately as if for a ball, informing her rather tentatively that Mr. Dampier had left early that morning and wouldn't be back for some hours.

"Indeed?" Sabina stared at the reflection of a fashionable young woman in her looking glass, noting with concern the defeated stoop of her shoulders. She straightened them immediately, asking offhandedly, "Was I left any message?"

"No, ma'am. Not that I know of."

"Excellent," she said briskly, and meant it. "I mean to take a walk this morning, Maria. So stout shoes, if you please."

The stout shoes thumped angrily all the way along the great gallery and down the staircase into the small breakfast room. Not that she suspected her husband of cowardice in his sudden absence from the Hall. Oh, no! Instead she suspected he had left merely to annoy her.

When she opened the door, and found Mr. Marney cozily seated at the breakfast table, she was convinced of it.

Mr. Marney rose to his feet, his mouth widening in what

she could only suppose *he* supposed to be a smile of welcome.

"Mrs. Dampier. This is a delightful surprise. I had been told that you would breakfast in your rooms."

"A barracuda!" Sabina announced triumphantly.

Marney paused in the middle of his greeting and studied her suspiciously.

"I . . . beg your pardon, ma'am?"

"Nothing at all, Mr. Marney. I was recently reminded of something, and it's taken me a little while to remember what it was."

He displayed all of his pointed teeth, and his pale eyes glinted unpleasantly.

"Will you be joining me, Mrs. Dampier?"

"It looks that way, doesn't it?" She ignored the chair that he had pulled out beside him, and plumped down in one that looked to be beyond his reach. Then she spread her napkin over her lap and attacked.

"I want you to do something for me, Mr. Marney."

The bony fingers made a little steeple under his chin as he studied her through half-closed eyes. "I am always happy to be of service, Mrs. Dampier. You must be aware of my . . . devotion to the family."

Sabina resisted the desire to run her napkin hard across her mouth. Instead she schooled her features into the look of bored hauteur that Myles used with such devastating effect.

"I want you to bring me something."

He seemed impressed by the seriousness of her tone. "The head of John the Baptist, presumably."

"Nothing so difficult. There is a harp in the house in Brook Street. A great gold harp in one of the upper rooms. I want you to have it brought here."

"But that is no task at all. That is a job for a porter. I thought at least, at the very least, that you were going to ask me to slay you a dragon."

"My husband slays my dragons for me, Mr. Marney."

"Does he indeed, lovely Sabina? But unfortunately, not

sly, *creeping, crawling* ones." His voice was soft with a quality that made her flesh prickle.

"You were listening? With your ear against the library door?"

"I would have had to be lying in the crypt under the old chapel not to have heard. You have a very clear voice, ma'am. You would have created a sensation on the stage."

"It seems I've created one here."

She threw her napkin down on the table and stood up, unable to bear the loathsome man's gloating. But before she could move, he shot out of his chair, throwing himself against the door with a dramatic flourish. She stared at him amazed.

"Are you mad, sir?"

"I forgot to ask you what my reward would be for fetching you the harp." The pale eyes gleamed with a light that made her take a step backward. "What reward can you think of that I would like?"

Sabina fought down a wave of nausea and panic. *This isn't happening to me,* she told herself fiercely. *I'm not being bailed up in my own breakfast room by a man who I'd put my foot on if he were only a few inches tall.*

"Get out of my way."

"Not until you tell me what my reward is going to be."

"Your reward will be that I don't tell my husband about your behavior this morning!"

To her consternation, the sharp face suddenly creased, and he emitted a thin, wheezing sound that she could almost mistake for laughter.

"You find that amusing?" she demanded angrily. She judged the distance between her knee and the man's groin, wondering if somehow she could make contact without making herself vilely ill.

"Of course, I find it amusing. Good Lord, do you think he would care?"

"Let's ask him and see!"

"Oh, let us do so, by all means, Mrs. Dampier. And see what is more important to him—his plan to wipe his cousin from the face of the earth, or this farce of a marriage."

The man's insolence was overwhelming. "What do you mean, farce?" she demanded angrily. "What do you know about our marriage?"

But Marney had already begun to back away from the door, his palms lifted and turned outward in a mocking sign of surrender. "I yield! I yield! Better to run away and live to fight another day, eh, Mrs. Dampier?"

She threw the door open and ran out of the room, uncertain of where she was going, only determined to leave the spiteful little man and his venom far behind her. She found herself trapped at the end of a long corridor that led to some disused rooms. Panting in her mindless panic, she wrenched open a door. A large window led into an outer courtyard, and she flew to it.

Minutes later, she was running through the south garden and into the park, stopping only when she felt sheltered by the safety of a grove of trees. She lay back against the comfort of a tree trunk, trying to control her breathing.

Amazingly, she felt like laughing. Healthy, life-affirming laughter.

It wasn't hysteria. It was a simple hilarity born of shame at her unreasoned panic, and the realization that she must have left the Hall looking like a furtive housemaid absconding with the silver.

Marney was an obnoxious toad who made her skin crawl, but she had met other Marneys during her travels. Both her looks and the minimal protection afforded by a father more interested in the local birdlife than in whether her honor was being assaulted, had led her to hone her skills in deflecting unwanted attention.

No. What had made her take flight like a gothic heroine fleeing a lustful monk were Marney's vicious, wounding words about Myles.

Because, God help her, perhaps they were true.

She would not think about that now, she decided stoutly. She shaded her eyes as she looked at the land beyond the trees—flat, green, rolling land that invited her to lose herself in the joy of a day where the sun beat warmly and the only shadows were those lurking behind her at the Hall. Sabina didn't bother returning to fetch either her hat or her cloak. Instead she began to walk, finding some sort of release for sore muscles and restless longing in the exercise.

Before long, she could look back and find the Hall no longer visible. That was when she noticed that the birds wheeling overhead were seabirds. Her breath caught in excitement, and she pressed on, drawn by the faint tang of the sea in the distance.

The sound of an approaching horse stopped her in her tracks. It didn't occur to her that it might be a stranger; instead, she waited for it to draw near, philosophical in her expectation that it would be her husband.

It wasn't. It was Richard Dampier.

He saw her, and his horse plunged. When he quieted it with a soothing word, he cantered nearer, concern written across his handsome face.

"Mrs. Dampier? Are you lost? You are some distance from the Hall, you know."

"I know. That was deliberate. As for being lost, I'm not quite certain. I suppose I am somewhere between Lysons Hall and the sea."

He swung off the gray gelding with the enviable confidence of a competent horseman. "Yes, you are. You are also skirting my lands."

She smiled at the boyish pride in his voice. "I see. I am being warned off, am I?"

"On the contrary. I was never so happy to see a trespasser before. In fact, I was on my way to see *you*. I wanted . . . I wanted to apologize for last night."

"Last night? Oh, of course, last night. I had almost forgotten." She wasn't being polite. So much had happened the previous night that the farce around the dining table at Curstone Abbey had already faded into insignificance. "Lady Dampier was exhausted when we arrived. We should have realized."

"She is herself again this morning," he said heavily. "And extremely embarrassed at what took place. She isn't . . . she isn't always like that, you know. She wanted me to write a note and apologize, but I thought that a note would be so cold. . . ."

"I was right," Sabina said softly. "You *are* summer to Myles's winter, aren't you, Sir Richard Dampier?"

He stared at her, clearly alarmed that the conversation wasn't following an expected course. "I'm not sure what you mean."

Of course he wouldn't. He didn't have Myles's twisty mind, or his talent for understanding what she said, even when it made no sense to herself. She sighed, turning her face toward the sea so that the wind whipped her uncovered head, dragging her hair from its pins and lashing it against her face. She pushed it aside, asking bluntly, "How long has Lady Dampier been taking laudanum?"

She heard him suck in his breath as if receiving a blow to the stomach. "Upon my word, Mrs. Dampier . . . you take a great deal upon yourself!"

"Myles blames you for everything, you know," she said steadily, continuing as if he had not spoken. "Your wife's addiction is merely one of your crimes. He believes you betrayed him to your father fifteen years ago. He also thinks you were instrumental in having him transported to Australia. He thinks you did it so you could marry Sylvia and possess her fortune. I don't believe it. Not in my heart. Not now that I've met you. But I want you to convince me, Richard Dampier. I want you to tell me that you played no part in Myles's transportation."

She turned around to face him, to gauge the effect of her words. He wasn't looking at her. Instead he leaned shaking into his saddle, his head buried in his hands. She waited patiently until he lifted his face, his skin blanched to the fine white quality of paper. Only his eyes were alive, burning into her like twin blue flames.

"I knew," he whispered. "I think I always knew, but I was too much of a coward to find out for sure. It's because . . . I came out of it with everything, I suppose, while he

256

lost everything. That's why he refused to see me when I came to the prison. That's why he wouldn't answer any of my letters. I thought he was too ashamed to reply, but . . . I should have realized the truth."

The anguish in his voice was too real to be a hoax. "Then you didn't betray him?" she demanded eagerly.

"I swear to God, no! That's not to say that I couldn't believe my own luck when it all went wrong. You're right, of course. I always loved Sylvia, but she would never even look at me while Myles was around. And I was too frightened of her laughter—her pity!—to ever tell her how I felt. But after the elopement was discovered—even before Myles was transported, I was there to give her comfort. A shoulder to cry on, you understand. She began to depend on me, more and more . . . and eventually she married me. I didn't give a damn about her money. Why should I? Why should anyone? You've seen her. How could any man not love her?"

"You have to tell him," Sabina said flatly. "You have to tell him that it was none of your doing."

"If it wasn't mine, it was my father's," he said wearily. "And I could have done more to help him if I hadn't been so obsessed with winning Sylvia. But I was, and I didn't. So I suppose mine is the sin of omission. Isn't that just as bad?" There was a painful silence as they both digested the enormity of this confession. Then he added quietly, "I did do one thing for him, though, when I attained my majority. I urged a mutual friend to write a letter to the governor of the colony, explaining the circumstances and . . . and requesting leniency. I never heard if it did any good or not. I could never bear to make inquiries." He saw her expression alter and harden, and he said ruefully, "I told you I was a coward."

"And you never expected him to return, did you?"

Richard's lips twisted into a reluctant smile. "I was never more shocked in my life when someone told me they had seen him in London, living like a king and escorting a breathtaking beauty on his arm. That's when I knew who the Hall's mystery purchaser was. He shouldn't have had to do it in secret. I would have been glad to sell it to him. But how am I to convince him that I am . . . glad that he—and you—are there now."

"You can't," she replied roundly. "No one can. But you need to talk to him, Richard. You need to try to make him see reason."

The look of unease that spread across Richard Dampier's features would have amused her at any other time. Now it just emphasized the fact that Myles's cousin was not going to be the most useful ally in her fight for his redemption.

"Let's walk," she suggested quietly, and they fell into a steady gait, the gelding plodding patiently behind his master.

They walked in silence, each, she supposed, too busy with sorting out their own thoughts to intrude upon the other. So she was startled when Richard said quietly, "You are right, you know, about the laudanum. It's not widely known, of course. I've had . . . I've had a doctor see to her, but as far as he was concerned, if she was quiet and happy he couldn't see what all the fuss was about."

"But your wife is not happy, is she?"

"No, she isn't." It must have been difficult for him to admit it, and Sabina admired the courage it must have taken for him to continue doggedly. "You see, my wife and I are childless, but that . . . wasn't always the case. There was a son, once, but he only lived a few hours. Since then there have been many . . . disappointments. Too many. Sylvia has found it difficult to come to terms with them. You see, she had always longed for a child so desperately."

"I'm so sorry," Sabina whispered. She felt like an intruder, trampling over his pain in her comfortable walking boots, and she tactfully turned her head away to give him time to recover his countenance. No wonder he had responded the way he had when Myles implied she was with child.

Another brick slipping easily into the framework of his plan.

"Damn Myles Dampier! He needs a sound thrashing!"

She was aghast to find that she had spoken the words aloud, and met Richard's eye a little shamefacedly. However, his mouth was stretched into a reluctant grin. "I've seen Myles thrashed many times as a child, and I'm afraid it only makes him even more stubborn."

"I was afraid of that," she sighed.

"You love him, don't you?" He said the words gently, and it was the pity in his tone that most disturbed her.

"You think I'm a fool, don't you?" she said ruefully.

"No. I don't. You forget—many people loved him once, because he possessed qualities that made him very easy to love. I know. I remember."

"Or easy to hate."

"That too," he agreed solemnly. "No one could ever be halfhearted about Myles."

"And you, Richard? What did you feel about him?"

"I loved him. I was jealous of him. But I loved him."

The sincerity in his voice made her shiver and turn away. "You know that he plans to ruin you," she said, all emotion drained from her voice. Even now the words seemed too full of wickedness to utter.

"Myles hasn't ruined me, Sabina. I can't let you lay that at his door, no matter how much I should like to shift the blame to someone else. The truth is, I ruined myself."

"I don't understand."

"Speculation, Sabina." He reached out and took her hand, holding the fingers lightly. "It's just a different form of gaming. It can prove just as ruinous. I invested my money in a number of foolish schemes that I knew could prove disastrous. They did. I lost all of Sylvia's money and most of my own. My estate is mortgaged, and I have been forced to retrench. It's a story familiar to the very best families in England. And I have no one but myself to blame."

She wanted to believe him, but the evil image of Mr. Marney's sharklike features appeared in her mind's eye.

"I wish I could help," she whispered.

"So do I," he said frankly. He was silent, and then suddenly he raised his head excitedly. "There is a way you can help. Come and see Sylvia. Come and see her and tell her she is forgiven for last night. Offer her the same friendship you have offered me."

"Would she want to see me?" Sabina asked wonderingly. "Knowing what you now know, would she want to see me?"

"My wife is as good as she is beautiful," he said simply. "She will want to see you."

"Then I'll come."

He leaned forward and placed a chaste kiss on her forehead, before releasing her hands. "Bless you," he said.

He remounted his horse and smiled down. "When will you come? Today?"

"Tomorrow. I promise."

"Shall I take you up before me? Are you tired? Do you want a ride with me back to the Hall?"

She remembered the last time she had shared a horse with a man. Myles's arms had been around her, holding her safely. She couldn't bear to be in anyone else's arms, however innocently offered. She smiled up at him. "No, and no, and no to all three questions. I want to continue my walk."

He made her a graceful salute and, pulling the gray around, cantered away, a fair young knight setting out on a quest for his lady's sake. The beautiful Lady Sylvia, a prisoner, not of a ferocious dragon but of her own feverish weakness for the juice of the poppy.

Sabina watched him ride out of sight, and then turned once more in the direction of the wheeling seabirds. Myles had promised to show her the sea near his home. She faltered, wondering if there would ever come a time when he would do so. Since his return to Lysons Hall, he had become someone completely different from the man she had known aboard the *Ellen Drury*. The cynical part of her whispered that it was because he had been courting her then. Although it had been a strange courtship, with no pretty compliments or tender words of love. Instead he had given her companionship, and laughter, and the rare gift of a generous mind, answering her questions about the world with wit and warmth.

And now all she wanted was his soul.

As if on cue, a horseman seemed to be summoned up from nowhere, riding a roan gelding that pranced and threw its head, arrogantly delighting in its own strength and beauty.

The black knight, she thought fatalistically. *That's all I need.*

He reined in close enough to make her step back nervously, and stared down at her, his nostrils flared with even greater effect than his horse's. Something had annoyed him.

"I thought you would be with your beloved Mr. Marney," she said flatly.

"Indeed? Is that why I find you making assignations with our neighbors, Mermaid? That was very quick work. You've met—what? Two, three times? Or do I forget the meeting at the posting inn when you so touchingly recognized each other as kindred souls?"

His tone was distinctly sour. He sounded, if she could believe it, *jealous*.

Myles Dampier, jealous? The thought was so ludicrous that she let out a little silvery laugh she had learned from a Brazilian lady famous for her charm.

"Really, Myles? Assignations? You sound like something out of a farce."

"Husbands are often farcical, my dear," he said smoothly, the undercurrent of anger barely perceptible. "But you might want to warn my delightful cousin that the next time he wants to kiss my wife he had better do it somewhere more private."

"What? Myles, did you have a *telescope* trained on us?"

"I was watching from under the trees."

"You saw us and you didn't make yourself known?"

"I was about to, when Sir Richard Charming took your hand and started giving away free kisses."

She looked up at him, slack-jawed with disbelief. The

impossible had happened. Myles Dampier was displaying a common human failing.

Stupidity!

She turned on her heel and began to stride away, not really caring where she was going. The jingle of a bridle alerted her to the fact that she had company.

"Go away," she called out. "I'm too angry to speak to you."

"Sabina—"

"No! How dare you accuse me of impropriety with your cousin? Of all the stupid . . . ! I could hit you!"

"I'm sorry."

"You're always sorry about something, Myles Dampier. The only trouble is, you're never sorry enough!"

She walked on, anger giving her steps a spring that they might not otherwise have had. She was conscious of being on her own only when she heard the sound of hooves moving off into the distance.

Myles had taken her at her word.

For the first time, he had asked something of her, and she had refused him.

That was good, she told herself fiercely. It was time he didn't get everything his own way. It was time she finally said no to him.

She just wondered why something so good could make her feel so empty inside.

CHAPTER TWELVE

"Your friendship," Lady Vantry said airily, "has done Sylvia a great deal of good over these last few weeks. I did not expect to see her here this evening."

Sabina, from her vantage point on the settee she shared with her hostess, had her attention directed to where the beautiful Lady Dampier held court with half a dozen gentlemen in the far corner of the Vantrys' gracious drawing room.

She forced a smile to her lips. "I really can't take the credit for it. I have called upon her several times, and gone riding with her in her carriage—that's all. I am hardly a celestial visitation."

Lucilla Vantry's sharp eyes grew sharper. "Nonsense. You have offered her friendship. And, believe it or not, Sabina, she has had few friends in her life. When you look like she does, women tend to avoid you, and gentlemen fall in love with you without seeing you properly at all. If you can find one true friend in this life, then you are doing remarkably well!" She leaned closer so that the waving plumes of her turban tickled Sabina's forehead. "I take it that the other . . . problem is being addressed?" Her Ladyship watched Sabina hesitate for a moment before adding impatiently, "Oh, come, my dear. You might as well tell me. You know I will only ask Richard about it and reduce him to stuttering idiocy."

"I convinced Richard to call in Dr. Martin, a local man. He seems eminently sensible about the whole matter."

"Good!" said Her Ladyship. "I never approved of Richard burying his head in the sand over this whole business. As I always say, 'He who refuses to be guided by the rudder will be guided by the rocks.'" She paused dramatically, then asked, "Which reminds me, my dear. When will that husband of yours return home?"

Sabina pasted a smile on her face. "I don't know, Lady Vantry. He has business in London."

Her Ladyship snorted. "Yes, well. My husband once had business in London, too. She had red hair and was as fat as mud. He thought I didn't know, but there is not a great deal that escapes *me*. You must write to Myles and bring him home."

Bring him home. The words reverberated in Sabina's head like the lyrics of an old, sad song. He had left her after that brief, disastrous meeting on the edge of the estate, taking Marney with him. There had been no explanation, no fond leave-taking. His curt, brusque manner had been searingly polite.

"Myles will return when he has finished what he set out to do." She shifted in her seat uncomfortably, wondering where else this grilling would lead, when her eyes widened and she stifled a small gasp. Mrs. Cedric Carstairs was fast approaching them, her face a mask of disapproval.

"Ah," said Lady Vantry cordially, "there you are, Harriet. I wondered where on earth you had got to."

Mrs. Carstairs cast a disgruntled glance over her shoulder to where her husband stood amongst a group of gentlemen, his entire attitude one of profound pleading. He nodded to her encouragingly, and she turned to Sabina, saying tightly, "The weather is remarkably warm for this time of year, Mrs. Dampier." And, obviously having said more than she would have liked to, she swept away before Sabina could respond.

"Well!" Lady Vantry commented lightly. "That went well."

Sabina felt herself tremble, and realized that her shoulders were shaking. "I think," she said firmly, "that I am going to laugh."

"No, you aren't! You are going to sit there and look as though no amount of attention is more than your proper due. And then, when the card tables are set out, I will make Hatty partner you as her punishment for wearing such a distasteful shade of bronze. She may be my sister-in-law, but the woman has absolutely no idea how to dress!"

Sabina did laugh then, and the sound caught Richard Dampier's attention. He left the small group of neighbors with whom he talked, and bowed gracefully over her hand, retaining her fingers just a trifle longer than was necessary.

"Lucilla, Mrs. Dampier." He smiled and looked to where his wife reclined on a low settee, chatting animatedly to her little court. "Thank you, Sabina. You are responsible for this. I don't know how you managed to coax her out of the house this evening, but . . . you have my gratitude, just the same."

"I wish people would stop endowing me with magical powers. I assure you I did nothing! I merely said how much I needed her support, and . . . there she is."

"I suppose the harp was nothing! If you could have seen her face when it was delivered! I can't thank you enough."

"What's this? What's this about a harp?" Lady Vantry's features were razor-sharp with curiosity. Sabina expected her to grow whiskers and twitch her nose at any moment.

"I'll let Sir Richard explain," she said cordially, rising to her feet. "I think I need to get some air. Especially now, as the weather is remarkably warm for this time of year."

Lady Vantry chuckled, but made no protest. "Yes, yes, go, my dear. Richard and I have things to talk about."

Sabina hardened her heart to the look of horror that passed across Richard's face, and determinedly skirted several knots of people before finding her way through the doors onto the garden terrace. Once there, she heaved a sigh of relief at her solitude and ruefully reflected that being a social pariah had been a lot less exhausting than being a social success.

People had been kind, of course. Surprisingly so. Lucilla Vantry and Richard Dampier had led the way, and gradually the cards and calls which had begun as a slight trickle were promising to become a flood, and the ten or twelve families she had once been prepared to scorn were threatening to take her to their collective bosom.

For Myles's sake, she was glad. And as for herself . . . well, it was an entirely new experience for her. She realized that her life, as adventurous as it had become over the last five or six years, had always been rather lonely. It was almost impossible to make friends when she and her father were on the move all the time. That was why the Marchands had been so important to her, and their loss all the more tragic. They had been her first real friends, and to have had them swept away by the ocean, wiping out all trace of their lives . . .

She drew in a shuddering breath, remembering what could have been her own fate. Chastened that she could be so sad when she had so much to be grateful for, she left the terrace and its warm, comforting arc of light, drawn farther into the shadows.

It made her understand all the more keenly how Myles must have felt all those years ago, separated from friends and family, not only by distance but by his bitter belief that he had been abandoned by them. And now she knew how that feeling of abandonment could eat into your soul, causing you to imagine all sorts of dreadful things, even here under the gentle moonlight amidst the perfume of late-summer flowers.

He came up behind her with the stealth of a cat, but her senses seemed so attuned to the darkness that she was prepared for the light touch on her shoulder. She didn't need to turn around to know who it was. His fingers burned through her like a branding iron, marking her forever as belonging to him.

"When did you get here?" she asked in a low voice.

"I came through the door just as you left the room. I watched you leave. Politeness made me pause to acknowledge my host and hostess at least."

"Of course you know I came out here to be alone," she said quaveringly. It was too much. The feelings, spiraling through her like a small whirlwind, made her feel as if she had been stripped to the bone. "I've made an assignation with Richard Dampier, as you might have guessed. He should be here any minute."

"I'm sorry. I'm so sorry for what I said that day. I don't know what madness came over me." His words were low, and reverberated with something that sounded like shame. She was so surprised to hear it that she wheeled around to face him. He was immaculate in evening clothes, the white starched collar catching the moonlight. The rest of his body, garbed in black, blended into the darkness so comfortably that she put her hand out to make sure he was real, softly touching his cheek with shaking fingers.

He didn't move. He was as still as the great marble gladiator, and she withdrew her hand, curling her fingers up into two small fists. "I'm sorry, too," she said sadly. "I don't often get angry, but the circumstances seemed exceptional."

"No," he said in a flat, emotionless voice. "You don't get angry often, do you? You don't hate. You don't get bitter. You don't find any joy in hurting people. You rush to protect the weak, and you shield those you love with a fierceness that would do credit to a bulldog."

She could not interpret the tone of his voice. He sounded unutterably weary, as if he were a thousand years old.

She tried to laugh it off. "Indeed, Mr. Dampier? Did you merely follow me out here to give me a list of my virtues?"

"No. I came to tell you . . . something that I should have told you a long time ago."

She was chilled by his unnatural formality and braced herself for the worst. "What is it?"

"No. Not here. This isn't the place for you to hear it. Come home with me, Sabina. I've called for your carriage to be brought around. Get into it and come home."

"No! Not the carriage!" The protest was instinctively torn from her, and for one heart-stopping moment she saw his teeth gleam white through the darkness.

"I'll ride back, Mermaid. You will have it entirely to yourself."

"But what excuse will I give? I can't be so rude—"

"For God's sake, Sabina." His patience, barely held in check at the best of times, seemed to crack. "A sudden headache, an attack of the gout! Throw a wifely tantrum and leave in high dudgeon. You're a woman! You must know a thousand ways to leave a social function."

"Perhaps you could just throw me over your shoulder and carry me out! That way I wouldn't *have* to make excuses!" she shot back sarcastically.

"Every now and then, Mrs. Dampier, your intelligence exceeds your beauty." She barely had time to cry out before he bent slowly and hoisted her over his shoulder.

"Myles! No! I was joking!" She beat at him with her fists and kicked her legs in a futile effort to break free. A firm slap on her rump made her cry out indignantly, but as he bore her farther away from the house, she submitted with as good a grace as she could muster, saying in long-suffering tones, "If anyone sees us, they will write us off as madmen."

"Nonsense. The rich are never mad. Only charmingly eccentric."

His lengthy strides had brought them round the side to the entrance of the Vantrys' house, where Sabina, craning her neck around uncomfortably, saw that her carriage was waiting to take her back to Lysons Hall. John, the coachman, and her two footmen, who had been engaged in idle gossip with one of the Vantrys' liveried servants, watched the approach of their master and his wife with open mouths.

"Let me down, Myles! I don't have to be thrown through the door like a sack of wheat." Wordlessly she was lowered to her feet, but he kept a firm hold on her shoulders, drawing her into his tall body. She looked up at him and said breathlessly, "I think we have already provided our servants with enough amusement, Mr. Dampier."

"It's not their amusement I was concerned about," he replied thickly, but he let her go, and, before either footman could recover enough to leap to her assistance, she clambered into the carriage and shut the door with a snap. She heard Myles's sharp orders, and then the vehicle jerked into life, leaving her to ponder on what her husband had to tell her that could necessitate her abduction from the Vantrys' dinner.

Sabina walked through the Hall's ancient entrance, conscious that she had left yet another expensive evening cloak at a host's house.

"You know they will be short one lady for dinner," she said to her husband accusingly.

"They are short of *several* ladies in that gathering, Mermaid, our delightful hostess amongst them. I wouldn't worry about it. Go and wait for me in the library. I'll be with you soon."

He strode up the stairs without waiting to see whether she would follow his orders, and she stood dumbfounded, flushed with annoyance, and debating the wisdom of going straight to her room instead. However, her curiosity won over, and she began to peel off her gloves as she slowly made her way to the library.

She opened the door and found only a single brace of candles lighting the room. Somehow it didn't seem enough to dispel the natural murkiness of the darkly paneled room and its moldering volumes of books.

Nowhere else was the fact that the house had been left to slip into decay more evident than in this room. Here, Thomas Bradshaw, the infamous tenant, had used the pages of Milton and Shakespeare to kindle his fires, and had conducted target practice at cornices and carvings from his chair behind the great oak desk. Mice conducted feasts, and rats gnawed at the wainscotting. All it needed was a secret passage and a mad monk to complete the picture of gothic gloom.

Or a snake. Uncoiling from its recumbent position on a sofa. Sitting up and shaking its head to get rid of sleep. Drunkenly lurching to its feet where it stood swaying and smiling in the flickering of the candles.

"Mr. Marney!"

"Mrs. Dampier. You must forgive me. I seem to have fallen asleep. The journey from London was . . . most exhausting."

Polite words. Obsequious tone. It had the effect of making her retreat several steps.

"My husband wishes to speak privately to me. He will be joining us in a moment."

Marney lifted his hands to his mouth in mock fright. "Oh, my stars! He will, will he? And what is that supposed to do to me, *Mrs. Dampier*? Put me in my place? Frighten me? Make me leave?"

"I think you had better go, now."

He didn't seem to be listening. His pale eyes were fixed on her with an intensity that made her feel suddenly naked and unclean. Then he began to speak, his mouth working like that of a man in pain.

"You always seem to be asking me to leave the room, my pretty. Even when I do things for you. I have, you know—done things for you. I got you your damned harp, didn't I? Like a little lackey. And what do I get for it? I can do more for you. You don't have to stay here. I've made myself a wealthy man in my own right. You can have whatever you want. I won't ref . . . fuse you anything!"

He slurred on the last word. Sabina, who had barely been able to comprehend anything he said, registered one fact with shocking clarity.

The man was drunk. Her eyes sought and found the

evidence of an empty brandy bottle and the single glass on a small table beside the sofa.

"How dare you!" she cried out, incensed. "You insufferable, drunken creature. What makes you think you can insult me like this in my own home! When my husband comes in—"

"You don't understand, do you? That's the greatest joke of all." He threw back his head and let out a thin bray of laughter. Then he closed his eyes and announced in a sibilant whisper, "You beautiful little fool. You don't *have* a husband! You never did!"

Sabina stood still, her feet embedded in the floor. "That's insane! I was married on board the *Ellen Drury!* There are witnesses!"

"Stupid! Stupid! Stupid!" His voice rose ecstatically. "It wasn't *legal!* A marriage at sea isn't legally binding if performed by the captain! Didn't you know? I thought every woman knew the Marriage Act by heart! No marriage is legal unless performed by an ordained minister. No court of law would recognize it." Marney began to wheeze with great gasps of laughter, slapping his knee and tottering back to the sofa, where he collapsed in a little heap of pleased chuckles. "It's no more legal than if he had married that damned monkey the old whoremonger sent you. If Dampier has already bedded you, then you are nothing but his doxy, my dear. His beautiful, foolish doxy."

He spat out the last words like a snake spitting poison, and her stomach heaved.

"I don't believe you," she whispered.

But she did.

Marney wouldn't have to make up a lie to destroy her. He was far too clever for that. This time, the truth was enough to succeed.

She swung around, blindly seeking to leave the man and his vile revelations far behind her. She was stopped, confronted by a broad chest that backed her slowly through the door. Myles took one look at her face and grasped her arms, shaking her until her head slumped forward like a puppet's.

"What the hell has he been saying to you?" Myles gave Marney a look so full of venom and blackness that the lawyer shot out of his seat and backed against the window. "Look at me, Sabina. What's going on here?"

"The truth!" Marney shouted. He clutched at the tattered curtains as if they could shield him from Myles's wrath. "That's all. I told her the truth!"

"The truth! You wouldn't know the truth if it lay down and died in your arms, you poxy-faced whoreson!"

He shook Sabina again, forcing her chin up to look at him. But she closed her eyes, refusing to meet his eyes. "Sabina! For God's sake, listen to me."

"I can't," she moaned. Not this time. This time she was utterly defeated. "Every time I listen to you, you rip my heart out!"

She felt her legs buckling even as she spoke, and then she was in his arms, held high against his chest, where she curled up into a tight little ball of misery.

"I'll kill you for this. God help me, Marney, I'll hack you into little pieces and throw them to the dogs."

If he had shouted the words, Marney might not have taken them so seriously, but the quiet, practical tone of his voice made the man sidle along the wall, searching for an exit.

"Don't threaten me, Dampier. By God, I know too much about you for you to threaten me and get away with it. I could destroy you if I revealed everything I know."

"Destroy me?" Myles laughed bitterly. "Do you think I would have been so stupid as to use a creature like you if I didn't think I could control him when it was necessary? I could crush you like an ant, Marney. Legally or otherwise. And don't forget, my acquaintance with the London underworld is a little more extensive than even yours will ever be. I could have your throat quietly cut while you were still wondering where the breeze came from!"

With that, Myles left the room, holding Sabina close to his chest. She had begun to shiver, and her teeth were chattering, and by the time they reached her bedchamber, she felt as though she had been pulled from a frozen lake.

"Where's your abigail? Damn her."

"B . . . b . . . bed. I told her . . . not to . . . wait up."

"Your timing is impeccable, Mermaid," he said gently, and laid her down on the bed, pulling the covers over her and tucking them in around her like a child. He went over to the small fire burning in the grate and stirred it into life, adding more fuel.

He came back and watched her shiver, the dark face inscrutable.

"What . . . what's wrong with me?"

"Shock. Are you still cold?"

"Y . . . yes." Even that one word was difficult to say when she couldn't prise her teeth apart. She became aware that he was methodically removing her clothes when he propped her up and started to undo the buttons at the back of her gown.

"What . . . what . . . are you doing?"

"Getting you out of this. What damn fool removed the buttons from the front of the bodice?" He eventually succeeded in jerking her out of the sleeves, and then dispensed with the rest of her gown and her petticoats with the same ruthless precision. There was nothing loverlike in his actions, and it was only when he started to remove his own clothing that she tried to protest.

"Shut up."

"I don't have to! I don't have to do anything you tell me! I'm not your wife!"

"Stay under the covers, you little fool. I'm not going to touch you. Well, yes, I am, but only for medicinal purposes." And he slid under the covers and pulled her into his arms, sending his body warmth seeping into her shivering limbs. Eventually the shaking stopped, and she relaxed against him, her cheek against the coarse hair of his naked chest, wondering what strange alchemy made it possible for her to hate this man and love him so much at the same time.

"Myles?"

"Yes?"

"Why did you do it?"

"I don't know."

She tried to turn in his arms, but he held her fast. She wanted to struggle, just to prove some sort of point about her anger, but in the end she gave up and relaxed against him, savoring the warmth of the long, male body pressed against hers.

"Was it because you thought that if you returned and you discovered that you still loved Sylvia, you might one day want to be with her?"

He was silent, not answering, and she felt her heart shrivel up into a tiny burr within her chest. He moved onto his back and lay staring up at the ceiling, one arm supporting his head while the other continued to hold her, firmly, but with none of the passion that usually characterized their encounters. "I couldn't be sure of anything until we reached here," he finally said in a low voice. "I couldn't make any kind of commitment. I was still too wild with anger. I couldn't afford to make any mistakes."

A mistake. Now she was a mistake.

She didn't understand why she couldn't cry. Except that she was so tired and empty, she just wanted to curl up like an injured animal and sleep.

"Did Captain Scully know?" she whispered. Another betrayal. She had trusted the old sea dog.

"He thought it better than my making you my mistress. At least you would have the protection of a public declaration of intent."

"But I am your mistress, Myles." She was surprised that her voice could sound so reasonable. "If I'm not your wife, I must be your mistress."

"You are my wife, Sabina. In every way that's important."

"But not legally. And that's why Captain Scully sent us Jezebel. He had a guilty conscience. That was the only way he could salve it. He wanted to give me something he valued."

"She was more likely a gentle reminder that I had promised to take care of you."

And he had. He had taken care of her very well. He had given her a fine carriage to drive in, and beautiful clothes to wear, and servants to carry out her wishes. He had made her the mistress of a large estate and taught her the sensual pleasures of the body.

And he had lied to her in a way that reduced her to the level of a pretty puppet, dancing to a cleverly manipulated set of strings.

He had made her part of his plan to destroy his cousin, and in doing so had attempted to destroy that part of her where her pride in her own strength and independence existed. She had become as much his creature as Marney was.

There was no marriage to save. No life to build together. Only a love built on lies.

She stopped struggling to keep herself away from him and gave in to the tempting warmth of his body, flattening herself against it, her head resting on his shoulder, her arms flung across his chest. She heard his indrawn breath and felt him shudder deeply, his muscles flexing beneath her hands.

"Myles?" she murmured.

"Yes?"

"I'm so tired."

"Then go to sleep."

Sometime just before dawn she awoke.

Groggily she sat up in bed, half aware that something important had happened to her, before consciousness charged at her like a hussar and she felt the sharp saber slash of pain. With a small moan, she subsided back against the pillows.

She was aware that Myles stirred next to her, his tall body warm and drowsy with sleep. He flung an arm across her shoulder, and then she felt him lurch into wakefulness.

She turned her face, and in the half-light of a new morning, her eyes reluctantly sought his. They were fixed on her with a burning intensity, his emotions no longer hidden, the sapphire brilliance glittering with a mixture of regret and longing.

"Mermaid." His voice was low, and hoarse, and full of passion.

"No," she whispered. She closed her eyes and felt his fingers delicately trace the soft contours of her breast, and then move to cup her chin with a gentle hold.

"No," she murmured when his lips brushed against hers and his body moved over her, his hands warm and caressing, his mouth a revelation of fire and need.

"Yes, Sabina."

"I . . . can't." But she found that she could, and, siren-like, she wound her arms around him, her hold so fierce that she eventually pulled them both into the churning waters of desire, loving him until she cried aloud with the wonder of it.

When she awoke again the sun had risen, and he was gone. She rolled over and examined the crease in the bed where his body had lain next to hers, and made her decision.

She had to leave.

She couldn't remain here. Not now. She couldn't stay and be a part of whatever he was planning for the Dampiers. And neither could she stop him. He had made sure of that, in a way calculated to drain every drop of self-respect from her. He had made her a part of his design for destruction. She had never been a person to him. She had been a useful tool, and an expendable one.

And that, she couldn't forgive.

Sabina went through the motions of ordinary life, functioning normally on one plane of existence while on the other she shivered and sobbed like a helpless child. Maria helped her climb into her habit, accepting with equanimity her mistress's plan to go riding that morning. During the last fortnight, Sabina had taken daily lessons from Curtis with a critical Gammon in attendance, and the maid had no reason to suspect that anything different would occur today. She handed Sabina her hat and her long leather whip, with the news that Mr. Marney had left that morning with a regular flea in his ear.

"Really?" Sabina said indifferently. "I expected them to find his body in the coal cellar."

Maria, who seemed to find no fault with this scenario, sniffed. "It's a pity they hadn't. Squeezing the chambermaids and trying to kiss them . . . James said Marney and Mr. Dampier had quite a set-to this morning. Do you think Mr. Dampier found out about all his weaseling ways?"

"Possibly, Maria. Do you know where Mr. Dampier is?"

"He's waiting for you in the breakfast room, ma'am. He says he wants to speak to you, if it's convenient."

"It's not."

Maria's eyes widened, as a new respect for her easygoing mistress dawned in her eyes. "He was very insistent I give you the message."

"You gave it to me. And you can give him one back. Tell him . . . tell him . . ."

Maria's face was so hopeful of sensation that Sabina couldn't choke back a small, bitter laugh.

"Tell him it's a *husband's* privilege to wait upon his wife's pleasure."

On that cryptic note, she made her way to the stables, her plan for flight forming gradually in her brain like a well-executed battle strategy.

She couldn't do it alone. She knew that. And there was only one person she could think of who would be likely to help her in her quest. If she could get to see her this morning, then she could put her plan into action.

However, she ran into a brick wall when she announced her intention of riding to Curstone Abbey on her own. Curtis, the head groom, shook his head. "I don't think so, ma'am."

"I don't understand you, Curtis."

"Well, I'll rephrase it, like. *No*, ma'am."

Sabina looked into the grizzled face and began to cajole. "But you said I was coming on so well!"

"And so you are, Mrs. Dampier. But it'd be more than

my life's worth to let you go out on your own, without one of the lads in attendance."

"What about Gammon? Would you let him come with me?"

"He'd be no more use than that there monkey in case of emergency."

But in the end they reached a compromise, and Gammon was soon astride an aging horse that had suffered under Mr. Bradshaw's regime and now desired only a quiet life. The boy's excitement at being allowed to escort his goddess was almost palpable, and Sabina was able to reflect sadly that if only one good thing had come out of her disastrous association with Myles Dampier, this boy was it.

Gammon, who seemed entirely ignorant of the fact that a groom's presence was meant to be quiet and unobtrusive, announced, "I ain't called Gammon no more."

Sabina was startled from both her thoughts and her need to maintain what seemed to be playfully termed "an independent seat" on her horse. "Indeed? What are you called now?"

"Curtis. Jack Curtis. It was Mr. Curtis's name when he was a boy, before he become just Curtis, he says. No one uses it anymore, so I can 'ave it."

She was touched by his pleasure and said sincerely, "That's a very fine name, Gammon . . . er, Jack."

"Oh, you can call me Gammon," he conceded graciously, "and so can the guv'nor, but no one else can now." He added excitedly, "I got a book guv to me, missus. I'm going to read it one day."

"I know. You are going to the Dame school in the village of a Sunday, aren't you?"

"Yus, and she read us a story, about a boy who always said his prayers and go to heaven."

"That," she sighed dismally, "is called fiction, Gammon."

The boy looked at her sharply, his eyebrow snaking up in a movement so heartbreakingly familiar that she nearly cried out with the pain of it.

"Are you all right, missus? You ain't sick or nuthin'?"

"No. I'm not sick or anything."

"It's just that you don't look the same."

Because she wasn't the same. She smiled brilliantly and asked lightly, "Tell me, Gammon. What does a doxy look like?"

Gammon shifted uneasily in his saddle. "What do want to know that for?"

"Just curious, that's all."

"Well . . . often they don't 'ave no teeth. And they like the gin."

"Don't . . . don't tell me any more. I'm sorry, Gammon. That was inexcusable of me."

Gammon looked at her as if she were crazy, and then very carefully used phrases that he must have noticed calmed down females in the grip of the megrims. "Very well, missus. As you say."

Sabina smiled a little sadly. It *had* been inexcusable of her to involve the boy in her own misery. But for the first time, she suddenly thought of what the future might hold for her.

Nothing.

Cousin Sarah of Bournemouth, if she was lucky. A position as a governess or a companion in someone else's household. Perhaps she could get Sylvia to write her a reference to the effect that she was honest and hardworking and always gave satisfaction in the execution of her duties.

But unless she passed herself off as a widow, no other man could ever accept the fact that she was no longer a virgin. Perhaps she would be forced to fulfill that longago prediction that Myles had made about her future as a courtesan. Perhaps she *would* make the perfect whore.

God knows, Myles seemed pleased with her performance. Perhaps he would keep her on. . . .

She gave a small sob as she doubled up over her horse and stayed there, shaking and gasping for breath.

"You are sick! I thought you was."

"No," she gasped, "I'm not sick, Gammon. But you must do something for me."

"What is ut?"

"Go back, and stay there!"

The boy stared at her as if she had run mad. "They'll kill me."

"Then go back and say I lost you on purpose. Yes, they will believe you if I say it's so. But for heaven's sake, go! I need to be alone."

Swearing fluently, Gammon turned his horse and drummed his heels into the animal's sides, forcing it into a reluctant trot. Sabina readjusted her leg around the top pommel and urged her mare on with her whip, a sudden recklessness lending her the courage to break into a gallop. Soon the Palladian magnificence of the Abbey broke through a grove of trees, and she prayed that Sylvia Dampier was in her right senses this morning.

She was.

When Sabina was shown into the salon, Sylvia was seated at the great harp that had stood beneath her portrait in Brook Street, her fingers resting elegantly against the strings, her face a study in pleasure.

"Why, Sabina, my dear. How early you are! Not that you aren't welcome . . . but, my dear! Your face! Is something wrong?"

Sabina looked at the older woman and fought back the terrible temptation to throw herself on the stool next to her and weep out her entire story. Instead she asked steadily, "Will you help me, Sylvia? I didn't . . . I don't know who else to ask. But I want . . . I *need* to leave Lysons Hall. Secretly, you understand. He won't let me go otherwise. I know him too well. And I have to get away, you see."

"No, I don't see!" Sylvia rose and came toward her, the beautiful face a mixture of horror and sympathy. "What is wrong? What has happened? Is it Myles? Has he done something to you?"

"No! Nothing like that—it's just . . . I can't bear it anymore." She put her hands over her face and began to cry; great gasping sobs caught in her throat and made her double over in pain. She felt herself led to a small sofa, and she collapsed onto it, unable to stop the storm until she was finally cried out. When it was over, she leaned against the brocaded back of the seat and stared limply as Sylvia began to bathe her face with a cologne-soaked handkerchief.

"Poor child," she cooed. "How terrible everything seems when you are young. I thought my heart was broken once, but it wasn't. Hearts don't really break, you know. Won't you tell me what is wrong? Then I can help you."

Sabina dragged in a raw breath and told her.

The whole story sounded extraordinary, and she felt like some modern-day Scheherazade before the Sultan, facing a terrible punishment if she didn't tell it properly. When she had finished, she turned her head and watched Sylvia's delicate features quiver with outrage.

"That's a terrible story, Sabina. I can't believe it of Myles. None of it. He was always sweeter than the angels. All this talk of vengeance and ruin—it's preposterous!"

"Well, now he's angrier than the Devil." She blew her nose vigorously and mopped her cheeks. "Will you help me?"

"Is that what you really want? To leave Myles?"

"No. Of course I don't. It's what I have to do."

"You should stay and *make* him marry you. You could have a secret ceremony somewhere. Go to Norwich! It's charming at this time of year!"

"Sylvia! You don't understand . . ." She broke off and regarded her friend ruefully. Of course Sylvia didn't understand her motives. She couldn't quite always understand them herself. "It's not just the fact that he lied to me about our marriage. That was merely the . . . the straw that broke the camel's back. I'm leaving Myles to preserve my own sanity! Now, will you help me?"

Sylvia turned to her, determination shining in her blue eyes. "I will. I will do it. Even if it's only to make Myles realize what a fool he is. When he discovers you gone, he'll understand what it is to *really* suffer. Just as he's made you suffer! And then he will have to go and beg you to come back . . . on bended knee!"

"No, he won't," Sabina said sadly. "He'll be angry because it isn't part of his grand scheme that I go away. But he'll forget me soon enough, and then he'll find someone else whom he can marry *for good*. Not like you and me! But at least he wanted to marry you! He couldn't even bear to have me as his real w . . . wife!"

She wanted to start crying again, but Sylvia, for all her air of fragility, showed a healthy interest in the practical side of things.

"Where did you say you were going? Oh, that's right. Bournemouth, to some cousin. I'm sure that will be very pleasant. We won't tell Richard about this, of course. He would be very shocked. It will be our secret. Of course you will need your coach fare, and some way of getting to Wells to meet the Mail. And a valise, with clothes and necessary items."

"I'll pay you back. It's just that I can hardly ask Myles for the money to leave him."

"Of course, dear. Most improper. I will meet you in my carriage by the old churchyard at . . . midnight, I think, so you can catch the early morning Mail Coach from Wells. I will have to swear *my* coachman to secrecy." She clapped her hands like an excited child and exclaimed, "What an adventure! I feel like a young girl again."

It was arranged, Sabina realized with a dawning sense of horror. Today would be her last day at Lysons Hall. After tonight, she would never see Myles Dampier again.

She celebrated this fact by putting her head on her friend's shoulder and crying as if hearts really could break.

CHAPTER THIRTEEN

Myles was waiting for her outside the stables when she returned, his face like thunder.

"What the devil did you mean, riding off like that?" he demanded roughly. "Curtis tells me you sent Gammon back without any explanation."

She reined in and kicked her left foot free of the single stirrup, sliding to the ground before he could assist her down from the saddle.

"I felt like it," she replied coolly, hoping that the ride back to the Hall had helped eradicate some of the telltale stains from her face. "I've decided to be just like you, Myles Dampier, and do whatever I please." Curtis emerged from the stables, thin-lipped and glowering, and she held out the reins with a smile of pure sweetness. "Here you are, Curtis. I feel much better after my ride."

She swung around with something that resembled a flounce of pure petulance, and started off for the main wing, only to find Myles's hand around her arm, forcing it up above her shoulder so that she was obliged to stop

283

and stand on tiptoe. "You . . . are . . . hurting . . . me," she informed him through clenched teeth.

"I'd like to do more than hurt you! Curtis was just about to send some men to look for you. He sent for me to see if I might *possibly* know where you had gone!" He shook her, hard. "Do you know how worried I was?"

"Why? Did you imagine me lying somewhere with a broken neck?" She lashed out at him, determined to touch some part of him in that damned impenetrable fortress he had built around himself. "Wouldn't that spoil all your plans? Or am I expendable now, Mr. Dampier? Can you do without my services?"

"Sabina—"

"It's *Miss Grey* to you!"

He slackened his hold on her arm, and she wrenched herself free, flying across the courtyard, stumbling through the ancient side door that led to a warren of corridors and the main section of the Hall. She picked up her skirts and continued to run, fleeing down the long gallery and into her bedchamber, before slamming the door shut with a crash that reverberated for a full minute.

She had to get away from here. Of course she did.

But why had her heart beaten such a devil's tattoo of longing when she saw him? Would she always feel like this? When she was far away from him, would she continue to want him with such a wretched hunger that her insides ached? Or would it gradually fade into nothing more than a quiet, anguished yearning when she was alone with nothing but her memories for companionship?

The knock at her door was deceptively gentle, and she scrambled to her feet, pushing back the hair that had fallen from its pins in her wild flight up the stairs.

"Go away!" she shouted, but instead it opened wide as she knew it would, and he stood in the doorway, his shoulders held stiffly, his face guarded. If she hadn't known better, she would have sworn he looked . . . *uncomfortable.* Indecisive. Uncertain.

She was hallucinating, she told herself sternly. Myles Dampier was as certain as the seasons.

"We have to talk, Sabina."

"There's nothing to say to each other. It has all been said for us, hasn't it? Mr. Marney was remarkably eloquent last night."

"And . . . afterwards?" He advanced a step and then stopped, gauging the effect of his words. "What was that about? Can you forget what happened in your bed? What will always happen?"

"Oh, our bodies are always *remarkably* eloquent, Myles," she said smoothly, brushing over the joy she had found in his arms as if it were nothing more than a cynical exercise in lust. "But then, you are awfully good at . . . communicating, aren't you? And as you know, I learn things very quickly."

She sashayed over to her looking glass, pretending to preen a little at her reflection. She drew back, slightly shocked by her appearance, but she practiced the silvery little laugh and spun on her heel to confront him, leaning her hands on the edges of her dressing table for support.

"In fact, I feel you could have been right about my eventual destiny all along," she continued blithely. "Sabina Grey, *courtesan*. It has a ring to it, doesn't it? I can ride with all the other high-class trollops in Hyde Park, advertising my wares, and maybe, if I am very lucky—but only if I'm *very* lucky, mind—you will be one of my first clients. Don't be afraid that I would ever embarrass you with talk about love. I wouldn't. Because I think I hate you, Myles Dampier!"

Delightedly she watched his expression darken, and noted the supreme effort it took to control his breathing into a steady rhythm, and to unclench his fingers from the two fists he had made. "Have you finished, Sabina? Do you feel better now?"

"Yes! I feel wonderful. I haven't felt this happy since the *Margaret Rose* sank!"

"I want to make arrangements to get married . . . legally," he continued, disregarding her bitter sarcasm. "I don't know why I didn't do it before. I have no excuse for it. After we came back to England, I suppose it didn't seem important anymore."

Her breath caught in her throat. She couldn't look at him, and she found herself studying the toes of her riding boots as she said coldly, "I decline your beautiful offer of marriage, Mr. Dampier."

"Don't be a little fool."

She shook her head, still unable to look at him. "I've already been a fool. A big fool. I don't want to be one anymore."

"We will be married, and everything will continue as before. You can't tell me you were unhappy before you found out we weren't legally married."

"Oh, yes! I was happy. Like a canary is happy. Because I didn't know any better."

His mouth twisted bitterly. "And now you do know better, is that it?"

"I want to leave here," she said quietly. "I want to go away."

"No!"

The word was the crack of a whiplash. She jerked her head up to look at him, noting the intractable set of his shoulders, the hard mouth, the blue brilliance of his eyes, wide with anger and denial.

"No," he said more quietly. "You won't be leaving."

"You can't stop me," she cried out, incensed. "You have no hold over me, no legal right to prevent me from doing anything I want to do."

"Don't I?" he said silkily. "Try me." He smiled his devil-saint smile and sauntered over to where she leaned against her dressing table. Placing one long finger beneath her chin, he lifted it until she could stare into his face. His breath was warm, his mouth so close that if she leaned into him she could join her lips to his. "Everything can be amended, Sabina. Everything. It will all turn out well in the end, I promise you."

He let go of her chin and turned to leave, but she stopped him with a question that had lain dormant in the back of her mind since the previous evening. "Is this what

286

you wanted to tell me so badly that you had to carry me off from dinner last night? That I wasn't really your wife?"

He paused a moment and then smiled, saying softly, "Of course. What other great secret would I have to reveal to you?"

She was still searching for an answer to that question when he turned and left the room without so much as a backward glance.

The rest of the day passed with torturous lethargy.

She was right, of course. Myles had no legal hold over her. Legally, morally, she was as free to walk through the great entrance portal of Lysons Hall and down the driveway to freedom as Maria or one of the maidservants was. But knowing Myles as she did, she couldn't guarantee that he wouldn't have her stopped and brought back on some trumped-up charge of stealing, or with a contrived tale of her not being in her right mind.

This was going to be hard enough to do as it was. She didn't need any added complications to hinder her flight to freedom.

She counted down the hours with an impatience that would have done credit to a condemned man, making it easier on herself by pleading a headache and taking her meals in her rooms. Myles most probably thought she was sulking, and avoided her, which was a stroke of unlooked-for luck. She couldn't be sure that at the last hour, a word, a look from him, and all her resolve would crumble into nothing.

She waited until the great house was still and dark before she put her plan into operation. She dragged out the small valise she had hidden under her bed, and hurriedly packed it with a small quantity of items. There were so many things she didn't want to take—the lovely gowns, the fine underclothes, the combs and necklaces—all belonging to Mrs. Myles Dampier of Lysons Hall, not to mere Sabina Grey of nowhere in particular.

But there were a few things she wouldn't leave without. That she *couldn't* leave without.

She found the shawl with its bright exotic colors and dazzling embroidered birds at the bottom of her drawer, cast aside in favor of more fashionable items of wear. Now she held it to her cheek, feeling once again the soft sensation of silk, and remembering her delight when Myles had given it to her aboard the *Ellen Drury*. It had been the first present he ever gave her, something feminine and beautiful to replace the rags the sea had left her.

Stop it! she told herself severely, crumpling the shawl between determined hands. *It's only a piece of gaudy material that doesn't even look well with any of your gowns. The fact that you wore it as your wedding garment on the ship should make you hate it. If anything could prove to you how farcical that entire episode was, this silly shawl should remind you! You might as well have worn the skull and crossbones for all the good it did!*

But she ended up draping it around her shoulders, tying the ends carefully together so that it wouldn't slip from under her cloak.

She had never had to dress in the near dark before, and while that proved a handicap to haste, it was as nothing to the challenge of trying to creep down the dark corridor without a candle. She attempted to solve the problem by keeping her back to the wall and inching along it, her valise clasped awkwardly in her arms to prevent it from banging on the wainscotting.

Every now and then she passed a high window where the moonlight streamed in, making the shadows move where no movement should occur. And at night the mice seemed to exchange their little pattering feet for bronze-capped boots that made the stairs snap and the floorboards creak. It took all her courage to walk down the long gallery step by quiet step, expecting discovery at every moment. She was just about to congratulate herself on a job well done when her questing hand rested on something warm and fleshy, like a human arm.

She stifled her rising scream with her hand flat across her mouth, but she couldn't prevent the strangled yelp that the little burglar gave.

"*Ssssh!* Keep your voice down!" she hissed.

"Missus?"

"Gammon?"

A scraping sound suggested that the boy was trying to use a tinderbox, and when he struck a light and kindled the candle he held in one shaking hand, she was able to confirm his identity.

"What are you doing here at this time of night?" she demanded, relief adding sharpness to her voice.

"Lookin' for Jezebel. She won't come to the servants' quarters, not 'less I fetch 'er. Too much the lady, she is now." His eyes narrowed against the flame as he assessed her cloak and the valise she carried. " 'Ere. What are you a doin', missus? You look like you're ready to take off with your ears back!"

She faltered, casting around for some story that would explain her hasty flight. Then she looked into the bright hazel eyes and sighed. She was tired of lies.

"I'm going away, Gammon. Tonight. I'm going to . . . somewhere else. And if you have any care of me at all, you won't give me away. You won't . . . you won't *rat* on me."

She used the phrase deliberately, hoping he would reassure her, but he didn't. Instead he held her with a look that nicely blended suspicion and contempt.

"You ain't fixin' to lope off with some other cove, are you? Like that swell over at the Abbey!"

"If you mean, am I running away with another man, no. You may rest assured that I'm not."

"Then why? Why are you goin' away. This place . . . this is heaven!"

She looked into Gammon's earnest features, and a bitter smile trembled on her lips. To a boy pulled from the bleak poverty of London's rookeries, Lysons Hall would indeed be heaven. For a while, it had seemed it could be hers. But no longer. She was just too tired of fighting Myles Dampier's stubborn determination to turn it into hell.

She tried to explain it to the boy in terms he could understand. "I'm not leaving because I want to, but because I have to, Gammon. I . . . I've discovered I don't really belong here."

The boy shook his head stubbornly, and his face was as severe as an old man's. "That ain't a reason. If you go, you'll break his 'eart. Mr. Dampier, he loves you, missus. He loves you something fierce!"

She leaned against the balustrade of the staircase as the force of his childish words struck home. It was the first time she had ever heard those words spoken. By anyone. None of the others had dared to suggest it—not Richard, nor Sylvia, nor Lucilla Vantry—because, of course, it wasn't true. If it was, he would have told her so. He wouldn't have backed away from her own declaration as if she had offered him a poison cup.

"Myles Dampier doesn't love anyone, Gammon," she said flatly. "The sooner you learn that, the less hurt you will be in the future."

The boy seemed to be prepared to argue the case, but she put her fingers to his lips and slowly shook her head. Silenced, he stared at her pleadingly. Even when she removed her hand and began to back away from him, one step at a time down the great staircase, he remained rigidly at the top, like a little sentinel, his eyes following her descent until she could no longer see him from the base of the stairs.

The rest of her flight was uneventful, and, despite her conviction that every bush harbored a footpad and every tree sheltered a murderer, she made her way unmolested to the abandoned churchyard, less than a mile from the Hall.

The church had been destroyed nearly two centuries ago, she knew, when Cromwell's army decided that its statues and ornate religious decoration were an abomination. The soldiers had burned it to the ground, and its stark ruins now served as both a rendezvous for local lovers and, it was rumored, a dropping-off point for local smugglers.

It had obviously appealed to Sylvia's inherent sense of romance to meet here, but to Sabina, standing in the moonlight not twenty feet from the crumbling headstones, and clearly able to remember every ghost story she had ever been told, it seemed a particularly bad choice. She was therefore relieved when the sound of an approaching carriage told her that Sylvia had not failed her.

She was thankful to see that it was a closed carriage, although the fact that it sported the revised Dampier crest caused her some concern. If Lady Dampier had expected to travel into Wells and back incognito, then she had made a very bad choice of vehicle, but Sabina was too grateful for its services to point this out. She waited until the driver, rigid with disapproval, descended from the box and opened the door. She climbed in carefully, landing on a pile of fur that turned out to be Her Ladyship's ermine muff.

Sylvia was in an extreme state of excitement. Flinging her arms around her friend, she cried, "Oh, my dear child! I half expected you not to be here. How very brave you are to follow this thing through!"

Sabina winced at the delighted enjoyment in the woman's voice, but merely replied, "I'm not brave at all. I can assure you, I squeaked at every sound."

"No, you are brave. You are a regular . . . h-heroine. That's what you are, a h-heroine."

The slight slurring of the word instantly alerted Sabina to the fact that something was wrong. She leaned closer to the woman to examine her in the uncertain light cast by the carriage lamp. The beautiful face was composed, but seemed unnaturally flushed.

"Sylvia," she demanded, "have you been taking laudanum?"

Lady Dampier looked indignant at the accusation, drawing back her hand as though Sabina had bit it. "Certainly not! Dr. Martin won't let me. He says it is very bad for me, although I can't see . . . but anyway, I don't take my tonic anymore." She slid her eyes away and lifted her hand to her mouth as she choked back a titter. "But I had a little brandy before I came. It helps me feel better when I want my tonic . . . it's not the same, but it makes me feel better. And I want to feel better, Sabina."

Sabina closed her eyes and counted to ten. When she opened them, her traveling companion was sitting giggling in the corner.

"You are drunk, Sylvia."

"I am not! How can you say mean things to me when I've brought you money? Look! Lots of it. All my housekeeping, and some of the money Richard keeps in the metal box after rent day."

Sabina's jaw dropped as she realized the riches she was being offered. "You took the *rents* from Richard's strongbox?"

"Well, he never said I could not," Sylvia replied with tipsy logic. "And I know where he keeps the key. If he didn't want me to have it, he should have hidden it."

"Sylvia, I can't take all that money. I don't want it. Just enough for my fare back to London and then to Bournemouth—that's all I asked for."

"You think someone is going to bail us up, don't you? You think we will fall victim to highwaymen. But Evans has a blunderbuss, and I took *this* from Richard's drawer!" To Sabina's horror, Sylvia unsteadily pulled a pistol from a pocket in her fur-trimmed cloak. She leaned forward conspiratorially and whispered, "If we are bailed up, they won't get the money. I'll protect it."

"Put the pistol away, Sylvia," Sabina said calmly. She prayed that it wasn't loaded, and wondered if at some time during their journey she might be able to convince her inebriated friend to hand it over to the long-suffering Evans. "I'm sure we won't have need of it."

Sylvia shrugged and slipped it back into the folds of her cloak with exaggerated care. Then she leaned out the window and grandly ordered the horses put to.

Sabina fell back against the squabs with a sigh of relief as the vehicle jolted into movement.

It was working, she thought unhappily. Whether Sylvia was drunk or not, her plan was succeeding. Within a few hours, she would be in Wells, waiting for the arrival of the Mail Coach, which would take her on to London. Away from Lsyons Hall. Away from Myles Dampier.

She wondered what he would do when he found her gone.

Would he try to find her?

Somehow she didn't think so.

Someone with Myles's stiff-necked pride did not run after the women who left him. But she could easily imagine his anger when he learned that all his carefully laid plans for her had vanished into the night. He might curse and brood over one more wrong inflicted upon him. He might add her name to the list of people who had betrayed his trust. But he would not want her back again. Not after this escapade. Of that she was quite sure.

And that, she told herself severely, was exactly what she wanted.

She was so involved in her own misery that Sylvia's drunken chatter had merely been scratching at the corners of her consciousness. However, as the stream of prattle continued unabated, Sabina gave in and began to listen.

"I was never more terrified in my life, my dear. Truly. I felt just like I did when I was a young girl all those years ago, eloping with Myles. Only this time I did it much, much better. Much, much, *much* better. I didn't tell anybody this time. Not a soul." She paused for effect.

"Well done," Sabina supplied automatically.

Satisfied with the faint praise, Her Ladyship continued, "I wanted to tell my maid, but I remembered what happened last time. So I didn't. I said I wanted to go to bed very, very, *very* early, and I wouldn't need her until morning. Wasn't that clever?"

Sabina straightened against the seat, her misery falling from her shoulders like a great weight as the import of those few words sank in. "What do you mean—'*what happened last time*'? Sylvia, are you talking about when you eloped with Myles?"

"We're not supposed to talk about it," Sylvia said moodily. "It's still a scandal, you know."

"Did you tell someone you were eloping with Myles? Is

that what happened? You told someone and they betrayed you?"

"My maid told Sir John. That's why I didn't tell my maid tonight. I told her I was going to bed very, very, *very*—"

"Sylvia! Never mind about that! Do you understand what this means?" Sabina clutched at the woman's hands excitedly. "Of all the stupid things! It was so obvious! Of course, your maid would say something if she was concerned for you, or even thought to get some sort of reward for it. Richard *didn't* betray Myles! He was innocent of everything that happened to him."

"I love Richard," Sylvia declared angrily. "He's the best husband in the world!"

"I'm sure he is," Sabina said soothingly, "but the thing is, Sylvia, I can't run away now. We have to go back."

"Go back? Did we forget something?"

"Yes! I forgot that there were more people involved in all this than just me. I acted like . . . like a little fool. We have to go back and make Myles see the truth. Somehow we can put everything to rights!"

"I want to go to Wells!"

"We will go to Wells, but not tonight." Sabina stifled her impatience and continued calmly, "We have to go home. You have to tell Myles what happened that night fifteen years ago! It's vitally important that he listen to you. . . ." She broke off as the carriage suddenly lurched and then changed its pace, the horses whipped from a trot into a gallop. "What on earth . . . !"

She put her head out the window to speak to the driver, and was startled to see the carriage was being followed by a lone horseman, who seemed, despite the increased gait of the horses, to be gaining on them.

"It's highwaymen!" Sylvia shrieked.

"It's Myles Dampier!"

It was undoubtedly Myles. There could be no mistaking the elegant lines of his roan gelding, or the fierce thrust of his shoulders as he pounded his horse into the wind. Sabina called out to the driver to stop, and after casting a suspicious glance at their pursuer, Evans began to reluctantly rein in the horses, and applied the brake.

"It's Myles. He came after me." She realized that her voice sounded completely normal, which was remarkable when her heart seemed to be wedged so firmly in her mouth.

Sylvia, however, was backed against the squabs, her face white with fear. She was shaking. "It's not Myles. It's a highwayman. You shouldn't have made Evans stop the carriage!"

"Calm down," Sabina soothed, conscious that she herself was anything but calm. "Of course it's Myles. I should know my own . . . Myles when I see him."

But Sylvia was beside herself with fear. "No, no, no, no, no," she moaned, and she made a small movement with her hand toward the pocket of her cloak.

At the same time, the carriage door was flung open and a man's head and shoulders emerged out of the darkness.

Afterwards, Sabina thought of what happened next as very akin to drowning. There was the same sense of helplessness, the same distortion of time that allowed her to move with all her force but, at the same time, far too slowly. She screamed a warning as the pistol fired, only to find her body slumped in Myles's arms, his hands covering her breast. His fingers were bright red.

She looked down to where her cloak had fallen open and saw that the brilliant colors of her shawl had become dulled by the liquid that stained the fabric a dark, muddy brown.

Her head fell back and she managed to look into Myles's eyes, which were wide with horror and anguish.

"I think that's blood," she said clearly, and then she acknowledged the pain and descended into darkness.

CHAPTER FOURTEEN

The sea was in her mouth.

She tried to get rid of it, spitting and gasping, but it remained just the same, filling her lungs and hurting her chest.

Of course, she thought. *I'm actually under the sea.* A dark, roiling sea pulling at her body like a piece of flotsam, trying to suck her down into the vortex below.

She tried to swim to the surface, but the waves were too high, breaking above her head and forcing her back down. Stubbornly she tried to reach out for the light shining just above her, but someone held her arms down and she couldn't break free of their grip.

"Hold her, man! For God's sake, hold her down!"

She creased her forehead and tried to make out the identity of the voice.

"Blood in the chest cavity ... not sure ... beyond my skill. But I'll try ..."

"Try! For God's sake, try!"

It was her father's voice, she realized lovingly, and

waited for him to save her. But he didn't, and she moved restlessly in the water, afraid to breathe, afraid to move in case the pain prevented her from reaching the surface.

The boat bobbed toward her just as she had decided to stop her struggles. She was glad, because she was so tired of swimming now. Her father and Mr. and Mrs. Marchand sat in the bow, waving to her, smiling at her, as jovial and happy as she always expected them to be. But when she tried to reach up her hand, they would not let her in.

"Why? Why can't I come with you?" she asked tearfully.

Her father shook his head. "You have to swim, Sabina. You have to swim for a long, long time."

"But I'm tired! Please let me come with you!"

But he merely smiled his pleased, loving smile and the little boat sailed away, leaving her cold and shivering.

She began to sink, and in her panic flailed and moaned because she had been left abandoned in a lonely sea. She couldn't swim it alone. She didn't want to.

And then the hands were on her, warm and strong, dragging her back to the surface through the dark, churning waters, supporting her body until the light broke over her head in a warm wave of pain.

"Myles!" she called.

"I'm here. Hold on, Mermaid! For God's sake, hold on!"

She tried. She gripped his hands like a lifeline, but she was too weak, her grasp threatening to slip from his.

"I have something to tell you," she whispered urgently. "Something to tell you."

"Hush. You have to rest."

Rest? If she rested, she would be dragged down into the depths, cold and alone. Eternally alone.

"I love you, Myles."

"Then don't leave me, Mermaid. Don't leave me."

"I don't want to leave."

She wanted to explain it, to make it clear that it had never been her choice, but the pain suddenly caught up with her, pulling at her with a hold that was too strong to fight, casting her into a whirlpool of darkness.

*   *   *

It was morning when she awoke.

She tried to move, noting how stiff her entire body felt, and how dry her mouth was. A pitcher of water stood on the table beside her bed, and she stretched out to reach it, exclaiming at the shaft of pain that shot through her from the simple action.

"Mrs. Dampier! You're awake!"

Startled, she turned her head, to find Mrs. Ferris rising from a chair on the other side of the bed, her face a study in pleasure and concern. The housekeeper fetched the water for her, helping her to bring the glass to her mouth, and Sabina was glad for the assistance, noting how weak her hands and arms were.

"Have I been sick?" she asked dazedly. Her voice was hoarse with disuse.

"You don't know? You don't remember?"

"I remember being at sea . . . of course, that was just a dream. But I seem to remember . . . I think I was shot?" She finished the statement as a question, her eyes widening as memory returned with unexpected clarity. Sylvia's white face, the smoking pistol in her hand, Myles's eyes as he looked at her . . .

She groped for the woman's hand, asking urgently, "Myles! Mr. Dampier! Is he all right?"

Mrs. Ferris hesitated before answering slowly, "He's not injured, if that's what you mean, ma'am."

"That's what I mean." She closed her eyes and sank against the pillows, wondering if she had possibly forfeited the right to ask where he was. But she wanted to see him, as badly as she had needed the water. "Will you fetch him, Mrs. Ferris? Will you bring him here?"

"No, ma'am."

Startled by the refusal, Sabina stared into the older woman's placid face. The housekeeper continued serenely, "He hasn't slept for nearly four days, and the doctor said if he didn't get to bed, there would be another invalid on his hands. Once we knew you were out of danger, we made him go to his bedchamber. I wouldn't disturb him for all the tea in China."

Four days. She closed her eyes as if the dull ache in her shoulder was paining her, but it was the thought of him sitting beside her for almost four days that caused the greatest ache.

"I wouldn't want him woken, either, Mrs. Ferris." She watched the woman smile and move toward the door, and asked in a small voice, "Are you going to leave me alone?"

"Now, now, Mrs. Dampier. I'm going to send word to Dr. Martin. And then I'm going to tell Lady Dampier the good news. She's been beside herself with worry, you know."

"Poor Sylvia," Sabina said quietly. "It wasn't her fault. She was just so frightened, she didn't know what she was doing."

"Yes, well. I think it cured her of playing with pistols. As well as cured her of ... other nasty habits a lady shouldn't indulge in. It's about time Sir Richard took a firmer line with Her Ladyship." She broke off, realizing that she had spoken improperly, but Sabina's rueful smile seemed to reassure her. She added a little more kindly, "and if you are wondering what is being said, ma'am, it was put about that Lady Dampier was rushing to the side of ... of a sick friend in Wells with you as her companion. The gun went off when she displayed it to alleviate your nervousness at traveling at night."

"Believe me, Mrs. Ferris. It did nothing to alleviate my nerves."

"No, ma'am." With a swift smile, the housekeeper bustled from the room, leaving Sabina to wonder what the servants *really* made of the whole incident. Working for the Dampiers, she decided bleakly, was never dull.

Sylvia's arrival at the door told Sabina that her friend had been keeping a close vigil. She crept in with that curious reluctance people display on entering a sickroom, and then tossed caution aside, flying to Sabina's side in a flurry of blue silk and ermine. Not even near tragedy could prevent the beautiful Lady Dampier from dressing for the occasion. She knelt on the dais, and putting her silver-gilt head on the covers, promptly burst into tears.

"Sylvia, please don't. It's all right. I'm going to be fine. Truly."

"But you nearly died!" Sylvia said between sobs. "The doctor who saw you first said he couldn't do anything and we should be prepared for the worst! And Myles began shaking him, and we had to get the doctor out of the room for his own safety—well, Richard and Mrs. Ferris did, and then he refused to come back in unless Myles went away, and he wouldn't, and so we had to send for Dr. Martin, and there was so much *blood* . . ."

Sabina couldn't help but laugh at this ingenuous description of events, even though the simple act of laughter caused her much discomfort.

"I'm sorry about all the blood," she teased. Sometimes it was hard to remember that Sylvia was almost a decade her senior.

"Don't! Don't be nice to me. I don't deserve it. I was such a fool!" She raised her face from her hands, and Sabina was startled by her haggard appearance. "I nearly killed you, and it's no use saying it was an accident. I was a drunken fool. I know that. And it's made me take an awfully long look at myself and what I've been doing—to you, to Richard, to anyone who cares about me."

Sabina reached out to touch the gold curls with a shaking hand. "For your sake, I'm glad. But last night—"

"Last week!"

"Last week," she amended solemnly, "was just as much my fault as it was yours. I didn't have enough courage to stay here and try to fight for what I wanted. I thought it would be too hard. And it might yet be. But fighting for something you want to keep beautiful . . . and alive is very important, Sylvia."

"I know that! I'm glad that you do, too." Sylvia rose from her position by the bed and swabbed at her face with the edge of her fur tippet. "I'm going to go home now. I want you to get some sleep, and we'll speak later. Only . . ." She paused, and Sabina encouraged her to speak with a gentle pressure on her hand. "Well, promise me that you won't leave again until I see you. And if you must leave, you will come to us first!"

If you must leave.

Sabina closed her eyes against the pain. "Of course," she agreed quietly. "You may rest assured I won't try to slip away again."

Sylvia leaned down and kissed her, her expression as unclouded as if she had confessed and been shriven. But before she left, she paused at the door, turning her head slowly to look at her injured friend. "By the way, my dear. There is something I forgot to tell you." She drew in a deep breath and met Sabina's eyes squarely. "I remember from that night—I told you something, and you seemed to think it was important. And then you asked me to tell Myles. Well, I did. I did tell him. I told him about my maid informing Sir John that we had eloped."

"And . . . ?" Sabina used the simple word to break the lengthening silence.

"He said it didn't really matter anymore. Does that make you feel better?"

"Of course."

It didn't, but she thought about Myles's cryptic words long after Sylvia had gone and Mrs. Ferris returned with a tear-stained Maria to help bathe her and wash her hair. She thought about it while the bed was made up and her bandages changed, and she thought about it when she was coaxed to slip between cool, white sheets and sleep.

"Is Mr. Dampier awake yet?" she asked Mrs. Ferris tiredly.

"No, ma'am. Best you sleep, as well."

She did sleep, although she had an odd dream that Gammon was in the room, with Jezebel high on his shoulder, and that they were ushered out by an exasperated Mrs. Ferris. Then she dreamed that there was a gentle rapping on the door, and it opened and Myles Dampier entered the room and made his way to the chair next to her bed with his quiet predator walk. She whimpered, tossing her head from side to side, not wanting to awaken from this particular dream, but aware in the manner that dreamers often are that she was about to do so.

He leaned forward in the chair, his broad shoulders hunched like an old man's, his head bent over his chest, his hands clasped together like those of a man in prayer. He was such a portrait of defeat that she couldn't suppress her sharp intake of breath. Immediately, his head shot up, and he looked at her, the cornflower eyes red-rimmed and brilliant with what looked like tears. He was haggard, unkempt.

He looked like a man who had been shipwrecked.

Myles was the first to break the silence.

"You look dreadful," he said quietly.

She swallowed at his characteristic bluntness. "So do you."

"I guess you have an excuse. The doctor extracted a cannonball from your chest."

"Yes, it feels like it." Once again her reply was mechanical.

"He wasn't sure he could stop the bleeding." He sounded like a medical student contemplating a strange corpse, all emotion drained from his voice. "There was a moment when I . . . when we thought you were gone."

She closed her eyes. *Gone.* What a tepid, useless expression. As though she hadn't been fighting with every fiber of her being to stay.

"What happened to my shawl?" she asked wearily.

"What?" Her question seemed to rouse him from his stupor, and she watched him rub a lean cheek that hadn't been shaved in days. He tried to focus on her. "What shawl?"

"The shawl you gave me on the *Ellen Drury*. There was blood all over it. They didn't throw it away, did they?"

He stared at her, the hard angles of his face turning even sharper, his jaw working hard to maintain its rigid, inflexible line. He seemed to ignore her question as the ravings of an invalid, and said stiffly, "You know I won't stop you if you really want to go. I'll send you to Bournemouth if that's what you really want. I know I have . . . no right to hold you here against your will."

Wonderful. It was just what she wanted to hear.

She must have made some sound, because he suddenly turned on her, his fury barely held in check. "Did I seem such a monster to you that you had to *escape* me? When Gammon came and told me you were creeping out in the middle of the night like a sneak thief . . . !"

"They threw it away, didn't they?" she said quaveringly. "The shawl you bought for me in Teneriffe. My lovely shawl! It's gone."

"Stop going on about your damned shawl! What the hell does it *matter?*"

"It was all I had left!" she yelled back at him. "It was the only thing I had to take with me! And now it's gone. Everything is gone!"

She began to weep then, great gulping tears that made her wound ache and caused her to cry out in pain.

"Don't cry, Mermaid. Please," he whispered. The bleak, agonized look had suddenly disappeared from his face, replaced by something profoundly different. Something that resembled the sun rising. "I'll get you another one. Even if I have to crawl all the way back to the Canaries to do it."

"I was married in that shawl," she whispered.

"No, you weren't, but if I can find the damn thing, you will be."

She shook her head. "I can't. You don't love me."

Myles Dampier didn't follow the prescribed rules governing the treatment of invalids. He didn't sit sedately in the chair provided for attendants, or kneel discreetly by the bed. Instead he sat on the covers, leaning over her with a look of such fire in his expression that she suddenly forgot all about the pain. She forgot about everything, reaching out to grasp frantically at the collar of his jacket, bending him toward her so that she could be certain she heard him properly.

"You don't love me, Myles," she repeated.

"That's right, Mermaid. I don't," he said hoarsely.

"That's why when I saw you lying in my arms with a bullet hole through you, as white as a corpse, I wanted to take the pistol and put a bullet through my own head." He let out a frayed breath and tried to draw back, removing her hands from his coat with fingers that shook cruelly.

She held on to his hands in a death grip, refusing to let go. "That's not enough, Myles," she said relentlessly. "That's not nearly enough."

He stared at her, his eyes narrowed into blue slits of light. The sweep of dark lashes curtained every bit of emotion from her questing gaze. "You want pretty speeches, do you?" There was more than a hint of anger in his growl.

"Yes. I do. I'm *owed* pretty speeches, Myles Dampier."

"Very well. If it's speeches you want!" He drew in a deep breath as if about to launch into a theatrical proclamation, but when he spoke his voice was tight and restrained. "I love you, Sabina. I love you so much that my gut fairly aches with it. I love you so much that when I wake up, the first thing I think about is being with you, and I'm excited as a child. I think about you the last thing at night . . . when I don't feel anything remotely like a child. Whenever I touch you, I feel like I'm about to burst into flame. When I don't touch you, I still feel like I'm about to burst into flame." He leaned over her, his eyes bright with resentment. "I love you because you are the only woman in the world who has never bored me, or demanded, or taken from me. I love your courage. I love your wit. I even love that damned stubborn streak of yours, which will probably end up driving me insane one day, if I'm not moved to shoot myself. I never wanted to love you. If I had my way, I wouldn't love you. But I do, and I can safely say I've never felt so damned helpless about anything in my entire life!"

His chest was heaving with the effort to hold his emotions in check. They were, she realized with profound gratitude, not weak emotions. Like everything about this man, they were sweeping, intense, as powerful as the sea. But now it was all there for her to see, everything on display. His love for her, his strength, his humor, his arrogance, his pride—except that now it seemed somehow stripped right down to the bone, honed by suffering into something fine and life-giving.

"Do you think," she asked tremblingly, "that you can kiss me without hurting me?"

"I can't promise anything," he said, his eyes springing to life with secret laughter, "but I can try." He bent over her, his fingers brushing her lips, then moving slowly to trace her eyes, her nose, her cheeks, until they buried themselves in her hair, holding her face still. "For the rest of my life I can try not to hurt you."

"Don't promise me anything, then. Sometimes trying is enough."

In response his mouth descended on hers like a desert dweller to an oasis.

Later, when they had worked out how he could lie beside her with the least discomfort to her injury, she held up the large hand threaded with her own small one and asked sleepily, "When did you know?"

"Know what?" he murmured obtusely.

"That you loved me, of course."

"Do you know, Mermaid, I think I forgot to mark it down on my calendar." His smile had nothing of a saint about it at the moment. It was pure devil.

"You aren't going to tell me?" She couldn't keep the disappointment from her voice.

"I can't tell you. Since the first day I saw you I haven't been able to figure out whether I was on my head or my heels." He dragged their interlocked fingers to his mouth and managed to differentiate between them, pressing a kiss on each of her fingertips, before starting the whole procedure all over again. "You have that effect on me, you know."

"I'm glad," she said simply. She was content to lie there beside him forever, basking in her newfound happiness. This was how it was meant to be, she realized—two people who no longer used pride or fear to keep the other at a distance.

However, something stirred at the edges of her mind, something she needed sorted out right away. "And you know about Richard, don't you? Sylvia told you."

He looked at her ruefully. "That came out of nowhere, Mermaid. Do we have to talk about that tiresome couple at this moment?"

"I need to know. I need to know if . . . the poison is gone."

"The poison drained a long time ago," he said quietly, "but I was too stubborn to admit it. I found I could look at Sylvia as if she were merely any other woman—a little foolish, a little weak, and completely commonplace beside you. I found I couldn't even hate Richard anymore. And that frightened me a whole lot more than I could bear to admit." He added tightly, "You don't give up fifteen years' worth of hatred without a struggle, Mermaid. It was my food, my shelter—my existence!—for so many years that I didn't know how I would manage without it."

"And how will you manage?" she asked steadily.

He seemed to retreat into a place she could not follow, but only for an instant. He answered slowly, "That night when I took you from the party, I had something to tell you that I knew couldn't wait. You thought I was in London with Marney, making the final arrangements for Richard's ruin, didn't you?"

"And weren't you?"

"No." The word emerged with a vehemence that seemed to startle himself. "I had already told Marney his services would no longer be needed. I suppose his little outburst that night was the result." He looked down at their joined hands as if seeing them for the first time, and began to rub his finger across the pale circle where her wedding ring had once been. "I wanted to tell you that I had just been elected to the position of Chairman of the Select Committee on Prison Reform for Juveniles."

It was so unexpected that she could only gape at him. "Myles! Why—"

"Why me?" he interrupted. "I suppose the Home Secretary feels I might have an insider's view of things." He grinned at her astonishment, and added wickedly, "Most of the committee members seem more than happy to take my word about what it's like to be a convict. It saves them the trouble of experiencing it themselves."

"*Why* didn't you tell me?"

"You seemed so determined to hate me, it didn't seem important anymore. I thought I'd finally turned into Uncle John, just like you said I had, destroying everything I touched." His grip on her hand tightened. "Nothing mattered after that. Not Lysons Hall, or the Abbey, or Sylvia, or even poor, bewildered, innocent Richard. I truly thought I'd lost you. But I couldn't let you go like that, hating me, thinking me some sort of a beast." Remembered pain deepened his voice. "And then, in that damned carriage, when I thought I'd lost you for good . . ."

He sounded so completely vulnerable at that moment that she put her free hand to his face, smoothing the dark curls from his forehead, and then tenderly placed her fingers on his lips.

"You were a fool to think that, Myles Dampier. You must have known you could never lose me, unless you truly wanted to." She searched his face as it stared into hers, all the bitterness finally wiped clean from those remarkable eyes. They were a young man's eyes now, understanding love for the first and last time. She added softly, "How could you not know? 'A lover's eyes will gaze an eagle blind; a lover's ear will hear the lowest sound.' "

"What's that?"

"A quote," she said mistily.

"A quote, eh? Well." He leaned into her, his eyes no longer young. There was something older than time burning in the sapphire depths. "If you can quote at me, my love, I must not be doing it right." And he pressed his lips to hers, a benediction for the future.

EPILOGUE

Emily Dampier, eight years old and an authority on everything, looked at her cousin through a screen of branches and complained bitterly, "I don't see what all the stupid fuss is about. Babies are born all the time. It's just another one."

Master Bertram Dampier, who, at six, wasn't at all sure he *should* be sitting in a tree, shrugged. Since he was an only child, doted on by his fond mother and father, he didn't in the least feel threatened by babies.

"Maybe this is a special one," he suggested hopefully. "Maybe it's a boy, and we c'n play soldiers and things like that."

"No, it's another girl again. I heard Nurse say so. That's four of us now. And Papa said to Mama that it means they will just have to keep on trying."

"What does that mean?"

"I don't know," Emily admitted reluctantly, "but Mama got all silly and started kissing Papa so I left. I *hate* kissing. They do it all the time. Do you want to see the baby? I'll let you!"

Bertram nodded vigorously, and the pair shinned down the tree in a manner that would have put gray hairs in his mama's silver-gilt tresses.

They ran past the inner courtyard, where Jack Curtis led out a showy black stallion with a bad temper and a proud bloodline. Emily would miss Jack, who let her ride in front of him, and taught her tricks with disappearing handkerchiefs. But he was going away to someplace called Cambridge, and he wouldn't be back for years and years. She wanted to stop and talk, but Bertram was running at least two lengths in front of her, and she hated to be beaten by anyone.

They sprinted through the Great Hall and along the gallery and then up two flights of stairs to the nursery. There they stopped, peering in to make sure that Nurse wouldn't catch them out.

"Wouldn't you know it! Mama and Papa are in there with it!" Emily exclaimed disgustedly. "You'd think it was the only baby in the world!"

"Are you disappointed?" Sabina asked anxiously, watching her husband hold the child in his arms.

Myles stared down into the miracle of his daughter's sleeping face and laughed softly. "Mermaid, are you mad? I wouldn't exchange her for all the sons in the Western world. I wouldn't exchange any of them."

Sabina smiled and fumbled with the blankets until one tiny foot was exposed. Gently she moved a small toe and displayed the slight webbing.

"Just like her great-great-grandmamma," she said softly. "Our own little mermaid."

Myles grinned down at her. "Only forty-five more mermaids to go, my love." And he bent down until their lips met in a kiss that deepened until they were both slightly breathless.

"Ugh!" Emily Dampier exclaimed in disgust. "Kissing again!"

SWEET RELEASE
PAMELA CLARE

Though Cassie hates the slave trade, her Virginia plantation demands the labor, and she knows this fevered convict will surely die if she leaves him. But Cassie realizes Cole Braden is far more dangerous than his papers have indicated—for he can steal her breath with a glance or lay siege to her senses with a touch.

Abducted and beaten, Cole goes from master of an English shipbuilding empire to years of indentured servitude in the American colonies. And while he longs to ravish the beauty who owns him, his one hope of earning her love—and his freedom—is to prove his true identity. Only then can he turn the tables and attain his sweet release.

PERILS OF THE HEART
JENNIFER ASHLEY

Sent to seduce the captain of the merchantman *Aurora*, Evangeline Clemens trembles in her innocence. Her stepbrother's life—and the life of the rugged sailor she must tempt—depends on her success. She swears to surrender her body, her virtue . . . but she never expects to relinquish her heart.

Austin Blackwell suspects the timid temptress is a skilled spy ordered to sabotage his plans. She plays the part of an untried miss to perfection. But after sampling her sweetness, the commander vows to navigate any course to discover the truth. For his soul mutinies at the prospect of sailing into the future without the lady by his side.

WANTON ANGEL

SHIRL HENKE

A devoted artist, Elizabeth Blackthorne has earned a scandalous reputation with her free-spirited ways—she's been known to run about unchaperoned and even pose nude. But Englishman Derrick Jamison is uncharted territory. He acts like a foppish dandy, yet his disarming smile and intoxicating touch inspire feelings more extraordinary than her reputation.

Beth Blackthorne bowled him over the day they met. True, the fire-haired American didn't mean to topple him, but the fit of her lush body against his completely distracts Derrick from his mission of spying against Napoleon. From the United States to Italy to England, her siren call beckons until he knows the only safe harbor he will find is in her arms.

WICKED ANGEL — SHIRL HENKE

A gawky preacher's daughter, Jocelyn Angelica Woodbridge is hardly the type to incite street brawls, much less two in one day. "Holy Hannah," as those of the *ton* call her, would much rather nurse the sick or reform the fallen. Yet ever since a dashing American saved her from an angry mob, Joss's thoughts have turned most impure.

The son of an American Indian and an English aristocrat, Alexander Blackthorne has been sent to England for some "civilizing." But the only lessons he cares to learn are those offered by taverns and trollops. When a marriage of convenience forces Jocelyn and Alex together, Joss knows she will need more than prayer to make a loving husband of her . . . wicked angel.

___4854-X $5.99 US/$6.99CAN

Dorchester Publishing Co., Inc.
P.O. Box 6640
Wayne, PA 19087-8640

Please add $2.50 for shipping and handling for the first book and $.75 for each book thereafter. NY, NYC, and PA residents, please add appropriate sales tax. No cash, stamps, or C.O.D.s. All orders shipped within 6 weeks via postal service book rate. Canadian orders require $2.50 extra postage and must be paid in U.S. dollars through a U.S. banking facility.

Name_____
Address_____
City_____State_____Zip_____
I have enclosed $_____ in payment for the checked book(s).
Payment <u>must</u> accompany all orders. ❑ Please send a free catalog.
        CHECK OUT OUR WEBSITE! www.dorchesterpub.com